THE EDUCATOR

a Novel

by Marty Andrade

THE EDUCATOR

Published by Red Publishing
4413 Tabony St., Ste. B
Metairie, LA 70006. U.S.A.
info@redpublishing.com

ISBN 10: 0615505228
ISBN 13: 9780615505220
First Edition

The Educator
www.redpublishing.com
educator@redpublishing.com

Printed in U.S.A.

Dedicated to the real Big Ten Crew,
and college conservatives everywhere.

Author's Notes

Readers who are not Minnesotans may get confused by the initialism "DFL." The DFL is the Minnesota Democratic-Farmer-Labor Party. Our Democrats. When Farmer-Labor merged with the Democrat Party, the former was the majority group. Many DFLers still have more loyalty to Farmer-Labor than they do to the Democrats, so "DFL" is here to stay for a long time.

Some of the characters in this book are kinda-sorta based on real people, but the real people will vehemently deny this, so don't ask them. The antagonist Malcolm Paulson is entirely fictional, and not based in any way on any holder of the office of President of the University of Minnesota. This is a work of fiction, none of these events ever happened, even the ones that did.

I should also mention that the University of Minnesota-Twin Cities is an odd campus. The main Minneapolis campus is bisected by the Mississippi River, then bisected again by a major thoroughfare, Washington Avenue. The satellite campus is located several miles away, in Saint Paul. They are connected by bus. There are two students governments as well, the Minnesota Student Association (MSA) and the Student Senate. The Senate doesn't actually do anything, neither does MSA. However, MSA was more entertaining to participate in and easier to irritate.

Also, I know there are some anachronisms in this book that people who attended the U of M-tc in the mid-1990's will notice right away. Just ignore them, and please don't tell me about them. I have better things to do with my time. Thanks.

Acknowledgments

Lots of people helped turn my error strewn manuscript into something that could pass for a novel. Bill Gilles, Josh Taylor and Ben Wetmore did a lot of the heavy lifting in regards to style, grammar and continuity. Dan Nelson, Jenna Stocker, Marty Wingard, Orlando Ochoada, Aaron Solem, Peter Swanson and my parents provided endless editorial feedback and encouragement. Thank you. Hank Long and a young lady named Chloe on Fiverr.com helped as well.

My employers, Bill Capp and Bob Ingebretson, deserve a mention here for putting up with an employee who was more interested in studying or writing than in doing any actual work. While I never studied literature or took anything more than the minimum number of writing courses in college, one professor gave me great advice and confidence that bettered me as a writer, John Dickey. A professor of Astronomy, of all things. Scott Fodness, an incredible high school English teacher, taught me to love literature and read good books. Kudos to him.

I would also like to thank the numerous coworkers I worked with at the Leadership Institute. All were great conservatives and fantastic human beings. We shared so many stories and experiences in a very short period of time. They don't know it, but those stories and experiences inspired me to actually write this book. Another name I'd like to throw in here, but with no other details, is Joe Basel.

Any book is the product of countless hours of solitude but many years worth of experiences shared with many people. The people of the real Big Ten Crew deserve a book devoted to their exploits. But because many of those exploits were kinda illegal, they have this one instead. Needless to say, the good parts of this book are good because of the help I have received, any faults found herein are mine alone.

Marty Andrade
Summer 2011

There are no facts, only interpretations.
    --Friedrich Nietzsche

Youth is a blunder; Manhood a struggle; Old Age a regret.
    --Benjamin Disraeli

THE EDUCATOR

Prologue

1982
Rochester, MN

A tall black man stood outside a side door of St. Mary's Hospital smoking a cigarette. The lights of the clinic illuminated a soft snowfall in the dark February night. A row of small businesses was visible in the distance, their fluorescent lights shining into the ether. Most were still open, serving the needs of a 24/7 hospital staff. Rochester was built around the Mayo Clinic, and St. Mary's stood on a slight hill a few miles away. The lights of the city reflected off the clouds and snow creating an indirect and eerie glow.

The Black Man took a long drag from the cigarette before flicking it into the darkness and entering the hospital. He walked up two flights of stairs and down a hall. Despite the late hour there were numerous people about the Intensive Care Unit. None paid him any attention and he entered a small room abuzz with the beeps and sighs of medical equipment.

"I remember when a man could actually smoke in a hospital," stated The Black Man as he took a seat next to the old man attached to the beeping and sighing medical equipment. In the bed, he looked absolutely ancient. His hair was thin and white. At one time he was obese but the cancer had consumed his body. His skin was papery and translucent. Wrinkles marked his weathered face and his teeth and hands were stained yellow from nicotine. He had lived a hard and unhealthy life. Every mile showed.

"And I remember a time when a man could buy cocaine at the local pharmacy," The Old Man said, trying to chuckle but beginning a coughing episode instead. The kind of coughing episode reserved for those in hospice care. He recovered and continued, "Shit, if I'da known smoking was going to be such a pain in the ass I woulda picked a different vice."

The Old Man's words made the pack of cigarettes in The Black Man's jacket feel just a little heavier.

"At least you'll make a good looking corpse."

The Old Man laughed, in the form of an intense sputtering of coughs.

"You're such a sweetheart," The Old Man said, taking a few moments before continuing, "The attorney the hospital sent up just left with my final papers but I wanted to tell you myself. It shouldn't come as a surprise, but most of my estate is going to Hillsdale College. They've been hounding me for two years and can use the money. My grandson gets a stake in the firm. Twenty percent of the voting shares held in a trust, run by you. Make sure he has enough for college if he wants. Don't worry, I'm leaving you some money as well. I wanted to make sure you have enough to get through law school. I can't thank you enough for what you've done for me the last few years."

The Black Man squirmed a bit, uncomfortable in the knowledge a friend was preparing to die. He tried to lighten the mood. "You're not going to keep me here with a bunch of crazy deathbed requests are you?"

"Just a few. It might be cliché but a man wants a legacy, something that lives beyond his years. I was thinking you might be able to help me accomplish mine. I couldn't tell the lawyers any of this, but I have about a quarter million dollars in cash hidden away in a safe deposit box in a bank." The Old man smiled as he said this.

"Shit."

"Bah, walking around money. Chump change. But I'd like it to go to something useful. Working for Nixon made me realize these young people today aren't getting it. They're scaring the hell out of me." Another coughing spell took over and it took a couple of minutes for the old man to start speaking again.

"Those fucking hippies killed my son Ernie. You know that. He took the drugs, but they took his soul. It almost killed my grandson too. They're just communists. Smelly, lazy, pot smoking commies. And they'll destroy this nation.

"Anyone can see it, those fucking hippies who just went through the universities are going to be professors. They'll have free reign to propagandize all they want. All those lawyers. Hell, you know, we've talked about it enough...The modern campus is an antediluvian world. One of sin. The Lord is a man of war...

"Ernie, I want you to use the money to make war on these bastards, at least at the U. Give them a taste of their own medicine. Turn Saul Alinsky on them. Feed them their own tactics."

"Nice to know you had something easy in mind, 'just make war on the hippies,' sounds simple enough." The Black Man smiled and looked The Old Man straight in the face, "Don't worry, the money will make an impact. Your presence will be felt at the U for a long time. I promise."

"I knew I could count on you. If I gave the money to anyone else, half of it would end up going to pay for some politician's vacation or some fundraising guru's car. With you every dime will do some good. You're also getting my cabin on Camp Lake. And I'd like you to stay with the firm. I've ordered McCarty to keep you on and give you a raise."

"I think you had a little too much money."

"What do you mean 'had'? I'm not dead yet," The old man smiled. "Anyway, you'll find in the desk of my cabin directions on how to get the money. The bank is nearby in Big Lake. And I'm hoping you'll use the cabin for some good, besides fishing and entertaining all the women you have following you around."

The Black Man was about to say something but thought better of it.

"Anyway, I didn't want you to come all the way down here just to hear me prattle on about collectivists and hippies. I've got a chess set in the closet. Why don't you take it out and stay a while?"

"Don't you think the nurses are going to chase me out of here long before we finish?"

"Nonsense," the old man said, "there's nothing a substantial monetary donation to the right people can't accomplish." The Old Man smiled and took out a flask.

*   *   *   *   *   *   *

"So, how's The Old Man?" The short Asian man spoke without an accent.

"He hasn't got too long, high spirits though." The Black Man pulled out a pack of cigarettes and lit one. They were at a 24-hour roadside diner just outside of Rochester on Highway 52. Despite the late hour the restaurant was half full, mostly truckers.

"How's he gonna handle the estate?"

"Grandkid's getting a trust and money for education. Hillsdale College is getting the bulk of his estate. The old coot named me the executor." A smile crept across the Black Man's face. "He also left us with a mission."

"Sounds like him. Melodramatic. Conspiratorial."

They were interrupted by the waitress bringing their food. An omelet and fruit for The Asian Man, eggs and steak for The Black Man. As soon as the waitress was out of earshot the conversation picked up again.

"Apparently Morton Blackwell came knocking a few days ago," The Black Man said, "and the Old Man told him off, but not before Blackwell gave him some ideas. Morton wants to start a college campus program, send out people to try to organize conservatives on campus. Mainly to keep Morton's classes filled; The Old Man didn't think it would work.

"But, he thought maybe it could work on one campus, given the right support. You know how pissed off The Old Man got after his son OD'd. This is where we come in.

"We're getting cash, a lot of it. And the Camp Lake cabin, and everything there too. He wants us to work the U, create an organization to counter 'progressive hippie bullshit' and provide stability for the organization. One campus, one battleground, in his words."

"And you're going to do it?" The Asian Man was playing

with his food, pushing it around with his silverware. Occasionally would he take a bite.

"No, we're going to do it."

*   *   *   *   *   *   *

The Washington Avenue Bridge is Haunted

Footsteps follow in the dark
       Shadows Quietly whisper
       Imagination is sense decayed,
       Complaints are for the cosmic giver

            There is no resting in the River

The Final leap
       the world turned 'round
       'tis nothing more than Fury and Sound
       A short life earns nothing for the Believer

            All is swallowed by the River

Flags are thrown throughout the night
       A dozen Souls wait for light
       Timeless is time for the shade
       Life is motion from the unmoved mover

            Churn splash churn goes the River

Laughing still the Moon's Face
       There is no resting place
       One. two. three. end.
       echos of voices silently whimper

            We are all sinless Sinners,

            We belong to the River

THE EDUCATOR

Part I

Spring, 1994

CHAPTER 1

12:30am Thursday; February 24th, 1994
Washington Avenue Bridge; Minneapolis, MN

"I can't believe we just did that."

Sarah Stevenson was a petite woman in her mid-thirties. Five feet tall and too thin for her frame. Sopping wet with a backpack full of rocks she might make eight stones. She was an artificially well-tanned brunette with sparkling white teeth. She never stopped smiling, displaying the small gap in her front two teeth.

She was an attractive woman who had worked on-and-off as a stripper while in college and after. Eventually she escaped that dreadful work. For the last six years she had been working as a waitress for a trendy downtown Minneapolis bar before she met Malcolm Paulson, the President of the University of Minnesota.

She went to college for a while but never graduated. Her lifestyle as a youth was expensive. Stripping was good money but she was never able to balance work and school. After dropping out of St. Thomas University in St. Paul she continued to work as a stripper for a few years. Eventually she quit, getting a job offer at O'Callaghan's Irish Pub and Grille.

It was never her intention to work in restaurants all her life. And she hated being a stripper. Things just happened. Time flew. She began thinking about her life. It kept her up at night. In high school she had been popular and smart. National Honor Society. Soccer team captain. Pep band. A plethora of other extracurriculars. When she was young she dreamed of opening her own business, a bakery.

Years passed. All she wanted was a stop, a do over, a timeout to change the direction of her life. She met Professor Paulson only three months ago. He was handsome, smart, a good tipper and funny. They hit it off right away. He offered her a way out, a job and another chance at school.

Sure, he was leveraging to get sex, but she was attracted to him anyway. It wasn't a fair trade at all.

He helped get her a job as a library assistant at the U. Paulson's name was never used, of course, he just told her how to cheat the system. The 'hiring process' reviewed job candidates' resumes and cover letters by keywords rather than by anything qualitative. Interviews were conducted in a rigid format that was easy to practice for and backgrounds were almost never checked. References weren't called, employment history was never confirmed and qualifications were rarely challenged. For system gamers, it was easy.

After getting a full-time job she was eligible for a full-ride Regents scholarship. Most employees at the U of M went to school part-time for free, all of them had the option. She could finish her undergrad degree in a few years of working and he promised to help her get into a grad program somewhere. It was all too good to be true.

And Paulson was an exciting man. Other than a bulbous and oversized nose, he had movie-star good looks. In his mid-fifties, Paulson sported a full head of salt and pepper hair which was always perfectly groomed, combed off to one side with a razor sharp cut. Extremely athletic for his age, he had the libido of a much younger man. He spent ten hours a week swimming to stay healthy. The greatest of his natural aphrodisiacs was his money. Paulson was worth upwards of ten millions dollars. He also had power; Paulson was a major player in state politics, along with his leadership of the U.

The Dean Martin good looks and porn star libido were just bonuses compared to his wealth and influence.

During the 1980's he made millions by playing the stock market. A math professor and early computer programmer, he revolutionized the use of derivatives and used his knowledge of computers and statistics to find market inefficiencies. Opportunity met preparation. The market eventually caught up and the inefficiencies disappeared. He soon left business and returned to academia, his fortune still intact.

Later he was picked as the interim President of the University. The previous guy was forced to resign after a money scandal. The move from interim president to president was anti-climatic. The Regents were embroiled in a fight with the Minnesota legislature over racial quotas and they just weren't interested in putting any effort into a nationwide search to fill the position. After interviewing three other candidates they went with Paulson.

The couple had just made love in Wilson Library. It was something Paulson wasn't comfortable doing, but there wasn't anybody around. The library was large. Public sex made its own excitement, and almost being caught by a janitor just added to the rush. Stevenson loved to drink and a little whiskey from Paulson's flask lubricated the affair. Now her breath was heavy with alcohol.

They were walking hand in hand along Washington Avenue Bridge. A double-decker bridge with a pedestrian level above the road; the bridge offered an enclosed space for walkers going over the Mississippi River between the east and west banks of campus. It was cold, a few degrees below zero. But no wind. Nothing to stop self respecting Minnesotans from enjoying the walk outside.

THE EDUCATOR

"I'm glad you enjoyed it," Paulson said, a broad smile sweeping across his face.

It was met with a bigger smile from Sarah. He pulled her close and they kissed passionately. He was comically tall in comparison to her and he had to stoop his head down awkwardly. The kiss lasted a long time but eventually they started slowly walking along the bridge again.

Paulson loved the cold. There was something refreshing and clean about it. Minnesota could chill you to the core. It was deadly. It linked him to the ancient savage. In the modern world of electricity and microwaves a walk from your workplace to your car in the Minnesota Winter would remind you vividly of your mortality and of the life and death struggle of your ancestors.

It was nearly 1am which bothered neither person. Paulson was a night owl who lived off a few hours of sleep and Stevenson was a stripper. Bedtimes for both could be well past three. Stevenson was forced by her junior status to work the library until close. Paulson had just attended a black-tie banquet in St. Paul. He returned to campus around 10pm to visit Stevensen in the library. One thing led to another.

"I was talking to my office manager," Sarah started talking again, something she did a lot. "And she was telling me I'll be eligible for the Regent's scholarship in a few more weeks. I'll get my six months in well before I start classes in the summer. I can't wait. You're so awesome. We should find somewhere else to fuck, you know, for next time." Sarah couldn't have felt better. This was it, she was climbing out of her hole and could finally begin living her life the way she envisioned it as a young girl.

"That's good." Paulson once again pulled her into an embrace but this time left it just as an embrace. As they hugged Paulson looked around. There was nobody in sight; he hadn't seen anyone since the library. Normally there was some activity on campus, even this late at night, but the cold did a good job of driving the heartiest insomniacs indoors. The sky was overcast and the glow from the city provided enough light to walk by. The lights on the bridge were getting replaced thanks to a large makeover project started by Paulson. The day had been unseasonably warm, above freezing. The frigid nightfall created a heavy fog below the bridge, shielding the Mississippi River from view. The condensing moisture off the river made it impossible to see either bank from the center of the bridge. It was a rare opportunity.

The atmospheric situation wasn't unusual; the Mississippi River created its own weather inside the small valley which separated the two sides of the campus. Paulson knew this well from years on campus. But he hadn't really been paying attention lately.

He looked around again. He couldn't have planned this better. Normally he didn't have the urge to kill his mistresses. Killing was for strangers, at opportune times and in areas far away from work and home. But the cold, the slight fog and the lack of people were too much.

Besides, he thought, *I'm a pro. Killing in the middle of a city is part of the art.*

It'd be so easy.

The hug lasted a little too long even for lovers.

"What are you thinking about?" There was something innocent and sensual about the way she asked.

"Nothing, just reminiscing a little."

"Well, let's hurry up and get to your car, you can reminisce there. We could even have some more fun together."

"You are so naughty, I could just kill you." With that he embraced her for another kiss, his right hand slipping behind her back and grabbing her belt. His left hand cupping her breast as they kissed again. As he pulled away from her lips he said gently and lovingly "you're about to die."

Then, swiftly and with little effort he pulled her up with his right hand and pushed her with his left. It was just enough to get her body to clear the bridge railing and send her tumbling down to the Mississippi waters below. It was awkward and she began screaming the instant she felt the sudden movement. It was 3.1 seconds before she hit the Mississippi.

Paulson's hands clutched Sarah's purse. The strap had broken and he was barely able to hang on while he was throwing her. But he did. Paulson was running before she hit the water. The air above the river was thick from the fog and the scream was muffled. But he didn't want to take any chances.

He ran back along the river until he got to Fraser Hall and he began to walk. There weren't any sirens. There wasn't a patrol car or policeman to be seen. He relaxed and continued to make his way to the Northrop garage where his car was parked. Pilfering through the purse, he snatched up several photos Sarah had of herself. Paulson left her driver's license and other cards though. He planned on throwing the purse into the river later.

As he was passing between Fraser and Wulling Hall he saw a group of people walking towards Northrop Auditorium. They were all dressed in dark clothing and could have been quite clandestine except for the fact they were talking loudly. Paulson couldn't make out what they were saying but every few seconds the whole group would burst out in hearty laughter.

The group approached a communication kiosk, a board where student groups were allowed to put up posters advertising on-campus events, and started spraying something. At first Paulson thought they were vandalizing the kiosk but then he noticed one of the men putting some large posters on the board. Normally student groups used staple hammers so this scene surprised him.

Soon enough the group started on their way and were out of sight, their path leading them towards Washington Avenue. Paulson began walking again, wary of the world but the adrenaline was disappearing. His fears were beginning to subside. No one heard Sarah on the way down. Or at least they didn't care enough to call it in. As he got nearer to the parking garage he could just make out the picture on the new poster. It looked like a coat hanger.

When he finally got close enough to read the posters he stopped, dumbstruck. They read: "If abortion was criminalized and you needed an abortion, would you?" Below this was a drawing of a coat hanger. Below the coat hanger, the poster continued "Yes you would, you Godless Baby Killer. Sincerely, the Traditional Values Coalition"

"Those Republican assholes." Paulson mumbled to himself.

*   *   *   *   *   *   *

A metallic blue 1988 Nissan 300zx slipped into the Oak Street Parking Ramp near the University of Minnesota campus. The car looked good at a distance but when given a closer inspection spots of rust were evident. The Z-car, as it is known to its fans, is a wonderful car to drive, but not one suited to Minnesota's February weather. The driver took it to the second level of the cold concrete parking ramp.

Jonathan "Zan" Chin-Wu stepped out. Standing five foot four and weighing somewhere near 120 pounds, he wasn't the most intimidating figure. He was no pushover though. Over the last 20 years he had worked hard to get black belts in several different martial arts including Jiu Jiutsu and Karate. He studied Muay Thai and Eskrima. As a boxer he had once been a golden gloves state champion as a teenager. Like many short men, he felt there was always something he needed to prove, even if he couldn't quite understand why.

Zan was adopted; he never knew his real parents. Growing up comfortably in the northern suburbs of the Twin Cities he always felt like he was missing out. On what he didn't know. The first chance he got he moved into the city of Minneapolis. He went to the University of Minnesota and graduated with a bachelor's degree in political science in 1981. A partial scholarship to the law school brought him back to the University of Minnesota.

But he dropped out of law school.

He now did *this*, whatever this was, exactly.

Taking the stairs down, he stopped by the parking lot attendant' booth.

"Tass!" Zan greeted.

Chet Larson, known as 'TAS' among his friends, was in his late fifties and had been working at the U for almost a decade. TAS stood for 'The Angry Squirrel,' though few people knew this. Chet actually got a nametag with 'Tass' on it and that was what everyone called him. No one really knew what he did before he came to the U, but whatever it was, it made him *different*.

This made him Zan's friend.

TAS was standing outside his booth smoking. He flicked his cigarette and returned the greeting "Jesus Christ on a crutch...Zan, you bastard, how's it going? Hey, have I got some shit for you, you're going to love this..." Chet opened the door to his booth and pulled out a black backpack. "Check this out." he opened the backpack to reveal a mess of dirty paper, all one long sheet of dot matrix print.

"A bag full of dirty paper?" Zan asked

"Just read the fucking thing."

"Let's say I forgot how."

A car rolled up to the gate, the occupant impatiently honking the horn. TAS started to turn red. This sort of thing aggravated him.

He shouted towards the car, "Can't you see we're talking?" his voice heavy with indignation.

"I can't let myself out, asshole" came a reply.

Chet walked over to the gate arm, opened a panel and pushed a button. The gate arm lifted up. As the car drove out Chet tossed a cigarette butt through the open window, a middle finger found its way out the window as the car pulled away.

"Hope that wasn't your boss."

"Relax, we're friends," TAS stated, "he's one of the maintenance guys...And fuck you too, just read some of that." TAS pointed to the papers in the backpack.

Zan started to read. After a few moments he stopped.

"Holy fuck."

TAS smiled and said "Damn right Holy fuck."

*   *   *   *   *   *   *

'The Organization' came from nowhere.

That's how it appeared anyway.

A group of conservative activists, not affiliated with the Republican Party and preferring issues activism to pushing political candidates, suddenly appeared where nothing had been before. As if conjured from thin air. And no one could be sure who ran it. Where it got its money. Or why it existed at all.

They weren't typical College Republicans. They didn't care

about winning votes and making the Republican Party look good. In fact, they fought with the CRs relentlessly. The Organization followed different rules; if they even had rules. This group was tight-knit and uncooperative with everyone. They ran a conservative newspaper and occasionally pirated a radio talk show on the AM band. Because there was no official student group, their activities fell outside of the control of the U.

Few knew the entire story, including those on the inside. Zan provided the money and the marching orders. He was 34, old by campus standards, but he looked young enough to get by. He did his best to stay out of the spotlight.

The Organization was an old-fashioned right wing conspiracy.

And Zan loved it.

*   *   *   *   *   *   *

The Big Ten was a semi-popular dive at the University of Minnesota. All-wood paneling blanketed nearly every surface on the inside of the bar. TV sets were scattered about, hanging from mounts on the walls. Random sports programs flickered across the screens. Old black and white photos of former Gopher athletes with cheap wooden frames littered the walls, along with occasional pieces of sports equipment. The highlight of it all was a wooden plank from old Memorial Stadium, the long destroyed on-campus football venue.

The bar featured excellent toasted subs and the typical array of bar and grill confections that hardened the arteries of the regulars. It was a great locale for cheap beer, depressing atmosphere, lukewarm service and poor lighting. Exactly what The Organization needed.

In the back of the bar, away from the busier sections, was The Roundtable. The largest table in the place, it could comfortably seat nine people. Every Wednesday night The Organization met at The Roundtable for merriment and strategic planning. New recruits, current leadership and graduated alumni intermingled between rounds of cheap beer and appetizer samplers.

The meetings came in stages. Early in the evening, after the College Republicans meeting, the younger members and current leaders met. Around 9pm or so the riffraff, the worthless do nothing socialites who hung around for pathetic attempts at fraternization, typically left for greener pastures. Zan didn't normally make an appearance until after 10pm. The promising underclassmen, those being groomed for future leadership spots, stayed until the bar closed with the elder members.

Then the party moved elsewhere. The Perkins on County-D offered convenient 24-hour hospitality just twenty minutes away.

Only the hardcore initiates did their dues at these sessions. It wasn't uncommon to have one or two people do the entire shift, from the CR meeting to sunrise. The weekly ritual was no accident. It was done to test dedication. Also, the conversations provided opportunities to gauge a person's psychology. Political activism is a form of mental illness; it takes a special kind of self-hatred to eat so much shit for so long. It was important to weed out the weak, quickly.

Without fanfare, Zan sat down.

"Hey look at this asshole," a short fireplug of a man said. "We were just talking about you. We need money motherfucker. We still haven't made any preparations for a big speaker this semester."

The man was Orson Henning. He was picking at a chef salad. Short, almost as short as Zan, but with broad shoulders and an athletic build. His sandy blond hair was cropped close; short enough to avoid any curls. A Minnesota Twins baseball cap sat atop his head, bill adjusted slightly to the side. The outgoing senior always wore a big smile on his pale babyface, Naturally easygoing, his calm goofiness hid an edgy controversial nature that enjoyed pushing people to apoplexy.

"I say this with no measure of floccinaucinihilipilification, but we all need money you fucks, so settle down." Zan smiled into the silence vocabulary could produce. "We'll get to business soon enough... so...where is everybody?"

Zan had expected more than just three people. Besides Henning there was Rachel Anderson, an attractive brunette, and her boyfriend Horace Brown. Horace was a tall black man, about six feet six inches, give or take. More of a Republican than a conservative, Horace had found himself hanging around the organization thanks solely to his relationship with Rachel. The group liked having Horace around since Black Republicans were a valuable commodity and notoriously difficult to out.

Late in the previous school year Horace participated in a debate on Affirmative Action that was televised on a cable access show. When he said "Affirmative Action calls into question all minority achievement" a group of students from 'Africana' rushed the stage throwing Oreo's and Lincoln Logs and calling him an Uncle Tom. Africana was a radical Black separatist group that received a lot of student fee money at the U. Later, Horace received a bunch of death threats. He stayed out of the limelight after that.

Rachel and Horace had become inseparable but Henning could still get Rachel to participate in the occasional exercise. Rachel was adopted, and like most adopted children she came to believe abortion was the greatest evil in the world today. Since The Organization was the only campus entity doing regular pro-life activities, she was stuck.

THE EDUCATOR

She had a pretty face and great tits, so The Organization was glad to have her. Pictures of her had graced the frontpage of the Minnesota Daily several times and she was always featured in some way in the campus conservative paper. At one point she flirted the group out of getting arrested during a Planned Parenthood protest that went wrong.

"The boys are out postering with Nolan," Rachel said.

Zan gave Henning a cold stare.

"Hey, outgoing Senior." Henning said, pointing to himself with his thumbs, "I don't have to poster in February."

"Well, what the hell are they doing out there so early?" Zan, "the fucking womynists will tear down those posters before sunrise."

Zan promoted early morning postering. Students were night owls; the bars closed at around 1am and it only took one left winger to see conservative posters up and organize an impromptu censorship lesson. Normally postering was done after 2am and before 8am classes.

Henning took sip of Grain Belt Premium, the official beer of the group. "It's below zero outside, nobody's out and about tonight 'scept us."

"When did they leave?"

"About an hour ago."

"So, they ought to be back shortly...alright then...conservative speaker...Let's work a budget and a timeline. Get out a notebook."

*   *   *   *   *   *   *

By 1am it was just Henning and Zan sitting at The Roundtable, waiting. Rachel and Horace left shortly after Zan arrived, leaving the Big Ten hand in hand.

Henning and Zan were planning the rest of the semester's activities. There was a student government election coming up, some counterprotesting opportunities and an upcoming battle over student services fees. Then there was the major speaker.

"Horowitz wants five thousand minimum," Henning said, "we can get Walter Williams for less, but he won't get the press coverage we want." Henning wanted a speaker who could start a campus riot, and Horowitz could do that.

"Between that and the paper, things will get tight," Zan said. "We'll need to do some fundraising."

"We've pretty much maxed everything out, there are a couple of grants we can go for, maybe a thousand. We could direct mail, maybe another 500 or so. That's it man."

"We'll get it done."

A woman sat down at the table and lit a cigarette. Slim and

attractive, but older. She was in her early forties, had a dark tan with a healthy supply of freckles and had sandy brown hair fashionably cut in a short bob.

It was Alisha Williams, the bar's owner and manager. Over the years she gained a reputation as an outspoken conservative. But she was more of a libertarian. A longtime friend of Zan's, on Wednesdays she let the group stay past close. And she normally joined in for a bit too.

"Where's the big crowd?" She asked. "Your bill was a little light tonight."

"They're busy with some inflammatory posters," Zan offered.

Time was filled with some small talk for a while. And drinks. The rest of the employees did their cleaning and left. Closing time was one. The rest of the crew arrived at 1:30am. Two Freshmen, Kayla Witold and Frank Wallace, the sophomore Gene Zeale and the current group leader Nolan Painter.

Zan was strict about group leaders, people he called his 'Lieutenants.' It was always a Junior, never a Senior, and they had to have three semesters of experience before taking over official duties. Seniors were too easily distracted by graduation, job hunts and the realities of life. Underclassmen were, as a rule, idiots. Juniors combined necessary experience with insulation from the real world another year of school offered.

Since not all the group's members were recruited as freshmen, this meant some members missed out completely when it came to active leadership positions. Others only got a semester of real leadership. There was always work to be done and outgoing seniors participated in almost all the activities, they just didn't carry the responsibilities. Their job was as a reference source for the others.

Zan's current lieutenant, Nolan Painter, was tall and lanky. Standing a few inches above six feet, depending on his current slouch, he weighed no more than a hundred and forty pounds. He had short curly red hair and shockingly blue eyes. Protestant, pro-life and foul-mouthed, his tenor voice was capable of incredible volume when Painter lost his temper, which was often.

"Hey guys, there are some subs on the bar in case you're hungry." Alisha was never going to be a mother, but she treated these college kids well enough to make up for it. The two Freshmen made their way towards the food.

After everyone warmed up, the two freshmen left. Wallace, all two hundred fifty pounds of him, walked Kayla all the way back to frat row. It was ten blocks out of his way but all girls got escorts home, group rule.

It was 3am before Zan, Henning, Painter, and Gene Zeale got to Perkins.

THE EDUCATOR

Zeale was a Sophomore who had been recruited right away as a Freshman. He was on the fast track to become Zan's primary lieutenant next fall. He had a reputation as a spaz. In fact, his nickname in the group was 'Spags.'

Spags was insane. Crazy. Hardcore. Not right in the head. He took things too far, pushing the envelope further than even Henning would. Zeale didn't necessarily have a political philosophy. The older members, the group alumni who helped the 'kids' out when needed, recognized him as a nihilist. There was nothing to him except his love of chaos. Whether The Organization could use his services was an ongoing debate, held when Zeale wasn't around.

Joining the group at Perkins was an alumni, a former lieutenant and current U of M employee, Chris Berg. Chris was working on a Masters degree in computer science and electrical engineering at the U while working as a computer specialist for Technology Services, the U department charged with keeping the campus wired. He was short, bald, heavyset and sported a junco goatee that stretched all the way down to his chest.

"Alright guys," Zan started, "we need to make plans for next year's big operation...And I wanted to introduce Mr. Zeale to Chris. Chris, Gene is going to be our main guy next year, assuming he survives the initiation."

The two exchanged quick greetings and Zan quickly took over the conversation again, "I'd like to try a Marilyn Monroe," he said.

"A what?" Gene asked, not up on all the lingo yet.

Chris Berg explained, "It's an operation; Marilyn Monroe 'supposedly' slept with JFK. In fact, there is 'apparently' a film of Marilyn Monroe giving ol' Jack a blow job. While it never played a political role, the Kennedy family was basically bulletproof, a film of JFK getting a hummer from anyone could have cost him the '64 election. It's a pretty common operation; the secularists tried to do it a bunch of times to Jerry Falwell. You find a whore, or at least an easygoing chick, and put her in the room with your mark. Add a camera and boom...you got a Marilyn Monroe."

"Worthless." Zeale said. "Why don't we do a fire alarm day. The whole crew pulls as many fire alarms as possible, disrupting classes. We could even add in an 'apparent' explosive device too."

"We'll keep that in the backup file," Painter said, "for the day we want to be put in fucking jail."

"The Monroe works against most public officials, even liberal ones. Hard to do though. It would be good for everyone to give it a try" Berg said.

Zan jumped back in, "The president of the U is already a well-known skirt chaser. With a successful Monroe, we'll make it tougher for him to lobby for funds from those uptight outstate DFLers for another goddamned construction project. So it's worth it."

"What about a woman, we using a stripper or something?" Henning asked.

"Had a different idea." Zan took a long pause. "I was thinking we could use Rachel"

"Have you talked to Rachel about this?" Nolan Painter asked.

"Horace is the problem" Henning added.

"Talked to Rachel, yes...Horace? No," Zan said. "But Rachel is game; she's hardcore. And it doesn't have to go any further than the President feeling her up and getting a picture of him pinching her ass. It'll be a one-night attempt. The guy's a boozer, we can catch him at the University Club."

"Details?" Berg asked, taking notes. He knew technical details were his problem.

"Rachel gets into a fundraiser," Zan suggested, "there's one coming up in late May, She can be a guest of a major donor, like our friend the Archbishop...Money is a problem though. We'll need cameras, small stuff we can hide on a person or somewhere in the U-Club."

"Tell us about it." Henning complained.

"I'll figure it out," Zan said.

"So, let's see if I got this right," Zeale said. "President Paulson drinks too much, it's late, and Rachel is her normal sexy self. The guy gets handsy, we get pictures of him feeling up a student. Rachel gets indignant and slaps the guy. Those pictures get put out on flyers, released to the press, sent to uptight legislators on the education committee, Paulson gets the reputation as a perv. Presto, instant mayhem."

"Right on," Berg said.

"Fire alarms. Cheaper, more chaos, more fun, just sayin'."

Henning showed some concern, "Does Rachel get hurt by this?"

"We black out her face, no problem. We control the pictures, that's the beauty of this job," Berg replied.

"What's the point of all this?" Zeale asked.

"Chaos, fun, training." Zan said. "This is the fun stuff Gene. At worst, we screw up and waste some time. At best, we embarrass the guy and make it harder for him to get tax money out of the legislature. And it's important to try big things. One big operation a year; every time the organization gets better. We create political hacks; guys who know how to get anything done. We create plumbers. This is how."

"Whatever helps you sleep at night Zan," Zeale said.

"What about money?" Painter asked, lighting a cigarette.

THE EDUCATOR

"We have a major speaker this semester, another edition of the paper, a student government campaign and we still need enough to make a recruiting drive next year. And we have, what, five hundred in the bank?"

"I've got a meeting with the Archbishop tomorrow, we'll figure out the financing."

Everyone appeared satisfied for now

Chris Berg looked down at his notes. "So what about the MSA campaign?"

*   *   *   *   *   *   *

Time flew. A few hours later Zan was driving Orson Henning back to campus.. It was 7am. The sun was just beginning to rise and the strange atmospheric conditions of Minnesota had produced a purple sky. The ride down I35W to the campus was a quiet one.

After nine hours of conversation there wasn't much left to say.

Henning lived in Centennial Hall, and had lived there for all four years of college. In fact, he had lived in the very same room for four years. Henning struggled his way into the dorm.

Zan parked his car on Oak Street. After putting a dollar into the parking meter he put on some workout clothes, gloves, sweat pants and a hoodie. It was jogging time. He ran through the Superblock, up past Washington Avenue to the Rec Center, then around frat row. Down from the Knoll area back to campus. Around the mall area, across the bridge, around to Middlebrook. Looped Carlson and made his way back across the bridge. Down around the Weisman Art Museum to East River Road near the river flats. Then he sprinted up the hill, back through the Superblock to his Nissan. Four miles. Thirty-one minutes.

A new low for Zan.

Zan jogged outdoors three times a week during winter. The cold was hard on the lungs, and it required twice the energy.

Then it was back to his place in Northeast Minneapolis. The house, located on Adams Street just south of Broadway, was long ago converted into a duplex. Zan lived on the top floor while the owner of the duplex lived on the bottom floor. After stretching he crawled up onto his couch and turned the television on to watch the local news. Before Rusty Gatenby could come on with a traffic report, he was sleeping.

*   *   *   *   *   *   *

Nightmare. Screaming. Zan was falling. Falling. Surrounded

by a gray abyss. Blue water below. Time stood still.

His screaming sounded a lot like a telephone.

He woke up.

Zan's phone was a classic black Bell rotary dial telephone, equipped with two large bells as ringers, louder than an alarm clock. It could wake a man out of drunkenness.

A glance at his VCR told him it was 12:00, before he realized it always said that. Hoping the cobwebs in his mind would be gone before the conversation got serious, Zan grabbed the phone and sat up.

"Yeah?"

"Zan, it's Ernie."

At that moment Zan remembered the lunch meeting he was supposed to have with Ernie Kessler, AKA 'The Archbishop.'

"I wanted to make sure we were still on for lunch today." Kessler's voice reflected a patient humor.

Zan again looked around his apartment for a clock. The truth of the matter was he never needed a clock.

"Ernie, good to hear from you. You know, I don't have my watch on me, and I've misplaced my secretary. When were we supposed to meet?"

"Half an hour ago."

"Fuck."

"Don't worry about it," Kessler replied, "I needed to get out of the office."

The market had been down, especially for Kessler's financial firm. A biotech boom had popped its bubble.

"Give me half an hour to clean up. Do you still want to meet at the 5-8 Club?"

"Matt's"

*   *   *   *   *   *   *

Matt's Bar and Grill is an iconic burger joint in South Minneapolis on Cedar. The self-proclaimed birthplace of the 'Jucy Lucy,' a cheese-stuffed burger served white hot, Matt's was a popular spot. A Big Ten crew favorite. The interior was dark and dank. Cold during the winter.

The bar was empty this time of the day. Zan and Kessler took the booth nearest the door.

"How was last night?" Kessler asked.

"Uneventful."

Zan hadn't decided whether to tell Ernie about TAS's big find.

"I thought you were planning the big event for next year, the

Marilyn Monroe. Did you get to it?"

"Yeah," Zan shrugged, "some of the guys were actually excited about it. I was even able to talk Rachel into doing it; all it cost me was a few beers."

"Incredible." Kessler stroked his chin as if he had a beard. He felt he needed to look a certain way in his business. People had a hard time trusting a Black man with their money. Regardless of past successes. "You know, I thought for sure we'd have to use stripper."

"Oh, and did you ask out Alisha yet?"

"No, but you can suck my cock." Zan was notoriously bad with women. Or maybe women didn't like the fact he had no future. Either way Alisha was the only woman he got along with well enough to have a relationship, he never pulled the trigger.

"Anyway," Zan continued, "this Monroe has some equipment needs. Mr. Berg wants to wire some hidden cameras around the U-Club. And we still need money for two more printings of the paper, an MSA campaign and a major speaker."

Kessler passed an envelope over to him. "We're now out of money. There's 8,000 bucks in there. The Old Man's stash is gone now. After this, you're on your own; at least until I recover from this bio-tech business."

Zan thought again about the social security numbers. "I have an idea about some fundraising, off the books."

"Selling plasma?"

"Maybe, but you're better off not hearing about it."

"Okay, but I am your lawyer. Try to give me a heads up before the police call." Kessler said. "There's also some non-profit stuff we can do, on the books. I'll get to work on some direct mail letters. But this stuff takes time."

Their Jucy Lucys arrived. Kessler expertly bit off a small portion of the cheese-stuffed burger, allowing the extremely hot cheese to cool. Fries were used to dab up some of the cheese that tried to escape. Eating a Jucy Lucy was an art.

Zan was mostly uninterested in the food.

Kessler's eye's lit up and he snapped his fingers. "We do have some money. From the James Campaign. It should be enough to send Kayla and Rachel to CPAC."

"What for? I thought we weren't sending anyone."

"We have a hard time keeping women around the group. Rewarding them with a trip to Washington might keep them showing up."

"CPAC starts next week Thursday. Seems last minute."

"It is, but I can make all the arrangements. All you have to do is tell them."

Zan stared at Kessler. "There's no need for pretense. What are you not telling me?"

"I had this idea two days ago, I've already made the arrangements and their hotel room is right next to Representative Grams' room."

"Dude."

"I'd like to get someone onto his staff. Using young girls is the only way to do it with any success."

"Neither of them is initiated."

"Nothing's perfect." Kessler said. "You work with what you have. I've already made a substantial donation to Rod and I told him some friends of mine would be going to CPAC. He said he wanted to meet them. The dullard responds to incentives."

"Seems like a longshot."

"Not really. If the DFL is really going with Wynia, then we have a great chance to keep Durenberger's seat. Wynia couldn't motivate a Hyena to laugh. Grams will win the GOP primary. There's no way Dyrstad wins. Not with all the Catholics in the party. Come November, call it a coin flip. If I get someone on Gram's staff now, load up his campaign with some of our guys, we'll get our own Senator for at least six years."

"You sound pretty confident."

"Grams is a Ted Baxter. His handlers will hold a lot of sway with him. If I can get one or two people close to him, he's mine."

"Who else you got working on it?"

"Just Shotgun." Kessler said. "He was Gram's volunteer coordinator in ninety-two."

"Still sounds like a longshot."

"Before I forget, I bought you this..." Kessler reached into his pocket and pulled out long, thick, black phone. "It's a portable phone, works throughout the Twin Cities. It's a dollar a minute, so be judicious."

"Cocksucker."

"Shut up and eat your burger."

*   *   *   *   *   *   *

CHAPTER 2

6:00pm Thursday; February 24th
Morrill Hall; University of Minnesota

University of Minnesota President Malcolm Paulson walked out of his office. He had a late meeting at the State Capitol. But there was enough time to add to his collection.

Quickly moving across Northrup Plaza, to East River Road,

he approached the darkened husk of the Mineral Resources Research Center, an archaic relic of the industrial age.

When more economical sources of iron dried up in the latter part of the nineteenth century, interest turned towards taconite. Taconite was only thirty percent iron and could be difficult to refine. For years, the Mineral Resources Research Center was at the cutting edge of taconite refinement. But all things come to an end, and in the late 1970's the Research Center became obsolete. The building was abandoned.

The University simply locked the doors. Equipment was left where it was, how it was. One day there were people working on taconite refining, the next day not. The building was on the Historic Register, and couldn't be destroyed. It was on a prime piece of real estate, next to the Mississippi River with a view of St. Anthony Falls. Soon enough, it was all but forgotten except by the brave souls who occasionally broke in to graffiti the walls and abandoned equipment.

It was Paulson's favorite place on campus. He would sneak in late at night, though he didn't need to. Unlike the graffiti artists, he had a key. The big brick renaissance style building had a couple of atriums where equipment had been used. There were plenty of nooks and crannies. Offices, bathrooms, closets. Security guards had caught Paulson in the building a couple of times, but the University President never had anything to worry about, he would just smile and tell them he was working on a renovation plan in his head.

There would be no renovation. Not while Paulson was in charge. The building had been abandoned since the mid-80's, before Paulson become University president. It hadn't happened under his watch, so there was no blaming him. It was out-of-the-way, so there were few complaints.

It was his sanctuary. He could get away from people here. Paulson entered through the loading docks opposite the river. He worked his way towards the north end of the building. An old bathroom, covered in graffiti, had no door. Paulson walked in. Standing on the remains of the lone toilet bowl, he stuck his hand through a large hole in the wall. Grabbing a thin rope attached to a nail, he pulled up a small metal box with a combination lock.

Paulson pulled Sarah's driver's license and a lock of her hair from his coat. He had painstakingly created the lock of hair from one of Sarah's brushes left in her purse. The hair was wrapped together by a small red bow. The purse would find its way into the Mississippi sometime tonight.

Taking a long inhalation from the hair, he could still smell Sarah's perfume. Opening the metal box, Paulson dropped in the two relics.

There were now eight locks of hair in the box, three driver's licenses, two Polaroids and one high school senior portrait. The first two women he killed, he didn't collect a memory. Since then, if he didn't get a memory, it didn't happen. Only once since his collection began did he fail to grab a memory. Those girls didn't exist. They didn't matter. But the women in the box, they belonged to him. They were his.

Forever.

And he wanted more.

*   *   *   *   *   *   *

It was nine in the evening. The temperature had dropped to ten below. Still, a comfortable ten below. Without wind the cold was just miserable, not unbearable. A man of average height and average build sat on a granite bench at the bus stop in front of Coffman Memorial Union. He had brown hair jutting out from underneath a stocking cap, long enough to cover his ears. His brown eyes stared into the cold nothingness.

He was improperly dressed. Blue jeans. Leather military jacket. There was no defining characteristics to the man. There was no reason to notice him.

And no one ever did.

Even when they did, his appearance was so plain nobody could describe him.

Zan Chin-Wu, dressed in sweat pants and three layers of sweatshirts and fleece pullovers, sat down next to the man. TAS's backpack was with him.

Zan didn't stay seated. The bench was too cold.

"Hello Joe." Zan said.

"This better be good Zan," the man replied, "I'm missing work"

"You'll like this, I have some information here I think you can find useful," Zan showed 'Joe' the backpack. "The names, addresses, phone numbers, and Social Security numbers of every member of the faculty and staff of the University, including the President of the U and all the Regents."

'Joe' nodded. After a pause he responded, "What did you have in mind?"

"We need money, I know we could do better things with all this, but getting cash should be our first priority; we have a sting planned that needs to get funded."

"The Marilyn Monroe?" 'Joe' asked.

"Maybe...but what I had in mind for this stuff was a real simple scam. Identity theft. It's the next big thing. We, and by we I mean you and the rest of the chaos crew, start filling out credit card applica-

THE EDUCATOR

tions for Regent Williams and Vice Provost Brackens.

"They both have nice homes with street mailboxes. Neither is married. No one will be home during the day. Applications take a few weeks to process, check the mail once a day before they get home. Take the credit cards when they arrive. We get a few weeks' use of the cards for cash advances and other purchases. Some fake IDs would seal the deal."

The featureless man sat and thought.

"I like it," Joe said. "We could even try to get a second mortgage on their homes and use that to buy some big ticket items too. What's our cut?"

"Tass gets the first ten thousand or so, I get the next ten thousand. The rest is yours, plus you get all the information to wreak havoc on whomever else you choose."

"This will take time. Winter makes it hard to wait around mailboxes without raising suspicion. We'll try to do something sooner than later, but you'll have to wait for summer if you really want to sneak twenty grand out of this.

"Do what thou wilt."

"I'll contact you when we have your money. I'll give Tass his cut first."

"Good enough" As Zan said this, a small shuttle bus with a gopher on it stopped in front of the two men. It was the Campus Connector, the bus that connected the far flung reaches of the University's Minneapolis and Saint Paul campuses.

Zan, leaving the backpack behind, got on the Campus Connector and left.

The other man got up, grabbed the backpack and walked back to Coffman.

On the bus, Zan picked up a copy of the Minnesota Daily left on one of the seats. The frontpage story was about a new University employee whose body had been found down river from the U. An autopsy was planned but a preliminary analysis suggested the woman had been drinking heavily. The U of M Police Chief was quoted saying he believed the girl been drinking and either accidentally fell from the Washington Avenue Bridge or purposefully ended her life by jumping.

The Police Chief suggested that to avoid such catastrophes one should confide in friends and never drink alone. Zan couldn't disagree with the man. Nothing else in the paper caught his interest, so Zan took out a piece of paper from his jacket and started jotting down some other fundraising ideas.

*   *   *   *   *   *   *

The ride to the St. Paul campus took about ten minutes this late at night. It wasn't much time to think. Zan was still left with a short-term money problem. He pulled out his new phone and called Kayla Witold at her dorm room.

After two rings a feminine voice answered, "Hello?"

"Kayla?"

"Just a sec." In the background Zan could hear the girl call out loudly for Kayla.

"Hello?" asked another feminine voice.

"Kayla, it's Zan."

"Hi!" It was probably feigned enthusiasm but Zan liked it anyway. "What's going on?"

"You have any tests tomorrow?"

"Well, no."

"Good, put something nice on and grab your purse, we need to do some fundraising."

"What?"

*   *   *   *   *   *   *

Joseph Svenson walked into Coffman Memorial Union with Zan's backpack. Down a flight of steps made of gaudy orange tiles, he emerged on the ground floor of Coffman and slipped the backpack and his leather jacket in a custodial closet. Underneath his jacket was a denim work shirt, well stained. He was scheduled to work until 11:30pm but he had already finished all his work except for changing out the trash bags, which he could typically do in about an hour. He decided to head to the bathroom on the basement floor and read a book on the can for awhile.

For Joe, the goal was not to make money working. It was to get paid to do the things he wanted to do. Read books. Listen to music. Nap.

Svenson was plain. average. unnoticeable. Thus his moniker 'Regular Joe.'

Joe was the leader of the self-described 'Chaos Makers.' Three men irrationally bent on causing the University to waste as much money and time as possible. Nothing else. No philosophical reasoning. Just destruction.

Each had a story.

Joe had taken classes at the U but after he failed to pay a library fine that was somewhere in the vicinity of a hundred dollars, the University prevented him from registering for classes until he paid the fee.

There was a problem. Joe had never been to a library in his life, and had never checked out a book from any of the U libraries. He refused to pay the fine.

That was eight years ago.

This put a hold on his registration. It forced Joe to miss out on three required classes for his degree. The hundred dollar fine would cost him several thousand dollars in tuition money.

So he never registered for classes again.

Eventually Joe paid off the fine. This allowed him to start working odd jobs around campus. Sometimes they were full-time, but often not. Either way, they were always union, with pension plans, health benefits, overtime. Good jobs.

A happy consequence of working at the campus he loathed was it provided him access. To stuff. Technology. Computers. Art work. Joe became quite the thief.   With every theft, act of vandalism or practical joke, Joe could feel the U being brought towards entropy. Just a little, but entropy nonetheless.

Nihilism attracts nihilism and Joe soon met others like himself.

Man number two in the Chaos Makers trio of terror was Mark 'Fats' Nelson.

Mark had gone to the University for five years. Near graduation, the University told him he didn't meet all of Liberal Education Requirements and couldn't graduate, not until he took a few more classes.

'Liberal Education Requirements' was the fancy phrase for left-wing propaganda. Everyone who wanted a liberal arts degree from the University had to take them. The goal of education had moved from teaching young people how to think to teaching them what to think.

The options forced upon students were limited in scope but limitless in expression. American Studies classes portrayed America as a modern Hitler state; literature classes required students to write leftist papers because teachers would openly grade conservative students much lower; theatre courses where professors assigned the Communist Manifesto and the Democratic Party Platform.

There was no avenue for escape.

Students could send grade disputes to the dean of the department and hope for the impossible. Complaints to leftist deans about leftist professors could, in a best-case scenario, be presented to a board of leftist professors to regrade the work.

Normally, the work was given the same grade.

Fats Nelson knew the process well. He had been through it with almost every professor he ever had. He never won, but it was fun. Fats was a contrarian. And, unlike Regular Joe, a conservative. But he wasn't a partisan. He just enjoyed being a contrarian.

Nelson's problem with the University, the reason he felt

driven to bring his wrath upon the campus, was a minor technicality with his degree. An English Major, he was given a specific schedule of classes to take, including his Liberal Education requirements. The same week he declared his major, the head of the Liberal Arts College changed the Liberal Education Requirements to include two additional 'Diversity Core' classes.

Diversity Core classes were lib-ed classes on steroids. They were just race-baiting exercises where all the white kids were made to feel guilty about the condition of minorities in society, regardless of their actual innocence. The minorities were taught to blame their problems on white people, regardless of the actual outcome. The uselessness of the exercise was superfluous to the intent. Hate whitey, even if you were whitey.

To Fats, these classes were the bane of of his existence.

The rub: Nelson signed his degree contract before the extra classes were added, but when he was a Senior the University told him to take the classes or they wouldn't give him a degree. Taking another set of classes would cost him several thousand dollars. So he didn't do it. He was done, degree or no degree.

Fats met Joe through 'Tass' Larson when they were all working as parking attendants. After sharing stories in a marathon bull session, they pledged revenge.

At first their attempts were amateurish. Slashed tires on University vehicles; broken gate arms at University parking ramps; arson. But after purchasing a book by George Hayduke, their activities became more sophisticated and effective.

Soon they were sending messages to department heads and faculty on official University letterhead outlining new policies for office workers. Like new and tedious expense report procedures. Or policies against reading newspapers. Regulations regarding chairs, banning wheels, found janitors busily removing all the wheels from office chairs.

Eventually department heads made changes to the memo 'procedure' and warned people about false messages. So the Chaos Makers sent memos asking employees to 'ignore the previous memo, it was not from the department.'

The 'ignore previous memo' gag was used randomly over several years to great amusement.

As much fun as the memos were, the pair's golden moment had come two years ago. Professor Richard McKean, a tenured Political Science professor, was a well-known communist. McKean used his classes to spread his Marxist philosophy and dozens of conservative students battled him to no avail. McKean graded on ideology instead of merit. This practice was not unique to McKean, but his pursuit of indoctrination bordered on persecution. Students who stood against him were failed. Period.

THE EDUCATOR

War was declared. Regular Joe sent Professor McKean magazines in the mail. Nothing obscene. Except, the covers of the magazines, featuring attractive models and celebrities, had their eyes cut or burned out. The effect was rather spooky. And cumulative.

Next, Joe sent satanic symbols, painted on parchment paper, to the professor's home. A little blood added to the effect. McKean was an atheist, so these were laughed at. McKean even wrote an article about the attempt at intimidation.

After a month of inactivity, the duo started again. Boxes arrived at McKean's office filled with nothing but congealed blood. The Professor reported the activity to the police. His mail was monitored. Patrol cars would stop by his house once a night.

Joe and Fats stopped again. A few months allowed McKean to relax a little.

Fats went to the Caribbean for a vacation. He brought back a couple of dried devil fish. The devil fish, when dried, looks sort of like a miniaturized, mummified human corpse. Frightening with the proper presentation.

One night, thanks to some duplicate keys picked up while working as a janitor, Fats left the devilfish, in young girl's clothing, covered in deer guts and blood, on McKean's desk. He stabbed a large knife through the fish. Blood covered almost every surface of the office. Satanic symbols were spray painted on the walls. Finally, a plastic bag filled with red paint was suspended from the ceiling of the office, just in front of the door. On the door, a large knife was duct-taped so it would rip open the bag of paint once it was opened.

The next morning, covered in red paint, the good professor decided to leave his full-time faculty position and pursue his life long dream of adding more manifestos to his already copious pile of scribblings.

His magnum opus, 'Imperialism and Churchill,' sold 124 copies.

*   *   *   *   *   *   *

Jose Romero Rodriguez was the third member of the Chaos Makers. New to the group as of November 1993.

He had no special story about getting screwed by the University's bureaucracy. Nor had he ever been maligned in the classroom. He was just a tough Mexican kid from Sante Fe with a 90 mph fastball on a baseball scholarship. A torn rotator cuff his sophomore year ended his baseball dreams. And it also left him without enough money to finish school.

Not that he cared, he was never good at school.

But his mother pressured him to stay, so his pitching coach

found him a job at the U working for Parking and Transportation Services (PTS) as a parking lot attendant. For working full-time for the University, Jose was offered a Regents Scholarship that paid for eight credits of classes every semester. It was a good job; it required no effort and gave Jose a chance to study.

Seven years later Jose finished his degree in creative writing.

Already five years into a posh twenty-year pension plan, Rodriguez decided to stay on with PTS full-time. It was at PTS where he met Tass Larson.

The story repeated itself. Tass introduced Jose to Fats and Joe.

Soon enough, Jose was causing problems too.

*　　　*　　　*　　　*　　　*　　　*　　　*

Joe, done reading for the day, went back to work in Coffman clearing trash. After he was done there would be time to call up Jose and Fats and get a start on Zan's little project. He looked at his watch. There was even enough time to rummage through some of the Student Organization offices.

*　　　*　　　*　　　*　　　*　　　*　　　*

Kayla looked at her alarm clock. 9:20pm.

Kayla knew the cadre of people she spent her time with at the Big Ten were unusual. It wasn't just the weird hours or the endless nights spent postering campus.

Those things were fun. Irritating mindless liberals was great.

The fact there were people in their thirties in the group, people who didn't seem to have a job or a life and spent their time around college kids, that was unusual. But they all were nice. And funny. That made up for the creepy.

But being asked to dress up, late at night, out of the blue, from one of those thirty-somethings? That brought the creepy back into the equation.

In her Freshman Anthropology course she remembered a long discussion about modern tribalism and how tribes existed despite other 'schema-like' states. Whatever the hell that meant.

Over the last few months though, the Big Ten crew became her tribe.

Kayla met Zan outside of Bailey Hall wearing a brown single-breasted trench coat in a feminine cut. Underneath the coat she was much less fashionable, sporting a black sweater and lined blue jeans.

Giving the biggest smile she could muster in the cold, she asked "What's going on?"

Zan didn't return the smile.

- 35 -

"We need to catch the campus connector to Minneapolis. You have credit cards and such in your purse right?"

"Yes, but why?"

"I'll explain on the bus."

*　　*　　*　　*　　*　　*　　*

Zan made sure he didn't show it, but he was impressed by how well Kayla cleaned up, when needed.

She often skipped wearing makeup at all. And physically she wasn't very attractive. Shorter, a little chunky, but not fat. She often she wore thick-rimmed rectangular glasses. When she did put on makeup, found decent clothes to throw on and wore contacts, she could pass for a looker. Her hair was jet-black, straight and shoulder length. It always looked the same, neither adding nor subtracting from her appearance.

They sat in the back of the bus. Only one other rider joined them for the ride. He stayed near the driver.

The bus pulled away from the St. Paul Student Center.

"Okay," Zan said with curt authority, knowing this would be a tough sell, "I asked you to bring your credit cards and everything else because we're going to rob you."

"What!?" She gasped, and immediately covered her mouth with her hands.

"Relax," he said, "it works like this: you're at a party tonight, maybe on a date. You misplace your purse. In it are your credit cards. We use the cards to get cash advances from ATMs, maxing out before midnight, then maxing out again after midnight. Using your pin number of course."

"And how do I explain that?"

"Easy. Ditzy girl routine. I bet your pin number is written down somewhere in you purse or is it something easy like your birth date, or maybe one-two-three-four?"

"It's my birthday, July seventh, seventy-five. Seven-seven-seven-five."

"Perfect. So you're off the hook. Just tell that to the guys from the credit card company."

"So you've done this before?"

"Every year. Haven't gotten caught yet."

"Can't we just embezzle some grant money or something? You're only going to get 600 bucks if you max out my cards."

"Every little bit helps." Zan replied. "You'll be rewarded for all of this later, but this will make a difference."

They sat in silence for a minute. Their conversation must have seemed suspicious to anyone watching, with all the whisperings, gasps and occasional exclamations.

But no. Neither the bus driver nor the other passenger took notice.

People were always lost in their own little worlds.

"Okay." Kayla did her best to sound a little indignant. "I'll do it."

"Great. So, where do you want to go? Frat row or downtown?"

"Let's stay on campus."

"Delta Tau Delta it is."

*   *   *   *   *   *   *

The bus passed into Minneapolis. Zan pulled the line to signal the driver to stop in front of Moos Tower. They walked to frat row together, Zan forcing Kayla to practice her frantic post-theft phone call. The temperature had dropped below freezing again. Once they got to frat row, Zan took Kayla's credit cards and her drivers' license. And some last-minute instructions.

"Remember, tomorrow morning, call in the missing cards. And lose your purse somewhere in the frat house. You might even be able to find it later. I'll take care of the rest. Don't call anything in before eight in the morning. And be ready, the credit card companies will grill you on the phone if they think anything is up, so be in a highly emotional state, just like we practiced"

"I'm a girl, I can do that easily enough."

"And stay away from any drinks you didn't pour yourself."

*   *   *   *   *   *   *

Sometime around three in the morning, at a drive-up Wells-Fargo ATM in Fridley, a tall black man wearing black, with a black ski mask, walked up and put a card into a machine. The first and second attempts to take money didn't work. The pin number was incorrect. But the third attempt proved fruitful.

Two hundred dollars were withdrawn.

An hour later, the same tall black man, not that the cameras could really tell, wearing a ski mask, made another withdrawal at the same ATM. Before the night was over, twelve hundred dollars in cash had been collected from ATMs across the northwestern suburbs.

At eight the next morning customer service representatives from TCF Bank received a frantic phone call from a student at the University of Minnesota who had lost her purse. The representative did her best to calm the young woman. The fact was TCF Bank was in more trouble than the woman. Earlier in the week they increased her line of credit. Now they had to cover all the losses.

*   *   *   *   *   *   *

CHAPTER 3

March 3rd, 1994
Washington D.C.

CPAC, the Conservative Political Action Conference, had been a tradition for young conservatives since 1973. Three days and four nights of conservative speakers, book signings, mini-lectures and networking, crammed between constant partying and drunken debauchery. CPAC was better known as an annual conservative fuck-fest where guys from across the nation tried to talk drunken teens into groping sessions and blowjobs. And those drunken coeds did their best to oblige, even if the ladies were outnumbered two to one.

Kayla Witold had no idea about any of this. But Rachel Anderson was a veteran.

She knew if one wanted to avoid sex, it wasn't hard. DC had plenty of other distractions. Museums. Cool Buildings. Bars. But it was always fun to get a lot of attention, and Rachel was prepared to tease her way through the entire convention.

The trip was a last minute surpise; but Ernie Kessler had an even bigger surprise--A private jet from the Coors Brewing Company.

Coors had been a regional beer until Kessler and a few other venture capitalists convinced Coors to go national in the mid-1980's, after Kessler had been elected CEO of The Old Man's financial firm. Kessler's firm was having a difficult time lately, but Coors didn't forget about the humble financial company executive from Minnesota. They were always happy to loan out the jet.

It also didn't hurt that Coors was one of the most openly conservative corporations in the United States.

Sadly, to the girls the flight just meant some quality study time.

There was one other passenger on board other than the girls and Kessler. Congressman Rod Gram's Deputy Chief of Staff Michael Cohen. Kessler had already maxed out his individual contributions, so now the effort was finding a way to send soft money donations from his financial corporation to the National Republican Senatorial Committee, then from the NRSC to Rod Grams. All the while trying to make the whole deal appear legal.

For the girls, the next ninety hours were a blur. Rachel enjoyed taking a tour of the Capitol with Congressman Grams. Grams enjoyed spending time with a young woman, and even gave her a heads up about a job opening in his campaign. Cohen enjoyed funneling money into the Grams campaign Kayla enjoyed all the attention from the boys. Neither of the two girls could remember Senator Dole's keynote address, though both enjoyed it anyway.

Kessler enjoyed the fact everyone else was enjoying themselves.

*   *   *   *   *   *   *

CHAPTER 4

1pm Monday; March 7
Riverside Perkins, Minneapolis

Sometime in the late 1980's, during one of Zan and Kessler's marathon bull sessions at the Riverside Perkins, a homeless woman was seated a few booths down from the pair. The odor surrounding the woman filled the entire section. The first waitress refused to serve the woman, who mumbled incoherently. A manager tried to talk to the woman, to no avail. She smelled so bad, customers couldn't eat. The manager asked a police officer, enjoying dinner in the smoking section, to talk to the woman. He eventually got the woman to lift up her shirt. Wrapped in cloth around her abdomen was the rotting carcass of an infant. Since then, Riverside Perkins had become 'Dead-Baby Perkins.' After this incident, Zan decided to do all their late night work at the County D Perkins. But Kessler had a dark sense of humor.

Zan sat, waiting for Kessler in a smoking section booth. He was reading a copy of the 'City Pages'.

Kessler, running his normal amount of late, slipped his tall frame into the booth. Before he could get settled a waitress was there attending to the pair. A few minutes of small talk, a little more fuss with the waitress before they could finally talk some business.

Zan started, "How was DC?"

"Fruitful," Kessler replied, "I think Kayla found her social side. And Grams took a liking to Rachel. He even asked her to apply for a job at his campaign office."

"Sure we want Kayla to get social? That's how we lose chicks."

"No choice," Kessler said, "she's future leadership and future leadership has to be social."

"Any word on Shotgun?"

"Not yet, but he's got really good connections. He'll get on the campaign somehow. Any news on campus?"

"We're preparing for the MSA campaign tonight at my place. There's some fees stuff coming up next week and Regular Joe said he and Chris are gonna start wiring up Coffman for the Marilyn Monroe.

Speaking of which, how did the Midnight Cowboy go?"

Kessler smiled. He enjoyed getting his hands dirty. "I left the money from Kayla's creditors in an envelope in your car."

"Hope you locked the doors." Kessler took out a cigarette and lit it before continuing.

"Uh, about our money problem. I signed an agreement with a developing company to build some houses on Camp Lake's eastern shore."

"The Old Man would have your hide," Zan said defiantly.

"The Old Man never allowed his money to be so highly leveraged. We'll still own over half the lakeshore and this deal should be worth almost a million bucks after taxes. Not to mention the property tax burden I'll be rid of."

"I liked the fact we had that entire lake to ourselves."

"Life goes on. This deal gets us past the breaking point."

"For a guy in dire straights, you've been throwing plenty of money around."

"I use the credit I have. Look, this shouldn't be for long; I'm negotiating a deal with an insurance company to run their 401k program. I just have to get them to ignore my finances and trust my track record. If it happens, the firm is saved."

"Just tell them you're black and that they're a bunch of racists if they go somewhere else."

"That's Plan B."

Their food arrived. A few minutes later Kessler started on business again.

"Any thoughts on Zeale's iniation?"

"It's Shotgun's show this year. Not sure what exactly what he has in store, but it's going to require a roadtrip."

"Shotgun and Zeale should get along well, same personality."

"Sure, unless they kill each other."

"It's win-win either way."

*   *   *   *   *   *   *

A buzzer went off. Zan moved from his kitchen to the door and pressed a button next to a speaker, "Yeah!?"

"Zan, it's Chris."

"Come on up."

Zan pressed a button until he heard a door slam shut through the speaker.

It was eleven o'clock at night. And the night was just beginning for the crew.

Up the stairs came Chris Berg carrying a tote filled with reams of paper; it was a list names of all the St. Paul Campus students, with their student numbers and addresses.

In Zan's flat, the 'kids' were busy using campus directories to find registered students attending classes on the St. Paul Campus who lived off-campus. These students never voted, didn't care and rarely ever read the Daily. Their 'signatures' went on sheets. The sheets would become complete when Chris gave them the student ID numbers that went with the 'signatures.'

The Organization made its own rules.

All of this effort was targeted at getting on the ballot for the Minnesota Student Association's upcoming all-campus election. The Minnesota Student Association, known best by their acronym MSA, was the self-proclaimed student government at the University of Minnesota.

This was contradicted by the existence of a student senate that was recognized by the Board of Regents. In fact, MSA was really nothing more than a student union. Over the years the organization evolved to become the recognized voice of students thanks to the 1970's and a sympathetic University President who liked the group's radical agenda.

Eventually the student senate became irrelevant. But this didn't change the fact that MSA still had no actual power. The organization was in perpetual purgatory, lost somewhere between toothless student union and useless student government.

The Organization loved interfering with MSA. Low voter turnout made it easy to win seats and dullard bootlicking establishment types made good targets for ridicule. MSA provided a regular opportunity for direct confrontation with the liberal status quo of campus.

It also carried with it regular and reliable media coverage.

MSA could also be used as a successful fundraiser. They consistently refused to display the American flag during its meetings and this fact alone was typically good for a $10,000 return on a direct mail fundraiser for the Traditional Values Coalition.

Every year The Organization bestowed the honor of making a mockery of MSA during the undergraduate student body presidential election to one of its outgoing seniors. Winning was unimportant, even counterproductive. The goal was to muck up the works and crash the party. Nothing stings more than ridicule and with less than five percent of students voting, there was lots of room for ridicule.

This year, in order to increase voter turnout, MSA was experimenting with online voting. Students would sign into a digital ballot using their email addresses and register their votes. The polls would be open for three days and students would only be able to vote once. Paper ballot polling stations would still be open but each student would be checked against the online database to make sure there wasn't any double voting. Everything sounded so simple, it was sure to be a success.

Orson Henning, The Organization's candidate this year, was preparing the initial stages of his campaign. The first project was getting the required number of signatures, 250, to get on the ballot. Gathering signatures was a lot of work. For a real candidate it could be quite rewarding; it was a great opportunity to do some face to face campaigning, create a viable organization and test out campaign messages. It was the only time the candidates were really forced to campaign in a grassroots fashion. Intelligent candidates could start a groundswell of support by actively seeking signatures from as many students as they could.

The Organization wasn't quite so vigilant.

In years past they would simply forge the required signatures using student directories. Soon enough the election board started requiring student ID numbers along with the signatures to stop the fraud. The Organization called the bluff, provided forged signatures with fake ID numbers. Word came this year that the election board was going to check all names and ID numbers with a computer database.

Zan held the door open for Chris Berg as he huffed to catch his breath.

"Why don't you talk the Archbishop into buying this fucking place so you can move to the ground floor?"

Chris Berg was a computer expert. He didn't get to the gym very often. But, he did hit a heavy bag every night for twenty minutes and once knocked out an unruly underclassmen for being an ass. That underclassmen was Henning, and the two had gotten along well ever since. Berg worked for the U as a computer specialist and had access to things. Things guys like him shouldn't have access to.

Berg plopped the tote on the table and found his way to the fridge and pulled out a beer for himself.

"Make yourself at home," Zan suggested incredulously.

"Okay, next time you can hack the University servers yourself, faggot," Chris replied.

Everyone except Zan and Chris were sitting around Zan's family-sized dinner table. Orson Henning, Gene 'Spags' Zeale, Freshman recruits Frank Wallace and Kayla Witold, and Nolan Painter. Zan's upstairs flat in the small Nordeast duplex was about as full as it could get.

In fact, there was only one open room to the apartment. The kitchen area was also in the living room. A couch, TV set and some folding chairs were the only furnishings other than the table in the room. The table took up a lot of room. A small enclosed balcony was beyond the living room. A narrow hallway led to Zan's bedroom and the bathroom. And that was it.

Even with Zan's lack of stuff, the apartment was cramped.

On the table, sheets of paper, the official forms used to gather signatures, were spread around. Dozens of different pens too. Among the pens and paper there were bottles of beer and paper plates filled with pizza crusts. Beer and pizza were as good as cash in motivating undergrads.

"So, how many signatures do we want to come in with?" Zan asked.

Cheating was a way of life for Zan. A welcome one. The deck was stacked against conservatives on campus, and he loved marking the deck.

"The UDFL candidate says they're up to 500," Henning replied, "we should probably come in below that. I'd say 350."

"Sounds good," Zan said, "Frank and Kayla, you two can get a start matching names to IDs. We'll join you in a minute."

Zan, not waiting for a response, led the rest of the crew to the four-season deck at the front of the house which sat over the porch to the ground floor apartment. Cheap and gaudy yellow outdoor furniture formed a rough circle on the deck. Zeale, the youngest, was forced to sit on an upturned paint bucket.

After everyone settled, Zan closed the old wooden door and started the meeting. "We need something different for the campaign this year. Last year's 'Angry, Judgmental and Proud of It' slogan didn't have the edge we were shooting for."

"I was thinking," Nolan Painter said, looking to the ceiling in feigned thought, "how about a monarchy-party gag? We run a guy to be king, so the students never have to vote over student government again."

"Funny, but not edgy," Zan said.

"Why not do a 'Fuck MSA' campaign this year," Chris Berg said, "just like I did back in the day. "

"Fuck MSA?" Zeale asked.

"Yeah," Chris explained, "it's a satirical thing where we play on normal student rebelliousness by running to end student government altogether. Tell them we'll return the money. Talk about how stupid student government is anyway. Point out it's just a toothless student union."

"I like it," Zeale said.

"Can't say 'fuck' anywhere," Henning said, "I'm the Values Coalition guy, remember?"

"That was last year," Zan said, "you run the Smoker's Society now."

"Why not an 'End MSA' campaign instead of 'Fuck'?" Henning said.

"Don't be a such a pussy." Painter quipped.

"How about we just use a different word, like say 'Fook MSA' instead, and spell it, uh, like P-H-O-K?" Zan suggested.

"Works for me," Henning said.

"Pussies." Painter again.

Chris Berg finished his beer and decided to drop the bomb he had been sitting on, "You want to win the election?"

"Excuse me?" Henning asked.

"I was the guy assigned to write the software for the election," Chris explained, "I can get and create fake digital ballots without getting caught. We can pick the winner this year."

"But there are still paper ballots," Zeale said. "What if they find out some people voted twice and they raise a stink?"

"We do the same thing we're doing now," Berg offered. "We use off-campus St. Paul students. Freshman and outgoing seniors. Turnout is only about five percent so there's little chance there'd be a problem."

"How little?" Zan asked.

"Let's see," Berg was well versed in statistics and probability, "I figure one in five. We do this gag five years, we get caught once. But there's little chance the election board finds out about the fraud. It'll look like some student accidentally voted twice. Hell, considering this is the first year they're doing this, there will probably be a bunch of that going on. Worst case? The board finds out campus servers are being hacked by someone off-campus. There's no way they trace it back to us. Not when I'm the guy they'll turn to solve the thing."

Berg was good. When he was in junior high, he put together his own Altair 8800 and programmed the quirky thing completely by hand. Computers had been his life ever since.

"Wait," Henning said. "Why not hold off on it this year. This year, let the election run. We find out what underclassmen don't vote so we know who to use next year to tip the election how we want. Then we'll be able to pick and choose the MSA president as long as they're using Berg's software, right?"

"Even if they try something else, I have enough access to break it" Berg said. "They could fire me and I'd still be able to run their servers for them."

"And," Zan said, a smile audible in his voice, "We choose the most incompetent liberal boobs we can find. Idiot ideologues who will provide us all the fundraising fodder we can handle."

"Why don't we let Henning win?" Zeale asked.

"Because I'm fucking graduating, asshole."

"Plus," Zan added, "we don't want to get bogged down in MSA. It'd be a waste of time."

"Still, we should use our access this year, in case they go back to all-paper ballots next year," Zeale said.

"Good point," Zan said. "I guess we'll have to wait for all the campaigns to file first, before we decide who to help along."

"All this computer bullshit is fine," Henning said with authority, he was the candidate after all, "but I'd like to pull a Sideshow Bob this year."

"Haven't done one since Shotgun," Berg said in agreement, "so it should be new enough to campus."

"And it will be good for the kids," Henning said, nodding towards the two Freshmen visible through the window. They were diligently working on the signature sheets.

"Speaking of which," Zan got up from his chair. "It's about time we helped them finish."

*   *   *   *   *   *   *

CHAPTER 5

Tuesday, March 8
Uptown Minneapolis

Paulson rolled himself out of bed. The clock read 4:22am. He was up before the alarm. Again. But it was a solid three and a half hours of sleep. He normally couldn't get much more than that. He shaved, showered, got dressed. Made a breakfast of eggs, toast and fruit. Paulson took breakfast seriously. An hour later, he was ready to beat rush hour traffic.

Taking his Suburban out of the apartment's underground garage, he drove to campus. The University President traditionally lives in Eastcliff, a mansion several miles south of campus, on the cliffs overlooking the Mississippi River. It was large, beautiful, and had 8,500 visitors every year. Not the level of privacy a serial killer needed. Eastcliff was saved for alumni celebrations, big donor fundraisers and athletic recruiting.

Lake Street to I35W to Washington Avenue. The ride took twenty minutes. Paulson's parking space underneath Northrup Plaza was ten paces away from the basement entrance to Morrill Hall. There were cameras all around the underground garage, allowing Paulson to create his own timeline. In his daily planner Paulson crafted a new storyline everyday. A detailed alibi any investigation was sure to find.

Two flights of stairs up from the basement was the sprawling space consumed by the Office of the President of the University of Minnesota. Dozens of people worked in the office; desks and cubicles were haphazardly set up throughout the entire second floor. Several other U officials had offices in the same space. In addition there were a half dozen conference rooms available for use.

THE EDUCATOR

During the day department heads and administrators were constantly coming in and out. It was a busy place. But it was empty at this time in the morning. Paulson's actual office, inside his office, was in the southwest corner providing a view of Northrup Auditorium and the Mall area all the way to Coffman Union.

Paulson went to the break room and started the coffee machines. It would be a couple of hours before anyone else arrived in the office. He used the time to prepare for the day. There was a budget to approve, buildings to renovate, proposals to propose, policies to implement and bureaucrats to satiate.

Time flew. Paulson's personal secretary, Stephanie Demay, poked her head into the office when she arrived a few minutes before 8am. "Remember the meeting about General College at nine."

"I'm still working through the new PSEO Admissions proposals, give me a reminder a few minutes before, huh?"

"Sure."

*   *   *   *   *   *   *

Vice Provost Martin Brackens droned on and on, repeating himself several times. "By eliminating General College we can improve our US News and World Report ranking by increasing our 6-year graduation rate, increasing our per-student spending and raising our standardized test scores and first year retention rates. This proposal is win-win-win. We save some money, better our rankings and attract better students. We can be an icon for education in the international community. Everything will snowball from there."

General College was originally an open admission college founded in 1932. It offered access to the University for students who didn't meet the criteria for enrollment in the degree-granting colleges at the University. Students were given access to intensive support services and GC classes were transferable throughout the University. Norman Borlaug, Nobel Laureate, started his career in the General College. It was an extremely popular part of the University to the community at large.

"And what happens to current GC students?" Paulson asked.

"They get absorbed into the Continuing Education Department," Brackens Replied.

"Forty-eight percent of General College students are minorities, what does this do to our diversity levels?"

"They don't change." Brackens gave a sinisterish smile. "That's what's so great about this proposal. We can continue to accept under-qualified students through ConEd on a part-time basis. We can double the number of students given the opportunity to enter the University system while weeding out the low ceiling achievers. We don't

need to count part-time ConEd students in our primary academic reports but we can count them as part of our campus diversity."

Paulson stared at Brackens for a moment. *I really should kill
him*, Paulson thought. But he didn't enjoy killing men.

"I don't think so," Paulson finally said. "The University is a
land-grant institution and it is our duty to offer the citizens of Minnesota access to higher education, even if it hurts us in arbitrary third
party rankings. General College works, and nobody here has suggested otherwise. Playing three-card monte with underprivileged
students is unacceptable and will not happen as long as I'm president
of this University."

*   *   *   *   *   *   *

After the General College meeting, Paulson was back in his
office. The entire University had just been through an independent
financial audit. The final report was due today. If the U's accounting
totals were within three percent of the audit's, then Paulson's next
budget would be greenlighted through the legislature without any
fanfare. If there were major discrepancies it would mean several more
months of headache.

He stared at a renovation request from the Naval ROTC to
fix the roof of the Armory. Paulson had been, and would be, ignoring
all renovation requests from Captain Bittner. The Armory was a low
priority in the budget, it wasn't like they would leave and if he gave
them money he would be attacked by the local hippie radicals. The
request was just something to stare at while he waited.

Demay poked her head in. She shook it solemnly. "Three
point six four," she said.

"Fuckit," Paulson said. "Alright, we need to call an all-depart-
ment meeting tomorrow and have them start preparing for a department by department financial review. Start calling around to some
accounting firms, see if we can't get some outside assistance--wait,
scratch that. Call up Ernie Kessler and ask him if we can use some of
his people. It'll be cheaper. We have three months before we go to the
State Capitol."

"Sure thing."

"And Steph, start freeing up my schedule. No more building
proposals or academic reviews for two weeks, we need to get this
done."

"Okay."

"Oh, and get me a copy of that audit before the end of the day,
I don't care if you have to drive out and get it. If we can pinpoint the
problem departments, we can save a few hundred billable hours."

"Don't forget about lunch with your brother today," Demay

THE EDUCATOR

said as she left the office.

*   *   *   *   *   *   *

Timothy Paulson was six years younger than Malcolm. He was Paulson's only sibling and closest living relative. He had Down Syndrome with severe cognitive disabilities. Paulson donated millions of dollars towards adult care facilities that helped hundreds of people like Timothy. Enough money was stashed away in protected accounts that Timothy would be taken care of no matter what happened to Paulson. They ate lunch together once a week at Eastcliff.

"Hey buddy," Paulson said, "How you doing?"

"hay."

"I brought some pizza with me, you favorite, thin crust!"

"Peeya?"

"That's right, from Campus Pizza."

"Saya nona grayna."

"That's right, no greens, no vegetables."

The two ate together. Timothy occasionally laughing at Paulson's teasings and clownings. Timothy's guardian, a heavyset woman in her late twenties, spent the luncheon reading in the Walnut Den, where she always stayed during these reunions. The life expectancy for an American with Down Syndrome was less than fifty. Paulson didn't quite know how he felt. Or would feel when Timothy died. Still, he tried to see his brother at least once a week.

As they got ready to leave, Paulson gave Timothy twenty dollars and tipped his guardian a hundred. It took ten minutes to get from Eastcliff to his office. Stacked on his desk were fifteen large binders, each three inches thick. The results of the audit.

Paulson sat down and began reading the first binder.

Demay poked her head through the door. "No reason to read the whole thing. Building and Grounds, Parking and Transportation Services and General College are the primary culprits."

"Figures."

"Kessler said he can loan us two of his corporate finance specialists, they'll be stopping by tomorrow."

Paulson nodded his head. The weight of the failure finally hit him. *Fucking PTS*. Paulson knew failure meant everything became more difficult, from getting alumni donations to presenting renovation proposals to the Regents. Lost for a while in thought, Paulson came back into the moment when he felt Demay rubbing his shoulders.

"It's not so bad," she cooed, "you knew the failure rate was over fifty percent for first timers. It'll be fine. In fact, you can spin this to the legislature. After you clean out the problem departments you'll

- 48 -

look like a hardnosed budget hawk."

She's right. She's always right, Paulson thought.

"If you want," she whispered, "you can come over to my place tonight. I'll make you feel better."

"You know, you're always right."

"I know. Now remember you have the IT guys coming in at three. They want more money to expand our server capacities."

"They must think our Gopher Protocol is going to catch on."

"Is it?"

"Nah, the Internet is just a fad."

*   *   *   *   *   *   *

It was 8pm when Paulson finally got out of the office. It didn't take him long to digest the results of the audit. There were some huge discrepancies between expected income from the parking ramps and actual ramp income. It looked like shenanigans. Paulson hated shenanigans. Heads were going to roll.

Paulson decided to swim a few laps at the Aquatic Center before heading over to Demay's apartment. She lived just two blocks away from Paulson in Uptown. She was quite a convenience. Originally working as an accountant for the Math Department when Paulson was a professor there, he took her with him to Morrill Hall. Since then she had been his best employee.

A short, attractive brunette who was midwesternly pale, she could recall important numbers from every departmental budget she had ever seen. She loved accounting as a baseball fan loved statistics. In Paulson's mind, she was irreplaceable. While she wanted no real commitments in her personal life and their relationship had been casual, on and off, for five years, she would hint on occasion that she wanted more. Paulson always shrugged the suggestions away.

Paulson ran up four flights of stairs to her apartment.

The door to her apartment was unlocked. He entered, to find Stephanie on the couch in front of her TV set. A pizza in one hand, a beer in the other.

I hate her so much, Paulson thought.

*   *   *   *   *   *   *

Lights out, missionary position, shirt on. Paulson hated sleeping with Demay. He often fantasized about killing her. *It'd be hard. I'd need an airtight alibi. It would have to look like an accident or a suicide. A suicide note would be really hard to get right.* Demay wrote everything in a very ornate cursive handwriting. *Besides, she would be impossible to replace in the office.*

THE EDUCATOR

He looked at her while she slept. He did love her body. The curves were all right. *She'd look good underwater.* Paulson slipped out of bed and put on his clothes. He didn't need any more sleep, and the more time he spent around Demay, the more he wanted to claim a memory.

The clock in her kitchen read 12:23. *Thank God, another Tuesday out of the way.*

Paulson hated Tuesdays.

*   *   *   *   *   *   *

Zan loved Tuesdays.

No campus obligations.

Nothing.

Nothing important happened on a Tuesday.

Zan rolled out of bed. It was 10:30 in the morning.

The next fifteen minutes were spent doing 100 push-ups and 200 sit-ups. The workout continued with ten minutes of skipping rope in the backyard. This was combined with twenty minutes of stretching. Another twenty minutes were spent hitting a heavy-bag set up in the small garage he shared with the property owner, who lived on the ground floor.

He took a quick shower and grabbed his gym bag. There was a lunchtime aikido class to get to. Aikido was all kata, but Zan enjoyed the complicated motions, holds and throws.

On Fridays and Saturdays he normally trained in jiu-jiutsu or judo.

Other days he did his best to get in some kickboxing. And he still put in one class a week of shotokan karate, something he had done for almost twenty years.

All this was in addition to the sparring he did in boxing, at least three times a week.

He was running late though. The crew didn't get out of his place until after three in the morning, finishing the signature sheets. Zan jumped into his metallic blue car and sped off towards St. Paul.

Outside of the campus activism, martial arts was Zan's life. In high school, Zan boxed competitively in the Golden Gloves program. But he stopped in Law School and never got back into it competitively. Since then, he did nothing but spar.

There were no goals to his activity.

It was just something he just did.

Rumors in The Organization suggested all the fighting was the only way he could deal with the facts of his life.

The Aikido class lasted an hour. It was held in the St. Paul Gym, on the St. Paul campus. There were thirty regulars and a few observers. After the class, where he spent most of his time being thrown around, he jumped on an indoor running track. Aged, dating to 1915, Zan spent thirty minutes running the suspended track at a brisk pace.

A shower and a half a Big Mac later, Zan decided to use his old student ID to get into a matinee at the Har Mar movie theatre fifty cents cheaper. 'Jurassic Park' was still playing and Zan hadn't seen it yet.

Like usual, he liked the movie about as much as he didn't like it.

He stopped by the Northeast Boxing Club, just a few blocks from his home, and got nine rounds of sparring in before finally calling it a day. Some Ramen noodles with a little butter was dinner.

Another 100 push-ups before calling it a night.

At two in the morning, there was a buzz. Alisha Williams, the owner of the Big Ten, didn't feel like driving all the way home. She didn't bring any pajamas either.

Zan loved Tuesdays.

*   *   *   *   *   *   *

CHAPTER 6

8pm Thursday, March 17
Minneapolis

The semester's activities slowed down. Schoolwork piled up. It was three weeks until the MSA election. The conservative paper still didn't have money. There was planning and paperwork to do for the major speaker. Not that there was money yet for a major speaker.

But the work was done. Grant applications were filled out. Rooms reserved. People were contacted. Schedules were made. Bureaucratic bullshit needed to get done early.

Some offensive message postering provided a break in the monotony.

The winter wore on people though.

The best remedy Zan and the crew had for the cabin fever was pirate radio. It was a pain in the ass to do and in a lot of ways it was a waste of time. But it was fun as hell.

During the previous night, Painter led a crew through all the dorms in the Superblock, taping posters everywhere. Pirate radio played to the naturally rebellious nature of undergrads.

Showtime was 8pm. The radio show was done out of the back of a minivan owned by local libertarian and radio buff Mitch Davis. Mitch once had his own radio show on the local a.m. blowtorch, KSTP, before being unceremoniously fired.

THE EDUCATOR

It was his van. His equipment. He did all the technical work. Driving the minivan, a 1990 Toyota Previa, was Zan. Doing the show was an Organization veteran known as 'Shotgun' and he was helped by another Organization member known only as 'King.' In black market politics, pirate radio and other criminal enterprises, real names are not preferred.

Rachel Anderson invited herself on the radio program. And no one says no to 38-24-36. She was using the handle 'Random Hot Chick' and was practicing her flirtsy valleygirl act in her head as the van drove towards the University.

Pirate radio was, generally, a misdemeanor. But it could get expensive. Over the last two years, the twelve 'Gopher Pirate Radio' shows had become a lightning rod of outrage on campus. Using equipment only Mitch really understood, the show was able to overpower the campus radio station, 770 AM, 'Radio K.'

This made campus administrators, and the folks at Radio K, very unhappy.

Radio K sucked. It did nothing but play the worst artistic-modern-hardcore-but-not-sellouts-boring-but-loud music on the face of the planet. Few people listened but all students paid. The Organization had tried several times to get a talk show on the station, to no avail.

Then they tried to cut funding for Radio K by loading up the Student Services Fees Committee with darkhorse conservatives. When the administration overruled them, they turned to Pirate Radio to surprising success.

Everyone wants to break the rules. It's even better when they can be passive about it.

Radio K was not so amused. They hired a private security firm to track down the illegal broadcast. During the last broadcast, Mitch and crew were almost caught; barely escaping from their hiding spot inside the University Fieldhouse. Five thousand dollars worth of equipment had to be abandoned.

That was early the previous semester. Compensating Mitch for the equipment was one of the reasons The Organization was short of money. A stubborn man, it was Mitch's idea to use a mobile broadcast platform. Mitch figured a moving target was hard to triangulate.

The security company was also using mobile trackers. With both cat and mouse moving, the guess was they'd be able to broadcast much longer. Mitch had one other trick. He had set up a small radio transmitter and antenna on the roof on one of the parking ramps. A pre-recorded message would be broadcast teasing the actual show.

Mitch looked down at his watch. The recording would start in thirty seconds and would last two minutes.

"Okay guys," he said, "showtime, put your gear on."

Mitch was sitting in the back of the minivan where his groceries normally went. He started pushing buttons on his equipment. Four car batteries accompanied the retro-looking transmitter.

"Zan," Mitch ordered, "get us to 4th street so we're in range of the dorms."

At the wheel, Zan obeyed the command.

The car started moving eastward from Dinkytown. Shotgun, King and Rachel put on headsets and Mitch started doing sound checks. The audio quality was low enough that any listeners would likely not realize the studio was a minivan with some blankets stretched over the windows to dampen outside sounds.

Mitch waved at the crew, "And we're live in three...two...."

"Good evening students, professors and innocent citizens, this is The Shotgun," Shotgun emphasized his name like a rock star would, "and you're listening to some hardcore Pirate Radio!" Shotgun had a deep voice and could make it resonate thanks to help from Mitch. He was short, a little taller than Zan. Broad shouldered. Enormously overweight. He took up a lot of space in the cramped minivan. His excessive hand motions were icing on the discomfort cake.

Some music played for a few seconds, something from Van Halen. Then King started his opener: "Joining Shotgun is me, 'el jefe,' your lord and master, 'the King.'"

King's voice was unnaturally deep, very good for radio. King was actually David Langston, a horticulture professor at the U of M who was good friends with Zan when they were undergrads. Zan had included King in a lot of The Organization's projects.

However, If King was discovered doing the broadcast, he'd be immediately fired.

Luckily no one important ever stopped by the horticulture department on the St. Paul campus. And horticulture students and faculty rarely ventured onto the Minneapolis campus. Still, King kept his voice very deep and Midwestern; totally unlike his natural and obnoxious Jersey accent.

"And me," Rachel raised her voice a little whenever she ended a sentence and exaggerated her lisp, "Random Hot Chick. So...Helloo boysz, have you been bad since we were last on the air?"

"Oh we have," Shotgun replied, "But not nearly as bad as your friends at Boynton Health Services."

"What is 'Boynton?'"

"I'll explain it, Hot Chick," Langston said.

"Thanxxs King," Rebecca lisped, "thinking is soo hard."

"Boynton is the socialized healthcare service on campus. Supposedly it's available to all students, but even though everbody pays, Boynton is only used by ten percent of University Students."

"Wow, I'm no good at math, but even I know that's a small

number King." Rachel said.

The next ten minutes of the show went well. Mitch decided to go for a break at that point. Just some music while the cast checked their notes.

Zan kept the car in motion, circling around campus. University Ave, Washington Ave, 4th Street to East River Road. After a few minutes Mitch started up the broadcast again. The conversation revolved around Student Services Fees, a campus conservative obsession. The topic was the only one where the conservatives found consistent popular support. Students paid hundreds of dollars in fees every semester but few ever utilized the services provided.

"...and that, boysz and girlsz, is why you should show those utopian hippies that socialism doesn't work. Get down to Boynton and flood them with requests and they crumble."

Rachel ended her bit and flashed a smile to everyone else in the car.

It was short lived.

"Yo!," It was Zan shouting. "Cut the broadcast."

"And we're off." Mitch said, turning off all the gear just as King was trying to start on another topic. "What's going on Zan?"

"We picked up a tail. Black van. Government plates."

"Okay, just take it easy," Mitch shouted to Zan, as calmly as he could, "don't give them any reason to pull us over." Mitch reached under the back seat and flicked a switch on another piece of equipment. It was a CB Radio. "Archbishop, Archbishop, this is the Northern Alliance, begin operation Poland. Over."

In a car a mile away, in the heart of the Superblock, Ernie Kessler flicked the switch on a small radio transmitter. A reel-to-reel recording machine started to play a message over the 770 AM band. It was a brief recording of a segment of the show. The tiny transmitter could only broadcast about a thousand foot radius. Enough to cover the Superblock dorms and hopefully pull the tail off the real crew.

Mitch loved playing games with government bureaucrats.

Ernie let the message play for a few minutes, then eased out of his parking spot and made tracks for I94.

* * * * * * *

"The van is still following us." Zan kept the Previa minivan moving along East River Road, moving towards the Knoll area of campus.

"Don't give them any reason to pull us over. Right now they have nothing," Mitch shouted, more for emphasis than concern. He was a longtime believer in civil liberties and knew his rights inside and out.

"Okay, I'm just going to loop around and get to the Washington Avenue Bridge. Then get on the Interstate. What do I do if they keep following?"

"Drive us to Fargo." Mitch said. "They'll quit following us eventually."

*   *   *   *   *   *   *

CHAPTER 7

9am Monday, March 21
Room 110, Blegen Hall, Minneapolis

The room was silent for a second. A woman, attractive and sharply dressed in a gray and purple pantsuit, reached across the table she was seated at and turned off a clunky tape recorder.

"You guys can't be fucking serious."

The speaker was Rita Singer, the chairwoman of the Student Services Fees Committee. Her hair was jet black, and straight until the ends curled around her conic breasts. Not an accident. Her face was long. Her chin ended in a sharp point. Her nose was like a blade. Everything about her body, was angled and sharp. Her look was basically a jumble of straight lines. Still, everything was proportional and some of the gentlemen in the room had a hard time focusing on the business at hand.

Across the table from Rita were Nolan Painter, Orson Henning, Kayla Witold and Frank Wallace. The group had just presented the Fees Committee their budget for the Traditional Values Coalition. The Fees Committee, along with giving money to underutilized administrative groups like Boynton Health Services or the campus gyms, also gave money to a few select student groups.

Those groups included the Queer Student Cultural Center, Womynists NOW, Africana, La Raza, the Asian American Student Cultural Collective, and other 'oppressed' identity groups. All the groups were unmistakably left-wing; yet the Fees Committee consistently claimed their programming was necessary to avoid violence and oppression. A few years ago, The Organization started applying for fees too.

Rita's response was typical for these situations, if more blunt and honest.

"That's right Madam Chairman," Nolan replied formally. Nolan was president of the group and had done most of the presentation. "We're requesting two million dollars to address the unfair allocation of student fees, retroactively. All fee money ever given to left-wing groups, adjusted for inflation, minus the ten thousand dollar grant we received from the fees committee two years ago."

"Okay," Rita looked around, shrugged her shoulders and started packing up her papers. "Looks like we're done here."

*   *   *   *   *   *   *

What Rita Singer didn't know was the Traditional Values Coalition was also recording their fees presentation. For the rest of the day, whenever anyone needed a laugh, they replayed Rita saying, loud and clear on the tape "You guys can't be fucking serious."

Kessler had set up a meeting at The Nook in St. Paul, a small sports bar known for their burgers. Zan picked up Henning and Painter from campus and arrived at 8pm, Kessler was already there. It was supposed to be a planning meeting, but it quickly devolved into a bull session. It was an hour before their conversation got back on track.

"So, Mitch was actually fined for being a radio pirate?" Zan started laughing again.

The entire table, Zan, Kessler, Henning and Painter had been reliving the Pirate Radio Show.

"Yeah," Ernie had just heard from Mitch Davis about getting the misdemeanor charges in the mail that very day. "The FCC identified the van as the source of the broadcast and decided to levy charges and fines against Mitch."

"So how much are we talking about?" Zan remembered the money problem again.

"A thousand dollars, give or take," Kessler replied.

"How's he taking it?" Painter asked.

"He told me he intends to fight the charges. Which tells me I'll be doing some pro bono work," Kessler was still licensed to practice law. "Mitch says he has a bunch of legal arguments about radio homesteading that he found in one of his libertarian manifestos. Well, I'd prefer he just pay the fine." Ernie took a puff from his cigar.

"Are we done with the radio show then?" Painter again.

"Nah, we'll just store it for a while," Ernie said, "in two years we'll be able to start up again and they won't be prepared for it." Ernie pointed at Painter and Henning. "You two just remember, there is nothing new under the sun. Every trick is old. Sometimes they get so old they're new again."

Zan jumped in with a new topic. "So I was talking to Frank on the phone this morning, and he was telling me the fees presentation lasted just ten minutes this year."

"Yeah," Painter replied. "That Singer chick just listened to our presentation, turned off the recorder, and asked us if we were 'fucking' serious. No other questions. They just got up and left."

"That's awesome." Kessler clenched his cigar in his teeth as he was smiling. The table started laughing again. "And you got it on tape?"

"Fuck yeah," Henning exclaimed.

Their food arrived, interrupting the conversation for a few minutes.

"Okay, so we're set for your MSA run?" Kessler directed his question towards Henning.

"Oh yeah." Henning said. He was already halfway through a Nookie burger, a burger stuffed with velveeta cheese, and did his best to talk while chewing. "Uh, and we found out they were bluffing about actually checking the student ID numbers. We put eighteen fakes on one of the sheets, and they didn't catch 'em."

"The year we catch them actually checking, we better be ready with at least a thousand signatures, and force them to check each one," Zan said, looking ahead.

"Is Chris finished setting up the Marilyn Monroe?" Henning asked, making another abrupt subject change. He was excited about the operation, the first one he'd actually get to work on.

"Don't know. He's got until finals week." Zan said. He had ordered a basket of fries, only, and was eating them with a fork. This was in stark contrast to Kessler, who was eating a Nookie burger with onion rings while smoking a cigar and sipping whiskey. The tall black man was starting get a little heavy as he neared his fortieth year. Daily jogging had helped control his otherwise unhealthy lifestyle.

"I heard some good news," Painter interjected, "Horowitz is coming to St. Johns first week of April. It's two weeks before our spring break. He'll talk at our campus for half his usual fee."

"Well shit, tell him we'll pay him in cash up front," Zan said. This was the best news he had heard in a while.

"In cash?" Painter said quizzically.

"Oh yeah, just tell his secretary. We've done it before." Kessler said. "We pay in cash and Horowitz can spend it before he has to report it on his income. Matter of fact, I'll call him personally."

Kessler wrote a note to himself on a napkin and slipped it into his leather jacket.

*   *   *   *   *   *   *

The Nook is a great spot. Good food. Cozy. Right next to the Cretin-Derham Hall baseball diamond where you could watch games in the winterish-spring. Rumor had it some high school freshman named Jake Mauer had knocked a ball 490 feet from homeplate to The Nook's front door. It was just a rumor. On the inside, pictures blanketed the walls. It was a great place. And the crew spent five hours there.

*   *   *   *)   *   *   *

Paulson shut down his computer and left his office. It was nine in the evening. The sun had long since disappeared.

Mondays were brutal.

He always put in long hours during the week so he could escape on weekends. Being president of a University was akin to being a CEO of a major corporation; it consumed your life completely. Even more than your whole life, if you let it. That's why he always made time for a workout, and never stayed around town on the weekend.

Alighting down the stairs to the bottom floor, where he could access his Northrop Garage parking ramp spot, Malcolm got into his car.

He always drove a big, black Suburban. It could haul his trailers and boats during the summer and provided reliable transportation in the winter. Driving out from the garage, he maneuvered his vehicle onto Pleasant Street and took a right on Pillsbury, eventually snaking his way to metered parking in front of the University Fieldhouse. From there it was a quick walk to the Rec Center.

The university Rec facility had several large gymnasiums, dozens of racquetball and squash courts, several weightlifting areas and scores of bikes, treadmills, rowing machines and other cardio equipment. Connected to the Rec center was an aquatic center with an olympic-sized pool along with a diving platform. It was an athletic Taj Mahal impelled by Paulson's predecessor.

And Paulson loved it. He worked out at least four days a week at the Rec. Paulson walked down to the basement floor where the lockers were located and entered the men's locker room. He had one of the few full-length lockers in the facility. A few minutes later he was taking laps around the pool. A former Big Five swimmer as an undergrad, he switched to distance swimming in grad school, completing several triathalons when the sport was just getting popular.

The pool closed at ten. Paulson took a quick shower and decided to try some running. The Rec itself stayed open until eleven every night, hours Paulson himself demanded. Paulson finished five miles in 44 minutes.

You're just not a young man anymore he thought to himself, disappointed in his performance.

With no time for any weightlifting, Paulson decided to walk around for few minutes before taking another shower.

The girls.

Paulson loved the Rec.

Sometimes people recognized him. On campus he could be a

bit of a celebrity. A young girl, a Sophomore, talked to him at a water fountain for a few minutes. She was short, curvaceous and flirty. A little too heavy for Paulson but he felt an attraction anyway.

He let it be, showered and drove home.

Within him something burned. He needed another prize.

It used to take a year or so but now it showed up every couple of months.

Paulson knew this was an inevitability. All killers entered this cycle. And the quickening cycle was how you got caught.

He drove. And thought.

*   *   *   *   *   *   *

CHAPTER 8

2am Thursday, March 24
West Bank, University of Minnesota, Minneapolis

Frank Wallace was running.

The Campus Election Board, seeing fit to abridge free speech however it wanted, regulated when MSA campaigns could start campaigning: no posters allowed, no doorknocking allowed, no spending money allowed, until thirty days before an election. It is the natural eventuality of any committee action, something will get regulated.

Tonight was the first night the election board allowed campaigning. Henning, Kayla, Horace and Rachel had postered around campus three hours earlier. They were seen by other campaigns and they were the first group to stop postering.

Simple strategy: put up a few posters, be seen, get alibi, leave early. The "Henning for Prez" posters would get covered up by other candidates before the fun began. Campus black ops were delicate operations.

Whenever there were shenanigans involving postering, it was always the last group out that took the blame. The key to getting away with dirty tricks was to look inept. A campaign so incompetent they couldn't figure out the basics never raised suspicion. It was the same rule when dealing with police: act dumb, forget things, look lost, ask for a lawyer.

Big Frank Wallace was part of the second crew.

Zan, Zeale, Painter and Wallace were tearing down some posters and vandalizing others by drawing inappropriate pictures or phrases on them. Sophomoric stuff.

Chalking was also popular. Campaigns would chalk their names on sidewalks since few students practiced good posture. A bucket of water, a sponge and some chalk could turn "Vote for Jenna

Summer Moonbeam" to "Jenna Summer Moonbeam eats fetuses."

It was all part of Sideshow Bob.

In previous years, two in the morning was late enough for black ops. With more campaigns trying to get fewer votes, things had gotten competitive. The last group to poster got their message out. Despite the cold, two in the morning was not late enough.

This was why Big Frank Wallace was running.

Caught red handed trying to rip down an "End Racism and Sexism; Vote Moonbeam" poster, Frank took off for the Washington Avenue Bridge. He was working alone near the Carlson building on the West Bank of campus. The four men had split up to cover more ground and were to meet up at the steps of Northrup Auditorium.

Running after him were three very irate women, waving staple hammers in the air and trying to take pictures.   They quickly fell behind the hulking Wallace. A former All-State tight end who had turned down football scholarships, the vegan wisps weren't going to catch him.

Wallace was wearing all black sweats and had on a ski-mask, nothing unusual in the well-below-zero-all-the-time Minnesota winter night. There was no chance they'd seen his face. Still, not many men his size were active on the campus political scene.

It was almost a mile to Northrup Auditorium and Wallace covered the distance in seven and a half minutes. When Wallace arrived on the steps of Northrup, the image of the big man coughing and panting made the rest of the crew start to laugh. Wallace had been the last to arrive since he was the only one on the West Bank.

It was a couple of minutes before he could spit out more than a few words.

"Jesus Christ," Wallace was still breathing heavily. "Ran into a group of womynists, they started chasing me, swinging their staple hammers and all...they had a camera too..."

"Perfect," Zan said. "We needed something like this."

"They were following me."

"The way you were running, I bet they quit before you hit the bridge," Painter lit up a cigarette before continuing. "Where'd you learn to run like that?"

"White boy in Racine, Wisconsin," Wallace panted, "on the Football team in North High, in practice all the defensive players were tough black kids who hated white cake eaters like me. Whenever they caught me, I got knee'd in the groin or worse. So they stopped catching me."

"So you're a big cocksucker who can run fast, big deal." Zeale picked up his backpack. "Let's get out of here before someone else sees us."

CHAPTER 9

11:30am Monday, March 28
Dead Baby Perkins, Minneapolis

"'Masked man caught oppressing Moonbeam,'" Kessler was reading the day's edition of the Minnesota Daily. "They even published a fuzzy picture of a man in black running away at night on a black background."

"Yeah," Zan replied. "It could be Mr. Wallace, or it could be a UFO. You can't really tell from the photo."

"Frontpage above the fold," Kessler said, "this is great, this Sideshow Bob is going perfectly. Pretty good crew this year."

"Best since Shotgun and Dan the Goy."

The two were enjoying another lunch at the Dead Baby Perkins. Kessler was waiting on a tremendous twelve breakfast, Zan was sipping coffee.

Kessler continued, "How about Chris and the Marilyn Monroe, does he have the equipment yet?"

"He does. He and Regular Joe are going to start installing the cameras on Spring Break. The camera's are pretty nifty, pinhole with some sort of wireless connection to a laptop Berg wants to set upstairs somewhere. Pretty technical. Only have three cameras too, so Rachel is going to have to lure him to specific spots. Speaking of, does she have an in?"

"Thanks to the Camp Lake deal, I just made a sizable donation to the Architectural Department. Got myself a last minute invite. Rachel would make a good date. Then all she has to do is get Professor Paulson alone, and the hard part is done."

"This op might actually work," Zan said.

"I told ya, good crew this year."

"Let's wait until we're *fait accompli* before celebrating anything."

*   *   *   *   *   *   *

CHAPTER 10

7pm Wednesday, March 30
Coffman Theatre, Coffman Memorial Union, Minneapolis

"It was the most embarrassing work of oppression this campus has seen since the BSMM applied for fees!" The shrill voice belonged to Jenna Moonbeam, Womynist and U-DFL endorsed candidate for undergraduate student body president. The BSMM group she spoke of was the Beastiality Society of Multicultural Multiculturalism. Two years ago, BSMM applied for student services fees. Their officers? a president, vice president, treasurer and zoo keeper. Orson Henning, a sophomore at the time, had been the zoo keeper.

The BSMM was not awarded any fees money.

Moonbeam continued, "This hate crime cannot continue to go unpunished. One of the campaigns in the race is responsible and I demand the culprits identify themselves and pull their campaign from the race."

"Okay," The moderator of the debate was Jeff Dyer, the current Speaker of MSA. Six feet tall and very heavy, he was sweating under the bright lights in the Coffman auditorium. "Uh, Mr Henning, any comments regarding the dirty campaign tactics recently profiled in the Minnesota Daily?"

"Absolutely Mr. Speaker. I want to add my voice to the chorus of those offended by the criminal acts of vandalism perpetrated on our fair campus. My campaign does not condone these tactics and we will be on the lookout for those responsible whenever we do any campaigning at night. Whoever is doing this will get caught. We have even purchased camera equipment. Our hope is to catch these bastards in the act."

Henning suppressed a smile by digging his thumbnail into his index finger as hard as he could. Almost half the debate had been spent on The Organization's Sideshow Bob.

"Thank you Mr. Henning. Mr. Stinson, your thoughts on the vandals."

"Clearly, our campaign is opposed to such tactics." Stinson was short, very thin but with good hair. He looked like most Frat-boy douchebags, vaguely approaching the essence of handsomeness but failing to actually be handsome.

He was the Fraternity and Sorority Organization candidate. The Greeks typically ran their own MSA candidates, despite never being involved in student government otherwise. The Organization liked this because their presence frustrated the U-DFL. This made up for the fact the Greeks were mostly douchebags.

"What concerns me though," Stinson the douche continued, "is that we have talked about the vandalism for a majority of this debate. What about the real mission behind this election, finding an MSA president who will use the organization's resources to create a better campus? Considering one of the candidates up here offers no solutions, but in fact he wants to destroy MSA. That's the real issue here."

"That's clearly you Mr. Henning," Dyer said, "so I'll let you respond."

"Thanks Mr. Speaker. And thank you Mr. Stinson for bringing this up. I do want to destroy MSA. After three years serving in MSA I can tell you the organization is unfixable. It doesn't matter who we elect, it will remain an impotent organization, nothing more than a soap box for boot licking, poli-sci establishment wannabes. So you might as well vote for the guy who wants to euthanize MSA and start student government anew."

"So that," Moonbeam interrupted, "is what you mean by 'Fuck MSA'?"

"Yes."

* * * * * * *

There was a quick celebration at the Big Ten that night.

Henning's debate performance was the reason.

They partied despite some bad news. Vice Provost Martin Brackens had upheld the Fees Committee's decision to award the Traditional Values Coalition zero funding.

But party everyone did. The Roundtable was full of people until Alisha Williams finally pulled the plug around two in the morning.

Then it was time for the Sideshow Bob's final act.

* * * * * * *

Chris Berg and Zan drove Henning, Painter, Zeale and Wallace over to Zan's house in Northeast. There they shared some beer and donuts while outfitting themselves for the night ahead.

None of the crew had noticed any of the other campaigns walking around campus past 3:30 in the morning. For everything to work, they needed solitude.

For the night operations they had a VHS video camera with four batteries and posters declaring "MSA; Yes it's just for losers." They were also dressing a vituperative Frank Wallace in a Gorilla suit in order to spoof the fuzzy picture Moonbeam's people took of him earlier.

Zan and Henning were also working on an official Press Release from the Henning Campaign condemning the dirty campaign tactics dominating the election.

Their final draft read:

```
For Immediate Release: March 31, 1994
Contact: Nolan Painter, Campaign Manager
```

THE EDUCATOR

paint1939@tc.gold.umn.edu
612-625-4452

Henning Campaign Condemns Dirty Tactics
Pledges an administration focused on
doing nothing the right way

(Minneapolis, MN)--Orson Henning, MSA candidate and Liberal Arts student, today condemned the dirty tactics being used by unknown campaigns as "tarnishing the tarnished reputation of that stupid and worthless organization, MSA."

"If there is one thing I know," Henning stated, "it is that MSA sucks. Students deserve better than to have pathetic brown nosers whoring themselves to the student body for a taste of bullshit personal glory and power."

Henning went on to suggest the vandals were targeting his campaign specifically.

"These people are trying to get me to take the fall. Already I have been interrogated by the election board, taking time away from my busy day playing videogames. I'm offended. I will not be a patsy."

Over the last two weeks, MSA campaign posters and sidewalk chalk advertising have been defaced and destroyed by unknown assailants late in the morning. A fuzzy picture of one of those people was recently published in the Minnesota Daily. Postering at University Kiosks is basically unregulated, but the Student Activities Offices bans anyone from tearing down posters.

Henning delivered an ultimatum to the people responsible: "So today and until the election is over, my campaign will be on the lookout for the culprits of these heinous acts. We will not rest until they are found."

###

Chris Berg had his own surprise, a Super Soaker the size of an assault rifle with a five gallon water reservoir that was carried like a backpack. The SS-300. This would be used on the chalkings. Wallace, dressed in the gorilla suit, carried another Super Soaker SS-300.

Painter had taken Zan's car to an all night Kinko's in St. Paul to print off their posters: a picture of Vendela Kirsebom in a bikini with the caption "Phok MSA Güt, Vote Henning"

The whole entourage drove back to campus at four in the morning. Chris Berg and Wallace walked around for half an hour washing the sidewalk of any chalk. Zan worked the camera and followed around Painter, Zeale and Henning as they tore down posters and talked about how much they hated the other candidates. Everything was videotaped.

Then, Wallace walked into view of the camera wearing the gorilla suit and Henning shouted "There he is, the vandal Moonbeam photographed!" and the last scene of the tape was the crew chasing down Wallace, tackling him then kicking the crap out of him.

The VHS tape and the press release were ducktaped to the employee entrance of the Minnesota Daily building on University Avenue.

The Sideshow Bob was complete.

*   *   *   *   *   *   *

CHAPTER 11

10am Thursday, March 31
Zan's apartment, Northeast Minneapolis

The phone was ringing.

It was the beautiful sound of real bells being struck by real clappers.

Zan scrambled around his apartment looking for the big black rotary dial monstrosity.

Barely awake, he answered, "Chin-wu"

"Zan, it's Ernie"

"What's going on?"

"How'd the Sideshow Bob go?"

"Pretty good. We played the tape on the camera and it was hilarious. The Daily was already calling around the campaign trying to figure everything out."

"That's good," Kessler said, "Wanted to let you know, I just got word from Mitch Davis, the charges against him were dropped. The judge decided driving around in a car and owning radio equipment wasn't illegal."

"Good for him."

"And...I was also talking to Shotgun, he's set Zeale's initiation."

"Great," Zan relpied. "Speaking of, has Shotgun found a way into the Rod Grams Campaign?"

"He's not sure. Spent the last few weeks writing fundraising letters for him though."

"That's something." Zan's head was still fuzzy from the late night.

"Just wanted an update. Get me a copy of the Daily article about the Sideshow Bob and keep me appraised of everything. I'll be at the cabin for a three day weekend."

As soon as Kessler clicked off Zan got another call, this one on the cell phone.

The sound of the ring had no timbre. No warmth. Zan did not like it.

"Hello?"

"Hi Zan, it's Kayla."

"What a surprise."

"Yeah. I figured you owed me lunch after the little stunt you forced me to pull with my credit cards. I'm sick of dorm food so you need to take me somewhere nice."

"Fine...I'll be there in thirty."

*   *   *   *   *   *   *

The Golden Nugget, hidden away on Excelsior Boulevard just past Interstate 494 in a wooded southwestern suburb, had great burgers. They were consistently voted the best in the Twin Cities area. Still, they lacked the big crowds places like Mickey's Diner or Matt's Bar attracted. Like most of the joints frequented by The Organization, it had colorful atmosphere and great food.

Zan and Kayla had talked mostly about the recent activities. But something else had been bugging her.

"Thanks so much for taking me out. My roommate was just sitting around the room without a top on reading some feminist crap. She creeps me out. Sometimes I catch her staring at me whenever I'm changing clothes. Eww. Next year, I'm finding a place."

"Glad to help."

"Also, I wanted to ask you...why you do all this stuff."

"What stuff?"

"The campus stuff. You're over thirty. Why aren't you out making money or having a family?"

"Not sure." Zan heard questions like this periodically. He never had any good answers. "Think about it this way, did you ever make plans about your life?"

"Sure."

"Well I never did. I never planned a thing. I did things at the last minute, on a whim, at random. No plan, no goals. I don't want to go anywhere. The world has nothing to offer me. I even got into law school by accident."

"By accident?"

"Well, not quite by accident. It was a pain in the ass getting it all done. I mean to say, I didn't get into law school to go into law. There was an internship at a local firm and they only took law school students. It's a long story. And not a good one, everything fell through.

"As I was saying, when you don't plan, you just accept the circumstances that come your way. I got involved in campus politics because I ran into The Archbishop when he was running a recruiting table for Reagan. Everything snowballed from there.

"Eventually, The Archbishop and I decided to stick to activism on this campus. I'd do the groundwork, he'd help out on the strategic level. We got lucky in the fundraising department. Now here I am."

"Don't you ever think about the future?"

"No."

"How can you do that?"

"All it requires is to not think. There's no 'doing' to it."

The two sat in silence until the arrival of their burgers. Kayla stared at the pint of Guinness brought to her. She was afraid to drink it. They weren't strict about ID checks at the Golden Nugget.

Zan decided to try to explain further, "All of us are a little nuts in this group, you know."

"What do you mean?"

"Take Henning. The guy could be going to medical school. Or law school. Instead he's trying to get a job in politics. Idiocy. He's abrasive, arrogant, temperamental. Politically he's just a normal conservative. Politics is insane. It requires insane people.

"Zeale's another perfect example. I'm not sure what he believes. He's just nuts.

"Then there's Painter. Abortion is the only topic he cares about. If it weren't for the fact violence is counterproductive, he'd be out there setting abortion clinics on fire.

"See, we're all basically the same. Zeale is crazy, Henning is anti-social, Painter is angry. Abnormality is normal in politics, but we're abnormal even for politics. There's a role for people like us, it's just hard to find.

"Someone like Zeale wouldn't function in the CRs. They're just a social club. Church groups don't care about this world, just salvation in the next. Most pro-life orgs just collect diapers and old cribs for fat trailer trash. Spags is one of a small population of people who need to act, to do something about politics, but have no home. Our little organization seeks out these people. We're all basically the same. We grew up reading the same books, believing the same things and are now stuck living in a democracy with people who shouldn't be allowed to vote because they no idea about the cost of freedom or the hell of slavery."

"So we're out to destroy the system. To ridicule it. To laugh at those who play the game. We hate the rules, we hate the ways things are. We are what Albert Jay Nock calls 'The Remnant'

"And guess what, you're here for a reason too. Normal girls don't commit credit card fraud. Whether you want to admit it or not, you fit in."

Kayla sat in silence for a second.

"I don't now if I agree." Kayla's voice was quiet, contemplating the fanatics she had spent so much time with this year.

"Think about it," Zan said. "This group it not about friendship. We're defenders of liberty. Guerrilla fighters against the left. Small battlefield on campus, sure. You need to know the whole story. Zeale, Painter, Henning, Wallace. All of us, we're not trying to get married or have a social life. Our life mission is dedicated to something else. You're a good fit, but you should know about the road you're on."

The conversation drifted back to the food after that.

*   *   *   *   *   *   *

CHAPTER 12

The Minnesota Daily's frontpage story, April 1, 1994:

Henning Campaign Dirty Tricks Videotaped
Vandals Videotaped Themselves

MSA presidential candidate Orson Henning left a video Friday morning at the Minnesota Daily office showing himself and members of his campaign tearing down opposing candidates' posters and erasing sidewalk chalkings.

Henning had previously denounced such tactics as "cheap tricks" from "vandals." The Henning campaign issued a press release with the videotape stating "...my campaign will be on the lookout for the culprits of these heinous acts. We will not rest until they are found."

When asked about the apparent contradiction between his video and press release, Henning stated "I stand by my campaign's message." And wouldn't comment further except to say "The other candidates suck."

MSA presidential candidate Andy Stinson, when told about the video and Henning's duplicity, called his opponent "an idiot."

Jenna Moonbeam, the DFL endorsed MSA candidate, was

more philosophical in her description of Henning's actions.

"This is common of conservative male hegemony. Henning, being completely self-centered and unable to relate to anything outside himself, is removed from anything of value. His satire is a strained compulsive attempt to impress the sad and unenlightened females in his little group." She said.

Moonbeam went on to describe Henning's actions as part of his patriarchal upbringing and that proper "consciousness raising" exercises will help his troubled spirit.

"It's too bad," She commented. "He's really disappointed all of us, and that's no surprise."

Andy Stinson, the MSA candidate endorsed by The Association of Fraternities and Sororities, described Henning's actions as "more proof Henning doesn't take MSA seriously."

The video concluded with Henning and his campaign volunteers tracking down and beating up a man in a monkey suit. It was an allusion to Henning's description of a photo published previously in the Minnesota Daily of a dark silhouette presumably responsible for vandalizing campus kiosks earlier in the campaign. At the MSA debate, Henning had described the photo as being a pitcure of "Sasquatch or something."

It is not known whether the election board will take any punitive action against Henning. The U of M police force said no charges will be filed as campus kiosks are not under their authority.

The MSA election will be held Tuesday, Wednesday and Thursday of next week.

*   *   *   *   *   *   *

CHAPTER 13

7pm Thursday, April 7
The Big Ten

Henning, Painter, Zeale, Wallace, Kayla, Rachel, Horace, Zan, Chris Berg and Minnesota Daily Reporter Matt Laderman awaited the results from the MSA election. A phone call from the Election Board to the Big Ten's bar phone would 'officially' release the numbers.

Of course, the results of the election wouldn't be a surprise to anyone sitting around The Roundtable. Chris had created 400 votes for Jenna Moonbeam out of thin air to push her over the top. The neo-hippie socialist crusader would be good fodder for direct mail fundraising letters.

The phone on the bar rang and Alisha Williams picked up the phone and took the call.

"Congratulations Mr. Henning, you received 292 votes." Alisha tried to put a positive spin on the news, she not being in on the conspiracy, "But Jenna Moonbeam won the election with 892 votes."

Henning lifted his beer to everyone.

"At least I don't have to be their Goddamned president."

"Wait," the Daily reporter was scrambling to write down the exact quote. "Can you repeat that?"

"I wrote it down for you."

*   *   *   *   *   *   *

CHAPTER 14

7pm Tuesday, April 12
Willey Hall, West Bank

"...I'm a former communist, I know all their little tricks and deceptions. The left is a political movement filled with meaningless gestures and intellectually dishonest charlatans. None of whom deserve the freedoms and opportunities of this country. Their hope and desire is for the destruction of this country and our way of life. I know. I was a communist and I wanted the U.S. to lose the cold war. Now we're seeing the remnants of that movement on college campuses. They can't save the Soviet Union, but they can try their socialist experiment again. And America will pay the price."

David Horowitz ended his hour long speech and took questions. What questions there were to take. One student went into a profanity laced tirade against racism and called Horowitz a "fucking fascist." Another student threw a water bottle at the conservative intellectual.

Painter decided this would be a good time to end the event.

Hosting speakers was the most important role The Organization played on campus. Speakers drove media. Good speakers started debates. Discussions would persist in the campus paper for weeks. It was the way to crack the liberal monolith on campus. High profile speakers were not easily ignored.

The College Republicans didn't do this. Sometimes a high profile office holder would drop by a CR meeting. But these weren't big media events. In fact, it was preferable for the CRs to avoid media exposure. The CRs weren't in the fight for the marketplace of ideas. They were a social club with entirely different goals.

The Organization was different. They were about debate. To liberals on college campuses, the debate was over. Their minds were made up; the decision of history was set: Wealth redistribution shall be the norm. Abortion on demand shall be available at any point in a pregnancy for any reason or even none at all. Fisting was not disturbing or perverse, it shall be part of a healthy and loving relationship. Guns are evil and shall be banned. There is no God, there shall be no churches. Unapproved speech is dangerous. The State is the Individual.

Conservative speakers put these ideas on trial. Normally, young conservatives were left to fend for themselves against older and more experienced liberal opponents enjoying lofty positions as faculty. Good conservative speakers were heavy artillery. David Horowitz was one of the most popular in the country. The former socialist intellectual for the 'new left' had seen the light after the tragic loss of a close friend. Since then he had become a proud agitator on campuses across the country.

After the event, Horowitz was taken to Grandma's Restaurant in the Seven Corners area. The entire crew attended. Kessler, Zan, Berg, Horace and Rachel, Kayla, Painter, Zeale, Henning, Wallace, Regular Joe, Mitch Davis. Two long tables were put together to seat the crowd. Horowitz sat at one end of the table surrounded by the youngest members.

Grandma's was spacious. Like all the joints The Organization preferred, the food was delicious. The decor was a quasi-colonial with large wooden tables and tall wooden chairs. Occasionally the service was even friendly, making it an upgrade over the Big Ten. It was also really expensive, but Ernie Kessler was footing the bill.

The senior members of the group sat at the other side of the table around Kessler and Zan. The kids got to talk to Horowitz. The seniors got to scheme.

"So we have a week and a half before Spring Break," Zan spoke loud enough to be heard over the background noise. "Are we set for the roadtrip?"

"Just heard from Shotgun, he's set." Chris Berg slurred his words just a touch. He was on his fifth beer.

"What about El Dos de Mayo?" Henning was smoking a cigar and drinking a snifter of cognac.

"Ernie, we have money for El Dos or are we borrowing?"

"No credit cards necessary boys," Kessler puffed on a cigar. "El Dos is on me this year."

*   *   *   *   *   *   *

CHAPTER 15

5pm Wednesday, April 13
Northeast Boxing Club, Northeast Minneapolis

THE EDUCATOR

Hit. Hit. Duck. Hit. Miss. Hit.

Zan couldn't remember how many times he had been hit. Fifteen or sixteen. That was a lot for one round. At least for him. A nineteen year-old middleweight, new to the boxing gym but not new to boxing, had been kicking his ass all day.

Zan was up against the ropes. Getting pounded. He pushed off the ropes and squeaked by two more jabs and finally got into the center of the ring. The kid, Markos Pavavorich or something, had won a golden gloves state championship while in high school in New Jersey. He moved to Minnesota for the climate.

His family emigrated from Russia when he was twelve. Unable to throw a baseball and too light for football, Markos started boxing. Soon he was going pro.

The two met again at center ring. Zan threw out a jab that came up short. Markos stepped in and threw a roundhouse with his right hand. Zan ducked down but Markos was already coming in with an uppercut from his left. Hit Zan square in the face. Zan motored back to gain some recovery time and suddenly was in the ropes again. Markos started throwing straight punches, lefts and rights, at Zan's body and face.

Rolling out to his right, Zan sprinted out from the ropes and stayed in the corner. Markos came aggressively and Zan dropped his guard a little. Markos took advantage with an overhand right that landed squarely on Zan's chin. Markos started throwing jabs but was caught off balance when Zan switched to a southpaw stance, pulled on Markos' left elbow with his right, then threw a quick punch to his exposed ribcage, knocking the wind out of him.

Zan started throwing a flurry of punches while Markos tried to get his bearings. It didn't take long for Markos to recover. A three punch combo pushed Zan away. Before the two could exchange more blows a buzzer went off, signaling the end of the sparring round.

The two tapped gloves and Zan worked his way out of the ring.

"When you show me dat move?" Markos shouted at him in a thick accent made worse by his mouthguard.

"I'll show you what I did Saturday, when I've recovered."

"Okay."

Another boxer, a former professional who taught at the gym, stepped into the ring to spar a couple rounds with Markos.

The Northeast Boxing Club was a classic boxing gym. Something you'd see in a old movie. It was located on Quincy street in Northeast Minneapolis. The building was an old brick industrial work, with high ceilings, overhead cranes on I-beams and a spacious interior. It was an old repair shop for railroad engines. There were two full-sized rings at opposite ends of the shop. A small weightlifting area was located in a far corner and there were a dozen or so heavy bags and speed bags located throughout the rest of the space.

Zan sat down on an old wooden bench along the wall behind the ring and started taking off his gear. Normally he tried to do ten rounds on sparring days but Markos stopped him at four.

A lanky man with a big grin and thick glasses took a seat next to Zan. The man had large round ears that stuck out from his head, was about six feet tall with a well weathered face that always had a clownish expression. His name was Steve Coombs, AKA 'The Lake Guy,' and was rather famous around the area for his regular appearances on Minnesota Public Radio in his 'Stump The Lake Guy' segments.

"Heya Zan, sawya got beat up a little there." Coombs always spoke in cheery tones amplified by a heavy Minnesotan accent.

"Yeah, Markos beat me up pretty good." Zan replied through the towel he was wiping his face off with.

"Liked that move ya did though, where you opened up his ribcage. Thatsa tough ta do."

"He wants me to show him how to do it later."

"So, whattaya think about him?"

"A little unpolished. New Jersey must be just brawlers."

Zan was digging around his bag. Pulling out a bottle of aspirin, he popped two into his mouth and chewed.

"Ha, I remember when you could spar ten rounds witout breaking a sweat."

"I don't see you doing rounds with Markos."

"And you're not gonna. I know better." Steve paused for a second to watch Markos pound away on another gym patron. "You know, it's a cruel sport. By the time you learna do it well, you're already too old to do it.

"Am I getting old?"

"Nah. Just getting older. Old? Ten years from now, probably."

"Thanks for the peptalk Steve."

"Hey, it's not a peptalk. I'm just saying you have to learn to accept things as they come. There's always gonna be some new kids with great stuff knocking at your door. But, it's our job to make great stuff into great results. You're a good coach. If Markos gets lucky as a fighter, you might make some money training him."

"I don't need a job. I have a job."

"Working as a political schmuck? Dealing intellectual smegma to kids who donna know better? That's not going to last. Ya gotta tink about your future. You haven't had a real job in well...as long as I've known you."

The two sat in silence for a bit. Then Coombs got up and continued working out. Zan unwrapped his wrists and packed all his stuff into his gym bag. He only lived a few blocks away and typically jogged the distance as a warm up and cool down. He waved goodbye to Coombs and started for the door when he heard Markos yelling at him "Zhan! You be here Saturday, Show me move?"

"I'll be here," Zan shouted back.

*　　　*　　　*　　　*　　　*　　　*　　　*

"You guys know a lot about local history, right?" Horowitz asked.

"Sure," Painter said. "Why?"

"I've always wondered, why is there a North and a South Dakota? they're both basically devoid of human habitation, right?"

Orson Henning and Nolan Painter were driving David Horowitz to the University of Minnesota campus in Morris. It was two hours northwest of the Twin Cities. Morris was a late partner; four other schools were also hosting Horowitz as a speaker. Late was better. The first school to bring in a major speaker normally paid full price. The second school in the area got a small discount. Morris' Conservative Underground, fifth in the queue, was paying Horowitz just a thousand dollars for the speech. Eighty percent less than what St. John's shelled out.

"Ever hear of the Great Dakota War?" Henning asked.

"No."

"Eighteen sixty-two," Henning started, "the United States is embroiled in the Civil War. In west-central Minnesota, from the Minnesota River to the Red River Valley, Swedish and Norwegian immigrants were fighting their own war."

"Swedes and Norwegians?"

"Yes," Painter said, "the two groups had been in conflict as soon as they started settling in the Midwest. You see, the Norwegians were ruled by Danish nobles serving under the Danish Monarchy. But after the Napoleonic Wars, The Danes, who were allied with France, were forced to cede Norway to the Swedish Crown. This started a little war between Sweden and Norway. A union was later formed, but it made neither side happy."

"Nor would it," Henning added, "until the two countries dissolved their relationship in 1905."

"Right," Painter continued, "so the animosity created a host of problems between the two groups and the problems found their way into America. In early 1862, a group of Swedes led by Olaf Fairhair raided a Norwegian settlement near a town known as Pigs Feet."

"Pigs Feet?"

"Yes Mr. Horowitz," Painter said, "Pigs Feet. Pigs are a big deal around here."

"After the raid on Pigs Feet," Henning continued, "the two groups created their own armies, gangs really, who fought relentlessly."

"This was during the Civil War," Henning said, "so there were very few troops available to handle this sort of uprising. A man by the name of Will Mar, a retired General and Mexican War veteran, led a group of Dakota Indians and Irish immigrants against the two groups. Peaceful Swedes and Norwegians were allowed to stay, but the gangs were forced into the Dakota Territories. At the Battle of Fargo, General Mar finally defeated the last remnants of the Norwegian Independence League. To keep the peace, Mar forced the Norwegians into the Northern Dakota Territories. The Swedes were vanquished to the Southern Dakota Territories."

"The town of Pig's Feet was renamed 'Willmar' in honor of the general," Painter said. "A few decades later, North and South Dakota entered the Union as two distinct states, instead of one. Despite being sparsely populated. All because of General Will Mar and the Great Dakota War."

"In fact," Henning said, "the town of Morris was a refuge for settlers, both Swede and Norwegian, escaping the conflict."

"Wow," Horowitz said, "I should mention some of this stuff in my speech tonight."

"Yes you should," Painter said.

*   *   *   *   *   *   *

Henning and Painter dropped Horowitz off behind Imholte Hall on the Morris campus, promised to pick him up in a few hours and take him back to Minneapolis. Once Horowitz was gone, Painter and Henning began to laugh uncontrollably.

*   *   *   *   *   *   *

CHAPTER 16

10pm Monday, April 18
Oak Street Ramp, Minneapolis

Springtime in Minnesota is a miserable affair.
Cold rain. Strong winds.
Wet, cold, muddy, rainy.
That's after all the slush and mush melts away of course.
Zan's metallic blue Nissan 300zx made its way to Oak Street Ramp.

THE EDUCATOR

The temperature hovered around 40 degrees Fahrenheit. Made worse by the rain. The weather forecast included freezing rain and icy roads as the night progressed.

And it was nicer out tonight than the previous day.

Entering the ramp, Zan drove parked close to the ramp attendants' booth. Tass Larson was smoking a cigarette as he approached.

"Zan! How the hell are ya?"

"Ambulatory and taking nourishment, how are you?"

"Waiting for opportunity to knock...Jesus H. Christ on crutch...you look terrible."

Zan smiled. Two black eyes. A large cut over his right eyebrow. Other bruises. It also looked like his nose had been broken again. Everything was held together with a little asymmetric swelling.

"Yeah, had a rough weekend at the gym."

"What, were you boxing a bus?"

"Close enough. I was trying to give this Russian kid some pointers. But the only way to make sure the lesson takes is to practice in rounds."

Tass started laughing through an exhalation of smoke. "I bet you're the only one dumb enough to teach someone else how to hurt you."

"Well, doing it for free anyway...yeah, I guess."

"Take a seat in the booth, I'll pour you some green tea."

The booth was small, no more than a few square feet. Just room enough for both men to sit. Zan took a beat up office recliner while Tass held court on a stool. All four walls of the booth were windows, providing a clear view of the cement forest. Large gray pillars rose from the asphalt, supporting the giant gray concrete cloud above. Lights hanging from the ceiling flickered, casting a yellow glow on the concrete. The occasional parked car broke up the gloom.

"Good ol' Minnesota," Tass said, "when you're not freezing to death, it's a cold drizzly hellhole. After this we'll get three months of mosquitoes and fat people in white tank tops. All for just three days of nice weather." Tass took a long drag from his cigarette. "Those fucking Swedes, desperate to find someplace like home. They coulda just stayed home and let me stay in Scranton."

Tass lit another cigarette to go along the one he was already smoking. Inhaling both deeply, at the same time, he then tossed the old cigarette out the window.

"Problem is, the Democrats control all the states with nice weather," Zan replied.

"They control this one too, zipperhead," Tass said.

"I prefer 'slope' to tell you the truth. But in Minnesota's defense, it doesn't matter who's in power up here, it's too cold to be homeless and the bad weather prevents a lot of crime."

- 76 -

"You're polishing a turd...Well, what's going on with you? besides the hamburger face?"

"Wasting time before I get over to Coffman. Regular Joe and I are installing those cameras for the Marilyn Monroe."

"So soon? I thought that wasn't until June."

"We have to get everything ready early, the Chaos Makers are going on vacation together after Spring Break."

"How'd they swing that?"

"Pretty sure Joe put in his two weeks' notice."

"Why?"

"He wouldn't say, but I figure he's got some scam going on."

"Something to do with Social Security numbers?" Tass said.

"Joe tell you about that?"

"Maybe"

"So what's he got planned?"

"I have no idea." Tass lit another cigarette, inhaled both new and old at the same time, then flicked the old one through the open window. "But it can't be that good, he wanted me to help him get a job with Parking Services."

"Maybe he just really likes the idea of a new exciting career."

"Yeah, something about being here really makes life worth living; it's the aesthetic beauty and the intellectual challenge." A car interrupted their conversation. After the transaction TAS turned the lights off in the booth and lifted the gate arm.

No more customers for the U tonight.

"How 'bout your new guy," Tass continued, "Zeale something, hows'zat going?"

"We're initiating him over Spring Break. Shotgun is going to drag him around South Dakota."

"A little far, huh?"

"Naw, we're taking our underclassmen to Mt. Rushmore, then maybe down to Colorado if we have some time. We're taking Kessler's RV, Henning's van, my car and Shotgun is already in South Dakota looking for fossils."

"That fat fuck is hiking around looking for fossils?"

"He says he likes it because he gets a lot of exercise."

"Yeah, I'm sure it helps him squeeze into those size 54 pants."

*   *   *   *   *   *   *

CHAPTER 17

6am Friday, April 22
Centennial Hall

THE EDUCATOR

Gene 'Spags' Zeale stood alone in front of Centennial Hall, staring into nothing really. There were a few people milling about. Some going to the nearby hospital. Some students walked by on their way to get breakfast.

Few students ventured out early enough for breakfast before 8am classes, let alone on a Friday; but those few had staying power. A freshman who could get to 8am classes on a Friday was a future academic all-star. Grad school. Corporate job. Social climber.

These were not the people The Organization wanted.

Zeale fit the mold. Not an overachiever. Went to bed around three o'clock in the morning. Six in the morning was the middle of the night for him.

The morning was gray. Overcast. Cool. Not miserable, not enjoyable. About as good as Minnesota gets during seasonal transitions; the Minnesota winter is dragged from the state like a demon from Hades, clawing all the way.

Zeale knew nothing about was was to happen. All he knew was he was getting picked up by Orson Henning at six o'clock in the morning.

Henning's big green Ford Econoline conversion van turned the corner and stopped in front of Centennial. Zeale grabbed his rolling suitcase, walked down the stairs and threw his stuff into the back of the van. As he hopped into the passenger side front seat, Henning started laughing.

"I guess they didn't tell you anything about this, huh?" Henning pushed the van into drive and started down the road towards St. Paul.

"No, I just packed five days worth of clothing."

"Okay then, we're going to have to stop by Cabela's and get you outfitted."

"Outfitted?"

"No worries, I'll cover the bill. You can pay me back later. We need to go pick up Rachel and Horace, then we're going to meet up with everyone else at the Perkins in Burnsville."

"They're not going to make me hike around in this weather, are they?"

"If you're lucky, it will be this nice."

*　　　*　　　*　　　*　　　*　　　*　　　*

Zeale didn't know what to think.

Before him were three hundred dollars worth of outdoor equipment. A large hiking backpack, hiking boots, several pairs of wool socks, a down jacket, a large buck knife, a small tent and a sleeping bag. A snake bite kit topped off the pile.

It took about a half an hour to get everything done and it was back on the road again.

They were 45 minutes behind the rest of the convoy when they finally hit I35 south. There were more direct routes to get to South Dakota, but comfortably traveling at 77 MPH along the Interstate was better than twisting and turning through the backroads of southern Minnesota.

West along I90 the land was flat and rocky, a brownish tan made bleak by the gray skies. Some trees were scattered about the route, providing something to look at. Occasionally.

Every once in a while a radio station could be heard.

The monotony was broken up by occasional flurries of conversation.

Then long periods of silence.

The trip to Rapid City was ten hours.

Half an hour away from their destination, and with Rachel and Horace both listening to music on their CD players, Henning decided to give Zeale a foreshadowing of his coming trial.

"Gene, I should talk to you about the initiation. I can't tell you too much, but as your sponsor--"

"Sponsor?"

"Yeah, I was the guy who recruited you, I'm your sponsor. I'm the guy who pushed to get you into the group. So it's my ass on the line in this initiation too. Anyway, I should tell you, no one has ever failed the initiation."

"That's a relief."

"There's always a first time. If you fail, you're out. This exercise is meant to test your ability to adapt to challenges. It's more of a mental test than a physical one, though it will tax your body. In the end, though, our goal is to let you see that your personal limits are much greater than you think."

"Any spanking involved?"

"You'll know soon enough, fucktard."

*   *   *   *   *   *   *

They traveled the rest of the way in silence. At the motel, a dumpy Motel 6 right off the Interstate with two stories of dilapidated goodness, everyone disembarked the van and helped get everyone else into their rooms. Zeale thought he was going to get a room but Zan was the first to tell him to keep his stuff in the van.

After everything with the hotel was settled, Henning, Chris Berg and Zan huddled up with Zeale at the rear of the Ford. Without comment, Zeale was blindfolded and had his hands tied behind his back. He was unceremoniously dumped into the back of the van.

THE EDUCATOR

The trip felt like a long time to Zeale. He couldn't tell how long. Only the sound of the engine and the road, with an occasional burst of laughter from the van's occupants, gave any clue as to what was happening. To Zeale it felt like an eternity. But only an hour and half later the van came to a stop and Zeale was dragged from van and dropped on the ground.

His blindfold was removed. The air was cold, the sky was black and the only light came from the lights in the Ford. The winds howled at thirty knots, making the fifty degree night feel much colder.

The three men stood over Zeale

"Spags Zeale," the voice belonged to Zan, "do you agree to undertake the initiation into The Organization?"

"Yes, and I'd like some fries with a vanilla shake."

One of the men kicked Zeale in the ribs. Hard.

Another one of the silhouettes threw Gene's hiking backpack on the ground next to him.

"Okay then." Zan took a deep breath. "The first part of your initiation is simple enough. You have to travel ten miles due south. Tonight, before the sun rises. It's about midnight so you'll have five hours to meet up with Shotgun."

"Shotgun? the guy from the radio show?"

"The same. He'll have instructions for you at that point. If you don't make the rendezvous, you fail." Zan tossed what looked like a gun next Zeale. "That's a flare, if you give up, fire the flare and we'll come and get you. Shooting the flare is an automatic fail. The terrain isn't too difficult, but be careful not to step on any snakes. Any questions?"

"Aren't you going to untie me?"

The three men laughed.

"Is that all then?" Zeale asked.

"No." It was Chris Berg's voice. The big man stepped forward and pulled Zeale to his feet. "You have to do this with a headache."

With that, Chris hit Zeale across the jaw with a gloved fist. The glove did little to lessen the pain. Zeale fell to the ground with a loud thud.

"Good luck, Gene" Henning was the last to talk. The three men returned to the van. Through the fuzz Zeale was dimly aware of the sound of the van driving away in the distance.

*   *   *   *   *   *   *

Jessica Brown checked her makeup in the mirror of her bathroom. She was shooting for 'whore' but wanted to avoid 'prostitute.' She was a prostitute, but she was the kind of prostitute who made a lot of money by not looking like a prostitute. There was a knock at her backdoor. She stood up, checked her naughty schoolgirl outfit again, and walked downstairs to the door.

In her field she was a specialist. She only worked a trick or two a week. Her client list was limited to 34 individuals. Starting her work in college, exchanging sex for grades, word of mouth advertising helped her grow the business until, ten years later, she was making six figures every year. Confidentiality, discreetness and a willingness to pander to any fetish were her top selling points.

Her home, a nondescript two-story in the Frogtown neighborhood of St. Paul, was a palace of fantasy. Every room presented a different decor. One room was known as 'Sheik's Dream' another 'French Villa' another 'Girl's Locker Room.' The basement was a fully stocked dungeon for her bondage enthusiasts. The main room on the first floor and her kitchen were classic suburban for those who wanted the 'sexy wife' experience while the main bedroom and bathroom provided the 'girlfriend experience.' The only part of the home she kept to herself was the attic which she used as her personal bedroom.

The backdoor had a mail-slot. This wasn't an accident. Her dates had to send the money through the slot before she would answer the door. Clients could park in her parking spot in the alley, or on the street. The backyard was very small, with two large trees, and an entranceway that allowed the client to wait in privacy. Discreet.

She picked up an envelope from the foot of the backdoor. In it were hundred dollar bills. She riffled through them quickly. As long as there were 40 or more bills, she was happy. It wasn't a business for accountants. She left the final price of the night up to her clients. It had to be more than $4000, that was it.

Jessica was fiscally savvy. Deposits of over $5,000 in cash were given a great deal of scrutiny by banks and IRS, so she never did that. She had three bank accounts at three different banks, never made a deposit of more than $2,000 and had a safe in the house and a safety deposit box where she kept the overflow. She lived within her means and avoided anything lavish.

On her taxes she listed her profession as an 'interior design consultant' and paid taxes on enough income that a person auditing her wouldn't be surprised by her comfortable lifestyle. Over the last decade she accumulated half a million dollars in cash. When she reached a million, she would stop working as a prostitute. She even thought about settling down with one of her clients. There were a few she had in mind, including today's date.

The envelope with the money was thrown into her freezer in the kitchen. It was a decent hiding spot. None of her clients had ever robbed her, but paranoia was a positive quality in her profession. She returned to the back door and opened it.

The tall and handsome figure of Malcolm Paulson smiled

back at her. He gave her a box of roses and she gave him a kiss. Taking his hand, she led him into the kitchen. There champagne was waiting and the two could negotiate the night's services. Malcolm was intense and enjoyed a wide variety of experiences. She never knew what he was in the mood for. Pleasantries were exchanged before business was discussed.

"I was thinking of a little bit of domination," he said.

"Ooh, you want me to tie you up?"

"Just the opposite."

The little blonde gave Malcolm a smile. "Whatever you wish."

*　　　*　　　*　　　*　　　*　　　*　　　*

It took a few minutes before Zeale gathered his wits. There was no moon or star light to illuminate the world around him, but two hours with a blindfold had turned on his night vision. He slipped the ropes off his hands. He had worked through them on the ride down. Gathering his backpack and the flare gun, Zeale took the compass out of his pack, and started due south.

*　　　*　　　*　　　*　　　*　　　*　　　*

A mile away to the west, on a slight hill, three figures watched Zeale through nightvision binoculars.

"Damnit, he already had his ropes undone" Berg's voice was a raspy whisper. The strong wind made it unlikely that they would be heard conversing, but no one was taking any chances. "I don't think I hit him hard enough either. We barely had time to get here and he's already jogging out of range."

"He didn't put on his jacket," Henning noted, "he better not get hypothermia. This wind will suck all the heat from his body."

"We'd better get moving. We have to pick up Shotgun's car in Ardmore, then set up south in case he fires a flare." Zan spoke as he was getting up. "He'd better not fire that flare tonight, the wind will make it impossible to figure out where he is."

"He's not going to need the flare." Henning spoke confidently, raising his voice above the wind.

"Tell that to the snakes," Zan said.

*　　　*　　　*　　　*　　　*　　　*　　　*

Zeale stopped to catch his breath.

He wasn't sure how far he had traveled. Normally his double-pace matched up well with the roman mile. One thousand double-paces was about a mile, he needed to do ten thousand double-paces before morning. He had lost track a couple of times.

Must be somewhere near three miles now, he thought.

Pulling out his compass, he got his bearings. The compass had a luminescent needle, it was easy enough to keep moving the opposite direction. There was no horizon, no stars, nothing to see. The grasses around him were knee high, sometimes higher. He had fallen over a couple of roads, a small crick, and several old barbed wire fences. The wind made it impossible to hear anything, even his own steps.

He peered into the darkness ahead of him, desperate for anything to see other than void. With no watch, he started jogging again.

$$* \quad * \quad * \quad * \quad * \quad * \quad *$$

The bathtub in the second floor guest bathroom was filled. The water was cold. Paulson's preference. On the floor was Jessica Brown. She was wearing lacy white lingerie and had her hands tied with rope behind her back, her legs were tied together and a ball gag was in her mouth. She had put everything on herself.

Paulson couldn't help but laugh at the result. She had taken him up to the master bedroom and let him watch as she changed and tied herself up. From there Paulson just lifted her up on his shoulder and carried her into the bathroom. It was the easiest capture of his career.

"Jessica, do you think a fish feels pain when it's on a hook?" Paulson was sitting on the toilet looking down at her. "You see, it flops around violently. It looks like its in pain. But how can we really be sure?"

Paulson paused and pulled out a pair of gloves. Putting them on, he continued.

"You see, the fish reacts the same way to its predicament, being on the hook, that you or I would if we were fish. I mean this literally. If we literally took our consciousness and transferred it to a fish on a hook. Neurologically speaking, we know a fish doesn't have the brain mass or structure to experience pain the way we do, but from a behavioral standpoint they react as we would. As if they were in real pain.

"You may be wondering why is this important? Well Jessica, there are only a few ways we can approach what is known as the hard problem of consciousness. The rich inner world we enjoy as humans appears to lack a truly scientific explanation. Even more difficult are philosophical questions related to the subjective experiences of others. There really is no scientific way to approach these questions.

"It's the only question I've ever really struggled with Jessica." Paulson knelt down and started stroking Brown's hair. "It's the last great philosophical mystery. Sure, there are ways of evaluating these problems. I've mentioned neuroscience. There's something called logical behaviorism. But both these methods are left wanting. Neuroscience tells us how a bat navigates, with echolocation. But do we really know what it's like to be a bat? Of course not.

"Logical behaviorism also fails. If we could put a human mind into an animal, say a pig about to be slaughtered, we wouldn't be able to differentiate between a regular pig and the human, would we? In fact, and I've performed this experiment by the way, if you put a gag on a woman and cut her throat while she's hanging from her legs, she reacts the same way a pig does when you tie it up by its hind legs and cut its throat."

Jessica started to squirm.

"Relax. The lecture won't last long. I just, I really needed to get this done. The last time I did this I didn't get to lecture. I'm a teacher first, you know? As much as I enjoyed having you as an on-call fuck, it's probably time we went our separate ways. And try to enjoy the time you have left, eh?

"As I was saying, there's a real mystery when it comes to consciousness. An autodidact like Daniel Dennett would say the problem doesn't exist at all. He promotes an idea called heterophenomenology which relies on neuroscience, behaviorism and self-reporting of conscious states by the individual. This, obviously, isn't going to help you.

"And that's the point, I have no idea how you're suffering on the inside. I have no idea what it will be like for you to die. You could really be a zombie. Or a complex robot. I have no idea if you have the same rich inner experiences that I do. I have no reason to believe it at all."

Paulson leaned over and got close to Jessica, face to face.

"But I do believe in you, Jessica. You are there. And I'm here to celebrate you. Your mind is not an illusion. Your experiences are real and important. I'm a property dualist, and you are my argument."

Paulson got up, looked at his watch.

"Wow. Already? Looks like I'm out of time. I really went through a lot of trouble to get here, you know. As far as anyone knows, I'm at my cabin up north. Once I get done here, I've got to get back up there. I took my motorcycle down, that way my truck is still in the driveway at the cabin. Not much of an alibi but a workable one.

"I wasn't sure exactly what to do with you, though. Normally I try to make my murders look like they're not murders. But this time, I can't escape it. There's just too much evidence at this house to avoid raising suspicions. Prostitutes don't auto-erotic-asphyxiate. I just have to hope my alibi holds up. It will be the speed limit all the way home for me tonight.

"Goodbye Jessica."

Paulson lifted the woman off the floor and put her into the tub, holding her head down in the water. Eventually she stopped fighting; Paulson kept her in the water a full two minutes past this point. Then he took her out of the tub and carried her into the master bedroom. Paulson knew about the attic and quickly went through her real bedroom. He took her appointment book and all the contact information he could find for all her clients. There wasn't much. He also found her safe.

It wasn't too safe. The key to the safe was in her underwear drawer. Paulson took a pair of panties and cut a lock of hair from Jessica. He also took some photos she had of herself on her dresser. In the safe he found an incredible amount of cash. And a diary. He took the diary. All this stuff was thrown into a backpack Paulson found. Then Paulson started on the kitchen.

There was very little of use to him there. Jessica clearly didn't cook. Paulson found and poured a full bottle of vegetable oil into a large pan and put the heat on 'high.' Then he remembered the stack of old newspapers in the entranceway. Grabbing the whole stack, he went back upstairs.

Paulson started crumpling sheets of the newspapers into little balls and stuffed them under the bed where Jessica lay. After a few minutes he had a sizable pile. Looking again at his watch, he took out a lighter and lit the newspapers. The bed soon caught fire.

Paulson sprinted for the kitchen. The pan full of oil was smoking. He lit a napkin and threw it into the oil. It caught fire. Paulson took a champagne glass, filled it with water in the sink, and chucked it into the oil from several feet away, running away as the water caused the pan to spew forth a geyser of flame. The ceiling, curtains, wall and floor of the kitchen were flaming. Paulson grabbed a flaming curtain and dragged it into the main room, throwing it onto a couch.

Then he swiftly walked out the back door and jogged to his motorcycle, parked on the street about a block away. It was two minutes from the start of the fire to the motorcycle. Two more minutes and Paulson was driving up Snelling. He would take I35W to Highway 10, snaking his way back to his cabin, avoiding I94 and a majority of the State Patrol vehicles on the road.

The first police car arrived at Jessica's house eight minutes after Paulson was gone.

*   *   *   *   *   *   *

Henning was sitting atop his van, looking out with binoculars. Zan was beside him with the night vision goggles. Chris Berg had departed, he was driving Shotgun's car back to Rapid City.

A radio crackled.

Henning picked up the bulky walkie-talkie and spoke into it. "Henning, go ahead."

"It's Shotgun, I found the kid. He's about three hundred yards out, you can head."

Zan flicked the light on his watch. "Three hours twenty minutes, that's incredible."

"We might get back in time to get a nap."

"You're such a pussy Orson."

*   *   *   *   *   *   *

Zeale could barely move his legs.

He figured he had to be close.

Suddenly there was a burst of light in front of him. It was a flare.

"Gene Zeale!" Came a deep voice, slightly modulated from being spoken through a megaphone. "This way."

Zeale started moving again, towards the source of the flare. It was up a slight hill. Another rusty barbed wire fence was an unwelcome surprise.

Eventually, he made it to the top of the hill. There was a small fire in the middle of what looked like a u-turn in a dead end gravel road.

Shotgun was sitting in an old rocking chair, sipping from a thermos. The light of the fire highlighted his enormous bulk. Zeale was shocked the rickety looking chair supported the man.

"Three hours and twenty minutes, that's good time."

"Piece of cake."

"We're not done yet Bobbo. You earned yourself a nap, that's it. We head out at dawn, about an hour from now. Sack up and try to rest." Shotgun took another gulp from his thermos and conjured what looked like a candy bar from a pocket.

"Don't suppose I could get some food, huh?"

"Cowboy up fag. You ain't hungry yet."

*   *   *   *   *   *   *

CHAPTER 18

7am Saturday April 23
Rapid City, South Dakota

"That is the most disturbing thing I've ever seen."

The voice belonged to Rachel Anderson.

The subject of the sentence was in Zan's hands.

It was a plastic baby doll with a noose around its neck. On its naked belly were written the words 'Abort me?'

Each rope was attached to a large hook.

Over the previous weekend, he and Ernie Kessler had created 400 of these little delights for use on this trip.

Their plan was to hike around Mt. Rushmore throwing the babies up trees.

The theory was simple: any press is good press.

Especially bad press.

At least when it came to abortion, the theory worked.

The reason was simple. After Roe v. Wade, the issue of abortion was taken away from the public. Abortion, for every woman in the country, for any reason, at any time, was legal. It was decided. It was history. The goal of abortion defenders was to let people forget it was even an issue. Abortion, the issue, didn't need to exist. Any mention in the public sphere about the issue was dangerous. Soon enough the very word 'abortion' became taboo. It disappeared from the media. Disappeared from polite discussion.

In a country built on having robust debates on controversial issues of public policy, abortion became anathema. Pro-life advocates became lepers.

The cure? Get noticed. Good press. Bad press. It was all the same. Every action, whether 'constructive' for the cause or not, became an impetus to discussion. The hope, to those who held this opinion, was possibility of a critical mass in the public sphere where a re-evaluation of the abortion issue could be made.

Gathered in the motel room with Zan and Rachel were Nolan Painter, Chris Berg, Horace Brown, Orson Henning, Kayla Witold and Frank Wallace. Only Chris Berg and Orson Henning had seen the dolls until this moment.

"I like it," Painter said.

"Couldn't we get some fake blood to complete the look?" Wallace added.

"We hadn't thought of the blood idea," Zan looked at the doll. "But at this point we'll have to use these as is. So here's the plan, we truck over to Mount Rushmore, walk around a bit, then, when the coast is clear, toss a few of these," Zan lifted up the doll, "around the park."

"That's insane." There was a fearful edge in Horace's voice. "How illegal is this going to be?"

"Well, if they catch any of us," Zan tried to remain nonchalant, "They'll have us on littering charges. Or trespassing, if they get moody about it."

"Could we get arrested?" Kayla asked.

THE EDUCATOR

"It'd be a nice silver medal," Zan replied, "but the grand prize here is if we get all of these guys up a tree without anyone noticing we're there. Then, as the park service goes nuts trying to find all of these things in their parks, we piss them off enough that they go to the media for help or just to be righteously indignant about 'our national heritage' being used so offensively. Pictures, media stories, offended liberals. Whatever. This isn't a precision operation, it's more of a dragnet. We're trying to get whatever we can from it."

"Besides," Painter jumped in, "It'll be fun."

*　　　*　　　*　　　*　　　*　　　*　　　*

Gray was the sky.

There was circumstantial evidence of a sun, the lack of absolute darkness.

The wind was blowing hard, which wasn't the only indignity: it was raining. Cold. Heavy. Freezing. Whipping.

Fucking Rain.

And Zeale was walking straight into it.

'Shotgun,' who had yet to give Zeale his real name, looked like he was enjoying himself. This just made Zeale that much more miserable.

At six in the morning they started walking north by northwest. Straight into the weather that had been plaguing the region for the past couple of weeks. The rocking chair was left at the impromptu campsite. Shotgun said he had liberated the chair from an abandoned farmhouse up the road.

Zeale couldn't believe anyone had ever lived out here.

What idiots had they been? he thought.

The walking wasn't strenuous but fatigue was building and Zeale wasn't sure how much farther he could push himself. And they had been walking for just six hours.

The grass tended to be about knee-high. Sometimes it got up to the waist. At one point they ran into an old dirt road and followed it for half an hour. Twice they had to make their way across muddy cricks.

Outside of the road and the occasional barbed wire fence, there was no evidence of another soul around.

"Hey..." Zeale's voice was barely a whisper. Shotgun didn't hear him. Zeale pulled on his jacket and tried again "Hey!"

"You're not quitting already, are you?" Shotgun's huge round face had a jocular quality, as did his deep baritone voice.

"No...but I need some water."

"Rain not enough for ya huh?" The big man stopped and took off his backpack and pulled out an old fashioned round canteen and handed it to Zeale.

Shotgun was shorter than Zeale. At least four inches shorter. But he seemed tall, by the way he carried himself. However, Shotgun must have weighed at least a hundred pounds more than Zeale. Dressed in dark green camo overalls, a gray hooded sweatshirt and a green rain slicker with a large leather fedora to finish the ensemble, the big man looked preposterous.

Zeale had put away the entire canteen and passed it back to Shotgun.

"Shit. Looks like I didn't pack enough water."

"That's all?"

"Got one more canteen left, and we got three more days of hiking."

"Who the hell planned this?"

"Relax." Shotgun pulled out two towels out of his backpack. "Tie them around your legs. They'll absorb moisture from the grass. It should fill up your canteen in a few hours."

"That's stupid."

"Unless you get really thirsty again."

Shotgun shouldered the backpack and the two started walking again.

"We still have some hiking to do," the fat man said, "but, I can get started on some lectures."

"Lectures?"

"Yeah, just some indoctrination. I was hoping the rain would die down, but..." Shotgun reached into his overalls and pulled out a packet of notecards. "A little rain will add to the dramatic effect."

Alright, let's see..." Shotgun took one of the notecards and read it, then slipped the rest of the pack back into his overalls. "Guess we can start with the political basics. Political technology is ideologically neutral. The same tactics and strategies used by communists to move public policy can be used by conservatives--"

"Just wait a second," Zeale interrupted, "I need to take a crap before we get too far into this."

*   *   *   *   *   *   *

Zan was on patrol.

Wearing blue jeans, a green windbreaker and a hiking backpack, he looked normal enough. Behind him was Mt. Rushmore. He was not there to see Mt. Rushmore.

Normally, two Park Rangers were walking around the Presidential Trail in the woods at the base of the mountain. Zan had traveled all the way around the trails, from the Sculptor's Studio to the Indian Heritage Village. Now he was almost to the the Grand View

Terrace again. Out of his bag he found a small 35mm camera and started taking pictures. He'd hold a scrimmage line for a few minutes while everyone else worked into position. His job was to find and distract any Ranger he met along the trail. Rachel and Horace were also on lookout duty, ready to distract any Ranger they found on the stairs between the Grand Terrace and the Borglum View Terrace. They had a dozen questions about squirrels prepared.

Henning, a regular jogger, was nearest to Zan. The two had the farthest to run. Big Frank Wallace was near the stairs heading down from the base of the Mountain to the Compressor House. Kayla held ground along the nature trail between the Borglum View Terrance and the parking ramps. In the parking ramps were Nolan Painter and Chris Berg. They were busy placing pro-life pamphlets under windshield wipers.

Painter had a bum knee. Berg was a fatass. They had to stay close to the wheels.

At exactly 11:11am, everyone was to start tossing the baby dolls into trees. The weather was miserable, lower forties with some rain and gray skies. Still, the site had scores of tourists milling about, most of them taking pictures of the monument from the Grand View Terrace. Zan had only seen a handful of tourists make the trek around the trails.

11:11.

No one around, Zan stopped and opened his backpack. In it were ten 'Hangin' Babes' as Rachel called them. As a lookout, Zan's load was light. A few tosses sent the doll-rope-hook contraptions into the trees. Just down the trail, he saw Henning and waved. Henning waved back, then the two went back to tossing the 'Babes' into trees.

     *   *   *   *   *   *   *

The Borglum View Terrace was the original studio, log cabin style, Gutzon Borglum used while sculpting the initial plaster models of Mt. Rushmore. Most of the structure, except for two fireplaces, had been stripped away to be used as a platform for viewing the mountain sculpture. A bust of Borglum adorned the terrace. Horace and Rachel had spent fifteen minutes adoring the bust. Anything to try to look like tourists not bent on violating the sanctity of a national monument.

A few other tourists mingled about. A red squirrel chewed through an old pine-cone. Horace took out a camera and started taking pictures of the squirrel, which ignored him.

More waiting.

A Park Ranger walked by. Rachel put on a smile and stepped in front of him.

"Excuse me, I had some questions about the local wildlife,"

she said.

The Ranger smiled. He was average height, friendly faced and gray-haired. "Sure, I'd be happy to."

*   *   *   *   *   *   *

"...How many species of squirrels are there...how do you tell the difference between a red squirrel and a chipmunk...what do they all eat...are they always making babies or is it seasonal...how come you can't feed them...what's the difference between red squirrels and gray squirrels...are all these squirrels indigenous to the US...are there any animals that eat the squirrels...where are the other animals in the park...have you ever seen a bobcat..."

For fifteen minutes, the Park Ranger enjoyed the attention of the attractive young woman and thought nothing of it. Though, he couldn't remember anyone ever being so interested in squirrels, even among kids. Then the woman's boyfriend looped his arm around her and the two started off, up the stairs to the Grand View Terrace, waving as they left. The Ranger waved back

The Ranger started down towards the Sculptor's Studio. There weren't many people around at all. The Studio was empty. Then he made the turn and started working his way up the Presidential Trail.

Panic set in.

At his feet the words "Your Mom was Pro-Life" were spray-painted in bright pink on the wooden boards of the trail. A few more steps, more graffiti. "Life is Prima Facie"

"Abortion is Murder"

"You wouldn't abort puppies"

Then he things in the trees. Taking a closer look he saw they were plastic baby dolls with rope nooses around their necks.

Dumbfounded, he just stood on the trail for a minute, unsure of what to do.

A short Asian man sprinted up to him, waving his hands.

"I'm so glad I found one of you guys," the man said to the Ranger, "there are a bunch of young people spray painting and throwing stuff into the trees, just up the trail." The Asian man pointed to where he just ran from. "If you hurry, I bet you can catch them."

The Ranger nodded and started sprinting up the stairs of the trail, in hot pursuit.

The Asian man calmly walked in the other direction.

*   *   *   *   *   *   *

The spray paint was a last minute idea from Henning.

THE EDUCATOR

*   *   *   *   *   *   *

CHAPTER 19

Sometime in the morning
Somewhere in SW South Dakota

"Ernest Erhard. We call him 'The Old Man.' Flew in World War One. A pretty good pilot too. An ace. Eight kills. After the war he returned to college and got a mechanical engineering degree. Ended up working up in the Iron Range. After a while, I guess he and a buddy realized the miners needed help managing their money. So that's how Erhard & Long got started. This was a few years before Pearl Harbor."

Shotgun was walking and talking. Moving his hands in exaggerated motions. Zeale tried to keep pace with the fat man. He could barely hear anything.

"During the war, The Old Man returned to Duluth and worked on a mining operation. He also consulted with weapons factories and the like. After the war was when his financial firm really took off. By the 1960's, he was the second richest man in Minnesota. Erhard first got involved in politics in 1964, on the Goldwater campaign. Money talks in politics. Pretty soon he was one of the most important Republicans in the country, but one of the least known.

"During the '72 Nixon campaign The Old Man helped funnel a lot of laundered money into the campaign. He took rich donors to local casinos, showed them a good time and cashed out millions to funnel into slush funds. The Old Man knew what he was doing, and never got caught up in the Watergate mess. Kessler, or 'The Archbishop,' met Erhard when he was doing an internship at his firm. Kessler was in law school at the time. This was in '78. Let's Just say Ernie and and The Old Man hit it off right away..

"Kessler loved stirring shit at the U. In '77 he was actually the chairman of the College Republicans on campus. So The Old Man started giving him money for events and stunts. Kessler and another guy, Tim Pawlenty, who's now a state rep, once took over MPIRG. This was in '81. As it was, the two were pretty close. Zan met Kessler around this time, in the CRs.

"In 1982, The Old Man found out he was dying. He was eighty-seven years old at the time. Lung cancer. Morton Blackwell, the Leadership Institute guy, first gave Erhard the idea of creating conservative groups on college campuses. Blackwell was just starting a nationwide conservative training organization, that later became LI. Blackwell also wanted to start a program where he could send out field reps to start these conservative non-partisan non-profits. Erhard didn't think his plan could work. But, he thought he could make it work on one campus. So he gave a bunch of money, under the table, to Kessler and Zan.

"Kessler figures the big reason The Old Man became so adamant about this was because his son died of a drug overdose. The stupid bastard got heavy into the sixties hippie movement. Left a baby grandson in Erhard's care. One of Erhard's nephews had to raise the kid after he died. Erhard never married, his son was from an affair he had with one of his employees. Anyway, that how our little group got going.."

Shotgun stopped for a second, cracked his back with a violent twisting motion, and continued.

"Ever since, Kessler and Zan have been at the U of M. We've built up a pretty good organization over the years. Lots of good people. Probably twenty or so initiated alumni. We're the only continuously operating conservative campus org in the U.S. At least, from what we know. Of course, no one's heard of us. And we have to keep it that way. Otherwise there will be accusations about corporate funding and Zionist whatever bullshit conspiracies from the lefty wackies. It's easier to stay under the radar. That's why there's all the secrets. That's why there's so few of us recruited every year."

Zeale stopped and unwrapped the towels from his ankles and did his best to squeeze the liquid into his canteen. "Are we done now?" He asked.

"Yeah, as far as the history of the organization is concerned. You'll be getting a little book, written by me, that has more information in it."

Zeale drained the contents of the canteen down his throat. "Couldn't you have just given me the book?"

"Sure. We're not here for the lecture. I just wanted to kill some time and get you caught up. We've still got to get your initiation done."

"This isn't it?"

"No. This is still foreplay."

"Fuck dude." Zeale had other thoughts, just not the energy to say them.

"First lesson of recruiting. Initiations have to be hard. The fraternities do terrible things to their recruits in order to win over loyalty. It helps fool the mind into believing everything was worth the effort. *Esprit d' corps* and all that.

"Notice, I'm giving you propaganda only after I've made you tired. See? That way your mind is too weak and confused to doubt the information. You're more likely to take it as fact. It's a method of persuasion the Stalinists mastered."

"You're bullshitting me?"

"No, as far as your concerned. But the story is hard to digest when fully lucid."

"Then what's the initiation?"

"It's coming, relax dude."

"Why aren't you hungry?"

"I'm fat, I'm always hungry"

*   *   *   *   *   *   *

The rain picked up. Shotgun looked unaffected; Zeale did not. For an hour Zeale had been complaining nonstop. Finally Shotgun reached his breaking point.

"For fuck's sake, Spags, shut the up ya pussy."

Zeale walked in silence for a bit. Shotgun felt joy at the silence. Then it was gone again. "Out of curiosity, how'd you get your nickname?"

"Oh, I had a car as an undergrad, so I drove people around a lot. Always had a shotgun in the back of my truck, behind the seat. People just started calling me Shotgun...Anyway, what kind of name is 'Gene Zeale' anyway?"

"My parents had a good sense of humor."

They kept moving up a small line of hills until they came to the top. From this point, a series of small tan buildings, bumps really, were visible in the distance.

"Where the hell is this?" Spags dropped his bag and sat down on it.

"That is the Black Hills Ordinance Depot. Big military installation. Abandoned years ago. Those buildings used to house all sorts of great American toys. Millions of tons of weapons. I like coming here, it reminds me of the stakes involved in politics."

"How so?"

"To give you some sense of the effect of government in the world. Numbers in a budget don't have quite the same effect as these endless little concrete igloos. Each igloo representing tons of bombs. Those tons of bombs representing the millions killed by government in this century."

"Point taken. Can I go home now?"

"No"

*   *   *   *   *   *   *

Shotgun stopped and pulled out a gold pocket-watch and checked the time. Zeale's initiation had started just under 24 hours ago. His ordeal had lasted longer though. He hadn't had any food in about 36 hours and in the last 72 hours he had only gotten a few hours of sleep.

They were walking amongst the concrete bunkers of the Black Hills Ordinance Depot.

"Just past five o'clock." Shotgun carefully put the watch back into his jacket. "I guess I should tell you the final test of this initiation."

"I'm shaking with anticipation." Spags said, with more than a hint of sarcasm.

"Or hypoglycemia." Shotgun tossed a granola bar to the beleaguered underclassman.

Spags greedily consumed the granola bar as they kept walking. Shotgun took him around one of the concrete igloos, to the side facing away from the remains of the road. There Spags took note of a simple tent made with the remains of a shower curtain and some wood planks, with a dirty blanket acting as a sort of floor. There were some more boards and cords of dry prairie grass near a small fire pit that had small wood planks set up in a small teepee with grass underneath, ready to start a fire.

"Your final test..." Shotgun spoke as he uncovered a motorcycle hidden under a large tarp, "Right now, someone identifying himself as a U.S. Marshall is calling the Fall River County Sheriff's Office to report an escaped convict who overpowered a U.S. Marshall, stole his car, and drove to an abandoned town in Wyoming. Tracks showed the murderous convict escaping into the prairie land heading east. The person will also mention this convict grew up on a military base near the Ordnance Depot. The caller will request the Sheriff send someone to check to make sure the offender is not hiding out around his old stomping ground."

Shotgun pulled out a map and a compass. "You are required to evade the police and meet up with an aircraft landing in 12 hours on the location marked on the map." Shotgun pointed to the spot then flipped the map and compass over to Spags. "It'll be right around sunrise. Our current location is also marked."

"Are you fucking serious?"

"Relax, you should be able to do it. There's lots of cover thanks to the bunkers and tall grass. They'll be able to track you, but stay out of their line of sight and you should be fine."

Shotgun straddled the motorcycle, a small green and white dirt-bike that barely took his weight. He flipped out a car flare from his backpack and lit it, then tossed it onto the prairie grass packed beneath the boards in the small fire pit. The fire started quickly and soon was producing enough smoke to be seen by anyone looking closely.

He then started up the motorcycle. He turned his head to say 'good luck' to the initiate, but the words never escaped his mind.

THE EDUCATOR

Spags leveled a roundhouse kick to the back of the fat man's head, knocking him out cold.

*   *   *   *   *   *   *

Two people atop horses plodded along the road passing bunker after bunker.

They were wearing tan pants, tan shirts and black rain slickers marked 'Sheriff.' Their pace was relaxed. There was a man and a woman. Occasionally a bright copper shield was visible from under their jackets.

The sun was setting, the weather finally nice enough to acknowledge the sunset.

In the distance, they could see the smoke from a campfire. Half an hour later, they were at the campsite, staring at Shotgun as he snored loudly next to the fire.

"Hey John, wake up big fella, what's going on?"

John. The name penetrated the haze and woke the big man up.

Shotgun rarely heard his real name.

"Hey Aaron, 'bout time."

"Ve thought vee'd give the leetle one zome extra time," The woman, a Swedish import named Natasha, shot a smile visible in the fading light, her teeth pearly white and almost fluorescent, "vhy ve find you here?"

"The capricious little bastard knocked me out," Shotgun realized he had forgotten the little bastard's name.

Natasha dismounted her horse and knelt over Shotgun. She took out a pen light and checked his eyes, then asked him questions about where he was, the date, and others. He didn't do so well, but Natasha had a lot to do with it. The attractive and vivacious buxom beauty provided ample distraction for any male.

"Yust a slight concussion, you'll be fine."

Amused by everything, Aaron dropped down off his horse, then he and Natasha helped the man up.

"Ever ride a horse?" Aaron asked.

"Yeah, but he died soon after."

*   *   *   *   *   *   *

Spags was sitting in a little diner in downtown Edgemont. The town was dying but had some life. A gas station. A convenience store. A motel. He enjoyed some food, thanks to a hundred dollar bill he had hidden in his shoe, and filled up the gas tank on the motorcycle. Then he drove back to the military installation in the dark, to find the pickup point. No one saw him on the empty roads back to the ghost town of Igloo.

*   *   *   *   *   *   *

Shotgun's fuzziness slowly melted away during the horse ride.

It was just past midnight when the trio trotted in to their destination.

The Kelley Ranch.

A few miles south of Edgemont, the place offered half a dozen small cabins for vacationers looking to get away from the city life. Cattle, horse stables, and open country were the primary selling point. The owners, the Kelley's, offered horseback riding lessons, cattle rustling, hiking, shooting, and pretty much everything someone could think to do on a ranch.

Aaron Wright was a longtime associate of Ernie Kessler. Aaron had been a freshman working on a Finance degree from the University of Minnesota when he received an internship with Kessler's Financial company a few years after The Old Man's death. Since then, Aaron's market insights had earned Kessler millions of dollars. A libertarian, Wright didn't share Kessler's moral vision, but as an economist he knew the more right wingers around, the better. So, he helped The Organization whenever he could.

Aaron was an avid outdoorsman and spent many weeks of his free time on the Kelley Ranch.

Before entering the ranch, Aaron and Natasha removed their Sheriff outfits. The two lovers shared a horse, with Shotgun riding Natasha's. As they approached the stable to return the horses, Big Sam Kelley, the ranch patriarch, opened the doors to let them into the stable.

"I know I shouldn't ask," Big Sam said with his booming baritone voice, "but how the heck diya leave with two people and arrive with three?"

"They were doing me a favor," Shotgun answered back, with his own booming voice in the bass frequency, "I was waiting for a bus."

"John Underhill," Big Sam walked up to Shotgun's horse and grabbed the reigns. "I thought I told you to stay away from my horses."

Shotgun expertly dismounted the horse with surprising grace for a man his size. "My bike broke down and I needed a lift. I was metal detecting out by Ardmore. I started for Provo, Got lucky and ran into Aaron and Natasha."

"I oughta charge ya for wear and tear." Big Sam took the

horse over to its pen and led him in.

"Oh, you can charge me for a night in one of your cabins." Shotgun didn't want to stay with Aaron and Natasha, the two had a reputation for coital prolificness.

"Fine by me. I'll go get your cabin set up. If you want, Mary can get y'all some supper." Ranch work was hard work. Shotgun and Aaron knew their hosts didn't get to sleep until one or two in the morning and they didn't feel bad about agreeing to a midnight supper.

Big Sam went out to the cabin while Aaron, Natasha and Shotgun went up to the main house. Shotgun got on the phone and called Kessler. He told him how everything had gone. The universal conclusion was Gene Zeale was going to be a fine addition to The Organization.

When Shotgun was done with the phone, he made his way to the kitchen where Mary Kelley was serving Aaron and Natasha. On their plates was a mixed grill of chorizo sausage, eggs, fried onions and hash browns served with toast and mugs of beer. Mary handed Shotgun a plate as he sat down. Big Sam entered and gave Shotgun keys to a cabin.

Then Big Sam pulled out a few cigars and passed them around.

Life was good.

*   *   *   *   *   *   *

Sunrise, just outside of the ghost town of Igloo, SD, a plane approached.

The plane circled for twenty minutes.

Spags admired the aircraft. It was a bright yellow with a dark brown stripe. A big engine chugged away on the aircraft's nose, turning a propeller. The fuselage was big and beefy. This wasn't a hobby plane, it was a work plane.

Spag's didn't know it, but he was looking at a de Havilland Canada DHC-2 Beaver. A true bush plane with a solid reputation among pilots in Alaska. It was a short-takeoff and landing craft and running examples fetched six-figures on the open market. The plane was the first thing Ernie Kessler bought after he made his first million. Those good times had been a long time ago, but Kessler had done his best to protect his favorite things after his firm was almost wiped out in the 1987 market crash.

The plane alighted the road and stopped just twenty feet from Spags.

The tall black man emerged from aircraft and waved the underclassman aboard.

Spags hopped into the aircraft and took a seat in the cockpit. Just as he got his seat-belt fastened the aircraft started down the road with a roar from the engine. In a few seconds the plane was airborne again.

The pickup took less than three minutes.

The plane banked to the right and Kessler pulled out small binder filled with maps. After a few minutes he put everything away and settled on a course. Then he turned to congratulate the new member.

"Welcome to the Israel Bissell Society," he said.

Kessler might as well have been talking to himself.

Gene 'Spags' Zeale was asleep.

*   *   *   *   *   *   *

CHAPTER 20

El Dos de Mayo, 1994
Sally's Bar and Grille, Minneapolis

El Dos de Mayo was a good fucking time.

It was the most important date on The Organization's calendar.

Celebrating is important in any organization, but more so in political ones. The business of politics is so foul, only camaraderie and the promise of heavy drinking and merriment could motivate the rational person to participate. Even then, it took the irrational to stay.

Irrational not being bad.

El Dos was a good time. Lots of food, drink and endless hours of storytelling.

It was a way to release all the pent up frustration and anger conservatives experienced on a liberal campus in a socialist city in an authoritarian state. It was also part of the recruiting process. Freshman participants would see how the group could be fun, and could get alcohol.

Since many group alumni were also present, it offered a chance to disseminate the stories of previous accomplishments and create group cohesion.

And for the upperclassmen it was an excuse to barhop and get drunk.

The party started in late afternoon at Sally's Bar and Grill on Washington Ave.

A half dozen of the undergrads were already inside racking up a huge bill. Almost the whole organization was there, except Orson Henning, Zan Chin-Wu and Ernie Kessler. They were in the parking lot waiting for Chris Berg. After eight minutes of impatient waiting, Berg waddled into the parking lot.

"It's about time." Kessler stared down the trollish Berg.

"Fuck you, the stupid Maroon server crashed again and I'm the only one my department chair thought could fix it. That's what I get for staying in the office a half hour after I'm supposed to be done for the day."

"Hey, it's fucking El Dos," Zan said jovially, "So, let's have it Chris."

Berg's ever growing facial hair gave him an evil villain look as the two lengths of beard extended from both sides of his Fu-Manchu were waxed to pointed ends almost four inches below his chin. The heavyset man pulled a small box from his black trench coat and tossed it over to Kessler. Kessler fished out a small item from the box and gave it a good look, then handed it to Henning.

"Congratulations Orson Henning," Kessler said solemnly, "You're now a full member."

Henning took a close look at his gift, a gold ring with a large star sapphire at the crown. It looked almost like a graduation ring. He slipped it on his right pinky finger.

"If anyone wearing one of those rings asks a favor, you must honor it, as they will do in turn for you." Zan shook Henning's hand. "Less than twenty people have a ring from the Israel Bissell Society. It's an elite club."

Then each of the men put their hands on Orson's shoulders and together they recited a prayer together.

"Heavenly father, give us the strength to do your will on Earth and the strength of character to follow your commandments. For this we pray, Amen."

Then everyone entered Sally's, slapping each other on the back along the way.

*   *   *   *   *   *   *

Thirty people were gathered inside Sally's for the celebration. Some CRs. Pro-lifers. A few ROTC guys.

Most were not members of The Organization or even recruits. Conservatives were a niche community and everyone knew everyone.

And, normally, got along well.

They were fighting the same battle.

There are differences and sometimes the competition between groups for the scarce resources on campus got intense. There are only so many hardcore politicos around. Organizations that didn't get their cut of the good recruits suffered and died.

The Organization was both active in recruiting and very selective. They wanted hardcore people, but they also wanted hardcore people who were sonsofbiches. This thinned things out and made easy peace with the CRs and pro-life groups.

The guys in the Israel Bissell Society were those whom none of the other groups really wanted anyway.

*   *   *   *   *   *   *

"This paper is shit." Henning flipped a copy of the Campus Patriot, the conservative newspaper, to Nolan Painter. "Look at page eighteen. 'Analysis of Clinton's Balkan Policies.' Seriously, no one is going to read shit like that. It put me to sleep."

Painter picked up the paper and paged through it. His piercing blue eyes scanned the pages. After a few moments he tossed the paper back to Henning.

"Alright, what the fuck am I supposed to do with it?" Painter asked.

"It's your paper now," Zan interjected, "you need to make it into an actual paper. And no bitching about how no one will help you."

"Outgoing Seniors aren't supposed to do heavy lifting," Painter replied.

Zan sat down across from Painter and put on the warmest face he could.

"It won't be heavy lifting; it's an election year. We just need three good issues fall semester. One of those issues we'll put together this summer. Then, you're done. By second semester you'll be an at-large editor with no responsibilities."

"Fine, but I'm taking a stipend."

Everyone at the table rolled their eyes at the comment. Stipends represented avarice and disdain for the movement. The table was about to start giving Painter a lot of shit but they were interrupted by Ernie Kessler announcing a guest.

Congressman Rod Grams had stopped by.

*   *   *   *   *   *   *

Politicians did the same thing at every appearance. A quick speech. Some hand shaking. Some awkward small talk. Asking for support in the upcoming election. Etc Etc.

It was always the same crap.

Rod Grams was no different.

But Grams was popular. He was thinking big, trying for the open Senate seat.

THE EDUCATOR

Tall, broad shouldered. A friendly, understated smile behind friendly eyes. He walked slow, was very patient, and was surprisingly quiet for a politician.

He enjoyed some appetizers, which he made a point to pay for, then his handler, the unshakeable Michael Cohen, shuffled him out of the bar.

Kessler walked out with him.

"Rod, have you thought about adding Mr. Underhill to your campaign?" Kessler walked with the two men through the Sally's parking lot. "You know he did well on your congressional campaign. It would mean a lot to me."

"Absolutely not," Cohen said, "Mr. Underhill has changed his name twice in the last three years. It would be a distraction on the campaign trail."

"John changed his name after school because he was looking for a job and he thought the University thing, when he forced the previous U president to resign, would make it look like he was a troublemaker," Kessler replied. "He changed it back after giving up on the corporate world. That's not two name changes."

"It's enough for an unsympathetic media to run with it." Cohen said.

"Actually," Grams stopped their progression towards his car. "I like John. No one worked harder on the campaign. And besides, Michael, when was the last time the press made a stink about a communications director? They can't, they have to stay on good terms with the CD if they want information."

"John's already got an offer from Quist to run his primary campaign against Carlson. I told him to wait until I talked to you."

Cohen tugged on Grams' arm but the big man didn't move. Perhaps remembering all the money Kessler had thrown at him over the years, he decided on an action.

"I'll give John a call."

*　　　*　　　*　　　*　　　*　　　*　　　*

"I don't get it. Kessler has to be one of the best connected men in Minnesota. What's he doing hanging around the U with people like us," Zeale wondered aloud.

"Kessler's got his obsessions." Zan stated. "This campus is one of them. We promised The Old Man we'd stay, and we keep our promises. This is our mission. The Old Man is the only reason Kessler is running a financial firm instead of working as some real estate attorney. But it's also one of his windmills. It's a small world capable of manipulation. It lacks the great tidal forces of national politics, where you can't make changes."

"So," asked Nolan, "What keeps you here doing this shit?"
"I've got nothing better to do," came Zan's answer.

*   *   *   *   *   *   *

The party moved to The Big Ten. They took up the entire back room, including the roundtable. Zan, normally strict about his dietary intake, was putting down shots faster than Alisha Williams could serve him. Soon enough, he was inhabiting the men's bathroom, vomiting what poisons he could. Zan only drank once a year, on El Dos. Part tradition, part stress relief. It interfered with the Zan mystique, but it was all in good fun. Taking life too seriously made suicides.

Alisha was able to get Zan out of the bathroom and took him out back, behind the bar, for some fresh air. Much to the delight of the El Dos crowd, who at this point were almost entirely alumni. After half an hour, Alisha decided Zan needed to be taken home, so she did it herself. She left the group to her able staff and drove Zan home.

Alisha Williams was a friend.

The weird thing about friends is that you can't avoid making a few. Some people enjoy accumulating friends like they were pieces of jewelry. Friends become meters for self-esteem to the point where the term 'friend' loses it meaning. In reality friends are a burden. Should be a burden. If a friend needs a favor you go out of your way to help. Even if it puts you at risk. The converse is every friend is also an insurance policy.

Zan took friendship seriously. Friendships were burdens. Only those who could be relied upon in a crunch could earn the title of friend, and this left him with very few friends indeed. Zan and Kessler had gone to great lengths in teaching these simple truths to members of the organization.

Eventually the elders of the group shied away from other people altogether. The burdens of friendship often outweigh the benefits. Most of the alumni were incurable bachelors and often loners. This isolation drove people away from the group, and this added to the antisocial nature of everyone else. It was an interesting dynamic, one a psychology student would love. If The Organization ever attracted one, that is.

Still, friends were made.

Back when city governments began to restrict restaurant and bar owner's rights to allow smoking in their own establishments, right-wing activists on campus, led by Zan et al., began a crusade against the safety Nazis. Letters were written, protests were done and at one point a smokers' rights group was created on campus. The Organization passed out free cigarettes to incoming freshmen as soon as they moved into the dorms. It was fun, and quite a success.

THE EDUCATOR

But the efforts failed.

The local city government forced all restaurants to have a smoke-free section. They even required large and expensive air filters and barriers between smoking and non-smoking sections. Expensive, and it put people out of business and out of work. Alisha was one of the few bar owners leading the charge and she had worked with the young conservatives at the U for many of her events. In defeat she became good friends with The Organization, Zan and Chris Berg in particular.

Her downtown Minneapolis bar shut down thanks to the onerous requirements and she eventually sold it and became the night manager at The Big Ten on the U of M campus. A few years later, she bought the bar. Because of her, The Big Ten became an instant right-wing hangout; the only place were the first amendment was practiced on campus. No ideas were off-limits.

El Dos de Mayo 1994 continued without Zan, who left the party early for the first time ever.

Alisha never made it back to the bar.

*   *   *   *   *   *   *

CHAPTER 21

Tuesday, May 3
Bailey Hall; St. Paul Campus

Just like that the school year was nearly over. The Minnesota weather changed from miserable cold and snow to miserable freezing rain and muck to mildly pleasant spring. Fifteen weeks passed quickly for all students. For those working in The Organization it went doubly as fast. There was no rest. No Introspection

There was also no time for fucking.

Almost none.

Most college students found some time. But for many students the pressures and deadlines of college prevented these pursuits.

Biology can't be held at bay forever.

Towards the end of the school year students realize time is running out. In high school there was always the presumption you would see your classmates come fall. After high school is finished, for the first time this artificial network of friends and acquaintances is torn apart permanently. It is a harsh introduction to the fact the world churns away and at any time your social network can be completely scrubbed.

Students who originally ignored and bypassed the advances of classmates suddenly became receptive, often seeking out those who originally earned rebuke just a few months before. There was no more planning for the future. Students learned to live in the now.

Kayla Witold had gotten a fair share of attention from the boys in her dorm. Nothing about her was special. She was short, pale, with a friendly face. Generally unconcerned with her looks, she had a respectable figure. Attractive enough, though she was getting a little fleshy. The definition her body had in high school was gone. Sometimes she still wore contacts, but had otherwise switched back to her glasses because it saved time.

All year she had waited for the man she wanted to marry. Someone good looking, smart and charming, to find her. And all year she got hit on by the same group of douchebags living in the dorm. There was Jon, the tall and awkward music wannabe who ate lunch with her and her friends sometimes. *Musicians were worthless.* Then there was Lou. He lived just around the corner and she had taken freshman biology with him. They studied together for awhile. He wasn't bright, he wasn't interesting. He talked more about being drunk than he actually spent drunk.

She wondered if all the talk actually meant the guy didn't drink at all. He wasn't bad looking though. Lou was just a little taller than her, had a bit of a gut but that went well with his broad shoulders and massive arms. Lou spent a lot of time lifting iron at the St. Paul gym. He was a horticulture student, learning how to squeeze more sugar out of beets. Kayla didn't like the idea of spending her life with a man who pumped iron and worked with plants.

Fucking plants of all things.

But Kayla burned. She realized the fact she was thinking about sex meant it was time to stop studying for a while. She had spent the last fifteen minutes on the same page in her psychology textbook. Next week was finals week. During finals week you also had to move out of the dorms. Sometimes students were done with everything and out by Wednesday. Sometimes students barely checked out in time. It was a double-down of stress.

She got up and went down to the cafeteria. Her normal supper was a salad with sprouts, hard-boiled eggs, spinach and bacon bits with a bit of blue cheese dressing. And coffee, a habit picked up from The Organization. She took her tray out to the seating area and saw Lou, in a sleeveless t-shirt, sitting in front of several textbooks and notebooks. He waved her over and she sat down.

"...How are things...What are your summer plans...How's studying going...How many finals do you have..."

Small talk absorbed most of their conversation. Lou was trying to memorize different forms of turf grass and their properties. Kayla was worried about her PoliSci class, the one with an infamous Marxist professor. Occasionally they sat in silence, eating.

After about half an hour Kayla got up to leave, Lou stuck to his horticulture books.

Then something pinged in her mind.

Kayla stopped. "Hey, I think I could help you with your studying. They say teaching is a good way to learn."

Lou lifted himself from his book. "That's a great idea"

He gathered his books. They dropped off their trays and walked up to Kayla's room. He set up his books on her bed. Then she joined him on the bed. Before she knew it, her pants were off.

*   *   *   *   *   *   *

CHAPTER 22

Thursday, May 12
Superblock

Orson exhaled a puff of smoke from his cigar. For Orson, moving from the dorms was going to be hard after four glorious years of co-ed proximity. Upperclassmen who chose to live in the dorms enjoyed privilege. If you were old enough, you were allowed to have alcohol in your room. Word got out. Even the less-than-social senior could easily find attractive young freshmen to spend time with, when alcohol was involved.

He was sitting on one of the picnic benches behind Centennial Hall, the dorm that had been home for four years. It was Thursday afternoon of finals week, the busiest time for students trying to get out of the dorms. The U required students to be out of the dorms 24 hours after their last final. Students absolutely had to be out of the dorms by 8pm Saturday of Finals week. This seemed cruelest to students who had Saturday finals, since they had to study and pack at the same time, but in the end no one cared. By the time a student got up the courage and spare time to complain, he was already halfway through the weekend and living out of his car. This happened to Orson once; he was happy it never happened again.

Orson blew a smoke ring up into the air and watched it disappear quickly in the spring breeze.

An obnoxiously girlish voice lisped "Ors'ee! Howzit goin?"

It was Tessa Olsen, a buxom Community Adviser he had known well, at one point intimately, during his spell in Centennial.

"Hey Tess."

"So, you moving out today?"

"Already checked out, my stuff is packed away in my car. I was just enjoying this last little bit here." He waved his cigar between his fingers.

The big curvy blond sat down next to him, and they sat watching groups of parents and students struggling with big blue laundry hampers filled with belongings. The hampers had wheels and were loaned out during move-ins and move-outs. They were a pain to push around as the wheels were more for show than any mechanical use. It was a comical scene.

"So," Tessa cooed, "have you figured out what you're going to do with your life yet?"

"Not really."

"Headed back to Wisconsin?"

"Yeah, for a few weeks anyway. A friend of mine says he has a job lined up for me at a think tank in D.C., I'll probably take that."

"Wow, Washington. That's cool. I knew politics would pay off for you, you were too good at it."

"I dunno, I'm still debating going back to my dad's lumber yard."

"Oh hush. You're going to love it." She leaned over and kissed him on the cheek.

"Getting a little sentimental, huh?"

"Maybe, I'm staying here for another year or so. I'm going for my education Masters. Staying in the dorms too. Crazy huh?"

"I hope things go well for you." Orson hoped he sounded sincere. Tessa was a ditz and the thought of her becoming a teacher gave him a cold feeling in his limbs.

They sat in silence again, watching several groups of students and parents trying to manhandle the laundry hampers through the narrow dorm doors.

"Gosh," Tessa observed, "This is just crazy. All the people moving out. It's pure chaos. No order to it at all."

"I love watching it. I've been amazed by it every year I've been here."

"I've never really watched it before. I was always too busy... There *has* to be a better way to do it," she said.

"Sure, you could take everyone in the dorms and force them to volunteer their time to help out a few of their neighbors. Maybe a schedule or computer system could keep the order. Then you could enforce it with something, maybe the threat of fines. That way everyone helps out everyone else. People would be out of the dorms on time, and none of the drama. Nice and orderly."

"Yes, that sounds about right."

"Of course, you'd have privacy concerns. Or theft. Maybe a student runs behind because of unforeseen circumstances. Maybe there's no way a student with a Saturday final is going to be able to help anyone until everyone is gone; you are dealing with human beings after all. Hundreds of them, each with their own preferences, timetables, values and incentives. Some of them value their time. Others are more laid back. Almost all would object to being forced into helping each other. And how careful would they be handling things that were not their own? Not very.

"No. I think it works out pretty well the way it is. Every individual works through their own preferences, in their own time, on their schedule. Many students help other students anyway. And the parents help too. Your computer would fail to account for the thousands of adults who would have to work around their schedules to help their kids.

"I love watching the chaos of move-out week. It's an example of the market at work. People going about their business, accomplishing amazing things in a short amount of time, with no director at all. It's beautiful."

"You're one odd duck, Mr. Henning."

*   *   *   *   *   *   *

Part II

Summer 1994.

Black bird singing in the dead of night
Take these sunken eyes and learn to see all your life
you were only waiting for this moment to be free
          --Blackbird by The Beatles

Beauty and Mercy are only recognized by people
Because they know the opposite, which is ugly and mean.
          --From the Tao te Ching

THE EDUCATOR

CHAPTER 1

6pm Friday, May 13
Morrill Hall

President Paulson powered down the computer in his office and stretched out his legs. University work was never done.

But summer slowed down the flow.

The legislature was in recess, there was some time before the summer sessions began. It was time to take to the road.

He was going to have a solid five days alone. Up North.

Paulson walked out of his office, downstairs to the underground parking garage and drove his big black Chevy Suburban across to Arlington Street to the East River Parkway and went north for a few blocks, parking his car in front of a meter by the abandoned Mineral Sciences building.

Walking around the building, he pulled out his special key and unlocked the chains around the loading dock entrance. Making his way to the ladies bathroom on the second floor, he found his box. His ladies. Right where they should be.

Sitting on an old wooden chair he had smuggled into the bathroom, he opened his box and remembered. Smelling each lock of hair. Rubbing underwear on his cheeks.

Then he lingered for a while on the photos.

He was hungry again.

It was happening faster and faster.

He had read about this, read about sociopaths and serial killers. For years he tried to contain himself. To stop himself. To learn about his compulsions. Instead, the education fed his lust.

There was something wonderful about reading the exploits of others. How long they worked and how many victims they accumulated before getting caught.

Now he wondered where he ranked among all the great serial killers of the past. He was in his golden years now. His prime. Age and wisdom combined with experience and enough athleticism necessary to carry out the deeds.

He put everything back into the metal box and locked it; put it back through the hole in the wall and attached the rope to the nail on the stud. There were no concerns about the box being discovered. If it was ever found, he was caught; he accepted that. If police ever got suspicious, he didn't know how he would react. Lay low? Why? You were as good as caught anyway, *might as well go on a spree.*

A Spree.

Normally he only killed one woman at a time. Serendipity would sometimes present opportunities he couldn't pass up. But a spree. *What an idea.* There were lots of women running and exercising everywhere, trying to lose the winter weight and get a tan.

He might give a spree a try.

Thoughts of future conquests floated in his head. Being a good killer took imagination. There were so many factors to consider. So many angles. It was just like writing computer software.

He worked his way out of the building and back to his car.

*   *   *   *   *   *   *

Loud ringing.

Zan couldn't firgure out why the sea was ringing.

Then he awoke.

It was his phone. The big brass bells on his black monstrosity of a phone had interrupted his life once again.

At least it was a phone he could control. His new portable phone followed him from place to place.

Zan answered. It was Alisha.

"Hey Zan, I was able to get a minute here to talk, you want to get out to Saint Anthony Main tomorrow afternoon? I want to see 'Maverick.' Three o'clock showing?"

"Sure, I'll be back from sparring by then." Zan was normally bleeding after a Saturday morning of boxing, but he figured that just added to the Zan Experience.

"Okay, gotta get back to work, bye." she hung up before Zan could reply.

He stared into the ether. Then he put on some running shoes and went for a quick jog.

*   *   *   *   *   *   *

CHAPTER 2

Friday, May 13
Monticello, MN

It was almost 9:30 in the evening when Paulson got to his storage garage in Monticello. The University President did most of his fishing and boating up north. And his storage was located on the way to two of the University's three other campuses. In fact, Monticello wasn't too far out of the way for a Duluth trip either. It was a great spot to store stuff in case he wanted to get in a quick fishing or snowmobile trip while charging the U for mileage.

The storage facility was huge. There were three boats, several snowmobiles, ATVs, a spare Ford 150, a sleek cherry red Porsche 964

THE EDUCATOR

Turbo and a couple of motorcycles located inside the steel structure. He kept the building heated in winter, to great expense. For Paulson, there was no point to wealth if you didn't find a way to enjoy it.

Paulson pushed his 1992 Lund 1600 Angler II Dlx fishing boat up to his Suburban and attached the trailer. The boat was painted a dull red with white trim. It was one of his few possessions that wasn't obnoxiously ostentatious.

On the road again, he made his way north on Highway 10 towards St. Cloud.

One of his favorite fishing spots was Big Fish Lake located about ten miles west of the city. He owned a small cabin on that lake. Fishing south of Interstate 94 was always a little more private than fishing north of the Interstate. Paulson never understood why.

Paulson opened the cabin, turned on the power and water heaters, and parked his boat. He decided on a quick hunt. There were lots of students around, even though almost all of the local colleges were done with their spring terms. The bars would be full, which was both good and bad. There was almost zero chance he'd be more noticeable to any witnesses. But, his face made the papers and there was a chance someone might recognize him.

A shower, a shave, and an informal dress of clothes. Dark, slimming and discrete.

At 11 o'clock he drove into St. Cloud and picked the first bar he saw, a large sports bar called The Ultimate. The bar was nearly full. Paulson ordered a beer and decided to walk around. The Ultimate had several levels. The basement was full of pool tables and dart boards. Almost all the basement dwellers were old men.

The ground floor had a small dance area and a stage. A DJ was working a table and the music was barely audible past the dance floor. In the middle of the building was a large island bar surrounded by stools. Tables were scattered about. There wasn't much organization to it. There were square and round tables, tall tables and some booths. Above the middle of the ground floor, spiral stairs next to the bar lead the way up to the loft. The loft provided a view of the dance floor, and in the opposite direction a view of large bay windows. Beyond the bay windows were outdoor volleyball courts and a frozen pond. A small bar served those in the loft.

Television sets, some hanging from the ceiling, others fastened to walls, were everywhere. Two large screen TVs, perched like ancient monoliths, flanked both sides on the ground floor. ESPN was the channel of choice. A few TVs had on CNN. Cigarette smoke hung in the room like a light fog.

Paulson made his was towards the dance floor. This was the only area with an acceptable male-to-female ratio. The DJ was entertaining several groups of women, dancing in a group, on the dance floor. The music was horrific to Paulson's ears. It was some kind of 80's metal. Walking around the periphery of the floor, he looked for good targets. There were few. No eye contact anywhere. The dance floor chicks were too young.

It reminded Paulson of how much of a misnomer 'Minnesota Nice' really was. Out-state Minnesotans were respectful, occasionally helpful, and generally humble. But they were also cold, indifferent, detached and self-involved. Classic Minnesota Scandanavians were anti-social, avoided eye contact, and were uncomfortable conversationalists.

It extended to the point of xenophobia. People outside the family or community were regarded with great distrust. Paulson hated people from out-state.

He turned to start working his way back to the front door, almost knocking the drink out of the hands of a woman directly behind him.

*　　*　　*　　*　　*　　*　　*

She was smiling at him. She turned to another woman to her left and said "I think you're right." Then she looked at Paulson and asked "You're Malcolm Paulson, president of the U of M, right?"

Paulson looked down at the petite woman. She had shoulder length black hair and bright green eyes. Her face was worn but still quite attractive. She looked to be in her late forties. Her friend was taller and thinner, her hair was brown and featured blonde highlights. He smiled back at the two ladies.

Game on, he thought.

*　　*　　*　　*　　*　　*　　*

Sandy and Ashley were their names.

Sandy was short and loquacious. Effervescent.

Ashley was tall and reserved. Supercilious.

Together they were quite social. They took Paulson to their booth and chatted. The two girls had known each other since high school, had gone to college together at St. Cloud State, became strippers together, and now they owned their own winery and bed and breakfast together. During the summer they were kept busy with their business. During winter they had much less work to do, and a lot of money to blow.

They asked Paulson about academia. The two girls had sociology degrees and were capable conversationalists. Drinks lubricated the discussion and Paulson poured his charisma on the ladies. Sandy got handsy with the Professor, while Ashley kept most of her attention on Sandy. Paulson could see the two girls were lovers. Maybe not partners. Close friends. He found their dynamic odd.

"You two seem very close to each other," he observed non chalantly.

"We're really good friends," Sandy said, eying Ashly, "And when we have a bad day at the bar, we go home to the same house. So we're never bored." Then Sandy leaned in and kissed Ashley.

"For that, I think I'll order another round of drinks," Paulson said.

The women excused themselves to the restroom while Paulson walked up to the bar and ordered another round of drinks.

The two women grabbed adjacent sinks and started working on their makeup.

"Coming on a little strong?" asked Ashley.

"Please, we hit the jackpot with this guy. The fucking president of the University of Minnesota, millionaire, in our favorite bar? And he's actually charming?" Sandy checked her teeth in the mirror.

"I don't like it."

"Pfft, you don't like any of the men we run into."

"That's not true, Ashley said, "It's just, we got a good thing going. Why are we still fishing for someone else?"

"You might not need a cock, but I do," Sandy worked some more lipstick on her face, "Christ, it's been two months since I fucked a guy. If you don't want any, go home. But I need some."

Ashley looked in the mirror. Then she looked at Sandy. "Fine. You're such a cunt though."

Sandy smiled. "But I'm your little cunt. I knew you'd come around, now smile pretty for the rest of the night. No more grumpy Ashley, okay?"

The two returned to the booth. Paulson did his best to entertain and charm. They talked about their business. Paulson described some of the stresses of his job. The night wore on. Sandy kept her hands on Paulson almost the whole time.

Last call was approaching. Paulson finished his drink and decided to shoot from the hip.

"They're about to kick us out, and I'm having too much fun, would you ladies like to show me your bed and breakfast?"

The two girls giggled at the suggestion.

"It's such a mess right now," Sandy replied, "why don't you just take us to your place, we're in no condition to drive?"

Paulson smiled. Sandy smiled. Even Ashley was smiling.

* * * * * * *

Paulson couldn't believe his luck.

In all his life he had never experienced something like this. It was a jackpot. Paulson even reconsidered killing the two ladies.

Then again, he never drank wine. And already had a place to stay in the area.

*   *   *   *   *   *   *

When Paulson was 24, he had already earned a PhD in mathematics. A prodigy. Started programming computers as a teen. Entered college early. As a researcher Malcolm earned several international awards for his probability and number theory work. At 36 he was offered tenure at the University of Minnesota. He turned his early success in academia into financial success as he applied his knowledge to the over-the-counter derivatives market starting in early 1984. In four years he earned more money playing with derivatives than he ever imagined. Eventually the pressures of being a part-time college professor and full-time stock market guru got to him.

Among the problems was the inability this lifestyle gave him to fulfill some of his basic desires. So he left the financial world to go back to teaching full-time. After a scandal ousted the previous University president, Paulson offered to be the interim president. As a respected professor, financial guru and wealthy benefactor, the regents felt Paulson was perfect to restore faith in the University bureaucracy. In 1989, the Regents gave Paulson the job on a more permanent basis.

Killing was easy; killing well was hard. Paulson didn't mind being away from the classroom. He hated teaching and mathematical genius often had an early expiration date. The worst part of being a professor was exposure to literally thousands of young women and not being able to have his fun. Students were easy targets, they did anything their professors suggested and Paulson had more than his fair share of lovers from this group. But if his students suddenly started going missing, it wouldn't be hard for police to figure out his role rather quickly.

Paulson did his best to make his murders look like accidents, create false story lines for police to follow, hunt in different locations, change his *modi operandi*, but these tricks were far from foolproof and Paulson had read about hundreds of murderers caught trying to be too clever. In fact, he did his best not to be seen reading books about murders. Luckily for him, he worked at a place with several cavernous libraries where a person could study in peace.

The drive to Big Fish Lake took twenty minutes. The girls kept talking, the same blather they had been spouting all night at the bar. The two sat up front, Sandy sat on top of Ashley. Despite the talking, Paulson could feel the sexual crescendo. The two girls were already warming up inside the car.

THE EDUCATOR

Paulson's cabin was surrounded by tall pines and had a long dirt driveway leading up to it. Parking in front of the attached garage, Paulson led the girls in. It was small, one bedroom with a bathroom attached. Another room, the largest, had a kitchen tucked in the corner with couches and loveseats in a half circle facing out towards the lake; full length windows giving a great view facing west. A sandy beach and a small dock finished the setting, but weren't visible in the darkness.

Ashley excused herself to the bathroom while Paulson made some drinks for the girls. All he had was gin and tonic. But these girls drank anything. Paulson pulled out a small bottle from a junk drawer. Inside was a white powder, ground Rohypnol. He put some of it into the drinks. Paulson never slept well, often only getting two or three hours of sleep a night. He wasn't bothered by it, but it did provide him access to prescriptions for any number of benzodiazepines. Rohypnol was the preferred date-rape drug. It caused anything from sleep to hypnosis to amnesia. Good stuff.

Paulson liked his victims lucid, but the drug helped him gain control. Killers in control didn't get caught. The ruin of many of Paulson's fellow travelers was the survivor; someone who fought their way free or were left for dead but didn't die. One woman wasn't a problem. two required precautions. He poured just a touch more Rohypnol into the drinks.

He walked the two glasses to the couch, where he found Sandy already stripped down to her panties.

"I see you've made yourself comfortable."

She got up from the couch, took the drinks from Paulson, downed both of them, and dropped the glasses on the floor. Then she pushed at Paulson's mid-section and he fell into the couch. She was on top of him instantly, pressing her lips to his. Paulson took a peek at a wall clock above the kitchen. The drug normally took fifteen minutes to take effect. *Fucking Bitch*, he thought to himself.

*   *   *   *   *   *   *

Paulson gave it a good effort, but was only able to waste ten minutes before climaxing.

He was distracted.

No condoms in the house so now there was physical evidence linking him to his intended victim. It was too late to call everything off. Sandy had taken the drugs. The dose she took wasn't going to kill her or put her into a coma. But she was going to be groggy for most of the next day. It would be very different from a normal hangover. If she got scared and went to a hospital, questions would be raised. Specifically, why would someone give a date rape drug to a woman desperate for sex?

For a few minutes after, Paulson lounged on the couch, Sandy lying on top of him.

What about Ashley? he thought.

"Where do you think Ashley is hiding?"

"Hmm?" Sandy was slow to respond, and groggy. The drugs were taking effect. "She's ssuch a bitcchh. Haf da time, she just hidthes in the bath-troom." She startled to giggle. "You sthought you were gedding a threesthome." More giggling.

"I'll go find her, offer her a drink."

Paulson rolled Sandy off to the side and got up. He put on his pants and slipped into kitchen again. Another gin and tonic was pre-pared; another roofie. The master bedroom was empty but the bath-room door was closed and the light was on. Paulson knocked.

"Hey Ashley?" He waited, heard nothing. "Look, I thought you might want a drink"

Still, nothing stirred.

"I figure, if you want, you can sleep on the couch. Or I could give you a ride home. I'm sorry if you didn't want to be here."

Ashley opened the door. Her makeup was smeared. She had been crying.

"I'm sorry," She said.

"No, it's no problem," Malcolm's voice was reassuring and fatherly, "want a drink?"

"What is it?"

"Gin and tonic."

"Yuck, I'll pass. If you don't mind, I'll just stay on the couch tonight...I don't want to...but...I...Well I don't really like men, you know? Not a lot, anyway."

"I understand," Paulson said, putting the drink onto the toi-let. "Come on, I'll set you up on the couch."

Paulson wrapped his arm around her waist and led her into the bedroom.

Suddenly, he threw her into a wall, hard. Before she could react, he punched her in the gut. Her face contorted with pain. Lifting up her head by the hair, he struck her face. Then he threw her to the ground. Falling to his knees, he lifted up her left arm and struck her underneath the armpit, knocking the wind out of her. Gasping for breath, she couldn't comprehend what was happening.

He lifted her entire body and flopped her unto the bed, face up. As hard as he could, he dropped his fisted right hand like a ham-mer just below her navel. The blow broke her pelvis. The attack lasted about ten seconds and Ashley couldn't even release a scream. Still gasping for breath, she rolled off the bed. The pain in her abdomen shot into her brain and she stopped moving. She wished desperately

THE EDUCATOR

to pass out.

A few moments later, Paulson re-entered the room and wrapped her mouth in duct tape. Some kind of bag was put over her head and she could no longer see. More pain. She had been rolled over on her belly. Paulson kneeled on her butt, causing excruciating pain in her pelvis. Then she felt her arms being wrapped in tape behind her back. She was rolled over again. Paulson pulled her upper body from the floor by her shirt, then hit her as hard as he could on her left cheek.

Ashley slipped into unconsciousness.

   *   *   *   *   *   *   *

Cold. Numb. Pain. Fog.

Ashley's last memories were a blur.

The pieces fell together. Ashley remembered in horror what happened.

She jerked her entire body and tried to scream, but nothing escaped from her mouth, which she couldn't open. Her eyes were open but there was no light. She jerked her body again but it caused tremendous pain.

Then there was a bright light.

Paulson had removed the pillow case from Ashley's head. The woman's eyes were red and inflamed, but the bright light of intelligence was evident from them.

"Nice of you to wake up. I hope I didn't hit you too hard"

Ashley's clothing had been removed. Her wrists were bound behind her, as well as her elbows. Her ankles and knees were taped together too. She didn't immediately recognize where she was. The light was still bright but the cold, concrete floor told her she was probably in the cabin's garage.

"I'm going to let gain your senses for a bit. I'll be right back."

As the fuzz waned the nightmare unfolded. She was in the garage, propped up against the garage door. In the middle of the small garage was Sandy. Her head movements were irregular and woozy, but she was conscious too. Sandy was sitting on a work stool, yellow rope was wrapped around her neck. Duct tape over her mouth. The rope was tied to a chain. The chain was attached to a wooden beam across the ceiling.

That wasn't quite right. Ashley focused on the chain again and realized it was connected to a chain hoist. Paulson re-entered the room, stripped of all his clothing. He was carrying a small vial, which he opened and waved under Sandy's nose. She jerked awake. Just as she did so, Paulson started pulling on the chain hoist, forcing her up off the stool to a standing position. Then he stopped.

- 118 -

He looked over his shoulder at Ashley and smiled at her. Then he pulled on the chains and forced Sandy into the air. She started kicking, her legs unencumbered. One kick hit Paulson on the knee but to no effect. He pulled the chain until her feet were about eighteen inches off the floor. Then he grabbed the small stool and slid it underneath Sandy's legs. She immediately stood up on the stool.

Breathing in big gulps through her noise, Sandy's chest expanded and contracted violently and often.

Paulson watched Sandy, then he left the room again.

Minutes went by. Sandy's breathing slowed down. Ashley tried moving again, but every time she tried the pain in her hip stopped her. The two stared at each other. Tears flowed down Sandy's face.

Paulson re-entered, carrying a folded lawn chair and a role of brown twine. He tied the twine to the stool, then tossed the twine towards Ashley. Unfolding the lawn chair, he lifted Ashley up from the floor and sat down on the chair, placing Ashley on his bare lap. Tears were now pouring down her cheeks.

He whispered in her ear, "Shhh, just relax. It's in my hands now."

Paulson grabbed the roll of twine and pulled the stool out from under Sandy. Ashley struggled and tried to kick with her bound legs. Paulson easily controlled her.

Paulson, watching Sandy kick and swing, caressed Ashley softly with his hands.

"Take a good look now," Paulson whispered, "Sandy is very thin, and petite. She's also in pretty good shape. You girls must get a good workout at this little vineyard of yours. Without a far enough drop, the rope fails to break her neck, see? Instead, she'll die of suffocation, very slowly. Very inefficient. I've read it can take up to fifteen minutes or more for someone to die from a hanging. I don't normally get this kind of opportunity. You girls really made my day."

Paulson kissed Ashley on the cheek. The taste of salt was left on his lips.

"Don't cry. You should be pleased. Look at all the trouble I'm going through for you. It means I care about you, I'm your friend. You're real to me. You're not objects, but people. Objects are simply discarded once they no longer serve a function. But you girls are worth savoring. Your last moments belong to me. I take them, they're mine. Forever.

"It's the most important moment of your life too, the summation of all you've ever done. Every experience, every memory. It all comes down to this. No more worries. No more burdens. It's all over. You should be calm about this. Admit it, it's partially your fault. You loved your friend, she loved you. But you shared her pursuit for Mr.

THE EDUCATOR

Goodbar. You remember that movie? Looking for Mr. Goodbar? No?

"No matter. Like I was saying, this moment serves as proof I admire and love you. You're more than a meat machine to me. There's something to you. A subjective experience. Unique. Entirely different from what other people get to experience. In philosophy, skeptics talk about the problem of 'other's minds.' How can anyone be sure others exist? They can't, according to skeptical philosopher. People could be zombies. But don't you see? This is my argument against it. You are not a zombie. This cannot be programmed by some grand deceiver. You're real. Sandy's real."

Sandy's face was tense with pain, but she wasn't moving her body anymore.

"Looks like she's about done. Fast. Probably the drugs...You know, I should tell you what an honor this is for you. Few people get to go through this. The apprehension. The stress. Your body is pumping out so many different chemicals right now, who knows what you're really going through. Sure, it's going to hurt at first. But as your brain is deprived of oxygen, you'll experience a high. It will be a trip. All those endorphins, adrenaline. The lack of oxygen. Your brain will enter a state of euphoria unlike anything you ever would have known."

Paulson paused and admired his work. Sandy's body and face had completely relaxed. Her expression dull but peaceful.

"Okay Ashley, now it's your turn."

*   *   *   *   *   *   *

CHAPTER 3

Saturday, May 14
St. Cloud, Minnesota

It was 3:30 in the morning.

Paulson was sitting in the garage with the bodies of his latest victims. In their purses Paulson found pictures, including one of the two ladies kissing each other. He kept them, as well as their bras and panties. He also took locks of their hair, wrapped together in the twine he used to pull the stools from their feet.

Their driver's licenses shared the same address, the same as the address on their business cards. Paulson hatched a plan. Leaving Sandy in the garage, he carried Ashley's body out to his Suburban and threw it into the back, covering it with a blue tarp. Then he threw some fishing gear over the tarp. Paulson knew the area, and found the girls' home. It was fifteen miles west of St. Cloud in a very remote spot. Except, it was adjacent to a golf course.

Paulson had to work fast. Golfers would be on the course at sunrise.

The large compound had one building, a single level, with a sign saying 'Sandy Beach Winery.' There was a large red barn too. The house, a big two story colonial monster, had no lights. One car was parked in front. Paulson drove up to the barn. He didn't expect anyone in the bed and breakfast. From what the girls had said, this was their last free weekend before the summer season kicked into gear.

The doors of the barn were unlocked. Inside, he found large metal things. *Caldrons?* He knew nothing about brewing or making wine. Finding a suitable anchor in one of the giant metal things, he tied a rope to it and tossed it over an exposed beam. On the other end he had tied a chain hook to it. Dragging Ashley into the barn, he lifted her up and looped the rope he had hung her with onto the hook.

It looked okay. Ashley's bruised face and abdomen added to the effect. The police would likely think the murder happened here. Except, no feces or urine. Ashley had cleared her bowels and bladder before Paulson's surprise, and had left nothing for him to collect and plant. So instead, he used a broom and bucket to sweep up the dirt underneath Ashley. The police would think the murderers had cleaned up the scene. He closed the barn door and walked over to the house. It was unlocked.

Moving quickly, he found two pieces of luggage. No flashlight and no lights slowed down his progress. He only had a small pen light, which he tried not to use. Upstairs he found a master bedroom with two separate beds. Pictures of the two women were framed in collages all around the room. There were two different dressers. The women slept together, worked together, dated together, but didn't share everything.

Sandy's was obviously the dresser with all the really small clothing and lacy underwear. Ashley's undergarments were more conservative. Paulson quickly packed as much of Sandy's clothes as possible. Then he looked for valuables. Endless boxes of shoes were under the beds. In Ashley's dresser he found a thousand bucks in cash. No jewelry. He remembered neither girl had worn any at his cabin.

Looking through the house, he checked five other bedrooms, all empty. In the kitchen he found some mail and checkbooks and other papers in a drawer. He took all of these. Finally, he found the business office. There were several ledgers filled with accounting numbers. He took these. There was a safe. He tried the handle.

The thing was unlocked.

He emptied everything in the safe into one of the luggage bags. In two trips, he took everything to the back of his Suburban. Then he remembered one last detail. He walked over to the barn, where Ashley's body was slightly swaying. In his hand was a tube of lipstick he had found on Sandy. He wrote 'Cunt' in generic block letters on Ashley's abdomen.

Then he drove off.

Paulson got back to his cabin just before sunrise.

He launched his boat from his private lake access. Paulson had been launching boats on his own for years, and it only took fifteen minutes before he was out on the water. He went to the southern part of the lake, and began bow fishing as soon as the sun was up.

By six in the morning, the lake had had at least two dozen other boats buzzing about. Every fishing opener was important to Minnesotans.

*   *   *   *   *   *   *

CHAPTER 4

11am Saturday, May 14
Northeast Boxing Club

Zan was sitting down on a wooden bench at his boxing gym.

He and Steve Coombs, the famous 'Lake Guy,' were watching a sparring match between two of the gym's professional fighters. Zan had spent the previous hour sparring with both of them, being their living target. Coombs had to drag Zan from the ring.

"Look at those two go," Coombs said, a tinge of envy evident in his voice, "And dammit, I don't want to have to keep dragging you out of the ring; Christ, you're tough enough. You don't need to prove it to anyone."

"I'm not trying to be tough, I'm trying to be good."

"Well, forget it. You're already past your prime as a fighter. Ya never had a prime. So ya might as well keep your wits about ya."

"Doesn't stop you from fighting."

"I have a lot more wits than you do. I have plenty to spare."

They watched a few rounds of sparring in silence. There was a huge difference between a professional fighter and an amateur--Even a bad professional. The pace was faster. The hits harder. Everything moved with lightning speed. Both men were in their prime.

Eduardo Monsante was a tough Latino from South Minneapolis, and had made enough money in four professional fights to buy a house. The flyweight was short, light, and liked to work the body. The other fighter was the Russian middleweight, Markos Pavavorich. Slower than Monsante, he still landed most of his blows. To Monsante's face.

All sparring has a purpose. For the flyweight, he was looking to take some heavy punches from a larger fighter. It made it that much easier to take good hits from fighters in his own class. For Markos, trying to hit the fast bobbing head of the quick Latino was good for his coordination.

After five rounds of pounding, Monsante had enough and quit for the day. Markos waved at Zan to get up and get into the ring. Zan got up and started putting on his headgear.

"Dontcha think you've had enough?" Coombs asked.

"He'll go easy on me. He wants me to teach him some counter-combos."

"Okay, but don't you have a date today? Don't think the little lady will appreciate a bloody mess for a companion."

"The fleas come with the dog."

*   *   *   *   *   *   *

Sex
Infrequent. Disgusting. Aberrant. Distracting. Expensive.
Relationships
Her stuff. Our stuff. Commitment. Romantic comedies.
Panic.

Zan, lying in bed in his flat, ignored his thoughts and decided just to stare at the ceiling

Alisha broke the silence, "Zan, can I ask you a question?"

The evening had gone fast, and it didn't take long to go from 'upstairs for a drink?' to pillow talk.

"No, I don't have any extra toothbrushes."

"Not that," she punched him in the shoulder, "I want to know what you are doing with your life? You can't do campus stuff forever. What are you doing for money?"

Awkward.

"Never really thought about. I'm fairly confident things will happen." Zan got out of bed and threw on the top of a black karate gi. "I'm getting some coffee, want some?"

Alisha jumped out of the bed. "Thank God. I never get to bed this early." She threw on a pair of Zan's boxers, which she barely fit into. She was thin but Zan was thinner.

Zan got the coffee and they sat down at his kitchen table.

Continuing the conversation, Zan said "I try not to think about the future; I guess I should, but I really believe it when Jesus says in the Bible 'God will provide.' There only exists the now. So whatever happens, I'll deal with it. There's no reason to think I couldn't. I have few needs, and I have no ambition for wealth or prestige. Simple."

Alisha stared at him for a few moments. "That's probably the worst answer ever. You might as well tell me you're hoping to play video games and live with your parents' basement the rest of your life."

"Hate video games, and my parents don't have a basement. Just an attic."

"You must've had goals, you went to law school."

"A delaying action. I just assumed 'get degree, get job.' But my life has led me down a path I enjoy. I'm free from a lot of earthly burdens and worries. It's all very Zen."

"I doubt you're really happy. How could you be?"

"Right now, I'm feeling pretty good. How could I complain about today?"

"What was the best part of today?" There was a sexual tone to her voice.

"There's still some 'today' left."

*　　　*　　　*　　　*　　　*　　　*　　　*

CHAPTER 5

Noonish, Sunday, May 15
Coffman Student Union

"Okay, there are three pinhole cameras hidden in clocks. Those were easy enough; they give a view of coatroom, outside the coatroom, and in the unisex bathroom by the staircase. Plus, I put another security camera hidden in a plant in the lobby. That one is in color. Rebecca has to get President Paulson into one of those areas. Otherwise, we won't get the shot."

Zan and Regular Joe were sitting in the basement of Coffman Memorial Union, by the bowling alley. Joe was talking. He was the one responsible for setting up the hardware for the Marilyn Monroe.

A group of Asian students were bowling at the farthest lane. Away from everyone else. A lonely student employee sat behind a candy and treats counter, reading a book.

"Kessler will have a camera hidden away in a briefcase," Zan said. "Plus, I'll be down here in the basement, just in case we have to follow them outside to get the shot." Zan sat looking at a plate filled with fried cheese curds, the most edible thing available in the bowling alley. He hadn't eaten any yet.

"Seriously Zan, I don't see the gain being worth the risk."

"You're too much of a skeptic. This operation goes well, we get pictures of Paulson feeling up a young girl. If it doesn't, we still get to keep the cameras."

"If anyone found out I put a camera in a bathroom, I'd never get a job again."

"It'll be fine. If anyone finds the camera, it's not like there are other cameras that they'd use to catch you. The only problem will be if anyone catches you watching the video feed the night of."

"Not a chance," Regular Joe stabbed one of Zan's cheese curds with a plastic fork and took a bite. "The equipment is hidden on the sixth floor in a maintenance locker used to store projectors and other electrical crap. No one is going to be in there until the summer term starts, and no one would notice the stuff even if they were."

"And you'll be watching the feed from the sixth floor?"

"Fifth, I'll be borrowing an office for the night. I'm the only janitor scheduled for that floor that night, so no worries. But I still think this thing is a waste of time and money."

"It'll be fun. We get to play with walkie talkies."

"I'd rather be bowling." Joe said gruffly.

"What, you want to bowl? We're right here. Let's bowl. Hell, Kayla's living near campus, let's give her a call"

*   *   *   *   *   *   *

Kayla's face was tan, she had no makeup on, and it looked like she had dropped a few pounds. She was hanging off the arm of a muscled man. Her new friend 'Lou.'

Zan and Regular Joe exchanged handshakes and greetings with the couple, who went looking for acceptable bowling balls.

"Damnit!" Zan whispered. He knew what the encounter meant. "She was turning out to be a good activist. Once they start the reproductive cycle, it's impossible to stop."

"That's what the kids do," Joe said.

"That delicate dance between men and women have claimed more solid activists than anything else I've encountered."

"People expect to meet Mr. or Mrs. Right while in college."

"Humbug."

"The liberals are all about fucking, they don't seem to have any problems," Joe said.

"Liberals and conservatives are different. Family values and all that bullshit. Liberals don't worry about making a family, getting a job, owning a home; if it happens, it happens, if not, no big deal. But Republicans see 'civic participation' as a way of finding their soul mates. Other people of like mind. Being a CR is like joining a dating service. What they don't understand is how serious the opposition is. Liberals aren't looking to create a life, activism is their life. It takes the place of religion or traditions. It even becomes their family. They are wholly committed. It's really something to behold."

"And disgusting and wrong," added Joe.

"It's why they succeed."

"The side with the most activists wins."

"Yeah that sucks," Zan sighed. "At least we can enjoy the fall."

"We should go bowling more often."

Kayla and Lou returned carrying two blue balls; their free hands in each other's back pockets.

*   *   *   *   *   *   *

CHAPTER 6

10am Monday, May 16
Somewhere near West River Parkway, just north of E. 34th Street, Minneapolis

Real estate along the Mississippi River is highly valued.

At least the parts of it that aren't industrialized and polluted.

Those who live along the West River Parkway in large modern colonials with a grand view of the Mississippi River are among the proudest of the local upper middle class. It being Minnesota, virtually all of these homes were owned by government bureaucrats. The farther north, towards downtown, the wealthier and more prestigious. Farther south, the homes and the lots got smaller; still homes for those of means. In a home just north of 34th street lived University of Minnesota Vice Provost Martin Brackens and his lover, Thomas Bredahl.

On Edmund Boulevard, which parallels the West River Parkway south from the University campus, sat a white Ford pickup truck, a long cab F250. On both doors and the tailgate were decals saying 'Anderson Gardening and Landscaping'. Three men sat inside the truck. Brackens had left for work at the U already. He normally left around eight in the morning.

The men continued to sit. The driver, a fat man, read a newspaper. The Hispanic fella next to him nodded his head rhythmically in tune to an unheard song being piped into his ears from a Walkman. A third man sat in the back, nearly invisible to any observers. A few more minutes passed. Then a Blue Ford Bronco backed its way out of the driveway of Brackens' home. Bredahl was leaving for work.

The fat man started the engine and drove the big truck the half block to Brackens' home and pulled into the driveway. The three men got out of the car, each dressed in white T-shirts and blue jeans. The Fat Man and The Spic started trimming the bushes around the house. The third man, of average height, average build and no outstanding features whatsoever, walked up to a door next to the home's garage, thrust in a key and walked into the house.

At ten-thirty the mail was delivered. The fat man grabbed the bundle from the mailbox and walked it into the house. After another fifteen minutes the men packed up and left. It wasn't the first time at the three stereotypes had been to the house, but it was their last.

*   *   *   *   *   *   *

CHAPTER 7

7pm Saturday, May 21
Coffman Memorial Union

Alumni functions suck cash.

The specifics change from function to function. The goal remains the same. Money and Prestige. Donors trade their money for the reflected prestige of the institution. Millions can be raised each year from high-end donors, though these donors are actually just a small percentage of the total amount of donations each year. But they are the best treated. Special tours of the latest building renovation. Access to executive suites at football games. Small plaques with their names on them attached to every bench, water fountain and potted plant on campus.

Every aspect of a donor dinner is carefully conceived to maximize potential donations and create competitions between the donors. There's a special choreography as the donors enter the building, ride the elevator, are greeted at the lobby, mingle with other donors, and even when signing in. Everywhere are helpful, friendly, attractive college women willing to assist in whatever the Old Money needed.

Name tags are given out at sign-in. Gold name tags for donors giving more than ten thousand dollars a year. Silver for those giving five thousand or more. Blue for everyone else. Most people write out checks to get the gold name tags as soon as they notice the stratification. The gold tags for the late donations are, of course, ready to go as soon as the checks are written.

Donors mingle in the lobby, where there is plenty of expensive booze being passed out. The mingling encourages competition, and provides peer affirmation to the donors that what they're doing is right. The donors create their own unique society of pomp and glitter. They do exactly what most rich people do, find ways to feel better and more important than anyone else.

And Ernie Kessler loved it.

He didn't love the culture itself. In private he mocked the sad predictability of human behavior. But in his world it was important to play the game and learn how to manipulate it. Kessler was a master too. It helped that he found his way into the beds of most of the women in this society. Both married and unmarried.

THE EDUCATOR

Tall and gregarious, open and friendly, he moved from small group to small group making women laugh and testing his charisma on competitive males.

Charm wasn't his only weapon. Kessler had money. Despite some rough patches where his own personal finances were stretched nearly to insolvency, his financial firm handled hundreds of millions of dollars in retirement and investment funds. Thanks to this, the fact Kessler was a well known Republican was generally forgiven. Republicans in the state of Minnesota weren't really Republicans anyway. They were 'Independent Republicans' with a history of moderate and cooperative behavior. Like prison whores.

Few knew Kessler's true ideology. And he liked it that way.

Rachel Anderson, Kessler's special guest and the bait in the Marilyn Monroe, was dressed in a simple black dress. A low cut neckline provided an almost unobstructed view of her ample bosom. The narrow skirt ended at the knees, slits climbing up the sides of her leg, nearly to her hips. The dress completely objectified Rachel as eye candy for lecherous old men. Which was exactly the intent.

President Paulson, mingling with other guests, noticed her immediately.

*   *   *   *   *   *   *

Zan lined up his cue stick. With some downward and left English, the cue ball would come off the three and knock in the nine ball. A quick and violent hit started the chaos.

"Damnit," exclaimed Chris Berg. "That makes three in a row. You really need to get a real job."

The bowling alley in the basement of Coffman was empty; except for a group of Asians bowling on the lanes farthest from the door.

Self-described Chaos Maker Jose Rodriguez sat behind the snack counter. Jose had just started working at Coffman a few days previous, and this had been a welcome surprise to Zan and Chris Berg.

Zan and Chris were at the pool table farthest from the door, and as far from the Asian bowlers as they could get.

Zan picked up a walkie talkie from their nearby table. "Anything happen yet J-man?"

After a pause, the gadget crackled back. "Nope. Prick hasn't introduced himself yet. But all eyes are on Tits."

"Okay, thanks." Zan put the device down. "Hey Jose, wanna play a round of cutthroat?"

"No way man, there's no playing with you," he replied.

A crackle. "Whoa." It was Joe on the walkie talkie.

"What is it?" asked Zan.

"You know that fat chick who works for Campus Activities?"

"Betty Buzzcut Butch? The lesbian?"

"Yeah. Guess what? She's not a she."

"You should probably not be watching the unisex cam."

"No kidding. J-man out."

    *   *   *   *   *   *

"Mr. Kessler, good to see you here," Paulson shook the big man's hands, "Thank you for supporting the Alumni Organization." Paulson's words were smooth and sincere. Sincere sounding, anyway.

"Thank you Doctor Paulson," Kessler slapped Paulson on the back. "I'm always happy to support the University in any way that I can."

Paulson's eyes were then drawn to the spectacle that was Rachel Anderson. "And who might you be?"

"May I present Rachel Anderson, one of my interns this year."

"Pleasure to meet you," Rachel said.

"The pleasure is all mine Miss Anderson."

    *   *   *   *   *   *

"What's going on?" Zan asked the gadget.

"Small talk. Prick is mostly talking to Archbishop," Regular Joe replied.

"What about Tits?"

"Tits is all smiles."

Rachel was not told about her radio handle.

"We didn't expect anything to happen right away Zan," Chris said. "We'll see what happens after the dinner."

"Start recording now," Zan told the walkie talkie. "Just to make sure we don't miss the shot."

    *   *   *   *   *   *

Everyone was ushered into the dining hall where they were seated to their assigned tables. A choice of Chicken Alfredo or some kind of vegan crap were served.

Then came the speeches.

First it was the Alumni Association president.

Then the Undergraduate Student Body President.

Then the Dean of Students.

"...Thank you for the support...Here's what we did last year... Watch our sports teams... You can continue to make a difference...

Academic excellence...Student experience...Diversity... International leader...Fine tradition...Progress..."

The bullshit never ended.

Finally, University President Malcolm Paulson gave his speech, reiterating everything that came before. He mumbled his way through it. No one was really listening anyway. He knew that. He couldn't get the thought of killing the busty brunette in the little black dress out of his head.

"With this in mind," he said, "The University of Minnesota will continue to lead in scientific and technological research at the international level throughout the next century, with your help. I know everyone is probably sick of hearing my voice..." Some polite chuckles drifted in from the audience, "So I'll wrap up my speech now. Please remain in your seats though, we have a special presentation for all of you. A forty-five minute video done by some of our students detailing their experiences at the U, I hope you enjoy it."

The lights were dimmed, two men dragged in a screen and a projector fell from the ceiling. The video was obviously not done by undergrads, but no one was going to say anything. Paulson slipped out of the hall, one mission on his mind.

*   *   *   *   *   *   *

"What?" Zan couldn't believe the last transmission.

"I said, Paulson is just sitting in the middle of the lobby, stretching his legs."

"In a tuxedo?"

"Yeah faggot, in his tuxedo. Do I need to repeat myself some more?"

"Maybe, I'll let you know."

"Maybe we could sell the pictures of him stretching to Yoga Magazine." Chris Berg offered.

*   *   *   *   *   *   *

Rachel felt a hand on her bare shoulder. Then the stranger whispered into her ear "Excuse me, Miss Anderson? Professor Paulson would like to speak to you for just a second in the lobby."

The usher, a woman dressed in black suit and tie, helped her up and led her out of the hall. Paulson was waiting on the floor, his hands stretched beyond his straightened legs, his body folded almost completely, his face nearly touching his shins.

"Miss Anderson for you Professor."

"Excellent, thank you." Paulson unfolded himself and got up from the floor. "You'll have to excuse me Miss Anderson, I have a bad back. These late nights are really hard on it."

"That's no problem with me, Professor," Rachel replied.

"Good, and don't call me Professor. I don't teach any classes. Just call me Malcolm. Rachel, after our little chat earlier, I was thinking, did you have any plans for after your internship with Ernie is done? It's over at the end of the summer, right?"

Paulson, obviously, didn't know the internship wasn't real. "Yes it is."

"And you said you had another year before getting done with your degree?"

"Yes, I switched majors and I need the extra year."

"Why don't you spend it working in my office?"

"Excuse me?"

"If Kessler found something special about you, then you must have a solid skill set. Besides, having a friend of Kessler's on my staff would be invaluable. The guy owns half of the higher ed committee at the Capitol."

"I appreciate the offer, but I hadn't really thought about where I was going to work after the internship."

"It would be full-time, probably worse than that. Your tuition would be reimbursed, so your last year would be free. You could take night classes, or just sneak out of the office for an hour or two for your coursework. Plus, if you do well...a personal recommendation from the President of the University of Minnesota could open a lot of doors." Paulson smiled and winked that last part.

Rachel just stood there. Stunned.

*   *   *   *   *   *   *

"They're just talking?" Zan was perturbed.

"Yeah...that's it...wait, looks like Prick just gave her something, a business card or something..."

Berg and Zan sat in silence, waiting for more information. The static from the walkie-talkie and the occasional sound of a bowling ball rolling down one of the alleys were the only sounds filling the air.

"Yeah, that's it. They just shook hands and parted ways. Operation over."

"Thanks Jay. Be sure to clean everything up."

"Willdo."

Zan put the walkie-talkie down.

"Sorry man," Berg offered. "We knew it was a long shot anyway. Nobody is that handsy. It'd take a total perv to feel a gal up ten minutes after meeting her, no matter how flirty she was."

Zan popped down from his stool. Opening his backpack he

pulled out a rolled-up black plastic bag that was stuffed with something bulky.

"What are you doing Zan?" Berg asked.

"Plan B."

Then he started for the door. He slipped out of the bowling alley and walked into the men's bathroom, kicking a garbage can over as he did so.

*   *   *   *   *   *   *

After a few minutes, Zan stepped out of the bathroom, dressed in a tuxedo. He walked into the elevator, and pushed the button for the fourth floor. As he stepped out of the elevator, there were a few people ready to go down. The movie was over and the event basically finished. Most people lingered, chatting in small groups in the lobby.

Zan was looking for Kessler and Rachel. Before he found them he ran into Paulson.

"Mr. Tvrdik, I didn't know you had an invitation," President Paulson preferred using Zan's adopted name. "Shouldn't you be embezzling grant money or filing another frivolous lawsuit?"

"President Paulson, how good to see you again. Sorry I missed the dinner and your speech. Kessler really wanted me to be here, but I got hung up in traffic."

"What Kessler sees in you I have no idea Mr. Tvrdik. But I do hope he sets you straight one of these days. A man of your age shouldn't be spending so much time with college kids. It's creepy."

"I dunno. From what I hear you enjoy spending time with young people too. Especially the ladies."

"It's always a pleasure to talk to you Mr. Tvrdik, but I need to say my goodbyes to the other guests."

Paulson walked briskly by Zan. As he walked by, Zan called him a "motherfucker" under his breath; just loud enough for Paulson to hear it.

*   *   *   *   *   *   *

Years ago, Zan got sick of his given name, Jonathan Olaf Tvrdik. He had been adopted by loving parents as an infant and raised in a big family of real and adopted Tvrdiks. But throughout school, Zan got shit for being a 'zipperhead' with a remarkably unAsian name. So he changed it when he turned eighteen to 'Zan Chin-Wu' after doing absolutely no research. It sounded Asian, which was all he wanted.

*   *   *   *   *   *   *

After a bit of looking, Zan found Kessler and Rachel sitting at a table in the dining hall. Kessler was smoking a cigar, Rachel was sipping red wine. There were a few other people still around. A pair of attractive women in suits and ties were waiting on the remnants. At five thousand dollars a plate there wasn't going to be any scrimping on service.

Zan sat down at the table. He grabbed a lone bread roll still left in a basket on the table and buttered it. One of the waitresses came by and he ordered a drink. A diet coke.

"So Zan, did you drop by for an early debrief?" Kessler's deep voice had a calming effect on Zan.

"Actually," Zan replied. "I wanted to get a better look at Rachel in her dress."

Rachel smiled.

"Rachel was just telling me, Zan, that Paulson offered her a job in his office over the next year. Eighteen bucks an hour, benefits and tuition reimbursements."

"And you won't have to get groped," Zan added.

The trio chuckled at this.

"This might be better than a straight up Marilyn Monroe," Kessler continued. "We've never had anyone in his office before. That's a lot of intel."

Just then a man in a tuxedo interrupted them.

"Excuse me sir, you cannot smoke in here, it's against the law."

"Call the police," came Kessler's reply.

"Excuse me?"

"I said call the police."

The man in the tuxedo stood there for a second, dumbfounded.

Kessler spoke again, "maybe I should call the police for you, would that help?"

The man in the tuxedo regained some of his composure. "Sir, I could have you banned from the U-Club."

"Go ahead, tell your boss, Bob Ingebritsen, you had Ernie Kessler banned from the U-Club. Let me know how that works out." Kessler took a long drag from his Cuban robusto. After another awkward pause, the man in the tuxedo left.

Zan broke the silence,"One of these days Ernie, they're going to call your bluff."

"It's no bluff. I know Bob and I donate more to the Minnesota Police Federation than anyone else in the state. I've put more of their kids through college than any government grant program...Now, if he'd threatened to unleash the Attorney General on me, then I'd be worried."

THE EDUCATOR

*   *   *   *   *   *   *

CHAPTER 8

11pm Thursday, June 9
Fourth Street Ramp, Minneapolis

Zan's metallic blue 1988 Nissan 300zx rolled into Fourth Street Ramp.

Tass had transferred to more remote, more private real estate farther away from his superiors. The move worked well. Tass preferred doing as little work as possible. Everyone in Parking Services knew this, but Tass was also union and nearly immune from discipline. As long as he showed up nearly on time and didn't steal, there wasn't much to be done.

Parking Services was also happy to get Tass away from their offices too.

Out on Fourth Street, Tass was isolated from other employees so his insolence couldn't spread. A weekly visit from his supervisor was the only contact Tass had with his employers.

Zan parked his car just inside the gates and walked through a door marked 'employees only.' There was a short hallway, bathrooms were at the end, Maintenance and Facilities had an office off to the left, and there was a rarely-used conference room to the right. Into the conference room Zan walked.

"Hey, about time. Your new ball and chain keeping you from watching the clock?" It was the loud, gravelly but friendly voice of Tass. "Sit down, let me get you some tea, Joe should be here any minute."

"Shouldn't you be watching your booth?"

"Nah, there's not enough people here during the summer to care. I always open the gate around ten anyway. As far as Parking is concerned, I have Crohn's disease."

"What a lovely thought."

The next thirty minutes were filled with standard male bullshit. Chicks, cars, sports. Tass was a reader and Zan was erudite, so politics slipped in. Tass also loved food and had an assortment of authentic Italian cheeses and sausage with him, which he shared. Tass, never without a cigarette, filled conference room with smoke by the time Regular Joe arrived.

Joe was dressed in a black suit and tie. He was wearing thick eyeglasses with a thick black frame. Three day's worth of stubble gave him the look of a fashionable yuppie. A black suitcase finished the costume. Joe had one of those faces which could become completely unrecognizable with a few small changes. His face lacked any unique features, so people only remembered the peripheral features.

Dressed as he was, no one would be able to remember him as anything more than an average-build businessman with glasses and a beard. Stone-faced most of the time, around Tass and Zan he wore a smile.

"If it isn't Donald Trump in the fucking flesh," Tass opened. "Do you like being late, or did you have to learn that from someone?"

"Is that how you greet one of your betters?" Joe said.

"I'll let you know when I actually meet one."

"Well played sir. But..." Joe flipped his briefcase onto the table. "I think you won't mind my tardiness."

Regular Joe tossed two bundles of hundred dollar bills at Tass, then another two bundles at Zan. Each bundle was held together with rubber bands, the bills well-circulated. Zan flipped through a bundle and estimated it held a hundred bills. Twenty thousand dollars cash money, untraceable.

"Jesus Christ on a Crutch Joe, where'd you get this?" Tass asked.

"Don't ask, just take it, it's your finder's fees"

"What's this out of?" Zan asked.

"It's ten percent, split between the two of you."

"Ten fucking percent?" Tass spoke with his normal forcefulness. "That means, what, you were, uh, four hundred thousand dollars up? With nothing but social security numbers?"

"And addresses, checking account numbers, routing numbers, phone numbers, relationship statuses. Identity theft is the next big thing,"

"So how did you guys get four hundred grand out of this?" Zan asked.

"Forty or so people who have given me and the rest of us a hard time over the past decade are going to be very, very unhappy when they start getting phone calls next month."

"And now, you, Fats and The Spic are done?"

"Yeah," Joe looked sad. "We figure someone must have gotten our appearances, car make and maybe license number by now. Police could pick up on the basic scam."

"Good assumption," Tass interrupted.

"Yeah, we were doing the same gag for a month. The car was a U vehicle, from Facilities Maintenance. We couldn't afford to be caught using a fake license plate, so we kept the U plates on there. The police will have a lead here at the U if they get that far. We're going to lay low awhile. Fats and I are leaving town. Spic is staying."

"You'll be fine," Tass gave a hearty laugh. "You can always get away with one. And fuck, a hundred thou' apiece. Plus ten years' worth of pension from all the fucking jobs you guys have done? You can go find yourself a nice little town and a shitty part-time job, and live without worries for a long time."

Joe snapped the briefcase closed and walked to the door. "I can't stay long," he said. "So I got to get going. I'll give you guys a call with any updates. Maybe we can hit Caps' Grille some weekend?"

"Sounds like a plan," said Zan.

And with that, Regular Joe turned and left.

        *   *   *   *   *   *   *

CHAPTER 9

Friday June 24
Camp Lake, Minnesota

The weather in Minnesota normally varies somewhere between miserable to unbearable, with occasional forays into the simply unpleasant. Winters are fiercely cold. When not cold, there was still the snow. Springs are wet, muddy, with prolific precipitation of freezing rain. In summer, humidity and high temperature combine to create a natural sauna. A sauna filled with mosquitoes and ticks. By Autumn, most Minnesotans, those who aren't hunters, have given up on the outdoors and have begun their indoor winter rituals again. Ironic, autumn being the most pleasant time of year in the state.

But, when the weather is nice in Minnesota, it is Really Nice. Low seventies. Gentle winds, just strong enough to blow the bugs away. A few fluffy cumulonimbus gently drifting in a blue sky. Nice.

Kessler sat on a lawn chair, on his dock. Cigar clenched in his mouth. Cooler filled with beer. Occasionally casting a line out into the lake. Fish don't like to eat in the mid-morning, after nine or so. But, throw enough lures enough times, they'll bite. Two small mouth bass, of edible size, had learned their last lesson already this morning. The peaceful quiet of the lake was disturbed by the sound of two jet skis dancing about.

Grumpy at the new truth of his once solitary escape, Kessler packed up his pole and kit, and walked back up to his lakeside cabin. As he was doing so, three vehicles turned into his driveway.

        *   *   *   *   *   *   *

The Camp Lake Cabin was built by The Old Man as a remote getaway in the early 1950's. It remained a humble cabin of a few rooms on a small lake. It was next to a small airfield, allowing The Old Man to fly in and out at a moment's notice. The Old Man piloted aircraft his entire life, starting out as a barnstormer before WWI. The cabin did not remain a humble hiding place.

After the Cuban Missile Crisis, The Old Man became convinced a nuclear exchange was inevitable. Spending millions, he had the cabin rebuilt into a fortress. There was a fully stocked fallout shelter. The Cabin was turned into a huge house, over ten thousand square feet between its three floors, not including the fallout shelter. Then he began buying up the surrounding land, until he had over 100 acres of woods and farmland spreading north from Highway 10.

It became a compound.

The airfield remained, nominally, in municipal hands. The Old Man purchased every hanger and only locals and friends could find accommodations at the field. Soon, everyone on the local airport board were friends, real or bought.

Despite his apparent paranoia, he brought many guests to the cabin, built several guest cabins in fact, and the Camp Lake Retreat became a regular stop for Republicans, state officials and other VIPs.

To inherit the cabin was to inherit The Old Man's scepter, a symbol of prestige and status. Ernie Kessler did his best to keep the retreat a special place. He remodeled the main building so it could hold conferences. There was a club and banquet area. A kitchen capable of feeding hundreds of people. A communications and computer room, several conference rooms and two master guest suites with private baths.

Kessler had sold lots on the eastern shore of the lake to developers in order to keep his firm solvent during a rough patch, but most of the land to the north was still in his name. It was prime hunting real estate, and it was only an hour outside of the Twin Cities.

Along with the small guest cabins, spaced every fifty yards or so on the north shore, there were three large metal storage sheds on the property. Tractors, cars, an unending collection of power tools. All the accumulated detritus rich people had. Kessler wasn't a handyman like The Old Man, but he liked having anything he could possibly need in case of a nuclear holocaust on-hand. It took several people to maintain such a facility, and Kessler used this as an excuse to put his conservative recruits on his payroll, thus providing money to his cadre and some legitimacy to The Organization.

These annual retreats at the cabin were great fun. A half dozen undergrads, another half dozen alumni. Sometimes a surprise guest. Planning, training, games. Every year he and Zan brought the Big Ten Crew here to continue the good fight.

Plus, the bomb shelter was cooler than fuck.

*　　　*　　　*　　　*　　　*　　　*　　　*

THE EDUCATOR

The undergrads, Rachel Anderson, Kayla Witold, Frank Wallace and Gene Zeale, now known to everyone by his nickname 'Spags,' were split by gender between two of the closest guest cabins. Nolan Painter and Orson Henning took one of the more distant cabins, which allowed them to come and go without being seen, their real-life responsibilities necessitating some flexibility. Zan, Chris Berg and Shotgun took rooms in the main cabin. Everyone was given an hour to unpack and decompress from the trip.

Kayla's appearance was a surprise. Normally, when someone in the group picked up a significant other, it meant the end of their involvement. Either the relationship with Lou wasn't serious, or it had already gone south.

After everyone was settled, they were brought to the banquet room on the main floor of the cabin for a high-class dinner of Domino's Pizza and Pepsi. Spread out in the banquet room were leather couches, high chairs and wooden coffee tables. It looked like an old-fashioned gentleman's club where rich white guys would smoke cigars and monopolize commodities to squeeze the proletariat into more severe squalor. The room could be filled with tables and a podium for fundraisers, or even emptied for press conferences.

Just a small corner of this 'Hall,' as Kessler called it, easily seated all ten members of the entourage. As everyone was distracted by the food and their conversations, Kessler brought in the special guest: Congressman and Senatorial candidate Rod Grams.

Light applause. Stump speech. Couple jokes. Handshakes. Pictures. A slice of pizza. Same old crap. Then Kessler excused himself and Congressman Grams. They, along with Shotgun and Chris Berg, went upstairs for a meeting.

Zan grabbed everyone else and took them outside. They piled in Chris Berg's van and headed north. It was time for some gun play.

*　　　*　　　*　　　*　　　*　　　*　　　*

Clandestine political meetings could get dicey. The stakes were high. Egos collided. It was tough. But a Senate seat was a valuable fucking thing. Too valuable to just let go.

Kessler did a lot of maneuvering, but the meeting came down to Chris Berg's computer models and how to sell them.

"I'm not sure I get what you're saying Mr. Berg." Congressman Grams had been silent through much of Chris Berg's presentation. Grams preference was to avoid saying anything, so this came as a surprise.

"It's idiotic, is what it is," Michael Cohen, Grams' chief hack, was more skeptical. "We can't ignore the primary and get an early start in the general. It's suicide."

"No, it's not. Based on the numbers I have, there's no way you lose the primary. My simulation software has you winning in ninety-nine percent of common election cycles, and ninety-four percent in abnormal. This is matched by polling data Ernie has..." Berg hated explaining things to people. He really hated people who didn't believe in math, trusting instead to intuition. Grams and Cohen were those types of men.

"Chris is right," Kessler added his gravitas to the conversation, "Durenberger is associated with the Republican establishment, which destroys any hope Dyrstad has of winning in the primary. Meeks will get the job done in the primary"

"So we need to start running the general election campaign?" Grams asked.

"Yes Congressman." Shotgun jumped in. "I've looked at Chris' data. For the first time in a long time a real conservative can win the seat. But the campaign must be flawless."

"Mr. Berg, you mentioned a little about your process, but I'm still not sure I understand everything." Congressman Grams stated.

"It's very simple," Chris replied. "Voter behavior is the same as any other emergent social-psychological property. While humans vary greatly between individuals, as a group patterns tend to emerge and become quite predictable. These macros, major sociological movers, can be regressed and computed within a significant degree of certainty. Currently, based on the demographic information, the current government and administration, and basic polling data and econometrics, there is a ninety percent probability the GOP will gain thirty or more congressional seats. I wrote these equations myself and they validly predict every national election result since World War Two."

Chris tended to talk very fast when explaining things and this was no different. Every point was thrown at his listeners in rapid succession and no one had a chance to slow him down. "In Minnesota, there is a four percent shift in DFL voter base; when combined with the independents leaning GOP, the Senate seat becomes a toss-up. So everything that can be done to gain an early advantage needs to."

"And how," Cohen asked. "Will it be possible to run a perfect campaign?"

"Campaigns are never perfect," Berg replied. "But, your message, language and voter ID can be crafted perfectly. I pulled some data on trending topics among swing voters and independents, plus basic language data. We can craft the perfect message and use focus groups to throw together the best slogans and marketing. Plus, I've been data-mining certain government and corporate databases and creating a resources voter-target list..."

"Is that even legal?" Grams interrupted.

"Oh sure, the university has some pretty sweet deals with

many private corporations, in return for setting up their corporate IT infrastructure, we get to use their consumer data for educational purposes." Berg finally stopped shooting words at the group and took swig from his coffee. "I estimate we can turn out an additional fifty thousand voters. Should be enough to win the election for ya."

The group sat in silence for a moment.

"I'm sure glad, Mr Berg." Grams said, very quietly. "That you're on our side."

*   *   *   *   *   *   *

"Okay, just relax. Slow down your breathing. Capture your target in your vision, now focus your eyes on your front site. Slowly, squeeze the trigger. Don't yank or pull. Just squeeze."

The voice belonged to Nolan Painter. It was soon interrupted by the crack of a gun shot.

"Atta girl!" Painter, normally soft spoken with a tendency to mumble, felt most at home on a gun range.

Tall, too thin, pale, but with bright blue eyes filled with intelligence, Painter's bright red hair was just long enough to curl. In sunlight, his hair and eyes overwhelmed the rest of his appearance and gave the spooky effect that he was nothing but his technicolor hair and eyes. On the range, his awkwardness disappeared.

Twenty feet away, a potato split open from the impact of a .22 round fired from the gun held in Kayla Witold's hands. Her plain but not unattractive face sparkled with pleasure.

For years gun enthusiasts had been trying to attract women into their hobby. And always, they did it wrong. The natural bravado a man shows when around a woman is amplified by the power associated with guns. Men, when teaching a woman to shoot, couldn't help but be boastful. To make a sexual display.

In the gun world, this means bigger guns.

Women, when first learning to shoot, are naturally uncomfortable by the whole situation. Even worse, they often have a difficult time with the overpowered magnums and ridiculously high caliber weapons men would give them as their introductions to the gun world.

Painter had long known the best way to learn how to shoot was with a small caliber handgun. A .22 pistol worked the best. No recoil. Cheap ammo. Anyone could learn to shoot this way. And women appreciated the surprising precision involved in shooting. Women had the patience and concentration to learn the art better and faster than men. Men, especially young men with testosterone pulsing about their brains, weren't natural shooters. Women and guns, however, were complementary.

Soon enough, Kayla was picking off potatoes, bananas and aluminum cans like a pro. She wasn't the only one. There were guns enough for everybody. Henning and Painter were the primary suppliers. Zan had brought a few of Kessler's favorites, including an authentic Soviet AK-47. Fully automatic, of course. It was old fashioned fun.

Rachel, dressed in black shorts and a white tank top that barely contained her, was manhandling the AK-47. It was her third summer at the cabin, and the Kalashnikov was an old friend of hers. The gun fired rapidly but you could hear the individual rounds leaving the gun. The big 7.62 mm pills impacted the ground in front of the group and kicked up dirt, potatoes, broken glass and pushed around an old milk carton, until the carton was gone.

"Hey Rachel, wait," it was Henning, "let me get the camera out of the car. This will be perfect for our recruiting posters." Henning was a shutterbug, something everyone found a little creepy. But he took good photos. Artistic. Something conservatives had a hard time finding.

When Henning got back with the camera, she started posing. Rachel knew the score. She was the group's sexual lure.

*   *   *   *   *   *   *

Time flew.

A couple hours at the gun range turned into a few minutes for dinner.

Then Zan and Kessler set up the main hall with a projector and screen for a movie.

'Goodfellas'

Afterwards Painter took the underclassmen out to the Zimmerman Walmart for a lesson in buying political materials.

Then another night of endless conversation and no sleep.

The next day was filled with lectures on the Overton window, fundraising, grassroots organizing, Saul Alinsky, recruiting basics, sign design, lit drops, pushing policy, force multipliers, earned media. The evening was spent in a game of paintball.

Another night, this one finally provided some sleep.

*   *   *   *   *   *   *

CHAPTER 10

7am Monday, June 27
Camp Lake Cabin, Minnesota

Kessler dropped some badges on the table. Orson Henning

picked one up and gave it a good look. It was silver, in the shape of a shield and said 'Private Investigator' around a gold star in the center. Another badge said 'Security Officer' and was in the shape of an old fashioned sheriff's badge. Another proclaimed 'Bounty Hunter'.

"Seriously?" Henning asked.

Ernie Kessler had gathered Painter, Henning, Berg and Zan for the morning meeting, held in the main cabin's kitchen. "Yes, it is for real," Kessler replied, "the state of Minnesota requires six years of experience before you can be a registered private investigator. But, South Dakota has no law. So I had Wright buy an office in Sioux Falls and set up a dummy corp. In six years you'll be able work in Minnesota."

"What's the point? private investigators are relics from old black and white movies, nobody will believe us if we pull these out." Nolan Painter said, holding one of the badges.

"But police officers will. It's another out," Zan replied. "Suspicious activity is less suspicious to a cop when he sees credentials."

"It might even keep you out of jail," Kessler said. "I'm also creating press credentials and we're working on starting our own publishing company."

"I like it," said Chris Berg, unhappy with the hour of his wakeup call. He grabbed the bounty hunter shield, "Can I keep this one?"

*   *   *   *   *   *   *

At nine in the morning, Zan started collecting the whole group together. They were going on a lit drop in RoCoRi, a set of three nearby towns so close to one another they went by an acronym. Rockville, Cold Spring and Richmond, Minnesota, were all conservative, rural and sparsely populated. The group was joining Rod Grams and some local candidates for doorknocking and lit drops. The day was already warm and thunderstorms were expected later. It was not going to be pleasant.

At the girls' cabin, he found Rachel alone, ready to go but with no idea where Kayla was. At the boys' cabin, he found a nearly unresponsive Frank Wallace, a sleeping giant with no interest in the world before lunchtime. And he found Kayla. With Spags.

Neither quite sure where their clothes were.

*   *   *   *   *   *   *

"Damnit Spags!"

Zan was waiting for Gene 'Spags' Zeale as he stepped out of the shower. Everyone else was already at the main cabin, waiting on them. But Zan needed to talk.

Spags, a tall, pale, hairy man, awkwardly tried to dry himself and keep his cool with Zan invading his space. "What?"

"Didn't Shotgun warn you about women? Didn't you get the lecture?"

"Yeah. So? You guys were serious about it?"

"Yes. And for some very specific reasons." Zan said. "We've had it pretty good over the last few years. But you don't have to go back far. It's the story of the Fridley Girls."

"Didn't get that lecture at initiation," responded Spags, "So fill me in grandmaster Zan."

"Fall semester, 1989. It was the year after Shotgun took down the University President in that scandal. Forced him to resign and all that, that's how we got stuck with President Paulson. We were riding pretty high, and it should have been Shotgun's big year. The Organization was bigger than it had ever been. We must have had fourteen or so good people. It helped that we were running the CRs at the time.

"Shotgun and company were able to recruit a bunch of people, including these three chicks from Fridley. We thought they'd be good activists. They were smart, attractive. They even did a lot of recruiting for us after they joined the group. We started getting tons of people to meetings. Thirty or forty. And everyone met up at the Big Ten after the meetings. It was great.

"But these chicks weren't looking to get into politics or save babies or anything. They were looking for husbands. Pretty soon they started dating members. Just about everyone got their chance. Over the next three semesters or so, these women dated three quarters of the male membership. Every time one of these chicks dumped a guy, we never saw them again. Eventually, all three found their husbands, got married, dropped out of school and we never saw them again.

"By fall semester 1990, it was just Shotgun...and Henning.

"Anyway, we got lucky, Shotgun was such a fat fuck that none of these chicks was interested, so we never lost him. But we lost a few good guys in that group. Shotgun had to come back an extra semester and recruit some more people for us. The Organization almost died. Those girls were around for just over a year, and it has taken us until now to get back on track. We didn't do any major speakers. Almost no campaign work. Not until they left. From my perspective, sexual relationships are the most destructive force to what we do."

*   *   *   *   *   *   *

Lit dropping is one of the easiest and cheapest forms of campaigning. Volunteers preferred it because there were few confrontations with homeowners disinterested in politics. No cold calls. Some exercise. Candidates liked it because lit pieces cost pennies apiece. And no postage. No big money. All one needed were volunteers willing to cover lots of ground.

Is it effective? Not really, but kinda. People had to see the lit pieces in order to throw them away, so there was a good chance the lit would be noticed. And whenever a lit piece is noticed, a candidate gets their name into another person's mind, if only briefly. Get into a man's head often enough, he might actually vote for you. If nothing else, he will remember you. Even if he's not sure why.

It got candidates votes, as long as voters weren't too pissed off for all that littering.

Zan and Chris Berg, both long experienced in political campaigning, knew exactly what to do. As soon as all the other volunteers were out of their view, they tossed all their lit pieces into a big blue postal service collection box and found their way into a bakery on the main drag.

They got coffee and a box of assorted donuts. There were a couple of tables in the bakery and the two men sat down.

"So, I hear Kayla was fucking around with Spags," Berg said. He was already on doughnut number two.

"Yeah."

"She's a bit of a whore."

"Yeah."

The two sat in silence for a bit.

"So, how long can we hide out here before getting missed?" Asked Berg.

"I bet we can go two hours."

"Race ya to the bottom of the box," challenged Berg.

"You're on."

*   *   *   *   *   *   *

A day spent lit dropping was an exhausting enterprise, even for young undergrads. Kessler rewarded everyone with a dinner at Olive Garden and a movie at the cabin. This time it was 'Dr. Strangelove.' Everyone was released for some free time, except for the undergrads.

Zan brought Frank Wallace and Kayla Witold down to the basement of the main cabin. The basement had always been off-limits, it was where Kessler slept; that was all either of the recruits knew. Walking down the stairway they noticed the bright orange shag carpeting awaiting them at the bottom. At the landing both students marveled at the bright, gaudy, pimpish décor of the basement.

Shag carpeting. Bright blue couch with matching loveseat. Big ass TV. Wood paneling. Pool table. Wet bar. Black velvet paintings of Elvis Presley and Spanish bullfighters. Blue and orange shag pillows scattered about along with beanbags and bar stools.

This was a bachelor pad straight out of 1978.

While the rest of the cabin was about style, the basement was about comfort.

"We allow very few people down here; it's the only area of the compound The Archbishop gets to himself. Just take a seat," Zan said.

Frank Wallace and Kayla took opposite ends of the big blue couch while Zan went through a set of swinging doors into a full kitchen, beyond which was a dry storeroom with its own bathroom. The storeroom had a small hatch in the middle of the floor which led to The Old Man's bomb shelter. The entire lot had to be engineered to keep water out of the basement and bomb shelter, an expensive accomplishment in The Old Man's day.

"Alright guys," said Zan upon his return. "We don't encourage a lot of reading, as reading ain't doing, but here are some required books. Finish them before the school year starts." Zan passed Wallace and Witold each a large stack of books. They got the following:

Barry Goldwater's 'Conscience of a Conservative'
Whitaker Chambers' 'Witness'
Saul Alinsky's 'Rules for Radicals'
George Hayduke's 'Get Even'
Thomas Sowell's 'The Vision of the Anointed'
Robert Heinlein's 'Starship Troopers'
Machiavelli's 'The Prince'
Ayn Rand's 'The Fountainhead'
The Communist Manifesto
Vladimir Lenin's 'State and Revolution'
P.J. O'Rourke's 'Parliament of Whores'

"That's a lot of reading to get done in a month." Wallace said.

"You can skip The Fountainhead if you want. Ayn Rand is as much bullshit as she is not."

"Still, all this before Labor Day?" Wallace was not a reader.

"Ignorance is dangerous. But...we don't want you wasting too much time as the year gets started; it's an election year..." Zan pondered a moment. "It will be okay to wait on some of the longer books until after the election. But you have to read Rules for Radicals and Get Even before the school year starts."

Kessler came downstairs carrying a case of beer. For the next few hours, it was nothing but laughs, popcorn, beer, pool and stories between the four of them.

In politics, fun is had in ephemeral bits. Most of the moments of an activist's activism is spent in boredom or anguish. Often both. The whole tapestry of a politico's life is such as to make any rational person wonder what possible motivation there could be to spend a life that way. Once the joy of the moment was gone, it was hard to recall exactly why it was so fun. But in the moment, there were few experiences better.

The four had a lot fun that night.

*   *   *   *   *   *   *

University President Malcolm Paulson hated working in the summer. Nice weather was for fishing. For hiking. For boating. For hunting. But the University of Minnesota was a multi-billion dollar affair and required a lot of attention, even when the state legislature wasn't in session. There was always some lobbying, some ass-kissing, or something else to do. Still, he kept his schedule open in summer, normally working only four days a week.

Walking from his office towards Washington Avenue, Paulson admired the construction work being done on several campus buildings. Relentless lobbying and constant requests for funds from wealthy donors who wanted to feel important provided the fuel for Paulson's great works. Two new buildings had been erected since he took over, and a dozen were receiving extensive renovation.

The weather was rather hot, humid. Walking briskly in a suit and tie, Paulson wandered without sweating. There was an informal dinner meeting scheduled with some of his department heads at the Big Ten. It was his attempt at a new tradition. Previous University presidents had been more formal and professional. Paulson hoped a laid-back approach would help open up the lines of communication between stakeholders. That's what he said anyway. Truthfully, he just liked hanging around bars and drinking.

The Big Ten was dark and dank. As always. The wood paneling, wood tables, wood everything gave the illusion you were sitting in a depression era lumber yard. Walking through the front door to the back, Paulson could already hear the cackle of Phyllis Caine, the district's state representative. Paulson shuddered. Caine wasn't the worst of the bunch either. Vice Provost Martin Brackens was also in attendance. That whiny man-bitch drove Paulson nuts.

Paulson was almost to the back of the bar when someone called out his name.

"Malcolm!" A woman shrieked.

Paulson turned to see Alisha Williams, the Big Ten's owner, step through the door separating her bar from The Village Wok. She dropped a bucket of soapy water and jumped into his arms and kissed him on the lips.

"Good to see you too," Paulson said.

"I missed you, you haven't stopped by in six months, find another mistress?"

"A gentleman never tells."

"That sounds like a yes." Alisha put her hands on her hips and pouted.

"And you, still looking for Mr. Right?"

"Actually, I am seeing someone on the side."

"Serious?"

"Not yet, might get there though."

"That's good, then you won't mind going out later? I got a big event at the Guthrie Theater next Friday, could use a date. It'd be a chance to wear that little black number you love."

"Ooh, sounds great," Alisha struck a demure pose while she spoke. "But I got to get back to the bathrooms, my work here is never done."

"Alright, I'll give you a call."

As Alisha turned around to grab the bucket of water, Paulson leaned over and pinched her ass.

*　　　*　　　*　　　*　　　*　　　*　　　*

"To that short little fucker," Shotgun raised a bottle of champagne, "who not only knocked me out and stole my motorbike, but left the fucking thing in the middle of a field with waist-high grass. I spent four hours looking for it asshole. And thanks for the concussion."

After a quick shake, Shotgun uncorked the bottle and the fizzy liquid sprayed all over the five men gathered in one of the metal shacks at the Camp Lake cabin. The other men, in return, uncorked their bottles. In a few seconds, all the bottles were spent and everyone was soaking. A few minutes of talkative celebration ensued. Most of the discussion dealt with Spags and his successful initiation.

After a few minutes Kessler interrupted the celebration, "Okay everyone, as you all know this is an election year. And you all know what that means." Kessler saw a few hesitant nods. "It's phone book delivery season."

"What's that?" Zeale asked.

"We do this every election year," Kessler said, "Phonebook Inc. delivers their phone books late in summer every year. I happen to own a huge chunk of their preferred stock. I bailed them out of bankruptcy a few years ago and so they give me first crack at their delivery routes. Because it's too expensive to mail the things, it's easier just to pay random people to hand-deliver them. So every year, in this state, I control who gets to deliver those phone books."

THE EDUCATOR

"I still don't get why you'd want that," Zeale said.

"Two reasons. First is, it's good graft. There are plenty of people out there who need extra work. You give a man a job, he's more open to helping you in other areas, like with his vote. An apathetic man suddenly becomes an advocate. Not only that, you typically get his whole family too. So a hundred votes turns into five hundred.

"The other reason is simple intel. The key to campaigning is to know where the voters are, who they are and if they'll vote for you. As we deliver these books, we keep notes on how many people live in the home, what their estimated income is, possible interests. We get a feel for the community. The phone books give us a legitimate reason to be on the property, otherwise we look suspicious. Good intel can get you three or four extra percentage points in a tight race."

"Besides, it's good exercise," Zan chimed in. "I'm sick of all you disgusting fat bodies."

The group chuckled at this, half of them overweight.

"One more thing," Kessler said. "Mr. Painter, it's time to give Mr. Zeale the *Operations* book."

"I have it in my cabin, I'll give it to him before we leave."

"Alright then, we start delivering phone books August eighth, Monday through Wednesday. Freshman Orientation is Thursday and Friday every week in August. Zan, You, Zeale and Painter are stuck doing Orientation. Everyone but Shotgun and Mr. Berg need to join me with the phone books."

After a few minutes of mingling everyone moseyed back to the main cabin.

Shotgun stuck his nose into the kitchen and cleaned out some leftover pizza. He and Chris Berg shared.

Zeale hung out in the kitchen with the two obese men, disgusted by their habit. Zeale was an athlete, as far as he was concerned. He played hockey and softball, did Tai Kwon Do and lifted weights. An average sized man, slim and without any muscle mass (to his frustration); his hair was already receding. It gave him a perpetual chip on his shoulder.

In high school he had learned to push back whenever he felt threatened or if his ideas weren't taken seriously. This gave him his spastic reputation. Whenever anyone confronted him about his behavior, he would simply reference 'Catcher in the Rye' and change the subject. But these old defenses didn't work in The Organization. They enjoyed pushing someone to the mental edge. Politics was a mean business, Zeale had learned, and eating was the easiest way to deal with the stress. Watching Berg and Shotgun eat, he promised he would never lose his discipline.

Painter returned to the cabin with a large three ring binder, over two inches thick, filled with paper. Painter threw the book unto the kitchen table. A simple black and white sheet with the words 'Operations Manual' represented the only outward identification.

"So what is this?" Zeale asked. He hated reading, rarely did it, and didn't like being assigned to waste his time.

"It's my book," Shotgun said, mouth full of pizza. "It's a how-to guide for campus activism, running a campaign, student government, student fees, non-profits, running a paper, the works. Everything a young conservative activist needs."

"You wrote it?"

"Hell yeah. Put it together my senior year. There ain't any good reference materials around. And be careful with it, there's some stuff towards the back that would look really bad if it got out."

Zeale opened the book and flipped to the last tab. "*Nixonian Enterprises,* Nice."

*   *   *   *   *   *   *

CHAPTER 11

11:30pm Friday, July 1
South Minneapolis

Paulson's big suburban pulled up in front of Alisha's house in South Minneapolis. Alisha exited the vehicle just as it came to a stop. She quickly ran to her door and entered the house before Paulson was even out of the car.

Paulson followed, walking up to the house while loosening the tie on his tuxedo.

As he entered the house he took off his jacket and threw it on a couch. Then he unbuttoned his shirt, slipped off his shoes, unbuckled his pants; Paulson confidently stripped down to his white boxers. Alisha entered the living room, wearing a white diaphanous negligee held together with a single pink silk ribbon. She also carried with her a bottle of champagne.

"This better be good," she said, "you know how much I hate the Guthrie."

She handed him the bottle. He dug around his coat and pulled out a pocketknife, sliced off the label and uncorked it. He took a large gulp of the fizzy liquid. Then he passed the bottle to Alisha, who did the same.

In one motion, he swiped the bottle from her hand and pushed Alisha towards the couch. She feigned pushing back, and Paulson wrapped her up in an embrace, kissing her passionately. Paulson was a seduction pro, in the kiss he stayed slow. Noninvasive. Sensual.

Slowly Paulson edged closer to the couch in the living room.

THE EDUCATOR

Once there he quickly turned Alisha away from him and pushed her over the back of the couch and lifted her garment out of his way. As he penetrated her he hit the timer on his Casio calculator watch. Eighteen functions including phone number storage. Paulson thought about all the functions of his watch. It kept his thrusting gentle.

After another long draft from the champagne bottle, he put it down and started to think about the next building on campus he wanted to renovate; his hands rubbing up and down Alisha's back.

*   *   *   *   *   *   *

The two lovers ended up on the floor in front of the couch, between it and a coffee table. Alisha lay on top of Paulson. A peak at his watch timer showed 22 minutes had elapsed. *Average effort* he thought.

Alisha pushed up from his chest, her negligee a twisted mess around her torso.

"I can't believe you're still timing yourself," she said, leaning in for a kiss.

"What can I say," he replied, "I'm a mathematician."

"Sexy mathematician," she said.

"Ready for another go?" Paulson rubbed his hands up and down her sides.

"Jesus Malcolm, you're gonna leave me bruised."

"How about this, you sneak upstairs and start the water on a hot bath, I'll make us a snack, and then I'll massage your feet until all the tension in your life diappears."

She smiled. "That's more like it." She jumped up, tried to adjust her negligee, then gleefully danced up the stairs.

Paulson found his jacket, took off his watch and put it into the breast pocket then he took out a small prescription bottle. Inside were several pills. Two aspirin, B vitamin, a gelcap filled with ephedra, and caffeine pills. He chugged the whole bottle. He had some amphetamine pills too, for backup.

In Alisha's kitchen, he found a ceramic platter and started filling it with chopped fruit and some Cool Whip. Alisha had plenty of fruit to choose from. It was almost all she ate. Paulson ate two bananas and quickly guzzled a glass of water.

Walking around the kitchen in the nude, Paulson started thinking about his collection of memories. Throwing Sarah off the bridge. Drowning Meghan in her own pool. There was that cute brunette who happened by his campsite in Yellowstone. Arousal returned.

Paulson grabbed the platter and a cheap bottle of Pinot Noir and started up the stairs, the image of strangling Alisha to death stuck

in his head.
　　She was going to have a very long night.

　　*　　*　　*　　*　　*　　*　　*

CHAPTER 12

10am Tuesday, July 5
South Minneapolis

　　Powderhorn Park is a cozy enclave of south Minneapolis, between Cedar and Hiawatha and Lake Street and 35th. Single family homes. Small, manageable yards. Parking on the street. Diverse. Affordable. The neighborhood was enjoying moderate gentrification after several decades of decline. Crime was a problem, but it was less a problem than in other areas.
　　Ernie Kessler sat in the back of Chris Berg's big white van. Instead of radio equipment, it was now filled with two computer monitors, three computer towers, four car batteries and an ashtray full of cigar butts. The very back of the van was filled with Phonebook Inc. phone books. Zan, Nolan, Henning and Zeale would deliver the phone books to houses, while making notes about those homes on clipboards.
　　Number of stalls in garage? Cars out front? Cars in the back? Bumper stickers on the cars? What was visible through the window? House empty or people inside? How many people? Dog? Dog door? Cat door? American flag? Christian symbols? Exercise bike? Garden? Vegetable garden? House size?
　　All the data got put into a computer database and cross-referenced with phone book and government records. Fishing license? hunting license? magazine subscriptions? All got mixed in. Then a computer program, written by Chris Berg, ran everything through an algorithm and identified political probability factors. A followup phone call would confirm if the phone book name matched the actual resident. Households were then cross-referenced with the MNGOP database, MasterMind.
　　Once enough cross-referencing was done, households could be identified for 1) doorknocking 2) volunteer requests 3) lit drops 4) phone calls or 5) further research. Households with a greater than thirty percent chance of "voting republican" were surveyed. More than fifty percent? Local candidates would specifically knock on the door. Especially important were irregular voters; those who only voted in presidential election years. Turning these voters out every election often paid off huge dividends for the investment.
　　People known as regular Republican voters were put on a

special list, they got candidate visits, letters requesting they volunteer with such and such campaign; 'Did you want a lawn sign?' Many were even asked to be election judges. And as always, they were pestered for as much money as they could possibly give. In 1992, the database helped turn out 14,000 Republican voters in the state of Minnesota. In 1994, Berg hoped he could triple the number statewide.

Why all the trouble? because nobody really wants to participate in democracy. Everyone likes democracy. They can recite the values of democracy as instilled by their social studies teacher. When asked, people showed a socially acceptable level of patriotism. Consent of the governed. Life, liberty and the pursuit of happiness. No taxation without representation. I like Ike. On election day a great plurality cast their votes to fulfill the expectations of their neighbors.

But there is very little value in the actual act of voting. Most people know this intuitively. While there is a cumulative effect in voting, where one vote per precinct can change the result of elections nationally, the individual was nothing. No one ever sees their contribution. Eventually, people become cynical towards the entire process. They join the apathetic and they stop voting. They were the true silent majority.

The real power in politics is not held by the voters. It's held by whichever side has enough activists to bother enough of the apathetic and cynical and pressure them to the polls. Apathy has many defenses. Phone calls can be ignored. Junk mail thrown away. The migrations of people confound Get Out the Vote efforts (known among politicos as 'GOTV'). Every year it becomes easier to avoid the political pests.

So the political pests develop strategies to cope with these realities. People are tracked, their interests listed into a database. Innocent-looking college students go door-to-door with surveys asking questions. The undertakings are tremendous resource users, so only narrow demographic or geographic areas are targeted. The parties rarely encountered one another.

In rural Minnesota, the two political parties didn't do much. Voter turnout was high in these areas, and the distances between homes made data collection prohibitively expensive. In the Twin Cities, the Minnesota GOP did next to nothing. Local party BPOUs, or Base Political Operating Units, were left to their own devices. And this normally meant absolutely nothing of value was done to identify, recruit and turn out Republican voters.

The MNGOP spent their money in the suburbs, in swing districts. Incredibly efficient. Tactically and logistical logical and economic. But the overall strategy was a losing one. More votes were lost for state and federal officeholders than was gained in the suburbs. The only winners in this strategy were suburban state legislators.

In the cities the DFL ruled. On election day, DFL activists would sit on buses and pressure people to vote. They would camp out in immigrant communities and drive hundreds of people to the polls; the majority of whom had never voted before. Most could barely speak English. But same-day registration in Minnesota made it one of the most voter-friendly states in the union, and the DFL manipulated this to great effect. The Republican refusal to engage immigrant groups created hundreds of thousands of permanent Democrat voters and put the Republicans at a huge disadvantage.

Kessler, trying to stop the bleeding, spent tens of thousands of dollars supporting different Hmong businesses, newspapers and tutors. The Hmong had reacted positively, and after Kessler recruited different Hmong people into the MNGOP, the community voted slightly more Republican than Democrat. It helped that the Hmong had been brutalized at the hands of leftwing philosophies, but it was still only possible because they were engaged by the rich Black Man.

Kessler learned a valuable lesson. Engagement Worked.

So he promoted doing more work in the Twin Cities. He believed the population density and lower voter turnout made the cities the place to target for statewide races. Which is why he did crap like this. Two weeks sitting in the back of a van, in front of a computer. In August.

It sucked.

But it was fun reporting to IRS agents, Kessler was routinely audited, about the 224 dollars he made every year delivering phone books.

* * * * * * *

CHAPTER 13

11am Friday, July 8
Freshman Orientation, Coffman Memorial Union

"What is this?" the question came from Student Activities Director Robert Pinkerton. Held in his hand was a sheet of paper with a dozen jokes typed out and a poorly drawn caricature of Bill Clinton as Porky Pig, pants free.

"It's a sheet of Clinton jokes..." Zeale tried to keep from laughing. "See, Clinton is there, drawn like Porky Pig. No Pants."

"I see what it is," Pinkerton said. "But this is disrespectful, and sexually explicit. Half these jokes involve oral sex. This is sexual harassment. It creates a hostile atmosphere."

Pinkerton was a fascist. Blue suit. Blue tie. Pastel shirt. Shined shoes. Lots of hair product. Aggressive in action. Effeminate in speech.

Arrogant. Tall. Loud. Uncompromising. Manicured. Immaculate. A proud practitioner of the school of persuasion by righteous indignation. With respectably broad shoulders and an exceptionally narrow waist, Pinkerton carried himself like a Lord Protector.

"Mr. Pinkerton, it's okay not to like our jokes, but we have the right to pass them out." Nolan Painter answered. Painter was tall enough to look down at Pinkerton, but this didn't stop Pinkerton's attempt at intimidation. "So maybe you should--"

"I know what I should do Mr. Painter. Kick you the hell out of this activities fair."

"Mr. Pinkerton," Zeale was more forceful. "You can't do that."

"Unless you stop passing out these fliers, that is exactly what I'll do," Pinkerton said.

"Well," Zeale continued. "We're going to keep passing out these fliers."

"Honest to God," Pinkerton put as much indignation into his voice as he could. "You're the fucking Family Values Coalition. One of these punchlines is actually 'cum cake.' I'm going to do you a favor and take these and throw them away."

Pinkerton sidestepped the two men and grabbed the pile of offensive fliers; he did so and started walking away. Zeale reached under the table. Hidden from view under the black table cloth was a plastic tub. He pulled it out and grabbed a handful of papers and started waving them.

"Hey Pinkerton, we got more!" Zeale shouted.

The blue suited man turned right around and got back in their faces. "That's it, you guys are outta here. If you don't leave the activities fair, I will have you arrested. Your table is forfeit, do you understand?"

"Alright," Zeale said. "Let's see it."

"See what?"

"The police. Let's see you call the police. I'd like to get arrested today."

*   *   *   *   *   *   *

"No, let me guess," the sarcasm was heavy in Kessler's voice. "You were the one who really shot McKinley?"

"Archbishop, I swear, it's nothing like what you have heard," Zeale was trying to sound pathetic, but he was actually enjoying the whole experience.

"You kill Vince Foster? Sell nukes to Saddam Hussein? Denver Mint Robbery? You're D.B. Cooper?"

"Will you just get us out of here," Painter pleaded.

"What? You don't like jail? Really? Then why were you arguing with that cop?"

"I wasn't," Painter said, "he was."

"He got the Constitution wrong." Zeale crossed his arms.

"Of course he got the Constitution wrong, he's a cop," Kessler said, "don't call the guy a 'fag' because of that. Call a guy a fag because he drinks cappuccinos or puts ketchup on his hot dog. And never say it to a cop. That will always get you arrested. For fuck's sake, he was a friend of mine."

"What if the cop is drinking a cappuccino?" Painter asked.

Kessler stared the two down. After a long pause he relented. "Okay, then you can call him a fag."

*   *   *   *   *   *   *

"What do you mean you slept with him?" Zan was turning red. The muscles in his arms were tensely folded across his chest. He tried to remain civil. But it was two in the morning.

"Easy now. You know what I mean. I slept with him. Fucked him," Alisha decided to tell Zan about her weekend rendezvous with University President Malcolm Paulson after copulation in hopes of softening the blow. She knew Zan was fairly conservative. But she also knew he wasn't a puritan. Hope springs eternal.

"Malcolm Paulson. You slept with Malcolm Paulson this weekend?"

"Yes."

"How long has this been going on? Have you been sleeping with him regularly?" Zan's normally mellow voice was raising in pitch.

"Off and on now for three years. I hadn't seen him in six or seven months. He stopped by the bar when you were away on that cabin trip." There was an awkward pause. "Look, it's okay, I was one of his mistresses. It's not serious. It was never serious."

Zan wanted to start yelling. He hadn't yet, not at this hour, with his landlord downstairs. But he wanted to. In fact, he wanted to break something, anything. He paced a bit, unsure of what to do. Alisha sat motionless at the table, sipping at coffee, wearing one of Zan's Led Zeppelin t-shirts and a pair of his white boxers.

"You've been banging this motherfucker for three years?"

"Yeah Zan, off and on, that's what mistresses do."

"And somehow it's okay to fuck around on me because you're someone's mistress?" Zan caught himself starting to yell and stopped.

"Zan, look...it's just sex, right? I know you don't like this guy but he's really sweet. But it's nothing. I want to stay with you. That's why I brought it up."

Zan left the kitchen area and went back into his bedroom. Returning a few moments later with a handful of clothes. He threw them onto the table.

"Get out. Take your shit and get out." His voice was low, slow. "I'm going to take a shower and try to wash the whore off. When I get out, you better be gone."

With that he turned and walked back into the bedroom and closed the door.

"Fuck you Zan!" She shouted at the door.

*   *   *   *   *   *   *

CHAPTER 14

7am Monday, August 22
Morrill Hall

And just like that, summer break was over.

Rachel Anderson was shocked how quickly they disappeared. The long summer vacations of her childhood had turned into short acquaintances with pleasantly unwinterlike weather. *Was it going to be like this forever?* she reflected while walking to her new job at the University President's office in Morrill Hall.

The second floor offices of the University President were an open scattering of cubicles, conference rooms, coffee and copy machines. Over a dozen people worked in the cubicles. The President had a large office to himself, guarded by the imposing desk of his secretary. Other bureaucrats were scattered in several adjoining offices. Rachel was disappointed. She didn't even get a cubicle. Her work station was one of a dozen computers lined up against the eastern wall.

It was her first day and no one had spoken a word to her yet. The President's secretary directed her to the work station and had given her an employee's manual. Over the next hour she reviewed it. Still no one to talk to. Of the dozens of workers that should have been in the office, she only counted eight. She played around on the internet. Nothing as usual. At nine-thirty she got coffee. At ten-thirty President Paulson walked into his office. Then left again right away.

Then lunch.

By two-thirty she had done her scheduled six hours of work and got up to leave. As she was walking downstairs she ran into Paulson.

"Miss Anderson?" said Paulson sweetly. "This must be your first day?"

"Yes it is."

"And how are you fitting in?"

"Well, there was nothing for me to do today. No one even talked to me..."

"Don't worry about that," Paulson slapped Rachel on her shoulder. "Your supervisor is on vacation until after Labor day. There's nothing for you to do anyway, the legislature is out of session for another month. Bring a book to read." Rachel's face changed to show some disappointment, and Paulson, an expert people reader, picked up on it. "I'll try to find you something productive to do for a couple of hours in the next few days. I could probably use some help with a proposal to the Regents for a new building. You could fact-check it for me." Paulson looked at his watch. "Well, gotta go, I'll see you tomorrow."

He leapt up the stairs two steps at a time.

Rachel stood there surprised for a moment, then started the long walk to her car.

*   *   *   *   *   *   *

Zan and Jose Rodriguez were walking along Como Avenue, just to the northeast of the main campus, where the U owned some large industrial lots. It contained some recycling facilities, the U's Printing Services Center, its vehicle fleet, a large equipment yard and special housing for married students. The U liked to keep all its junk in one spot.

Jose, AKA The Spic, was supposed to be hiding out after stealing tens of thousands of dollars from unsuspecting U administrators. Instead, here he was with Zan, checking out the locations of security cameras around the U of M large equipment yard. The day was hot, humid. Normally this would be considered nice weather, but the atmosphere was never nice around industrial parks.

After walking around the area for thirty minutes, they found a beat up picnic bench next to one of the Como housing buildings and sat down. Jose was wearing the Minnesota August uniform: white cotton t-shirt and tan docker shorts. Zan was in blue jeans and wearing a t-shirt featuring Homer Simpson.

Jose broke the silence, "So I hear you broke up with Alisha."

"Yeah, she was sleeping with Malcolm Paulson...and yes, *the* Malcolm Paulson."

"That's fucking awesome."

"Up yours."

"I don't know what your problem is *puto*, it's not like she's some holy virgin. Besides, you mighta talked 'er into that Marileen Monroe, huh?"

"I doubt it, she likes him too much. But I wasn't thinking about that. I was thinking about the fact she thinks she gets to fuck around on me."

"You think a woman is some sort of precious flower just because she's giving you head. Let me tell ya, it ain't true man."

"Just 'cause you're a swarthy Latino doesn't make you an expert on love."

"The hell it don't."

"Okay, switching topics. You sure you want to do this little job?"

"Oh yeah. This thing is set. It's perfect. I told you. I was the one who scheduled the transfer order for tonight. When they find the truck gone in the morning, no one will be surprised. I canceled the contract with the auction company, they won't know anything is wrong either."

"Joey, you're in enough trouble as it is." Zan said. "If anyone connects you to the identity theft stuff, you're toast. You shouldn't even be working for the U anymore."

"I got nothin' to worry about," Jose said. "It was Fats who was working for facilities maintenance. He's the one they can connect to the vehicle. And he's in Osakis or something. I'm just some Mexican working for the U. Hell, they didn't even interview me when I applied for the administrative assistant job out here. Just boom. Suddenly I'm running the Large Equipment Services Office. Shit man, as long as you ain't white, you can get away with almost anything on this campus."

"Just keep telling yourself that. Besides, why do you want that thing anyway?"

"Who wouldn't want it?"

"What are you going to do with it?"

"Nothing, but that's not the point."

"So, you're stealing just to steal."

"Why not?"

"Look, who am I to judge you for something like this, I encourage this sort of behavior. But you want me to help you. So there's got to be something in this beyond kleptomania."

The two sat in silence for a minute. Finally Jose spoke.

"Look, I got to do this sort of thing, and it ain't jus adrenaleen. Yeah it's exciting and all that. But, uh, doing this sort of thing helps me write."

"Write? You mean you want to come in here tonight, commit grand theft auto, steal something you have no use for, because you what? it helps you write?"

"Yeah. That's about it. That's why I do all this stuff. You can't write unless you do. And if you don't do, it don't matter what kind of writer you are, you don't do, you don't have nothin to write about."

Zan sat there for a moment. Then shrugged "That's as good a

reason as any."

"Quit worrying man," Jose said. "There's just the one camera, at the front entrance. We just take the back way out. No one will know we were ever here. I go back to work in the morning like nothing happened."

"Where are we going to put it?"

"I dunno, I thought you could figure something out."

"Alright, just a sec." Zan thought for a minute. "There's an old barn about a mile north of Ernie's cabin. It's empty, pretty big too."

"Excellent."

"Think we can make it up highway 10 without any problems?"

"When was the last time you saw the cops pull over a fire truck?"

"Most fire trucks aren't stolen."

"And neither will this one. It was going to be donated. The auction service was going to give the money to some college fund for the kids of dead firefighters. The U bought the engine for some kind of engineering research. It was used too much to be returned to service. I'll have paperwork showing the engine is being transferred to the auction service. Nothing can go wrong."

"Yeah, except those little kids won't get their college money."

"Did you get any college money?"

"Well, no."

"Then why you worried about some other kid? Should they get money jus'cause their daddy died?"

"I think there's a case to be made that the family members of those who commit to serve the community deserve some compensation too."

Another awkward pause.

"How about this," Jose broke the silence. "We steal it, I donate ten thousand bucks to their charity. Then those kids still get their money?"

"Seriously?"

"Sure man, it's only money."

*　　*　　*　　*　　*　　*　　*

Minnesota August nights were warm, pleasantly so, but very buggy. The bugs weren't normally bad in the city. Except around industrial parks. Wearing dark gray sweatpants and black t-shirts, Jose and Zan looked the part of late-night joggers. It was three in the morning when they got to the large equipment yard in the Como area. While there were few people out this late, it wasn't unusual to find people jogging or walking around the Twin Cities at all hours.

They jogged down 29th avenue, down to the food operations building, where there were no cameras, and went into the parking lot where they approached a fence. Both men jumped the fence with ease, getting into the equipment yard. Jose jumped into the large fire engine. It was red with a white stripe, had a roomy interior. Very cool.

It was your typical fire engine.

Zan started work on the fence. The main entrance to the yard was electronically operated and was guarded by a camera. On the east side of the yard was a gate in the chain-link fence that led to the maintenance facilities for the university's buses. There were no cameras there either. But there were a number of workers. The buses ran from six in the morning until two in the morning and required a lot of maintenance.

A universal law of thieving held that people were more interested in their own thing than noticing the world around them. This was especially true of night workers. Most of them worked such strange hours on purpose. Some were insomniacs, some were desperate. But mostly, they were city dwellers who enjoyed the city, but didn't enjoy people. Working at night provided a convenient answer to their quirk.

Still, someone was going to notice a fire truck.

Jose had the fire truck moving out of its parking spot, quickly working towards the gate. But Zan couldn't get it open. The key Jose had given him wasn't working. Jose jumped out of the truck. Zan told him what was wrong. Jose opened one of the compartments on the truck and pulled out a huge bolt cutter. Within minutes, with some heads following them as they drove through the bus maintenance parking lot, they were out of there.

And that was it.

An hour and a half to the cabin. No surprises. No police stops. Just one police car, and the officer waved.

That was the strange part, to Zan, of the whole ordeal. The real calm, quiet, when committing a crime; it never matched the adrenaline. Committing a crime was nerve-racking. The mind raced. Every imaginable threat was just around the corner. Fight or flight. The truth? Most people didn't care. As long as you weren't actually hurting them, they barely noticed you. Crime could be as relaxing as taking a walk around the park. If you let it.

The calm was unsettling.

*   *   *   *   *   *   *

Paulson parked his big Suburban in front of a meter in the knoll area of the east bank. He was dressed in his fishing clothes. Denim jeans and a denim collared shirt. He walked briskly to the abandoned Mineral Resources building. He entered through the southern docking entrance and wandered through the building. The machinery and the darkness made it difficult to navigate to the north end of the building.

Eventually he got up to the second story bathroom. Found the box. Opened it. Every relic was removed. He touched them all, smelled them. In the dark he could still tell the difference between the locks of hair. A flashlight lit the room. The relics he placed around him. From his pockets he produced three more. A pair of pantyhose. A drivers license with an unsmiling redhead on it. And a badge. Stearns County Sheriff Deputy #453.

He plopped down on the floor, staring at his collection. He relived the previous six hours. The redhead, smelled of sweat and beer. Young too. Twenty-five years old. Very thin, frail. Obviously a crack addict. The look on her face as he strangled her...

*   *   *   *   *   *   *

Paulson had arrived just as the bar was closing; the redhead told him so as he jumped out of the car. Then she asked if he wanted a blow job. Twenty bucks.

Sure. Why Not.

She walked him to the alleyway behind the bar. Dumpsters and empty boxes. As she went down, he grabbed her neck and pushed her to the ground. Then he squeezed. She put up no fight. He relaxed his grip, let her catch her breath. Then squeezed again. Repeat. Repeat. Squeeze. Relax. She was weak. Desperate to die. He almost let her live. Finally he finished her. Took her pantyhose. No bra, no panties. Just a beat up pleated skirt, a silver blouse, a purse with her drivers license and some vials of drugs. He wanted her shoes, but settled on the pantyhose.

When he returned to the parking lot, he found a cop looking at the girl's car. As he approached his Suburban, the cop yelled at him. He had questions.

Drinking tonight? What were you doing in the alley? Do you know who's car that is? The cop was fat. Old. Paulson waited. Dodged the questions the best he could. Over the radio, Paulson heard a disembodied voice report something. The cop had run the plates on the girl's car. Not his. Not yet.

Before he knew it, he was grappling with the cop on the ground. Much stronger than he looked, that old guy. Paulson got to the cop's gun first. The cop didn't make a sound. As Paulson got the gun to the man's temple, the old cop sprayed him with pepper spray. Shots were fired. One. Two. Five. Paulson didn't know. The cop was dead. Paulson pulled his badge and felt his way into his car. Crying. This was it. He was going to get caught.

He'd die first.

Then nothing happened. Five minutes creeped along. No one in the bar came out. No other cars went by. After pouring cold coffee into his eyes, Paulson was able to see enough to make the hour and a half drive to campus.

It was four fifteen in the morning. His face was still red, still hurting. Eyes burned. There was blood all over his clothing. Luckily, he kept a spare suit in his office. There was a shower in the basement of Morrill Hall, that the janitors used. He looked again at his collection, then dropped his pants and began to masturbate.

*   *   *   *   *   *   *

Part III

The sharpest sword is a word spoken in wrath;
the deadliest poison is covetousness;
the fiercest fire is hatred;
the darkest night is ignorance
　　　　--Gautama Buddha

He who fights with monsters should look to it that he himself does not become
a monster. And when you gaze long into an abyss the abyss also gazes into
you.
　　　--Friedrich Nietzsche

THE EDUCATOR

CHAPTER 1

9am Wednesday, September 7
Superblock, Minneapolis Campus

The first week in September was a busy time at the University of Minnesota. It was Labor Day Weekend. Students had to move in before the Tuesday start. The Minnesota State Fair was happening in St. Paul, right next to the St. Paul campus. There were books to buy. A campus to scout. Coeds to ogle.

Experienced upperclassmen preyed on coed underclassmen with promises of booze and computer help. Upperclassmen knew there wasn't going to be a lot of fucking the first week, it was about planting seeds for later in the semester, when the pressure and stress got the best of anyone.

Residential Advisers, RAs, had a long list of orientation and social activities. Open door nights. Group meals.

Student orgs were busy too. The first week was the best time on campus to do heavy recruiting. New students, particularly freshmen, were practically lost. The Minnesota Public Interest Research Group, or MPIRG, a liberal group founded by Ralph Nader, made an annual event of helping students move into the dorms. Dressed in yellow and white t-shirts, anyone who wanted help got it, along with an invitation to save the planet and end sexism, racism and capitalist oppression.

And it was a great time for thieves. New students had nice stuff like stereos and video-games, TVs and other electronics. Young women were moving their jewelry out of their parents' homes for the first time. Any youngish looking character could bluff their way into the dorms during the chaos and steal thousands of dollars worth of stuff. And they did.

It was also a great time for cons.

'Regular Joe' Svenson was sitting in the Washington Avenue Burger King, enjoying his coffee. He was not enjoying his coffee because it tasted good. It was crap. He was enjoying it because he paid for it with a cash advance he had gotten from the ATM machine in the restaurant. Using a credit card that 'belonged' to Malcolm Paulson.

Dressed in a dark gray suit with a blue tie and gray slacks, Joe looked a little out of place with the grungier student crowd around him.

A slim blonde woman wearing oversized sunglasses sat down across from him. She had on a white blouse, unbuttoned until deep down her chest. She wore a black pleated skirt that ended just above her knees. Fishnet pantyhose and black pumps finished the ensemble. Her blonde hair was bobbed just below her ears. Her eyes were hid-

---

den behind her sunglasses; her face was heavy with makeup.

On her right pinky finger was a gold ring with a blue sapphire.

"Jesus Christ Nicole, whoring it up enough?"

"Makeup is a necessity at my age, not all of us are ageless like you."

"I dunno, your getup seems more conspicuous than the last time we did this."

"A woman's beauty is short lived. This is all I can do to look less conspicuous around these kids."

Nicole Fielder was a single mother. A lawyer. Divorced. Outdoorsy. She and Zan had been friends in law school. She was the first female member of the Israel Bissell Society, and the only woman to have been initiated. She was a few inches shorter than Regular Joe, putting her just about the five foot mark. An aerobics addiction kept her in shape.

"I don't think anyone is going to notice your age," Joe suggested. "But they will notice you're dressed like a prostitute."

"An expensive prostitute."

Joe shrugged. "Okay, we ready?"

"Not really."

"Don't tell me you're having second thoughts."

"Of course I am," Nicole said. "The money isn't worth the risk. Especially since we're not even keeping any of it."

"Come on Nikki," Joe replied. "We do this because we hate those fucking students. Not because we want the money."

*   *   *   *   *   *   *

The pair walked into Frontier Hall, one of the four dormitories in the Superblock. It was a freshman-only dorm, along with Territorial Hall next to it. Walking past the front desk, they followed a student through the door that was supposed to prevent outsiders from sneaking in. The pair took the stairs up to the fourth floor.

Frontier Hall was a long box with three arms. Over one thousand students lived there. Almost everyone lived with a roommate. Most of the dorms were two person. Some suites had four people. The place looked like a prison on the inside. The walls were cream-colored, fluorescent lights provided gloom all year round. Dark green carpeting absorbed stains and took heavy wear well. The carpet only needed replacing every four years.

At the end of the southernmost arm of the dorm, the pair stuck their heads through an open door. One male student wearing black sweatpants and nothing else was lying on a bed playing a Game Boy.

"Hey there, how's it going," Nicole said cheerfully. The student immediately responded to the feminine sound.

"Hey, what's up," said the student as he got up from the bed. His words were slow, he sounded like a pothead. "What's going on?"

"I'm Marie, the vice-chair of the U-DFL and this is my friend Ralphie from the College Republicans. We're recruiting students together. It's an election year and we're hoping to get as many students involved in our democracy as possible, no matter what their political persuasion. We're hoping a good student turnout will make our elected representatives wake-up to our needs."

"So if you're interested in joining the CRs or the U-DFL, you can do so right now," said Joe quite professionally. Like a businessman.

"Yeah, well, uh, I'm prolly more Democrat than anything, you know?"

"Super," exclaimed Nicole. "Here's a flyer with our meeting time and place. Do you want to sign up officially?"

Nicole flashed the biggest smile she could.

"Yeah, alright." Nicole passed a clipboard to the kid who dutifully wrote his name and phone number on the paper.

"And if you want, you can pay your membership dues right now, it's two dollars," Nicole said. "That way, you can be a voting member right away. And besides, the CRs are asking for five dollars..."

"Uh, sure." The kid flipped some of his moppy black hair out of his face, and dug out some quarters from his desk.

"Thank you so much," Nicole said.

"Hey, what about my roommate, you should, uh, talk to him..."

"Oh, we'll come around again, don't worry," said Joe.

*   *   *   *   *   *   *

And so it went. Dorm room after dorm room. Sometimes nobody was there. Sometimes they talked to everyone in the room. Not everyone gave money. Not even close. But Nicole collected a healthy haul. It was not hard to motivate men to give money to a woman. Regular Joe's amount was not so impressive. Just sixteen people in Frontier were willing to pay CR dues.

To Territorial Hall. Same story. A sprawling dorm filled with lost, confused and vulnerable freshmen. Territorial was nicer than Frontier, just not by much. More sunlight filtered in. Nicole and Joe worked the same set up, started from the top floor and worked down. There were fewer students since it was lunch hour.

There was a hiccup. A know-it-all RA ran into them. Do you

have permission to doorknock? Yes of course. Who gave you permission? The girl working behind the counter.

After a minute of discussion, the short and fat woman left them alone.

It took just three hours to get through both dorms. The scam was complete. Freshmen were ignoranti. They were in the clear.

"What's our total?" Joe asked. The two were walking on Delaware Street towards Oak Street Ramp, where their cars were squirreled away.

"About eight hundred."

Actually, they both had been keeping track of the running total and knew it was actually around eight hundred fifty.

"You know," Joe said, "we're probably never going to be doing this again. It'll be a few years before it will work, and we'll both be too old to do it."

"We're too old now."

"Oh shut up," retorted Joe. "I say we keep going. We can hit Centennial and Pioneer. Might double our take."

"No way," Nicole said. "That's a terrible idea. Upperclassmen can smell a scam."

"But there aren't that many upperclassmen. They're still mostly sophomores and freshmen..."

They were silent again.

"Come'on, it'll be easy," Joe pressed. "Besides, I still have my Centennial Outdoor Entrance key. We can enter through the basement. Nobody in the office will see us at all."

Another long pause.

"Fine." Nicole turned around and they walked towards Centennial.

*　　*　　*　　*　　*　　*　　*

From the sky, Centennial looked like a four legged spider. From the inside, it looked like a fallout bunker. The dreariness of Frontier Hall was bright and happy in comparison. The lighting was poor. The carpeting older, more disgusting, no one was sure of its original color. The dorm was ancient. Like an asylum at the turn of the century where thousands were dying of TB.

It was a complex playground of five floors plus a basement area. The fourth and fifth floors were much smaller than the other floors; the fifth floor wasn't much more than two short hallways hugged close to the elevators. The people up there were particularly anti-social. No takers.

There was some luck on the fourth floor. It was one of the few smoking floors in the dorm system. Doors were open, people were smoking, happy. And some tobacco money found its way into the bag. The third floor started fine. The two eastern arms went quick. Most of the classes in the day were already done, professors not liking to work past three in the afternoon, so there were plenty of students coming into the dorms.

Fifty bucks was liberated.

Fortunes change quickly.

The center section of the third floor had a large open space between the two elevators where students could hang out in chairs and study. There were also unfortunate dorm dwellers there whose doors opened right into this space, exposing them to the sound of elevators running and loud conversations all night, despite a lights-out curfew at eleven.

Nicole was working over a lone room occupant, an affable little man with thick, black-rimmed glasses and a t-shirt that said 'Whence Cometh Evil?' when a group of people loudly lumbered up the stairs and into the central landing.

Nicole was too focused, but Joe saw the threat. Two police officers were being led by a short fat woman, wearing a yellow U of M sweater and gray sweatpants. *What is up with all these people wearing sweatpants?* Joe thought to himself, right after he had thought to himself *oh man we're fucked.*

*   *   *   *   *   *   *

CHAPTER 2

Centennial Hall

The fat chick stayed back, the officers did the talking.

"We'd like to know what you're collecting money for," said the male police officer. He was tall, six foot five at least. Salt and pepper hair underneath his hat, his face was well-weathered, but genteel, and his figure broad and trim. "According to the woman behind us, you don't have permission to be in the dorm."

"Sure," Nicole turned on the flirty cheeriness, "I'm from the U-DFL and he's from the College Republicans. We're recruiting members and collecting membership dues. It's an election year, ya know." Nicole winked at the two officers on the 'ya know.'

"See, that's funny," said the other cop. She was short, buxom, boxy, with a pretty face and long blonde hair bleached almost white. She didn't look much older than the fat chick behind her. "According to the woman behind us, you're not in the U-DFL."

"Pfff, whatever," Nicole rolled her eyes. "I'm in the U-DFL, Colin Tvrdik is the current chair. He's a little redhead, a bit taller than me. He's the one who asked me to do this. We do a big recruiting drive every election year, see?" She waved the clipboard at the woman.

"That's impossible!" shouted the fat chick. "I've never seen her in a meeting in three years. I'm the vice-chair, Colin woulda told me."

"Please ma'am," the Male Officer turned and spoke to her. "We'll handle this."

"And you," the Female Officer addressed Regular Joe. "I suppose you would know the College Republican chair?"

"Tony Meyers," Joe said "about five foot four, glasses, heavyset, looks kinda like a cartoon character."

Female Officer shrugged. The two mystery guests sounded the part.

"That doesn't matter, they need permission to be in here!" again shouted the fat chick.

"Ma'am, please," Female Officer scolded.

"You don't have permission to be in here, I take it?" asked Male Officer.

"Oh, you know how these things go," Joe explained. "You call one person, they tell you to call another, and another. Then there's three people and a form. Then another form. Pretty soon, you're given permission to set up a table out back where nobody goes. It's red tape, it goes in circles. But Minnesota law requires that political candidates and their representatives be given fair access to enclosed dwellings like apartment structures, like this."

"Suddenly you're a lawyer now?" asked Female Officer.

"No, just a well-trained political activist."

"Look," Mofficer said. "We're going to need to see some I.D., and we're gonna have to find a way to verify your story."

And that was the end of the conversation. Regular Joe jabbed his clipboard into Mofficer's gut as hard as he could, then sprinted down the hallway towards the west wing of the dorm.

Mofficer didn't stay down very long, "Watch her!" he shouted while sprinting after Joe.

Femicer had instinctively pulled her gun but wasn't going to take a shot in this environment. She watched Mofficer run out of sight. As she turned towards Nicole, a plume of chemicals hit her face. Pepper spray. Strong pepper spray. She was blind.

Charging the source of the spray, she ran into a body and tackled it. Her gun in hand, she shouted as loud as she could to stay still, and there may have been a comment or two about a 'fucking bitch.'

But she had tackled the little man with glasses, who had been watching the whole episode from his door.

*   *   *   *   *   *   *

Joe was fast. Not track and field fast, but he could easily beat most people in a sprint. This cop wasn't normal. The aging brute managed to stay just fifty feet behind him as he sprinted down the hallway. But Joe knew the dorm well; he had lived there for two years. At the end of the hall was a stairway that would lead down to a door which opened into the Centennial Hall grilling area, outside in a sort of courtyard.

And there was another staircase not fifteen feet from the other stairwell. It led up to the fourth floor. Joe hit the first staircase and went down one floor, then sprinted to the other staircase and took it up to the fourth floor, unseen by the cop, who was screaming 'stop motherfucker, stop' at the top of his lungs.

While the police officer was running up and down the first stairwell, looking for him, Joe was taking the elevator down to the basement. In the elevator he removed his jacket, dress shirt and tie. Underneath was a well-worn Grateful Dead T-shirt. Exiting the elevator, he was going to leave the building through a door that led to the loading docks at the sub-basement. But a group of freshman were leaving the dining hall underneath Centennial and were taking the tunnel to Territorial Hall. Slipping in with the group as they opened the locked doors of the tunnel, he was in his car driving on I-94 just five minutes later.

It cost him his suit, which was thrown in a trash can inside the tunnel, but he still had the clipboard and an envelope filled with a thousand dollars.

*   *   *   *   *   *   *

Nicole did not know the dorm well.

She ran to the staircase but decided against going down to the lobby to exit. That is where any reinforcements would be coming in. She alighted to the second floor and tried to calmly walk to another staircase which would hopefully lead to an exit. But she came to a stairwell and heard voices shouting, turned a corner and saw a group of students coming towards her. Walking away from this she hurried into her only available refuge, a men's bathroom.

The sound of a shower running was the only presence of life. She grabbed a stall and took off her wig, flushed it. Then flushed her glasses. Then her recruiting list. Then the pantyhose. She sat for a bit, trying to think, which she wasn't doing very well. Her mind was racing. She did her best to calm down, catch her breath. To her dismay, she realized she should have just walked out the front door like dozens of other students probably had.

She got out of the stall and went to the door. There were more shouts, and the sounds of people running. One ran right by the door. The window of escape had closed. She looked around. Then noticed the guy in the shower had a big purple robe along with a large towel. Nicole's lips curled into a grin.

*   *   *   *   *   *   *

CHAPTER 3

Centennial Hall

The bathroom was a long rectangle. There was three sinks along one wall, three stalls along another, a large basin and a urinal opposite the stalls, and the shower area was located along the wall furthest from the door. Two coffin sized shower stalls were hidden behind a cheap plastic shower curtain. There was a window, open and showing a view of the courtyard. Nicole could see two cops milling around, smoking cigarettes.

Nicole knew it was a longshot, but she believed a good looking woman could flirt, beg or whore her way out of anything. She got into the shower area, took off shirt and skirt, opened the second shower curtain to the occupied shower stall and stepped in, to the great surprise of the occupant.

"Please," she opened, "I really need your help, will you help me?" She immediately wrapped her arms around the man's shoulders, they were face to face in the extremely tiny space; maybe nine feet square. Naked except for her panties, Nicole hoped the sight of a desperate vulnerable woman begging for help would turn on his patriarchal extinct and give her a workable solution.

The man had yet to speak. It might have been the shock. It might have been the lady. She had moved fast, thrown words at him, and was now embracing him. Or maybe it was the feel of skin against skin. The man was tall, a shade over six feet. Boxy, robust, a little chubby. His chest was covered in brown hair. Well tanned, above the waist, his face was friendly. His eyes were deep brown, his head completely shaved. His nose was broad and large, roman, and his jaw line was masculine. Overall attractive, not handsome...masculine. Nicole figured she had hit the jackpot.

There was a pause; about twenty seconds but it seemed much longer. The muscles in the man's body eased their tension.

"Alright," he said. "let's hear it."

*   *   *   *   *   *   *

THE EDUCATOR

Nicole couldn't think of a good story to tell him that would sound believable, so she told him the truth. Mostly.

"...door to door in the dorms...political surveys...police...trespassing...panic..." Now she needed a place to hang out until they went away.

This took a couple of minutes. Nicole kept her grip on the man as she explained. She even felt his arousal from the situation. "Sorry about that," the man said.

"Don't worry about it, I'm an *experienced* woman, I bet I'm twice your age."

"You're fifty years old?"

"Uh, no," she said. "I'm thirty-six."

"And you're a good thirty-six. You don't look a day over twenty-five."

"Thanks," she purred.

*   *   *   *   *   *   *

With nothing to do but wait for things to calm down, the two talked.

The man introduced himself as Bob Restovich. Ex-military, army. On the GI Bill. Wounded in the Gulf War; his Bradley fighting vehicle hit an anti-tank landmine. Killed almost everyone aboard. There were some cool scars on his leg, if she wanted to go looking. 'Not right now' she replied. This was his second year in college, he had yet to declare a major and he liked living in the dorms, despite being older than everyone, including his RA.

There was a loud bang.

Someone had just entered the bathroom, the door slamming behind them. Nicole put her hand over his mouth to shut him up. A few seconds later a voice.

"Hey, you in the shower, Police Officer." The voice was loud, authoritative, and feminine.

"Yeah?!" Bob shouted back, "What'd you need?"

"We're looking for some people who might still be in the dorm, a man and a woman, have you seen or heard anybody in here since you were in?"

"What?! I can barely hear you," He shouted.

"I said, have you seen anybody else in the bathroom since you came in?" she shouted.

"No," he shouted back.

She approached the shower area and stuck her head through the privacy curtain. The two stalls each had their own curtain, and both were still closed. Only a thin sheet of plastic shielded the police officer from seeing Nicole. In fact, had she looked underneath the towel, she would have found Nicole's skirt.

Bob stuck his head out of the shower, pushing Nicole behind him.

"Was there anything else you needed?" he asked, annoyance in his voice.

"How long have you been in that shower?" the officer asked. She was as tall as him, blonde and broad shouldered. She looked like a tough ladycop, though she could be seen as attractive. Nordic. Viking. Someone Beowulf could love.

"About fifteen minutes."

"You know, it's the middle of the day?"

"Yeah, just got done working out. I take night classes."

"You couldn't shower at the gym?" the lady cop asked.

"With a bunch of guys? That's not really my style, ma'am." There was another pause. The two stared each other down. "You looking for an invitation?" Restovich winked at the cop.

She stared him down some more.

"Not today young man." She started to walk away. "Be sure to let us know if you see anyone."

*   *   *   *   *   *   *

"Well played," Nicole smiled. She liked this guy.

"You're going to owe me big, miss?"

"Nicole."

Bob noticed her face had changed a bit from his comment. "I don't mean you're gonna owe me something like that" he said. "I mean you're going to owe me dinner. This has been a terrible first date."

"I dunno," she smiled. "I've had worse."

"Look, we need to get out of here," he said, "My dorm room is across the hall from the bathroom, to the left, two doors down on the right."

"I'm calling the robe," Nicole said.

Nicole slipped out of the shower and slipped into the heavy purple robe. The shower had washed away her all her makeup, revealing a heavily freckled face. Her red hair was straight, and short. It barely covered her ears. Bob was next, throwing the towel around his waist.

"I'll go first, check to see if the coast is clear, and you can follow."

The two made a comical sight, creeping to the door of the bathroom. Bob checked both ways, then pulled her through the door. They half-ran to the door. Bob fumbled with the keys, but soon the door was open and Nicole scuttled in. Bob took one more look down the hall, and realized one of his neighbors had seen the girl. The man, a young Asian, had a big smile and gave Bob a thumbs up.

*   *   *   *   *   *   *

The weather was perfect for a game of toss. Painter, not too athletic and a little awkward, could at the very least throw a football with a good spiral. Gene 'Spags' Zeale was the recipient. He threw to Big Frank Wallace, who was surprisingly fast. Wallace then tossed the football to Kayla Witold. Wallace produced a perfect floating pass that fell into her arms. She, not terribly good at this sort of thing, was able to get a duck back to Painter.

And everything cycled around again.

The group was recruiting on the mall area of campus. It was an open field of grass, with some benches and trees, the crossroads of the main campus. A commons area for students to gather and interact. The perfect fall day made their exercise invigorating and fruitful. The football was a patriotic red white and blue. Several times random people joined in the game. Zan, and for an hour Rachel too, manned a table nearby.

Rachel just spent her lunch hour at the recruiting table. She was their best tool, as she attracted both men and women. The table had various bits of GOP and rightwing literature. There was a copy of the campus right-wing newspaper, a sign-up sheet and there was a big sign saying 'Conservative? So's the rest of America' sitting in front of the table.

It was a relaxing and fun way to find new people. Some came and signed up. Some chatted. Others argued. After four hours, they had found twenty-five new names. A few were interested in the paper. Some wanted to join the College Republicans. It would take some time to find the quality people The Organization wanted, and pass the rest off to other groups like the CRs or the pro-lifers.

The Organization itself didn't have official meetings, just the informal Wednesday night gatherings at the Big Ten. They did go to meetings hosted by other conservative groups, including the CRs. And they held official meetings for the student groups they operated; on Tuesdays the Traditional Values Coalition met, on Thursday it was Pro-Life Coalition, held right after a non-denominational Bible study. The weekends were spent on the paper.

It was a hectic schedule. Often classes were an afterthought.

That was the cost of understanding freedom.

At least the game of toss was fun.

*   *   *   *   *   *   *

Restovich's dorm was small. No more than ten feet wide, and not much longer. There was a desk, stacked with papers and books. One chair, wood. A bed, messy. Some small shelves on the wall were also filled with books. A large window looked out towards the space between Territorial Hall and Centennial. There were stacks of books around the desk. A basket of dirty clothes stood at the foot of the bed. Other than the books, it was a relatively well kept dorm.

Nicole plopped onto the bed and stayed wrapped up in the purple robe, which was incredibly soft and ludicrously large. Without any sense of shame at this point, Bob dressed himself in front of his closet. Although he faced away from her. She peeked. A wide reddish scar stretched from behind his right knee all the way across his butt cheek. Other smaller scars dotted across his legs. Surgical scars running parallel to his spine climbed up his back. His war wounds had obviously been life threatening.

He threw on an old gray Army T-shirt and black running shorts. He also hung up Nicole's blouse and skirt in his closet. She didn't want to wear those clothes again, for fear of them being recognized some day. He put on some cologne, it had a piney odor.

Looking around the dorm, Nicole noticed the books. Other than clothes, the books were the man's only apparent belongings. Most dealt with history. He had all three volumes of Gibbon's 'Decline and Fall of the Roman Empire.' A dozen bookmarks spread throughout the volumes suggested he had good familiarity with the epic work. A couple of Bibles were open on his desk. Then she noticed 'The Unmaking of a Mayor' by William F. Buckley. *What were the odds*, she thought.

"I hope you don't mind me asking," she broke the silence. "Are you political at all?"

"Uh," Restovich didn't know what to say. "I guess you could say that."

"Conservative?" she asked.

"Is it that obvious?"

"Seventy-five percent of military men are, the Bibles and your other books cinched it," Nicole said, revealing she wasn't an unobservant airhead, something she knew most men assumed about all women unless they were explicitly shown otherwise.

"You said you were doing political surveys," Bob said. "I take it you weren't doing it for any academic reasons."

"Nope," she replied. "We were trying to find Republicans."

What are the odds, he thought. "I can see why you might be unpopular."

There was a knock on the door. "Bob, open up," It was the voice of Amanda, Bob's RA. More knocking. "Let's go Bob, we need to talk."

Restovich silently approached the door, making sure not to let his feet come near the door, to hide any shadows that might sneak through the bottom of the door. Leaning in he took a look through the peephole and saw his Residential Adviser, with a police officer. Leaning away silently, he crept back to his bed, leaned over Nicole and whispered "Get naked."

*   *   *   *   *   *   *

CHAPTER 4

Centennial Hall

More knocking. "Damnit Bob, answer the door."

"Would you relax," he shouted back. "I'm trying to find some pants."

Bob removed his shirt and shorts. His boxers were short enough that some of his scars were visible. Going into his desk, he pulled out a chain. On it he had hooked his Purple Heart and Bronze Star medals, along with his old set of dogtags. He threw the chain on. Then he tossed his basket of dirty clothes onto the floor around his bed. He opened the door.

"What's up?" he asked.

"Bob," Amanda spoke first. "This is officer Nelson from UMPD, they've been searching the dorm for a couple of people--"

"Sir," Officer Nelson spoke firmly. "We're looking for two people, a man with brown hair, average build. Was searing a suit. And a blonde woman. Pretty, well tanned. White shirt, black skirt."

"I can't say that I have. Been in my dorm room for most of the day. Why ya lookin' for 'em?"

"They were scamming students out of money," The Officer said. "Then they assaulted me and another officer...We'd really like to track them down. Have you heard anything at all? We think the woman might have been on this floor."

"Nope."

"Can I ask," Officer Nelson's voice got stern, "you were seen with a woman coming out of the showers earlier. Are you alone in there?"

"No, I'm not alone," Restovich said cheerfully. "I'm in here with my ex-wife."

"Excuse me?" Nelson asked. "Your ex-wife?"

"Yeah."

Just then a naked Nicole walked up behind Restovich and put her arms around his waist. He lifted one arm and she popped her head to the side, giving the Officer and the RA a sheepish smile. "Hello," she said, "I'm Nicole."

Officer Nelson stood dumbstruck for a second. He stared intently at the freckled face and frizzy red hair. "So, uh, you two have been together most of the day?"

Nicole nodded her head.

Officer Nelson still looked surprised. But the look on the RA's face was even more priceless. She was a no nonsense black woman, short and heavy. She grew up in North Minneapolis. It took a lot to surprise her. The sight of a naked woman hanging on to the least social resident she had...Well, that was surprising.

The Officer was staring at Nicole. Her face was pale, covered in freckles, soft blue eyes. But mostly, her face showed age.

Bob cleared his throat and asked "is that all?"

"Yeah," Nelson said. "She's obviously not who we're looking for."

"I could have told you that," Bob replied.

"Look, if you see anything else, just call the security desk. We're going to have a policeman there for the rest of the day."

Bob began to close the door when the policeman put his hand out and blocked it.

"One more thing," The officer asked. "Where'd you pick up those medals?"

"Gulf War, I was with the 24th Infantry Division, mechanized, during Desert Storm. Our Bradley ran into an anti-armor mine. Take a look..." Bob lifted the right side of his boxer shorts, showing another scar on his thigh. "You want to see the one on my ass?"

"Maybe later son," The Officer said with a smile. "Have a good day now."

"We will." Nicole said.

They closed the door. Almost afraid to move, they stood as they were. They could hear the Officer and Amanda work their way down the hall, pounding on doors and talking to students. It was a full three minutes before they both began to breathe heavily; as if they had been holding their breath. Then Bob turned suddenly, grabbed Nicole by her waist and shoved her onto his bed. She covered up with a sheet.

Grabbing his chair, sitting in it backwards, facing Nicole, he scolded her with his gaze.

"Scamming students?"

Nicole nodded her head.

"I think it's time you told me the whole story. No more lies or omissions."

And she did. Regular Joe. Where the money went. What they did with the names. Why they did it ('because we really don't like most students'). Then she talked about the encounter with Officer Nelson. How she ended up in the bathroom. How she relied on his manly instincts and on her being a girl. At the end of it, Bob laughed. And laughed hard.

Then they just kept talking. About her job. About her kid. About his wounds. How his Medals on a Chain trick had gotten him out of a dozen speeding tickets. It was two hours before they stopped. He had classes. She needed to pick up her daughter from ballet. They walked to her car. They agreed this adventure constituted at least two dates. They set the third for that very night, at the Big Ten.

*   *   *   *   *   *   *

CHAPTER 5

Wednesday, September 7
Coffman Memorial Union, Room 303

Meetings weren't doing.

They gave the appearance of doing, but it was an illusion-- One many people fall for. Meetings were necessary, but were only successful if they led to a flurry of doing later on. Not only did the leader of a group have to know that meetings weren't doing. He had to convince his audience of the same.

The inability to accomplish this task was pejoratively known by The Organization as 'CR Disease.' The College Republicans got people to attend meetings. They were a brand, that was their power. But most of these people were worthless. They did not want to do stuff unless it involved beer or negotiating the reproductive act. The CRs were a social entity to these people.

And a good leader could use this to his advantage. Volunteering on campaigns could be very social. As long as you had a good supply of both genders. Worthless chair sitters were turned into useful assets. But no matter what, these people were a drag. They weren't smart. They weren't motivated. They were apathetic and lazy, a universal plague.

Nolan Painter, one of the CR vice-chairs, was attending the first CR meeting of the semester. And was bored to death. Nothing but introductions and storytelling. Frustrated, at the end of the meeting Nolan Painter asked for volunteers to poster for Allen Quist that night. Quist was the endorsed Republican candidate for Governor. Arne Carlson, though the sitting governor, had failed to win support of the GOP base. Carlson was running in the primary against Quist, and Minnesota had open primaries. You could register election day, without any ID, declare yourself in any party and vote in their primary. It was fun.

Carlson was a popular governor. Liberal. Irresolute. Everything to everybody. He was polling well, both in the general election and in the primary. But primaries in non-presidential years were notorious for low voter turnout. A few thousand votes could swing an upset. And there were forty thousand students on campus.

Three people volunteered to help Painter.

The rest went barhopping.

The curse of democracy.

*   *   *   *   *   *   *

Nolan took the three volunteers to the Big Ten and introduced them to some of the other undergrads in the group: Kayla, Spags and Frank. Chris Berg, Orson Henning and some other alumni were there, but they sat at another table. You have to be careful with your new recruits. You don't start out postering obnoxious prevarications at two o'clock in the morning in February. And you definitely don't introduce them to the misanthropes and nihilists in the group.

That's stuff you work into.

Zan was not there. The breakup with Alisha was going to complicate his mission on campus. Zan would meet up with Nolan and the new recruits on the steps of Northrup Auditorium at 9 o'clock that night.

At the Big Ten everything stayed informal. The conversation was mostly extemporaneous bullshit, with a little politico mixed in. Fifteen minutes to nine, Nolan, Kayla, Frank, Spags and the new recruits left to poster. The alumni stayed.

At nine Nicole arrived at the Big Ten, dressed in a black tank top and blue jeans. She figured there was no need to try to impress her date.

Restovich arrived not long after.

*   *   *   *   *   *   *

"Alright guys," Spags spoke softly; the acoustics amongst the huge pillars in front of Northrup were such that there was no need to talk above a whisper. "It's pretty simple. Grab a can of spray adhesive and a stack of posters."

The posters were big 11x17 inch bright pink monstrosities which said:

Help the DFL
Vote Allen Quist
In the GOP Primary

THE EDUCATOR

"Okay, let's see," Spags surveyed the crew. "Frank, you go with Red." Spags pointed a one of the new recruits, his hair bright red. "Kayla, go with Tall Guy; I'll take Buzzcut."

"We have names, you know," said Buzzcut.

"Not yet you don't," Spags replied.

*   *   *   *   *   *   *

"So Joe jams his clipboard into the cop's stomach and take's off like Carl Lewis," Nicole was retelling the story of the day's escapades to the crew. "Now we're in for assaulting a police officer and evasion. That dumb fuck. They only had us for trespassing. That's a fine. The burden of proof was on them to show we were running a scam. And no way that happens, we just needed to stop talking to them."

"So then what?" Chris Berg

"So then I took out my pepper spray and gave the other cop two seconds of peppery goodness. Then I ran. Get lost in that fucking mausoleum of a dorm, and hid in a bathroom stall."

"This is where I come in," Restovich said cheerfully.

"Yeah, he's taking a shower. I dump my disguise and try to sneak out. By this time the whole dorm is freaking out. There are people running, shouting. It's crazy...so I, uh" She began to laugh.

"You what?" Berg was loving the story, but Nicole's voice had suddenly changed. "Come'on, you're the worst storyteller ever."

"I take off my clothes, and jump in the shower with this guy." The table began to laugh. "It's the only thing I could think to do."

Together, the two expanded on the story. The cop in the bathroom. The confrontation with the other cop. More nudity. More laughter. Nicole failed to mention she had been scared shitless every moment from when Joe took off to the very minute she picked up her daughter from ballet. Nicole wore the blue sapphire ring of the Israel Bissell Society. She would never admit to being scared.

"Aren't you a little worried," Henning asked, "that they'll have your fingerprints from the flyers you were passing out?"

"Oh gosh," Nicole blushed at the thought. "I didn't even think about that."

"You ever been arrested?" Chris Berg asked.

"No."

"Then don't worry about it," Berg said. "We host the Minnesota Forensics Database on our servers at the U."

"What?" Nicole was confused.

"Yeah, we host the whole database. Every fingerprint taken from evidence or arrests in the state of Minnesota gets put in one place. I'll watch for the next few weeks. If they upload any new fingerprints from the UMPD, I'll just change them."

"You'll change the fingerprints?"

"Yeah, I was one of the grad students who developed the software. I'll just hit the server with a virus or something. Go in, change the code, and adjust a file or two. Piece of cake. Then they won't ever be able to link you to the assault. You just can't get arrested for the next year or so, until I'm sure everything has been added."

"What about the originals?" Henning asked.

"They don't manually do this stuff anymore," Berg replied. "They'd only check that if they caught her. There might be a backup copy of the originals on a computer at UMPD. They go through computers like crazy. We're always getting orders from them. But you'd be out of the statewide system. So, just don't get arrested on-campus by UMPD."

"Don't intend to," Nicole said.

"You can seriously do all that?" Henning was surprised.

"I could do all that even if I had to hack the thing off-site," Berg said. "All these systems have huge security holes. Doing it with the access I have is child's play."

Berg stroked his beard. Computers were the only thing that made him sexually confident. He waved at their server, who was not Alisha Williams this day, "Hey beer-wench, another Hamm's, huh?"

*   *   *   *   *   *   *

"Horace is gone, he and Rachel broke up."

Painter and Zan were walking back to the Big Ten. Seniors didn't poster when they didn't have to.

Zan wasn't going to the Big Ten, he was going to continue on to Oak Street Ramp to meet up with Tass. Zan didn't know the rules of breaking up, since he had been in relationships with women only a couple of times, so his strategy was avoidance.

"That means Rachel's basically gone to," Zan replied. "You never lose one or the other, you always lose both."

"Well that sucks," said Painter. "That means no hottie. And no Black guy. It handcuffs our recruiting plan, and without a Black guy we can't do any affirmative action stuff...Or anything else too confrontational."

"So we'll find one." Zan sighed. "Or not. It's an election year, so we won't have time to do anything crazy anyway."

"Yeah, it's an election year, and we're supposed to be recruiting lots of people. We should have access to hot chicks, Black guys, Mexicans and anyone else we'll need for trouble-making."

Zan shrugged; he was less and less concerned with these

problems. They walked for a bit without talking.

"So," Painter asked. "You seriously going to avoid the Big Ten until Alisha sells the thing."

"That place is a dump anyway."

As they walked towards the rear entrance of The Big Ten, they saw two people scurry hand-in-hand towards the dorm. Zan recognized Nicole as the little redhead in the black tank top. The man he didn't know.

"They're in a hurry," Painter observed.

"Yeah, she's running out of time to find Mr. Right."

*　　*　　*　　*　　*　　*　　*

Oak Street Ramp is a couple blocks from The Big Ten. Walking alone, Zan stuck to the alleyway. At night this stretch felt like the urban wastelands of T.S. Eliot. In the day it wasn't so dramatic. Zan enjoyed long walks. More so as he got older. He could be alone with his thoughts. Too soon the well lit concrete hulk of the ramp was before him. Lugubriously he walked towards the attendant's booth, expecting Tass and his normal irreverent conversation.

He wasn't expecting Regular Joe.

"Joe," Zan greeted. "I thought you were hiding out in the country somewhere."

Tass and Joe turned from their conversation and salutations were exchanged.

"I got something for ya," Joe said. He quickly ran over to his car and back. He threw a backpack into his hands.

"What's this?"

"The names and dorm addresses of a hundred and twenty possible recruits in the Superblock," Joe replied. "Plus a hundred bucks worth of slush fund money. Nicole and I pulled the Recruiter Gag."

Zan had not heard the story yet, and Tass insisted. So Joe gave a rundown on the entire episode from his perspective. It ended in a hearty laugh all around. Joe didn't know the details of Nicole's escape, but he paraphrased the profanity-laced message she left on his answering machine earlier that evening.

More laughter.

The three lunatics stayed at it until one in the morning.

Joe and Tass drove off.

Zan wandered around a bit.

Then he made a decision, and worked his way back to the Big Ten.

*　　*　　*　　*　　*　　*　　*

CHAPTER 6

Big Ten

Alisha Williams avoided The Roundtable crew all night.

But eventually their prodding was enough to get her to say hello.

First she sat with them for a bit. Then an hour. It sounded like they were taking her side over Zan's. They laughed at him. Made her feel comfortable. She didn't know if this was authentic or if they were just being nice so she wouldn't stop serving their minors. She decided it was a little of both. And she didn't care. They spent a lot of money in her bar, and she wasn't going to let the personal get in the way of business.

It took half an hour after closing time for everyone to filter out. She decided to do some paperwork, balance out all her registers and do a quick review of her alcohol stock. It was important to get everything set for the next weekend. Gopher football had their first home game. Thousands of students were going to be out searching for hangouts. It took an hour.

Her car was parked out back in a little parking area for employees and her renters, graduate students (her rule) who lived in the apartments she had above the bar. She drove a green Ford Taurus. She walked out the back entrance, around the chain link fence to her car. She hadn't noticed the dark figure leaning against her car. But when she finally did, she instantly recognized Zan.

*   *   *   *   *   *   *

Zan was trying to apologize. Trying to win her back. To ameliorate their longtime friendship. She was incredulous. Then angry. Then sardonic. Then angry again.

Then the shouting.

A peace agreement was not forthcoming. The argument danced on the edge of a domestic dispute.

Then it fell off the edge.

"What the fuck is wrong with you?" Alisha was shouting. "Did you really think I'd just forget what you did to me, how you made me feel, fucking seriously?"

"Alright, alright," Zan was retreating away from Alisha. "I was just trying to find a way to get along here."

She was silent for a second. Her face red with anger. Hair strands fluttered about her face. The night was quiet again.

"Look," She spoke softly, the tension left her body. "This sort of thing hurts, okay Zan..."

"Yeah, I know...But we can--"

Zan was interrupted by a scream and a charge. Alisha took two steps towards him while spraying him with Mace. It caught him off guard and he fell backwards, the only evasive maneuver he could think of. When he landed, he felt the sharp pain of his testicles being smashed by Alisha's steel toed low boots. Then another sharp pain as those same steel toed boots hit his ribcage.

"You think you can call me a whore!" She shouted. "Fuck you motherfucker."

He stayed down, blinded by the Mace. The sound of her car door opening and shutting. An engine starting. A car driving away. She was gone.

A minute went by. Zan got up, and was trying to wipe the chemicals off his face when someone grabbed him and stood him up against the chain link fence.

"What the fuck you doin?" A deep masculine voice asked. "What were you going to do to her, huh?"

The question came with a punch to the gut.

"You think you can pull this shit around here?" Another punch to the gut. "You can't."

The next punch landed across Zan's face. "Were you going to rob her?" A punch. "Rape her?"

Zan instinctively ducked.

He guessed right, the man had been winding up to hit his face. The man's fist slammed into the fence.

Zan's fists went to a body-body-uppercut combo. Right fist gut; left fist rib cage, right fist uppercut to the man's face. Zan was shocked, his upper cut found it's mark, somewhere above his own head. The guy was tall. And big. But the combo had knocked the guy out, and he tumbled to the ground, on top of Zan.

Crawling out from under the guy, one of Zan's hands found a tooth. He couldn't tell if it was his tooth or the other guy's. He tossed it as hard as he could. Then he stumbled his way back to his car, safely parked in Oak Street Ramp.

*　　　*　　　*　　　*　　　*　　　*　　　*

Malcolm Paulson admired his work.

The Bell Museum of Natural History was located across from the Armory on the U of M's east bank campus. Its West Gallery was the home of traveling arts and science exhibits. A new exhibit came by every couple of weeks. The latest exhibit highlighted the evolution of mankind. It contained fossils of human ancestors like Homo Erectus and a full-mounted skeleton of a Neanderthal; plus an assortment of human skeletal remains up to the last ice age. The exhibit also contained artwork devoted to the evolution of humans.

Paulson was struggling to find a way to dispose of Sandy's body. He'd been keeping her in the freezer at his cabin, underneath three hundred pounds of deer meat. This traveling exhibit didn't offer a complete solution, but it did get rid of one way of identifying Sandy's remains. He boiled the flesh off of Sandy's skull. Using the grime he pulled from his household vacuum cleaner, he gave the skull a faux-antique finish. He picked open a display case and replaced one of the human skulls on display with Sandy.

She was now on exhibit, next to a reconstructed skull from a Neanderthal.

Tomorrow, the exhibit would be packed up and shipped out.

Paulson dropped off the other skull in Pillsbury Hall, in an unmarked cardboard box.

Walking to his car, he could hardly contain his elation.

*   *   *   *   *   *   *

CHAPTER 7

11am Thursday, September 8
Coffman Memorial Union; Ground Floor Tabling Area

"So she Maced you," Painter was relishing every word of the story, "kicked you in the balls, and left. Then some random dude started kicking your ass, and you dropped him?"

"And I found a tooth. Don't forget that."

Painter started to laugh heartily. "And...you...thought this'd be a good idea...how?"

"I thought the bitch would at least talk to me before kicking me in the balls."

Zan sat back in his chair. A black eye decorated his face. Whenever he brought his can of pop to his face, his bruised and swollen right hand was noticeable. He and Nolan Painter were tabling on the ground floor of Coffman. Students filtered in and out of the food court area in search of lunch.

It was passive recruiting. There was a lot of serendipity involved.

It wasn't efficient. But it had upsides. It gave conservatives a noticeable presence on campus. It was a chance for interaction. Arguments sprang up. Tabling sharpened the persuasive charm or argumentative wit. It was also a chance to study, relax, converse. UMAH, the University of Minnesota Atheists and Humanists, spent their time at the tables playing Risk or Magic the Gathering.

THE EDUCATOR

"And what chick wears fucking steel-toe boats?"

On the table before them were life-sized pregnancy models, showing human development from seven weeks to nine months. Key-chains with little plastic fetus feet and pamphlets with pictures of aborted fetuses were available to interested persons.

Zeale and Kayla walked by, holding hands, and went to get lunch together. They waved at Painter and Zan.

"That just pisses me off," Zan said as the couple disappeared into the lunch lines.

"Two people eating lunch together pisses you off, but you think getting pepper-sprayed and kicked in the balls is something to brag about."

"I found the guy's tooth," Zan retorted. "How often do you get to do that?"

"Seriously, what's the problem with Spags and Kayla?" Painter asked.

"It's practically a death sentence." Zan took a drink. "And it's not some guy on the outer edges. It's my own lieutenant. Our top guy. And the chick is one of our future all stars...it's a fucking disaster."

"I dunno," Painter said. "I thought we had lost Kayla to that fat guy with the huge arms. But now she's back in the fold."

"Where's Horace?" Zan was lecturing now. "Where's Rachel? Single, they did a bunch of stuff. Dating, they still showed up, and sometimes were decent. Now they have to avoid us. We've been tainted with the memory of their bad relationship."

"Doesn't mean we're going to lose Zeale...he was initiated. You don't turn back after that."

"Look at my face," Zan turned to face Painter. "This is how an amicable sexual relationship is ended."

They were interrupted by a short and attractive woman who stopped in front of their table. She was almost as good looking as Rachel. Thinner, less curvy, shorter. Painter like to describe her as 'homegrown.' She had an attractive face that always carried a dour expression. Golden blonde hair stretched down to her waist in long waves. A plain white t-shirt and tight-fitting blue jeans finished the rural-girl-next-door look.

It was Melissa Hughes. She ran one of the pro-life pregnancy resource centers on campus; the Protestant one.

Momentarily, she smiled. This completely changed the shape of her face; for a brief moment it looked like she could star in a romantic comedy as the hometown girl who wins over the uptight city boy. But just as suddenly the dour face returned.

"Hey Zan, Hey Nol," Her voice had a melodic cadence. But cold, like a cheerful executioner.

"Hey Mel," Painter returned.

"It's good to see you guys tabling," she said. Neither gentleman responded. After an awkward moment, she walked over to another table and grabbed an empty chair and dragged it over. She sat down at the end of the table, perpendicular to the two men. A negotiating distance, but one close enough where both men could smell her perfume.

She could be quite intoxicating. Dour face and all.

She started talking.

No longer so intoxicating.

*   *   *   *   *   *   *

The old slur against pro-lifers, promoted most famously by George Carlin, was they were people you wouldn't want to fuck in the first place. It may have been true in his day and among his peers, but it wasn't true on modern college campuses. Pro-life activists, the women anyway, were some of the hottest chicks around. Among the campus activists, they were easily the most attractive. And conversely, the pro-choice activists were the opposite. Generally, the only attractive thing about the abortion advocates was they were whores.

The men were a different story. No one wanted to sleep with the pro-life guys. Most of them didn't like sex anyway. Didn't even enjoy having sex. Didn't like the thought of sex. Especially when having sex. They were disgusted by sex. Men without their natural sex drive lacked motivation or determination. Thus, in the pro-life movement the men were marginalized. They took a backseat to the women. There were consequences to this; Pro-life groups didn't have any edge.

They rarely participated in campus debates. Their speaker events were small and boring. Nothing was done to create discussion on the topic on campus. Mostly, these pro-life groups bought diapers, counseled pregnant students, held candlelight vigils on the anniversary of Roe or offered sidewalk counseling outside of abortion clinics. Legitimate? yes. Productive? not really. Some women were talked out of abortion. But opinions on the issue itself remained stagnant.

In The Organization, the chicks still ruled. They were the public face of The Movement on campus. But the men still had their say. Cocks think about politics differently. The men brought The Edge. The Edge was necessary to create discussion. It was impossible just to start a discussion about abortion. You had to force it. Pictures of aborted fetuses started conversations. Life-sized plastic fetuses hanging like Christmas ornaments from trees around campus? Arguments. The Edge worked.

These little events spurred a storm of earned media.

From there the women took over, with their soft lisps and

motherly demeanor.

The Organization had only nominal control over one of the pro-life groups on campus, The Pro-Life Coalition. It was made up of members from the other student groups; Life Affirmation was the Catholic group; The Campus Pregnancy Resource Center was the Protestant group. These groups did their own thing, in the background, earned almost no media and rarely changed a mind. The Traditional Values Coalition, always run by someone from The Organization, did most of the actual anti-abortion activism. Bringing in speakers and guerrilla advertising. Unfortunately, the Values Coalition was always spread thin, trying to cover all conservative issues.

Rachel Anderson had filled the gap. Pretty, smart and loquacious. The *joie de vivre* of the pro-lifers on campus. She led the Pro-life Coalition and did so well. She was a middle ground between the cocks in The Organization and the rest of the pro-lifers on campus.

No longer.

Now she was a senior, working a job and had worries beyond the campus. Life, the universe and everything. She was going to be pretty worthless. The question was how to fill her role. Managers needed to have a plan for every 'what-if' scenario. People change. They leave. They get sick. They go crazy. Zan, the presumptive middle manager, had been meditating on this problem.

Kayla Witold could take over The Pro-life Coalition. Zan couldn't tell if she wanted to, and he hadn't asked her yet. But, in the end, she was just not pretty enough to lead a pro-life group. Zan asked her to take a position in the Traditional Values Coalition, and she enthusiastically agreed. Her presence would deflect external accusations of misogyny in TVC while staying out of the spotlight. At least until she became more polished.

Sans Rachel, Zan was left with trying to find a new recruit to lead the group, let a man do it, or surrender control to another pro-lifer outside of the group. The best option was to let an outsider have at it for a year. There were dangers though. The Coalition had its own bank account with a few thousand dollars. Big money as far as student groups are concerned. There was also the chance the outsider would take the money and incorporate the Coalition into its own group.

Melissa wanted the group. She had called around. Left messages. Contacted the Student Group Activities Adviser. Been a pest. Zan had unilaterally decided the group should go to Melissa anyway, with no other options available it just made sense. But Zan knew he should not make it easy, either. The more hoops Mel had to go through to achieve her ends, the more appreciation she would have for the result.

Melissa kept talking.

Painter was nodding along with Melissa, pretending to listen, making eye contact. Melissa was the master of the filibuster. She spoke with no pauses. No breaks. No noticeable breathing Leaning in and out. Occasionally touching the arm of Painter. Zan figured she knew, had to know, that men just tuned out her relentless soliloquy.

Zan tuned back in,

"...and look, it's very important to not only deliver this message but deliver it in the right way. This is what I want to do with the coalition and I already have the support of the other officers, but the Activities Adviser showed us the constitution of the group explicitly states leadership changes outside of end-of-year elections must be approved by the rules committee, which happens to be made up of you guys from TVC. So I'd really like to get this transition done and revitalize the group without any delay."

She stopped. It shocked the male duo back to the conversation.

"What did you mean," Zan asked, "when you said the message needs to be delivered in the 'right way'?"

Melissa pulled a folded piece of paper out of the back pocket of her blue jeans. She unfolded it and tossed it into Painter's lap. It was a poster from the previous year, with the picture of a hangar on it and the words "Yes you would you Godless babykillers" in bold block letters.

"This is the sort of offensive nonsense that gives our movement a bad rap. I know what you guys think you're doing is right but it's no way to persuade people. Less confrontational methods will change hearts and I really think with your help we can--"

"Melissa," Zan interrupted. "Relax. We agree with you."

"What?" Melissa was a bit shocked.

"Sure. Maybe things got a little out of hand last year." Zan saw the look of disbelief on Painter's face but ignored it. "We'd be happy to let you take the reins of The Pro-Life Coalition."

Melissa was silent.

"Of course, we have to track down Rachel, she still has the checkbook and she's the only one with access to the account. Orson Henning, last year's treasurer, is not even living in the state anymore. But I'll get everyone on the rules committee to send a letter to the Activities Adviser that a change has been approved. Nol here will contact you when everything is set."

She shook hands with the men, thanked them and left.

Painter leaned over the table to watch her leave. "I do love those jeans," he said. "So what was all that shit about giving her the group? That's a lot of money."

"We didn't have anyone else," he replied. "Besides, we can find more money."

Painter shrugged. Both men knew Zan was right.

Unfortunately, it meant another year of pussy pro-life activism.

*   *   *   *   *   *   *

"I know you didn't get to meet him," Painter tried getting the images of a naked Melissa out of his head through talking. "But Nicole found a quality recruit during her little escapade...Bob Restovich."

"Ya ya, I talked to her about it on the phone this morning," Zan replied. "But I think it's trouble. They're already fucking each other. She's got a kid, he's going to school. He's in his mid-twenties. It's not going to work out."

"I dunno. I think it can. Restovich is going to help us tonight. We're lit-dropping the dorms."

"Military guys are never great activists. Sometimes they're good activists, but never great. They've got other things on their minds, and they consider themselves to have already served God and Country."

Spags and Kayla walked up to the table, hand-in-hand, their lunch done.

"What's going on?" Painter asked.

"Not much," Spags returned. "Any luck?"

"It's been alright," Zan spoke. "Fifteen signatures, a few of them had email. No hardcores among 'em though."

The four talked a while. About the pizza at the Pizza Shack. About Rod Grams. About Melissa. The weather. Lit-dropping. That communist who writes for the Minnesota Daily. Fifteen minutes later they said their goodbyes. Kayla and Spags walked off, hand-in-hand.

"Disgusting." Zan said. "Couplehood is such a disease."

"You're just mad because your little rose kicked you in the balls."

"That means I know," Zan said forcefully. "I know it's a disease."

Just then a woman approached the table, and without comment she put her name down on the sign-up sheet. She was just under five feet tall with platinum blonde hair pulled into a ponytail, a scattering of bangs on her forehead. Her skin was flawless porcelain. She wore a collared white dress shirt, unbuttoned to her bra line. She was chesty, with breasts larger than a girl her size should have, but well-proportioned. She wore a beaded rosary, the crucifix of which dropped provocatively into her cleavage.

Silver blue eyes reflected light like mirrors. She wore a perpetual smile on a classically feminine face centered around a button nose. The makeup on her face was very light, a touch of eyeliner and lipstick the only evidence she wore the stuff. She had a perfect hour-glass shape, postured with the help of high heels, which didn't take away from the grace of her movement. A black, knee-length A-line skirt finished the presentation.

"Hi!," she said. "My name is Tonya. Tonya Evans."

"I'm Nolan, the punching bag is Zan."

"Oooh, look at you," she spoke with real empathy. "Did some babykiller do this to you?"

"No," Zan replied. "Some random guy beat me up on the street."

"Seriously?"

"Yeah, people see me and they just have to start pounding my face."

She laughed at Zan. Infectious. She sat down on the chair Melissa had left at the table. She talked. And laughed. And talked. And talked. Occasionally she purred. She talked about herself. She was local. Freshman. Very Catholic. Hated Abortionists. Was disgusted by all the 'whores' on campus. Mentioned she had already gotten in trouble for arguing with a professor. Nolan invited her to do some activism, that day. They were going to be handing out flyers on the bridge that afternoon. She had a class, but would join them right after. Then she left, after spending an hour at the table.

"She's perfect," Nolan said after she left.

"No shit."

"You know what this means?"

"Yeah, we have replaced our Hot Chick with a Hotter Chick." Zan said. "Still, we gotta remain skeptical."

"Damnit, she's fucking *perfect*." Nolan reiterated.

*   *   *   *   *   *   *

A Jaffy. Until someone had some experience under their belt, they were just a Jaffy.

Jaffy was 'Just Another Fucking First Year' and it was the preferred freshman pejorative. All college freshman were accustomed to being the big fish in high school. They were smart, there were fewer people, they were often popular, did lots of extracurriculars. This made them narcissists. They had yet to deal with the challenges of college life, when they were no longer the big fish, and the pond was huge.

You had to break this attitude down, or you ended up with an insufferable blowhard.

And there were too many insufferable blowards in the world already.

Sometimes Jaffys respodend to their new environment by

shrinking from the challenge. To disappear. Avoid. This led to despair. People would wrap themselves in their own world to avoid the complications of life outside. Others turned to hedonism. Or nihilism. Few found balance on their own. At least not in the necessary time frame for campus activists. The cure was easy.

Work.

But this didn't come naturally.

It was a sad truth that most students at college did with their new-found freedom and independence what most people do with their freedom and independence. Nothing.

Marxists had been writing for years about awakening the proletariat and initiating the final revolution that would free mankind. Action was power. Once the masses realized their slavery a violent uprising would result in a utopia. Action! Power! Revolution!

In reality people preferred to stay at rest.

Change is hard, inactivity easy.

When given a choice between watching TV and taking a moonlight stroll in autumn, most people pick TV. It's not just solitary late night strolls people are lax on: working on cars, carpentry projects and even bowling have become endangered. Life throws more sedentary distractions at people than ever, and they yield to it without resistance.

This is the reason The Organization strictly enforces activity in its members. New recruits get very little downtime. It was a lesson learned from the Marxists. Their activists were the best, even if there weren't many of them. Zan made sure new recruits were given something to do right away, preferably within hours of the first meeting.

Social pressure worked magic. If a Jaffy mentioned a desire to host an event, they would be forced to attempt it. This once resulted in a Christian rock concert on campus, all done by the Jaffy. If someone expressed interest in learning a martial art, an upperclassmen would have them in a class the next day.

The Law of Do.

New members weren't allowed to waste time sitting in their dorm rooms. The older students found something for them to do.

At three-thirty, after getting lunch together, Nolan and Zan joined Zeale and Kayla on the Washington Avenue Bridge to pass out flyers for Allen Quist. Tonya found them, and immediately went about stepping in front of students returning from afternoon classes and thrusting the flyers into their personal space.

The flyers were the miniature versions of the posters the group had been putting up. They said "Help get the DFL into the Governor's Mansion, Vote for Allen Quist this Tuesday".

Zan and Nolan placed themselves strategically to watch Tonya. She fearlessly thrust herself into people's way, despite her small size. She talked. Flirted. Shouted. Intimidated. Laughed. Some of the men enjoyed having an attractive woman notice them. Still, most wanted to be left alone. It was hard to break down the walls of apathy.

Tonya was willing to do what was necessary to break those walls.

She was Jaffy, but Zan knew she was also a future All Star.

* * * * * * *

Zan drove back to his place in Northeast; he had enough time to go for a quick three mile jog and shower. There was a strategy meeting to get to, then he was going to help with the dorm lit-drops that night. The jog was slow. Knees were in pain. Age.

When he was done he took some aspirin and hopped in the shower. The phone rang, but he ignored it. There were a few messages on his phone, so he played them as he was getting ready.

"Hi Zan, it's me, Alisha...I wanted to apologize for last night, I'm embarrassed I did that...I'm really sorry, but, uh, you know, girls are the same...right? They're the same their entire lives, no matter how old they get. And I'm a girl. Crazy, you know?

"But I wanted you to know I'm really sorry, and I want you to start coming back to the Big Ten. There's no reason to avoid it, Zan, you've been going there for a long time...we've known each other for years.

"...I'd really like to stay friends..."

This continued for a while.

"Anyway, I gotta go. I'll try and call you later..."

Zan deleted the message. Then the rest of the messages, without listening to them.

Before he left, he went downstairs, to the backyard of the house, and punched a heavy bag he had set up back there. He let loose for ten full minutes, without stopping. No gloves. No tape.

His hands were bleeding by the time he was done.

Another shower.

* * * * * * *

You've never had a truly fulfilling burger until you've visited the St. Clair Broiler in St. Paul. On the menu the size of the burger is listed at a half-pound. But it is the heaviest half-pound burger in the state. The Broiler is family-friendly, has hearty portions, locally-grown ingredients and an atmosphere heavy in Minnesota Nice.

There are a lot of family-owned restaurants in Minnesota. Or at least, they pretend to be family-owned. But it was nice anyway.

Eating at one of these restaurants feels like a family reunion or a large neighborhood BBQ. Minnesotans never let anything get in the way of good food.

This was what politics in Minnesota was all about, food. Like any major city in the United States, the Twin Cities had hundreds of great restaurants. What was different was the kind of food you received. Minnesotans have high standards, but nothing fancy. Meat has to be fresh and of very high quality, vegetables too as they are available at farmer's markets, everything has to be flavorful, creams need to be really creamy. But most importantly, portions had to be huge.

Yes, food plays a major roll in politics everywhere. But it's a matter of degree. Minnesotans love the food more than the politics. Staff meetings are held at restaurants. Fundraisers are held in restaurants. Politicos spent their free time in restaurants. It takes a toll on one's physique. But when winter temperatures easily reach that spot on the thermometer where Celsius and Fahrenheit equate, people stop caring about their abs.

Spags, Zan and Painter were shown a seat. All three ordered a burger. After a few minutes of typical male bloviation, they were joined by a young man. Blue t-shirt and black blue jeans. Wore a beaded hemp necklace. Five and a half feet tall. Redhead. Blue eyes. Pale. Thin. The man sat down without introducing himself.

He didn't need to. Painter and Spags recognized him as Colin Tvrdik, the president of the U-DFL.

"Hi Colin," Painter said. "Whatcha doin tonight?"

"My uncle wanted to meet up with me."

"Who's your uncle?" Painter asked

"Him." Colin pointed at Zan.

*   *   *   *   *   *   *

Minnesota has a strange political history. One unique compared to other states. The Farmer-Labor Party had been a significant force in Minnesota, distinct from the Democrats in the state until a merger was negotiated in 1944. Now affiliated with the national Democratic Party, it kept its hybrid name, DFL, though there were no differences in policy matters between the two entities. This is why it is sometimes confusing to talk to a Minnesota Republican, who constantly complains about the DFL and DFLers.

The University-DFL chapter at the U was a formidable organization. It had access to thousands of potential activists. It could raise thousands of dollars, and they could raise it fast. Their favorite fundraisers were Date Auctions. In a U-DFL date auction, there was a pretty good chance for a fuck. So it was popular.

Colin had been elected U-DFL chair with ease. As the previous vice-chair he was popular and hardworking. And particularly brutal against Republicans in the press. Nolan didn't like him. At least, he assumed he didn't like him.

"You're Zan's nephew?" Painter asked, disbelieving.

"Damn right," Colin replied with a smile.

"Remember, I was adopted," Zan said. "My parents adopted three of us, but had four of their own. And all but me have kids now. Colin is my oldest nephew, an actual Tvrdik."

"Wait, you're a Tvrdik?" Spags asked Zan, a laugh ready to burst out.

"And that's the kind of bullshit that forced me to change my name," Zan replied.

"Uncle Zan and I have been preparing for this for like, uh, seven years, at least," Colin said. "I can't believe it's actually worked out."

"So you're a fucking conservative," Painter said.

"That's right," Colin said. "Saved by the Blood of Christ. A warrior for all that is right in the world."

"So you're really a Tvrdik? As in Zan Tvrdik?" Spags again.

"Jonathan Tvrdik, before the name change," Colin corrected.

"So how'd you come up with 'Chin-Wu'?" Spags asked.

"It sounded Asiany," Zan said.

"Wait," Painter interjected, "We have control over the fucking U-DFL?"

"Nominal control, yes," Colin said.

They all talked about the scam for the next few minutes. How long it took. How whack liberals were (most of them were good folks though, according to Colin). Why he had gone through it all for three years.

"Zan wanted me to meet up with you guys," Colin said. "I've got some goodies for you."

He reached into his backpack. He pulled out a binder filled with paper.

"I have the names of three hundred or so Republicans. We did a campus survey, the results of which, by the way, we'll be releasing to the Daily soon, for bragging rights. It shows how the campus is all liberal and all; anyway, I was able to convince the group that canvassing was just a bad idea, so we did the big survey instead. Helped us find a thousand people to register, but it's better than the alternative. Plus I can help you guys out too--"

"So you're sabotaging the U-DFL?" Spags asked.

"Not quite," Colin replied. "There's only so much I can do. We still have to be active. But I can waste a lot of resources on meaningless shit. I don't think we've sent a single person to a swing district.

We haven't done any real canvassing. After the primary, I'm hoping to keep everyone working on the John Marty for Governor campaign."

"Zan, this is absolutely brilliant," Painter said, impressed.

"Oh, it was his idea," Zan replied.

"Also, we're going to push the Allen Quist thing," Colin said. "I figure we should be able to turn out a thousand votes for Quist on Tuesday."

The excitement lasted for a few minutes, but then Colin got up from the table.

"Gotta go," he said. "You can't be too careful. And remember, you didn't see me, you don't know me, except you hate me, and I hate you."

Then he left.

*   *   *   *   *   *   *

CHAPTER 8

2am Friday, September 9
Centennial Hall's Basement

The basement of Centennial Hall was dark and cool. Lit by fluorescent light alone, like the rest of the aged dorm, it gave an atmosphere of melancholy and urban decline. That matched the basement, since it was in desperate need of repair. Half of the ceiling tiles were missing. Most of the other half were stacked in the corners of all the rooms in the labyrinth of rooms and hallways that made up what was supposed to be a collection of recreational and study areas.

Cobwebs filled with dust and grime hung from the skeletal framework which once held up the ceiling tiles. The carpets were worn out. Filthy. Disgusting. Instead of a nice commons, students at Centennial got a grim basement. It was a nice result for those who didn't mind dark places. Nolan and Bob were playing ping pong in a large and empty room, on an old table with fading paint and innumerable chips around the edges.

Restovich supplied the paddles, balls and the net for the table. The originals had long been lost to the tragedy of the commons. Zan and Zeale didn't care to play, but Painter was a closet aficionado of the sport. The two had been going at it for two hours.

The two noncombatants spent their time conspiring.

After the St. Clair Broiler, the crew hit The Village Wok, right next to The Big Ten on Washington Avenue. They stayed there, enjoying fried rice, tea and fried cheese wontons until one-thirty in the morning, when they had moved to the basement of Centennial. They were waiting for the witching hour; three-thirty in the morning, when they were least likely to encounter an embodied soul.

Politics was like war. There's a lot of downtime; a lot of boredom; a lot of tedious work; packed in between periods of unstoppable action. Except in politics the action generally wasn't lethal. It was waiting for war, in Kuwait, that made Bob a table tennis nut. Now it absorbed what little free-time he had.

Just after three, one of the campus security guards came down to the basement. Restovich greeted him, they shook hands, then the security guard turned and left abruptly.

"What the hell was that about?" Zan asked.

Restovich raised a large ring of keys and shook them. "I told you I could get access to all the dorms on the Superblock."

"Sonofabitch," Nolan said. "How'd you swing that?"

"That security guard is ROTC," Bob returned. "I saw him doing PT with a platoon of army guys one morning. So I introduced myself, showed him my ass, and my Bronze Star."

"And that worked?" Spags asked.

"Damn right it did." Bob said, "military guys speak their own language. But we better not cause any problems with the police."

"Well," Zan said, "When has that ever been the case?"

*   *   *   *   *   *   *

Malcolm Paulson clicked away on the Wilson Library computer.

It was after-hours, and Paulson had used his own set of keys to get in. He needed to access a computer that wasn't his own.

Forensic science was advancing in huge leaps. Five years ago, taking a fingerprint off a cadaver's flesh was a pipe-dream. Now it was fact.

The little redhead crack addict.

Paulson found out fingerprints had been taken off the woman's neck.

So, he was changing the fingerprint file in the Minnesota Forensics Database. Adjusting it just enough so the algorithm would fail to match his set, were he arrested.

Paulson's fingerprints were already in the system, as part of the original promotion of the system. Those fingerprints he had adjusted a long time ago. Still, were he arrested again, it was important not to get copped for any past crimes.

It took fifteen minutes.

Paulson was pissed it took him so long.

*   *   *   *   *   *   *

THE EDUCATOR

In groups of two, Zan's crew walked down the halls throwing 'Help the DFL, Vote Quist in the Primary' flyers under dormroom doors.

All doors except where there was a known conservative, not as of yet recruited. Under those doors was thrown an envelope, addressed to the person, with an anonymous letter inside:

"Want to fight the Left?
Want to make a difference?
Interested in becoming God's Warrior?
Meet us on the steps of Northrup Auditorium
Sunday, 1am

Yours in Christ
The Minnesota Sons of Liberty"

It took just ninety minutes to hit every room in the Superblock.

*   *   *   *   *   *   *

It was four-thirty in the morning before Zan got back to his place. He tried to do a few pushups, but gave up. He undressed down to his boxers and jumped into bed. It was a surprise to him to find someone already there.

*   *   *   *   *   *   *

"My God Zan, how late do you go to bed? I waited until three on you." It was Alisha, in all her naked glory.

Zan had jumped out of bed when he encountered the foreign body, grabbed a samurai sword, and flipped on the light. When Alisha jumped out of the bed, he put his high guard down. Now he leaned on the sword like it was a walking stick.

Alisha was shielding the light with her eyes, but continued talking, "You hadn't been answering your phone, and I didn't know if you had gotten any of my messages, so I decided to drop by. When you didn't show up, I went to bed."

"In my bed?" Zan replied.

"Well, it's not like I haven't been her before," she flirted. "I'm trying to apologize about the other night. I'm really sorry, and I wanted to make it up to you."

"What if I said I was still mad?"

"Then I'd point out your bottom half is disagreeing with you." She pointed to his crotch. "Why don't you turn off the lights and come to bed?"

Zan didn't normally let his penis do his thinking for him, but a naked woman in bed was a naked woman in bed.

*   *   *   *   *   *   *

Zan got up well before Alisha did. He made her bacon and eggs, and left it in the oven for her. He left a note on the fridge and went for a jog. His goal was to do eight miles in an hour. The route coiled its way through Northeast Minneapolis, down to campus and back on side streets.

Age is a cruel master. An hour and twenty minutes later he got back to his place. Alisha was gone, the breakfast found and consumed. On Zan's dinner table were three Polaroids and a note,

"Hope these brighten your day,

XOXO
Alisha"

One picture was a portrait. The next was a portrait, nude from the waist up. The third showed her nude and spread eagle on her bed in her house. Zan was impressed. He didn't think Polaroid cameras could be used with tripods. Either that, or someone took the pictures for her.

He decided he wouldn't ask her about that, though.

*   *   *   *   *   *   *

CHAPTER 9

1am Sunday, September 11
Northrup Auditorium

Behind one of the pillars on the front steps of Northrup were three small cardboard boxes with no top. In two of them were large 11x17 inch posters. In the third were staples and staple hammers. A note was taped onto one of the boxes, it read:

"Here are the tools;
Do with them what thou wilt."

The posters in the boxes said:

"Make Minnesota Safe for Pederasts,

Vote DFL.
Sincerely,
Phyllis Caine"

A picture of Phyllis, the district's representative, was included. A star and sickle was in the background. The posters were printed on red paper.

Zan stood on the roof of the Tate Laboratory of Physics, a large building on the east side of the Mall. He had a good view of Northrup from there, walkie-talkie in hand. Tate had a large dome with an old-fashioned optical lens telescope on the roof. It was open a couple nights a week for stargazing students. Zan had long ago befriended one of the astronomy professors he met as an undergrad and copied the key it took to get to the roof.

It came in handy.

The night was perfect for stargazing. Two grad students spent a couple hours with the old telescope. Luckily, with Monday looming, the grad students left the observatory before Zan needed the privacy. Somewhere in the darkness below, Bob Restovich and Frank Wallace were waiting.

This kind of operation was always hit or miss. The hope was a few of the people who received letters would show up, take the initiative and poster the offensive message across the campus. Then those people could be brought into the fold and recruited for more activism. From start to finish, it was asking a lot for someone to do stuff on a cold call. But anyone who did was quality. But they'd get some assistance.

Big Frank Wallace would be the second person on the steps of Northrup.

The first person would be allowed a few seconds to survey everything. If he stayed, Wallace would join him, claiming to also have been given a letter with the mysterious mission on it. Restovich would join up a few minutes later.

The last time Zan had done this, two years ago, they had a dozen people show up. None of them made it to initiation.

Bell chimed, signaling 1am. Nobody was in view.

The night waited.

*   *   *   *   *   *   *

"Big Frankie, Stargazer."
"Frankie here."
"See anyone?"
"Nope. Mall is empty Stargazer."
"It's one-thirty, nobody is coming. Let's call it a bust and get

---

those posters up."

"Roger that, see ya down here."

Zan turned off his walkie-talkie and pulled out his cell-phone. He dialed a number into the oversized brick and waited for an answer. On top of a building was about the only place he could get a signal on campus. Someone answered.

"Hello?"

"Spags," Zan spoke as loudly as he thought he could, "it's Zan, the operation is a bust. Better get down here, we have to get these posters up."

"Alright, I'll be over there in ten."

"And," Zan said, "get Kayla out here too."

"No problem. We'll be there momentarily."

*   *   *   *   *   *   *

By the time Zan got down from Tate, Wallace and Restovich were waiting behind the pillars on Northrup. A warm wind picked up. The heavy moist air from the day was slowly exchanged for drier air. It was a hint of fall, no more.

A few minutes later Spags and Kayla showed up, hand-in-hand. Zan shook his head in disgust, just out of their view.

There was time for small talk as they divided the posters and staples.

Someone ran up the steps.

"Hi," the man said, out of breath.

Everyone looked at him. The man was shorter than Zan. Asian, very slim, thick glasses, moved awkwardly, jet black hair in a bowl-cut. Oversized head on an emaciated frame. He wore blue jeans and a dark gray sweatshirt.

Everyone stood in silence.

The man tried again. "I got your letter, I'm Jason Kang, from Pioneer Hall." With a hint of an Asian accent.

"You're a little late," Zan said.

"Actually, I was here before you showed up. I watched you guys drop off your boxes."

Zan: "That was two hours ago."

"I know, my estimates were right on," Jason continued, "I was hanging out in the plaza over there," he pointed towards a small area to the north of Morrill Hall. "When nobody showed up, I decided to stay out until you guys came to clean up."

Members of The Organization were accustomed to a wide spectrum of unusual behavior, but this man was far out on the edge of the continuum.

"Anyway, I got to eavesdrop on your conversations. The

acoustics out here are really spectacular. I wanted to know what you were about."

Zan grabbed a poster and walked over to Jason and handed it to him. "Do you want to help us put these posters up?"

The man examined the poster. After a moment, he began to laugh. An awkward stereotypically geeky laugh. "Hell ya."

"That's all I needed to know," Zan said.

*   *   *   *   *   *   *

CHAPTER 10

11pm Wednesday, September 14
Big Ten

Things slowed down.

Arne Carlson carried the Republican gubernatorial primary with ease.

Only three hundred and eight votes for Allen Quist came out of the campus.

School picked up for the students.

With eight weeks to go before the elections, The Organization slowed down its operations for a bit. The important campaigning happens within three weeks of an election. There are few things activists can do to really change an election outside of this window. Only the candidates themselves held any sway with voters at this time. Doorknocking or a personal phone call could conjure a vote when none existed before. But it needed to be the candidate on the line. If not, it just annoyed voters more than anything.

The College Republicans went about their work of trying to register Republican students to vote. They also did a lot of crap work on campaigns. Stuffing envelopes. Phone calls. Lit-dropping. It was good work, but an ineffective use of resources. There were other roles outside of bothering people on the telephone for such energetic volunteers. But the Republican Party of Minnesota had long been masters of squandering and 1994 would be no different. The Organization kept its own priorities. Conservative activism was different from party activism, despite the occasional overlap.

The crew postered a couple times a week. And meeting at the Big Ten on Wednesday nights was fun. Tall Guy and Red disappeared. So it goes.

Restovich spent too much time with Nicole off-campus to be useful, but he still made the occasional appearance. Buzzcut had turned into a decent recruit; his real name? Matt Foley. He was a few inches north of five feet tall. Extremely thin, remarkably fast. He could run a five minute mile and not break a sweat. His hair always short, Buzzcut remained his handle. Eventually he came to accept it.

Jason Kang, a Korean immigrant and technophile, had so far kept up with the group. A libertarian with the excessive IQ and deficient common sense epidemic among their ranks, Kang still had been a solid addition. He knew electronics, gadgets, could pick locks, fix cars. A tinkerer. Was decent with computers. Didn't mind controversy. Not a natural English speaker, he had to translate everything in his head which made him a pain to talk to, but he fit in.

The future all-star in the group? Tonya Evans. 'Hotchick'

A nickname she soon found out about, and loved.

The flirtatious blonde, with the sparkling blue eyes, just a little larger, and a little farther apart than the average woman's, and a quick tongue, she hit the ground running with the group. She worked the tables, yelled at abortionists, postered late at night and looked great with a gun in her hands. A natural.

This was all the recruiting the group wanted to do. For now.

It was about quality, not quantity.

The health of any organization is built on recruiting. Normally, there needs to be twice as many recruits as spots. The Big Ten crew had limited openings.

The roundtable in the back of the Big Ten was full. Painter, Zeale, Wallace, Witold were joined by Buzzcut, Kang (who would need a nickname with a real name like that?), and Hotchick. Chris Berg and Zan were the only alumni present. Bob Restovich and Nicole Fielder were sitting together at a different table; Zan considered that better than nothing.

*   *   *   *   *   *   *

Alisha Williams delivered a round of beer for everyone.

A hand on Zan's shoulder the only sign of intimacy between the two.

Everyone momentarily distracted by the beer, Zan started the night's business.

He pulled out a box from underneath the table. "I have our Shetterly stuff."

"Shetterly?" Kang asked.

"Yeah, you weren't going to vote for Arne Carl were ya?"

"Actually," Kang said sheepishly, "I can't vote at all. I'm here on a student visa."

"Oh," Zan stumbled, but regained form quickly, "then you really shouldn't care either way. So here," Zan passed Kang a handful of Shetterly bumper stickers, "Start putting these up in Pioneer."

"Where do I put them?"

"Put them on the insides of bathroom stalls," Painter told him, "or anywhere people can see them but the janitors will have a hard time getting to them."

"Can I get a ladder?" Kang asked.

"Just use whatever's convenient." Zeale said. "Furniture or a crate or something. Just get it up as high as possible. Be creative. You'll need to do this sort of thing late at night."

"Yeah, I figured that part out." Kang put the bumper stickers into his backpack.

Zan passed out the bumper stickers to the table. Then he gave bottles of car-paint sealant and brushes in little plastic bags. "You can cover the bumper stickers with this stuff, while you're sitting on the can, and it will make it almost impossible to rip off the sticker. It will drive the janitors nuts."

"Dumb question," Buzzcut said, "why are we supporting this Shetterly douche?"

"We can't work for Arne Carlson," Zan answered, "a liberal Republican does more damage to conservatism than a liberal Democrat. We're not going to work for the DFL, John Marty can go fuck himself. That leaves the libertarian, which also hurts us, or Will Shetterly."

Buzzcut still didn't get the logic. "So we go for someone more liberal than the DFL?"

"It's not a matter of policies at this point," Zan said, "it's a matter of politics. The more college students we can get to vote for liberal third-parties, the better the GOP chances are. So for incurable cases, which is most of campus, we need to encourage radicalism. Thoughtful, reasonable moderates are worse than an environmentalist who masturbates to pictures of Ralph Nader."

"That is the most nihilistic thing I've ever heard," Buzzcut said.

"That's 'cause you're new to the group," Painter said.

*   *   *   *   *   *   *

CHAPTER 11

11am Friday, September 23
Coffman Memorial Union

An old man with white hair and an expensive looking suit got up from his chair at the front of the President's Room on the third floor of Coffman Union. Thin, willowy and ancient, he checked his watch, brilliant gold under the lights, and approached the podium.

"I guess we should get started...My name is Earl Prince, I'm the President of the Minnesota Civil Liberties Union. My colleagues and I are here today to give you a court-ordered seminar on the first amendment of the Constitution, its meaning, history and consequences. I want to first thank you all for appearing. Not all of you were required to be here, and it's always a pleasure for the MCLU to give these lessons on the civil liberties we enjoy in this nation.

"We're here because one of the groups on this campus, a conservative group, were passing out sheets of paper with information on it that some in this room found offensive. So offensive, in fact, that this group was told it could no longer pass out its literature. So offensive, that the police were called when this group refused to surrender its first amendment rights.

"More unbelievably, one of the young men from the group was actually arrested. Not for any physical violence, or threat, or other violation of the law. But merely for a playground taunt. We're not here to defend the student, or the offensive speech. The point of the matter is the student, student groups, and everyone else has the inalienable right to controversial speech in this country, and in particular the campus of a public university in this country."

The old man was the first in a procession of lawyers and legal scholars to lecture. It was sweet victory for Zeale and his lawyer, Ernie Kessler. Kessler smacked the University and the UMPD with a lawsuit a few hours after Zeale's arrest. The MCLU got involved, thanks to some prodding from Kessler. After a few weeks of negotiation, the lawsuit was dropped. Zeale had to apologize for calling the cop a 'fag' while every UMPD cop had to attend a short MCLU seminar on the first amendment as it relates to law enforcement.

The U wasn't so lucky. They had to apologize to Zeale. In writing. Then every employee of the Student Activities Office and a hundred other U officials had to take a longer seminar on the first amendment. Then the U had to pay for a full page advertisement in the Minnesota Daily with a statement affirming the principles of the first amendment and apologizing for trying to curtail the liberties of students. Even Dr. Malcolm Paulson, President of the U, had to attend the seminar. It had been a PR nightmare; it was even covered by Larry King.

Zeale and Kessler attended the seminars in good faith. Zeale got a picture of himself shaking hands with President Paulson, which went onto the cover of the conservative paper. Unbeknownst to the participants, Zan and Nolan Painter were in Church Street Garage putting Shetterly for Governor bumper stickers on all their cars.

*   *   *   *   *   *   *

The seminar concluded, President Paulson walked out quickly, avoiding the MCLU buffoons. He would send them a nice note later. Maybe. He walked quickly back across the Mall to Morrill Hall. The seminar had eaten up a huge chunk of his day, needlessly. Entering through the ground floor, Malcom hopped up the steps, two at a time, to his second floor office. Most of the staff were already gone, the office clearing out rather predictably at four-thirty on Fridays. His secretary had gone home, only two people were still milling about. One was Rachel Anderson.

"Rachel," he called out, "in my office please."

She dutifully trotted in and closed the door.

"There's a big project I'll be proposing to the Regents at their meeting in October." Paulson opened a drawer on his desk and pulled out a thick three-ring binder. "It's a proposal to renovate Coffman. I need you to review this," he shook the binder, "and write out an executive summary geared towards the Regents. I'd also like you to write a proposal letter about the project geared towards the legislature, in case we have to lobby for funding."

Rachel grabbed the binder and wrote some notes in a small notebook. "Who should I work with this on?"

"Just give it to Shannon," Shannon was Paulson's secretary, "I'll be going through most of this myself."

Paulson took out a leather day planner and opened it up. "Okay, there's a department head meeting on Monday night. Be sure to get those student achievement reports to them before the meeting on Monday. Let's see...On Thursday there's a lunch meeting with the people from Coca-Cola. I'd like you there keeping notes...let's see...

"Oh, I have a formal dinner at Coffman next Friday at seven pm. Can you join me?"

"Sure Dr. Paulson." Rachel sounded cheerful at the thought. Elegant dinners and fancy socials were one of the perks of the job. While Rachel was initially trying to help embarrass Paulson, she now found the man charming and good-natured. He hadn't laid a hand on her, despite taking obvious liberties with the body of his secretary, who seemed to enjoy it.

"Good, it should be fun. It's being held in honor of Bernie Cust. Former alumni, died last year. Left the U almost ten million dollars. His family, a dozen legislators and a bunch of local glitterati will be there. It's formal dress."

"Won't be a problem."

Paulson was looking again at his notebook. "Looks like that's it. For now...So how's school going?"

"Really well. This semester will be pretty easy."

"That's good, it means you can do more work for me," he smiled at her. "Anyway, you should get out of here and go find some trouble for yourself."

"Sure thing, thanks."

"See you Monday."

Paulson watched as she left the office. When Rachel was gone, he opened another drawer in his desk. A bottle of Jack Daniels was pulled from the darkness. Paulson drank straight from the bottle. He had two hours to kill before traffic let up and he could escape to his cabin. And he wasn't spending those hours sober.

*   *   *   *   *   *   *

Markos Pavavorich, the big Russian fighter Zan was coaching, was pounding Zan.

Fridays were a 'light' sparring day for the Northeast Boxing Club's professional middleweight. Left, left, right, left hook, right uppercut. Zan's series of combos failed to stop Markos, who ducked away from the uppercut and countered with a wicked right hook that landed across Zan's face, knocking him into the ropes where Markos pounded away with both fists.

Three seconds of this. Then it was over. The bell rang.

Zan crawled out of the ring, waving at Markos that he was done for the moment. Steve Coombs helped him out of his headgear and the two sat down on a ringside bench. An employee of the gym hopped in the ring wearing punch mitts and a body protector to give Markos some more work.

"You're sure taking a beating in there champ," Coombs said, his the voice of a confident and learned court jester, "I seem to remember most of my coaches were able to do their work witout giving demselves concussions."

"That's an unfair comparison," Zan barely spat back, "you don't hit very hard."

Coombs laughed.

The two sat in silence, listening to the sounds of the gym. Markos' bullet fast hands zipped into and out of the mitts and body of his target, a tall brunette woman who was an experienced fighter in her own right. The 'Zthwack' sound from Markos' gloves reverberated around the gym, overpowering the sound of other trainees jumping rope or hitting speedbags.

"Any interesting cases lately?" Zan asked Coombs.

Coombs was a biologist who specialized in lake and river ecology. His job was to work as a consultant, saving lakes from the many ills the world dropped upon them.

"Not right now," he replied. "But next year I'll be going to Israel ta investigate a fish shortage in the sea of Galilee. They're having a problem controlling Their zooplankton levels. It's hurting the whole food chain, including Saint Peter's Fish, the Mango tilapia."

"Sounds like it would bore me."

"Probably."

Markos came over to the ropes after two rounds of working on drills.

"Come on Zan, get in here and show me left-hand combo."

Zan got up, Coombs helped put his headgear on for him, and he entered the ring for some more sparring. Zan sweated through his white T-shirt. Sweat covered his face in a thick sheet. Zan boxed right-handed, but Markos had a fight against a tricky southpaw. Coombs, a natural southpaw, had done some work with Markos, but Markos could work full-speed with Zan in the ring. Normally a boxer can't fight well when reversing his stance, but Zan had been training ambidextrously his whole life.

A bell rang.

Zan flourished his right hand and tried sneaking in a quick left hook. Markos pulled away, then tried to push in closer. Zan kept him away, occasionally stepping on Markos' lead foot. Zan stayed evasive for most of the round, throwing some jabs, and that was it. But Markos' bloodlust couldn't be stemmed. He cornered Zan and pummeled him for a bit.

There was a tremendous pain in Zan's abdomen. Not normal. Zan was trying to tell Markos to stop, but the thoughts never escaped into words or action. Markos connected with his right to Zan's cheek, and Zan's world went black.

*   *   *   *   *   *   *

CHAPTER 12

Sunday, September 25
Hennepin County Medical Center

The inside of a hospital is surprisingly peaceful.

The ICU rooms are bright, white, comfortable. The bed and the TV have a remote control. The nurses are patient, friendly, if occasionally sardonic. If it weren't for all the people dying, it would be a spa.

Zan woke up for the first time.

He'd never been knocked down in a ring, let alone knocked out.

Let alone hospitalized.

Time dragged.

Markos stopped by during lunch, apologized. Zan ignored the apology, told him 'you're supposed to be killing people in the ring' and gave him some tips for his upcoming fight.

PART III: CHAPTER 12

A few hours later a doctor, a tall Pakistani, woke him from a nap.

"Ello Mister Wu," The Doctor had a thick Indian-subcontinental accent, "How are you feeling?"

"I dunno," he thought for a second, "nope, I really can't tell."

"Well, you were not doing very well at-all, I must say," he began, "when you were brought in you had suffered several severe injuries. A head injury, and we found an abdominal one."

"Sounds bad."

"It could have been much vorse. You suffered a traumatic brain injury with increased intracranial pressure. You were lucky, it was only a moderate injury. We did have to place a catheter in your lateral brain ventricle, to reduce the pressure. We took the catheter out this morning--"

"A catheter, in my brain?" Zan asked.

"Yes."

"Is it still there?"

"No, the nuerosurgeon took it out last night, but please don't touch the dressing on your head. We don't want to risk infection. Otherwise, that was the only major intervention required. We did put you on a ventilator for a while to keep your blood oxygen levels correct."

Zan was able to follow along, barely. The doctor was pronouncing everything correctly, but the inflexions of his voice, at odd points, combined with an irregular meter and incorrect syllabic emphases, made him difficult to follow.

"So I'm going to be fine?"

"You are amusing Mr. Wu," the Doctor said, "But I do not get called to help people who are fine. I'm afraid there are a great potential of problems here. Most people with these brain injuries experience some distress. Headaches, amnesia, confusion, personality changes, dizziness."

"But I don't feel any of those things."

"Do you remember how you got hurt?"

"I was boxing."

"With who?"

Zan was silent for a second. "It had to be Markos, the Russian."

"Do you remember getting hurt?"

"No."

"Do you remember who your visitor was earlier today?"

Another pause. "Not sure."

"It was your friend Markos," the doctor replied, "and he told you all about your fight. You see Mister Wu, we're just not sure what problems you're going to have, and if they are going to be chronic, or how severe or moderate they will be."

- 209 -

"Well, my memory wasn't good to begin with, I doubt it will matter much."

"Once again, very amusing you are."

"I do what I can doc."

"I keeping you here a few more days. We'll do some tests to get a clear mental picture of your problems."

"Uh," Zan interrupted him, "does this mean I'm outta the woods?"

"Yes, in a way. We still need to monitor you to make sure there are no more problems. And, I must tell before I forget...we also found you have an enlarged spleen Mr. Wu."

"What does that mean?"

"That you're stupid for one thing," the doctor sighed, "your spleen injury should heal and get better, but you have to stop all contact sports. No more boxing, Mister Wu."

"You can just kill me now then."

"Mister Wu, it's not just your spleen. If you box again, there is a chance you'll injure your brain. Again. And this time, it might kill you if you're lucky. If you're unlucky, you'll be a vegetable."

*   *   *   *   *   *   *

The doctor must have given him a sedative, because Zan didn't remember anything after being told he couldn't box.

Awake again, the TV was off and all the lights were dim in the hospital. The other guy in his room, an old Black man whom Zan had yet to see awake, was sound asleep.

After a few minutes of channel surfing. Zan found out the time from the Weather Channel: 9:30pm.

He swung his legs over the side of the bed and planted them into the cold tile floor. Standing up, there was no wobble. The only problem was the IV fluid bag Zan was connected to, and a urinary catheter Zan found, to his chagrin. Feeling really hungry and not very tired, Zan took a few tentative steps. Nothing bad happened.

Zan pulled the needle out of the vein in his hand. IV bag no longer a problem. Then he found his way into the small bathroom next to his room. Assuming the balloon was deflated, he pulled the catheter out. Painful. Very, very painful. But Zan had suffered through several bouts of kidney stones. The catheter wasn't as painful. But close. A few minutes of heavy breathing, and Zan was able to find his gym bag, which had a pair of sweatpants and a clean shirt.

Dressed, wearing shoes sans socks, he leaned out of the door. There was a nursing station several doors down to the left, and it was empty. Zan could see an exit sign a few doors to his right, marked with a glowing red sign that included a small flame and the symbolic representation of stairs. Zan walked to the stairs and went down. The door to the ground floor was marked.

It took a while to find, but Zan walked right out the front door.

It was a short two mile walk home.

At home, he ate two cans of Spam, which he promptly regurgitated. Giving up, he went to bed.

*　　　*　　　*　　　*　　　*　　　*　　　*

Leaving the hospital might have been a mistake.

Zan lay in bed, wide awake. It was impossible to sleep. His head throbbed with pain, and he was thirsty. Plus, he still hadn't regained bladder control; something he didn't expect. He took some painkillers, drank some water, which stayed down, and just laid in bed until the sunlight filtered into his bedroom.

It took twenty-four milligrams of Ibuprofen to stop the pain.

Leaving a hospital after a traumatic brain injury is a bad idea, Zan would later admit. But to Zan, people who constantly worried about their health and well-being were narcissists. You were going to get sick. You were going to die. If now, why not? Socrates was right, there was nothing to fear from death.

Around 9am his phone rang. It was the hospital, looking for him. He ignored it, the answering machine recording a message from his Pakistani doctor, laced with what he assumed were foreign curse words. It made Zan laugh. A couple hours later it was Kessler calling. He wanted lunch. And he wanted to know why there was a fire engine in a barn on his secluded getaway. The fatigue took him and he slept. Nightmares of flying fists, foreign doctors and fire engines. Sometimes he woke up laughing. Sometimes in a cold sweat.

The phone kept ringing.

*　　　*　　　*　　　*　　　*　　　*　　　*

Zan was a brain.

Walking in a ringing forest. And cold. And he needed to go to the bathroom.

He awoke.

Walking to the bathroom to relieve himself, it wasn't until he flushed the toilet that he learned he had regained his continence.

The headache was still there. But now it was just a dull pain. A little bit of pressure. A reminder he was alive. It was a good thing. Life affirming. He walked into the kitchen and tried to keep down some leftover Spam. It stayed down. The clock on his oven said it was just after two in the morning. He walked downstairs and outside to the front of the house, where he found his car, someone had brought it back from the gym for him.

The keys he found in his mailbox. Feeling no reason why he shouldn't, he drove out to South Minneapolis. Alisha lived in a small house near the corner of 36th and 24th avenue. It was a quick drive from Broadway, to 35W south, off at Hiawatha, to Ceder, past Lake Street into the Powderhorn neighborhood.

It was 2:30. Alisha would normally be driving home by now. Zan walked up to the house but no one was there. Zan waited. Dozed off. Lights in his face woke him up. A car had driven by. Remembering where he was, he was about to open his door when he spotted Alisha leaving her car. Then he saw the man. Tall, well built. Wearing a suit. Zan recognized him.

Dr. Malcolm Paulson.

He watched in disbelief as they walked up to the front of her house, and walked in together.

Zan sat in his car for a few minutes. Then he got out, opened the back, took out a metal softball bat he kept in there. Walking up to Alisha's car, he started swinging. Back window. Rear driver's side window. Windshield. Driver's door. Lights flicked on in the neighborhood. He jumped into his car and drove off at high speed.

*　　　*　　　*　　　*　　　*　　　*　　　*

CHAPTER 13

1pm Wednesday, September 27
South St. Paul

Political campaigning requires a lot of crap.

Most of this crap has to be purchased every election cycle.

But the one renewable resource for perpetual candidates is lawn signage. As long as your name doesn't change, a lawn sign can be used *ad infinitum*.

Statewide campaigns needed so many lawn signs that large storage facilities were rented to store them. Chris Berg had driven his van into one of these facilities, large enough to house a nuclear submarine, located in South St. Paul. With him was Gene Zeale and Nolan Painter. They were there to help out the Arne Carlson campaign.

The trio met with 'Tammy,' a hyper-personable thirty-something campaign worker. She gave them a list of twenty sign locations and together the group loaded the van with twenty very large four-foot by eight-foot signs, abbreviated as '4x8s'. Forty pieces of eight foot long, one inch thick, rusty-as-hell rebar joined the signs in the back. Goodbyes and well-wishes were said and they drove off.

They took their time through South and West St. Paul.

Up to Wabasha Street Bridge.

Stopping the van, on the south side of the bridge, Painter and Zeale got out of the van and opened the back. Chris shouted 'Go!' and the two awkwardly pulled the bundled 4x8s out of the van and they sprinted to the side of the bridge, and chucked the signs over, into the Mississippi.

Traffic was light, no cars were around.

Seconds later they were across the bridge and driving around downtown St. Paul.

Minutes later they were on the Interstate heading back to campus.

*   *   *   *   *   *   *

The crew met at the Big Ten that night.

No Zan.

No one knew what happened to Zan, why he didn't answer his phone or why he wasn't at his apartment. It was a bit of a mystery. Not a mystery worth solving of course. Not yet anyway. Painter and Zeale led the group to do some Shetterly campaigning. But that was it. Time off was time off. They'd worry about Zan later.

*   *   *   *   *   *   *

CHAPTER 14

Friday, September 30th.

There is no reason to answer the phone.

It was Zan's latest revelation.

He just let it ring. Threw out the answering machine the day before.

Zan was in the world, but no longer of the world.

The phone rang again.

But Zan decided to answer the phone this time.

"Hello?"

"Zan, hi, it's me," he recognized Alisha's voice, "I've been wondering what's been going on, where have you been?"

"I've had some family stuff to worry about," Zan lied.

"I hope it's nothing serious."

"It's not."

"Well, that's good," Alisha said awkwardly. She had noticed the lack of passion or interest in Zan's voice. "I want to see you, are you going to be around tonight?"

THE EDUCATOR

"Listen Alisha," Zan spoke in monotone, "I'm no longer interested in an 'us,' I don't see our relationship going anywhere."

"What?"

"I don't want to see you anymore, goodbye."

Zan hung up the phone. Then he ripped the cord from the wall.

With nothing else to do, he sat on the couch in his living room watching Jerry Springer. Then he took a nap. A few hours later he went for a walk.

The world became an empty stage.

*   *   *   *   *   *   *

Rachel Anderson was looking into a mirror.

Since she had started working for the Office of the President, she had been skipping the gym more and more often. All of her formal dresses, both of them, were revealing numbers that highlighted her curves. But now they were a little too revealing. Rachel's midsection had gotten soft. Her rear didn't look quite as shapely as she remembered. And her boobs barely stayed in place as she walked.

But at least she still fit into this dress. Her other black dress, with a longer and slimmer skirt line and more modest slits, was right out. She didn't have time to go out and find a new dress. To help add some modesty to the ensemble, she was trying to find a fashionable jacket to wear. Or a sweater. Something.

One sweater looked like it would work. She made herself a black sash to wear as a belt to streamline her midsection and hide her miniscule paunch. Black pantyhose hid her legs' paleness. After another ten minutes in front of the mirror, she decided this would be good enough. She swore to herself to spend more time at the gym, and to go out dress shopping this weekend. She put on her makeup and just before she left, she decided to call Zan. Maybe he'd want to meet up after the banquet. She didn't want to walk around at night, dressed as she was, without someone around.

But he never did answer the phone. She left her apartment in Uptown and drove to campus. It was a short ten minute drive.

*   *   *   *   *   *   *

"Rachel," Malcolm Paulson shined with enthusiasm, "don't you look spectacular."

"Thanks," Rachel acted embarrassed, "I'm not sure I have the legs for this dress anymore."

"Oh nonsense," he replied, "women see every flaw in their bodies, whether real or imagined."

They walked together for a bit without talking. Rachel was a little concerned with how much time she was spending with her boss, considering his reputation, which he never hid. But he always kept their relationship asexual. And honest. There was a distance there, a mental distance. It never appeared to her that he was anything but professional.

Rachel had stopped by the office to remind Dr. Paulson about the banquet. He wasn't going to forget, but he was often late to these things. He liked to get as much work done on Friday as he could, since he was gone almost every weekend. 'You have to find a hobby that gets you out of town on the weekends, or else people expect you to work' he always said.

This weekend it was the opener for the deer archery season. Malcolm wouldn't be back until Tuesday.

They were walking outside to Coffman in the cool autumn air. A slight breeze pushed around thousands of leaves. They danced around the Mall. It was just before seven in the evening. The skies were dark gray, but light rumored in. Winter was coming. But not yet. Rachel loved the Fall. The bugs were gone. The weather was comfortable. Everything was 'pretty.' Transcendent.

Paulson interrupted her meditation.

"I know I shouldn't ask you this," he said apologetically "but I just finished looking at your draft of the Coffman renovation proposal. I'd like you to take a look at it tonight, after the banquet."

"Really?"

"Yes, I know," he said, "but I was hoping to make a final review this weekend while I was at my cabin. Then we can finalize it when I get back on Tuesday."

"Oh I suppose," she replied, "I'll probably leave the banquet early then. I'd like to get home before eleven. I've got a big family thing this weekend," Rachel was lying, following Paulson's advice about protecting weekends, "so I'll be on the road early tomorrow."

"That will work out just fine," he said. "Just wait for me for a bit, I want to talk to you about some of the changes before you leave."

"Okay."

"Great," he paused. "Gosh, I'm so lucky I was able to steal you from Mr. Kessler."

*   *   *   *   *   *   *

The banquet was a typical bore. A half an hour of walking around, dishing out small-talk. Rachel felt lucky, she ran into Annette Meeks, a local conservative, very well-connected. They talked for a while, long enough to avoid any other conversations. Then dinner was served. Rachel got to sit with Joanell Drystad, Minnesota's

Lieutenant Governor. Drystad had recently lost in the GOP primary against Rod Grams. The campaign had gotten dirty, and Drystad got crushed.

Which was good. Rachel despised the woman. She was a liberal Republican and a strong abortion supporter. But Rachel smiled along. The food was good, and Rachel was served champagne, which she consumed greedily. After dinner there were speeches. Paulson gave one. Drystad gave one. Some relative of the dead guy talked. for. ever.

After the speeches were done, there was more mingling. Rachel did her best to escape, but youth and beauty attracts a lot of interest no matter where it is. Annette Meeks was able to grab her from a boring conversation with some old bald guy who said he used to be on the Minneapolis city counsel. She thanked Annette and slipped out of Coffman.

Morrill Hall was locked up and Rachel didn't have her keys. They didn't fit with the dress. But Rachel knew she could get into Tate Hall, then take a tunnel into Morrill Hall. The doors in the tunnel were supposed to be locked but could be opened without keys. Grad students in Tate had a habit manipulating their environment to avoid going outside in winter. A security camera failed to stop the vandals. Even the security guards gave up and just stopped locking the doors in that section of the tunnels. The homeless people spent their time in the libraries anyway, so it wasn't considered a big problem.

When she got up to the office, she found the Coffman Renovation Proposal at her work station, covered in post-it notes. She looked at the clock, 9:22pm, opened up to the first page of the proposal, and started her review.

     *   *   *   *   *   *   *

Paulson saw Rachel leave. He was working over the Lieutenant Governor, who had spent most of the conversation complaining about her recent loss to Rod Grams. She hated the man. Paulson tried to console her but there was nothing to do, the woman was terminally smug and couldn't handle the fact some people didn't see her the way she saw her 'genius' self.

Eventually he pulled himself away, after Drystad promised to help the U during the next session. Paulson talked to a few more people, but most had filtered out of Coffman already. Twenty minutes after Rachel had left, the party was over. Paulson personally thanked all the U-Club staff for working on a Friday night.

He had parked his car, the big Suburban, at the Coffman loading docks. His car was well-known on campus and he had special tags that allowed him to park anywhere, anyway.

Still, it didn't stop his car from getting the occasional parking ticket. Which really irked him. But there was no ticket this time. He drove his truck out to some parking meters behind Elliot Hall. Then he walked over to the abandoned Mineral Resources building. There was a University van parked there. Paulson had put it there two days ago. It was from the Building & Grounds department. Paulson drove the big white van over to Morrill Hall, parking on the sidewalk between Morrill Hall and Northrup.

Paulson checked his watch: 9:54pm. Rachel would probably be getting testy by now. *Good*, he thought. Over an hour separated his departure from hers. She left alone, headed in one direction. Paulson left later, in a different direction. Paulson was on his way to his cabin for the archery opener, according to his narrative. He, U alumni and nascent politician Tim Pawlenty, and Ernie Kessler were supposed to meet at Kessler's cabin at five-thirty in the morning.

Pawlenty was a young and good-looking man who had been trying to make a name for himself in the Minnesota State Legislature. As an alum, Paulson immediately recognized his potential and his importance. The two political parties were always exchanging power in government, although in Minnesota the Republicans didn't do so well. But it was important to be bipartisan anyway. Pawlenty was not a hunter and not an outdoorsman, but he needed to build up his Minnesota cred if he wanted to advance politically. Paulson recognized this, and invited him along on some fishing and hunting trips. Pawlenty also appreciated being introduced to Kessler, who was slowly becoming a kingmaker in the Minnesota GOP.

While he was sitting in some tree, hidden in the woods in central Minnesota, Rachel's body was going to be discovered. Paulson concentrated on the narrative. On the plan. The details had been worked out in his head a dozen times, but this had to be perfect. The girl worked in his office, so it had to be perfect. This wasn't some alcoholic whore from St. Cloud. It was his personal assistant.

      *   *   *   *   *   *   *

Rachel was at her workstation, plugging away at the proposal. Paulson walked up the stairs, instead of running as he normally did. She noticed him as he got to the top, and she waved. Walking over to her, he checked his watch, to try to hide his face. He could already sense the powerful adrenaline rush building within him. She got up from her chair and said something. He closed the gap.

Every step felt like an eternity. Paulson avoided making eye contact, because he knew she would see something in his eyes that would warn her. Five more steps, then four. Three. Two. He looked up. She had a quizzical look on her face. She said something. He heard nothing. He saw his opening. Ducking down just a bit, he swung his left hand, palm open, into her gut, just below her navel. It was his favorite move, since it almost always broke the person's pelvis right at the *symphysis pubis.*

She shrieked. Paulson grabbed her around the waist and lifted her onto his shoulder. Moving as quickly as he could, he ran to the stairs. They were a white marble, very hard. He took her to the railing, she was punching him in the coccyx, which was pissing him off. He lifted her off his shoulder and dropped her over the railing, where she landed on the hard marble fifteen feet below. He made sure she was going down feet first. She screamed.

Rachel landed like an uncoordinated sack of potatoes. Paulson rushed down the stairs. She was unconscious. But she was breathing. Paulson threw her on his shoulder again and brought her back up the stairs, into a conference room, where he threw her unceremoniously unto a table. Then he went and got a backpack from his office. Back into the conference room. He rolled up Rachel's skirt and removed her panties.

*   *   *   *   *   *   *

The world was gray.
Dull. Painful. Swirling.
Then terror.
Rachel didn't know life from death. Light from dark. Joy from suffering. She couldn't remember anything. Who she was. Where she was. The dreams of her mind were not her own. Her eyes were open. Her mind was cloudy. With concentration came terror. She tried to let go. To let darkness take her. It wouldn't
"Well, there you are." A voice. A male voice.
More terror.
Rachel couldn't return the greeting. Something physical was preventing her from speaking. Something foul and heavy in her mouth. A rag maybe. More words came into her mind. *Not good.* She focused her eyes. There in front of her was the friendly face of a friendly man.
"I was wondering when you would come around. I couldn't wait forever." Paulson was back to his calm confidence. He got up on the table with Rachel, and straddled her. Getting within inches of her face, he peered into her eyes.
"Things are going to be a little fuzzy, so try to focus on me, okay? I had to get you drunk. I didn't want you running away before I was ready to do this. It takes a while to set up, you know? You can't have a clean crime scene without some planning."
The senses were starting to turn on. Rachel began to squirm.

"Easy now," Malcolm spoke softly, "you're not going anywhere. I've wrapped you in velvet. Every inch of you, even down to your fingers and toes. You've been mummified, I think that's what they call it. Then guess what? I wrapped you in this plastic stretch wrap. Nope no more moving in your life. No more walking. No more running."

Paulson stepped down from atop the table and took a seat on an office chair.

"You see Rachel, I'm a monster. You're about to die."

There was silence. Rachel's world was the ceiling above her. Paulson had kept the main lights off, but there were always some lights on in U buildings. It was a pleasant level of lighting. Rachel tried to focus on the ceiling. She remembered something a friend had told her about The Now. There was no future. No past. Just The Now. Every moment was its own universe. A page in a book. If you concentrated, you could control how quickly the pages turned. Zan told her this.

She tried to forget everything. Forget Zan. Forget herself. Moments passed.

Each one timeless and eternal.

Paulson hovered over her, taking his hands and rubbing them up and down her wrapped body.

"You really are an attractive woman. That black dress, I tell you, it really is spectacular. I'm shocked you could get yourself into it, hard as it was getting you out. Not sure how I'm going to put it back on you after I'm done here. I'm lucky though, any marks on your body will be attributed to the ultra-tight dress"

He walked out of the room.

Rachel softened her eyes. Looked beyond the ceiling. Trying to return to the blackness. Paulson came back into the world.

"Are you sobering up yet?" He moved her head and looked into her eyes. "See, I had to give you an ethanol enema. Like the sound of that? I purchased an enema kit from a sex store. That's why you're going to be a little woozy for a while. I needed you to have some alcohol in your blood. I couldn't believe it when the sex shop lady talked to me about sherry enemas. And I thought my sexual proclivities were weird."

Paulson kept looking into Rachel's eyes, searching for a sign of intelligence. "Looks like you're there. I guess I can start.

"Let's have some fun. I've been planning this for over a month, you know. Ever since I first hired you. In fact, I've been dreaming about this since I first saw you. This took five weeks of planning and work.

"Look at this," he held up a piece of paper to her face, "it's your suicide note. You handled this paper a week ago, it has your prints on it. I saved it for now. I wrote up your suicide note earlier this afternoon. Wrote it on your computer. Printed it on the printer at your workstation. And guess what? You've even signed it," Paulson waved the paper again.

"I've been practicing your signature everyday for a month. I've done it ten thousand times. Didn't you wonder why you had to sign two sets of employment papers?" Paulson paused, waiting for a response he knew wouldn't come. "I guess not. I'm pretty proud of myself for this, in fact. They're going to find this note taped to your computer screen. The tape will have your fingerprints on it too. Even the pen I used is at your desk, you've been using it for a week."

Paulson leaned in close to her face again. Her breath was shallow, her eyes were tearing up. He got his mouth close to her nose. She exhaled, he inhaled. Then he exhaled and as she inhaled. He did this for a few breaths. She tried to stop breathing, but she needed to.

The soliloquy started again. "Everything has to fit a narrative. If something doesn't match the narrative Rachel, a cop will pick up on it, and then the fun is over for me. And this has been a great narrative."

Rachel tried to tune out the words. But his voice was reassuring. Scholarly. Intoxicating.

"You get a new job. It's a good job that you want to keep. I noticed right away that you're a workaholic. You like busywork. You hate doing nothing. That was fortunate. So I gave you tons of work. More than anyone else. And you did it. You stayed later and later. You broke up with your boyfriend. Lost track of your friends." Paulson laughed aloud. "You Republicans, I swear, you just don't get what life is about. You are not your work.

"The 'you,' the 'Thou' needs to be something more..." Paulson paused.

"But back to my story. Your personal life gradually disappeared. It's something people will talk about once they hear you committed suicide. You even gave up on your anti-abortion group.

"The police might ask your friends if you've been acting differently. And they'll say yes. That you've been distant. And tonight, at the party, Lieutenant Governor Drystad. I put you at her table on purpose. I know how much you hate 'abortionists.' Partygoers will say you were distant. Anti-social. That you left early. And those same people will say that you left alone, and that I left a long time after you had left.

"The narrative will fit. When the police find your body, they'll find injuries consistent with a fall from a bridge of great height into water. They'll find water from the Mississippi River in your lungs. Ooh, I haven't shown you that yet."

He left her field of vision, but soon came back, a large five gallon bucket in his hands.

"See this? It's water from the Mississippi. I've been storing in the office for a few weeks. Had to have it along in case an opportunity arose.

"They'll find out you drowned, Rachel. You jumped off a tall bridge and drowned. Because you were suicidal. Your life was changing. You became depressed. It's the perfect crime. Normally I just kill random women, you know? Whores I run into mostly. I rarely kill someone I know. It's too hard."

He hopped back on the table. Straddling on top of her chest. The weight hurt her, she must have injured a rib in the fall. Tears started flowing uncontrollably.

"I love lecturing, you know? I'm a professor. What can I say? I've often wondered why I do this, why I feel this need. And the only conclusion I can come to is that I'm a monster. This is what monsters do. There's no reason or rhyme. It just is. I'm fine with it. You should be too. Think about it, you deserve this. You abandoned your friends, sacrificed your personal life...and for what? For a job? You're just as responsible for your death as me.

"You died long before you appeared on this table. But that's okay. See, you're alive now. We recaptured it. Together. Really alive. Awake, you're there." Paulson leaned in again, wiped a tear from her face, and licked it. "This is the greatest moment of your life."

"See Rachel, there are still philosophical problems in the world. I never got into them while I was in school, but now I've had a lot of time to dwell on these things. Sure, there is no god, no good or evil and no meaning. But there is what is called the 'hard problem of consciousness.' The problem of subjective experience. Skeptics say we can't be sure of anyone's real identity or experiences but our own. It's a very difficult problem. See, you might be a zombie. A robot. Someone who looks and acts like a human, but doesn't enjoy the rich inner-world that I do. A 'Rachel' program acting out determined behaviors. No real feelings. No real 'experiencing.'

"Some say the hard problem doesn't exist; there's no reason to worry about subjective experience. The term itself is unscientific. Meaningless. They define the problem out of existence. They say it's just a masked man fallacy. Our thoughts, our experiences, our consciousnesses are just illusions, emergent phenomena of the parallel processes of our brains.

"An illusion.

"But this proves them wrong." Paulson adjusted his position again. She could feel his entire body on top of her. Belly-to-belly, as if they were making love. His face got very close again. Rachel's mouth had been gagged by something on the inside, and it was held in place by a wrap of velvet. It wasn't tight, but it kept her from being able to scream. He put his lips on her gag. Their eyes met. She tried screaming again.

"Rachel my dear, this is the essence of your subjective experience. Your terror destroys the idea of heterophenomenology. There is no way to observe or report or analyze your experiences right now. Your pain wipes away any thoughts of zombies. I even think this exercise gives credence to property dualism, my dear. I might be a monster, but you are a philosophical goddess in my hands.

"Rachel, this is a celebration of you, yourself. This is your honorificabilitudinitatibus. This is--"

A phone rang. It wasn't the rich timbre of a metal bell in a real phone. It was a digital ring. Fake. From a cellphone.

"Damnit." Paulson got off Rachel and jumped out of view.

*   *   *   *   *   *   *

"Hello, this is Paulson."

"Malcolm, it's Alisha." Paulson darted around his office, looking for a clock. There was one, it said 12:30am.

"Well, it's great hearing from you babe, what's going on?"

"Yeah, look, I know this is late notice, but I really need a fuck tonight."

"Okay," Paulson had to think. *What was the narrative?* "Look, Alisha, it's the archery opener. I'm on my way up north."

"Oh no," She sounded very disappointed.

"Relax, I'll be at my lake cabin. I know someone nearby, I'll be hunting with him tomorrow."

"So you're just going to be up the road aways?"

"Sure," Malcolm debated in his mind. He decided to take a chance. "Want to join me? I'll be hunting most of Saturday and Sunday, but we can spend the nights together. And I'm taking Monday off. So we can spend the whole day together, if you want."

"That would be great Malcolm. I've had a really bad week."

"Just drive on up then, I'll keep the lights on for ya."

"It's going to be three in the morning by the time I get there."

"That's fine."

"And I'm going to want sex. I need to be with someone tonight."

"Just be sure to wake me up for that."

"Great, I'll see you in a bit then." She hung up.

Malcolm walked back into the conference room.

"Well how about this Rachel," he said, "Tonight, my mistress and I are going to share each other's company." Malcolm got face-to-face with Rachel again. "And when I'm fucking her, I'm going to be thinking of you."

*   *   *   *   *   *   *

Paulson poured water into Rachels nostrils. She choked. Tried to cough, and couldn't. Water shot out of her nose. Paulson then grabbed her nose. She couldn't breathe. Just when the pain was too much, he let go and she breathed in again. More water. More choking. Paulson was dropping just a little bit of water, from a paper cup, into her nose. Every once in a while, he'd allow her to catch her breath completely. Then he'd start again.

Rachel didn't feel time anymore. This was eternity. Paulson had stopped talking. He was working now. The look on his face was of pure lust, and pleasure. Rachel prayed and prayed. One full Rosary, at least. Suddenly he pushed her off the table, and she landed on the floor with a thud. The lights came on. Paulson was doing something. She couldn't tell what.

"I almost forgot, I wanted to show you the pictures I took of you," Paulson was excited. "See, when you were unconscious." He flipped the pictures in front of her eyes, which were red with tears. She saw her naked body in the pictures. They were Polaroids. There must have been ten of them. All from different angles.

"These will be very important to me. I wanted to thank you for them."

He left her vision. More activity. He came back and put a bowl down next to her. It was a large clear plastic bowl. Then Paulson poured the water from the bucket into the bowl.

"We use it for Halloween candy," he explained.

There was a long pause. A silence she found most terrifying.

"Rachel, I've read about other serial killers, you know? Others like me. For most of them, this is about rape. Rape is a natural thing, found in nature all over the place. It's a legitimate means of reproduction. It's evolution at work. That's why so many women are the victims of multiple rape, far more than we would expect through random chance. Simple Darwinism.

"So a natural explanation of serial killers is that we are just on the extreme end of the rape-as-reproduction continuum. In fact, we could be a check on the system by removing ourselves and our victims from the gene pool, thus limiting the amount of rape happening, allowing complex social societies to develop. It's been an idea I've been interested in for a long time. This is all conjecture, of course...

"But for me, this isn't about rape. It's about power. Life and death. When I do this, I become more than a man. An *Übermensch*. I become more than the sum of my parts. I am better than other men.

"And who could argue? Did you know that I've actually ordered a major office renovation to start this weekend? It will contaminate the crime scene. It gives an explanation for why there's a van parked outside the door. It keeps the police from getting too curious about the lights being on; I told them there'd be crew in here all weekend, at all hours, trying to get everything done before the work week started.

"It's perfect. And once I kill you, I get to clean your body." He bent down to look her in the eyes. "And believe me, I'm going to enjoy that. Scrubbing off every foreign fiber and hair.

"I wish I had more time to chat. To celebrate. But I have appointments to keep"

He dragged the bowl closer to Rachel.

"Take a deep breath Rachel. It's your last."

She did. Then she closed her eyes, and was forever alive in that moment.

Rolling her face down, he got on top of her, lifted her head and put it face down into the bowl. Her body shook, fought, with an energy that surprised him. But die she eventually did. He pushed the bowl away from her. Then he just laid there next to her for a few minutes. He looked at the clock. Time was running out.

He cut off her gag and removed the fabric he had put in her mouth. It was her panties. She had worn black underwear, which Paulson found very arousing. He placed the panties into a ziplock bag. The garment and the pictures were his trophies this night.

Paulson never felt so good.

     *   *   *   *   *   *   *

Rachel's body was wrapped in an old rug. Paulson walked right out the side door of Morrill Hall, to the van parked on the sidewalk. He opened the back doors and tossed her in. You couldn't tell, from a distance, that there was anything amiss about the rug. Up close the guise would fail, but no one was around.

It took real skill to kill in the middle of the city. And Paulson was proud of every prize from the Twin Cities. The women he preyed upon out-state, they felt like cheating.

Paulson drove the van back to where his car was parked. Rachel's death was his masterpiece, and it was almost complete. He drove past his Suburban, down a dirt road to a small area where the rowing club berthed their boats. It was a great water access. But the nearby pedestrian bridge normally housed one or two homeless people.

Paulson had ordered the UMPD to crack down on the bridge-dwellers, but he had to make sure. Walking up from the water access, he found no evidence of life. He returned to the van. Opened the back, unrolled the carpet. Rachel's lifeless body flopped out. He had gotten her dress back on, but the straps on her shoes had broken. He tossed these far into the river. Then he tossed her purse into the river.

Except, he had taken her Rosary, and he put it around his own neck. He chuckled to himself, when he thought about the idea of God. *How ridiculous*. He took off his shoes and pants, then his jacket and shirt.

It was time to dump Rachel. Lifting her body up on his shoulder for the last time, he waded into the murky Mississippi waters. The current was fast and soon he was almost over his head. He pushed Rachel away from him, and the current grabbed her. He just hoped she would travel far down the river, so the police could believe she jumped off of the Washington Avenue Bridge.

Paulson had lost his footing on the rocks and the current grabbed him too, but he swam back to the launch area. He looked back. Rachel was gone, and he was soaked. He drove the van back up to the loading docks of the abandoned Mineral Resources building. There he switched back to his Suburban. The clock on his dash said 2:01am. He had just enough time to drive to his cabin and sneak into bed before Alisha arrived.

Based on his current level of arousal, Alisha was in for the toss of her life.

*   *   *   *   *   *   *

CHAPTER 15

Friday, October 7
St. Lawrence Catholic Church, Dinkytown.

Solemn is the funeral for a Catholic suicide.

To outsiders, the Church's reaction to suicide was callous. Unjust.

Suicide is caused by depression, mental illness. It's not the fault of the person. It's cruel to condemn those who fall victim to a chemical imbalance in the brain. Suicide is tragic enough without removing the victim from the benefits of God's Grace.

The tragedy of suicide is in fact served well by Catholicism.

Studies done from when statistical studies were a new thing, to studies done when statistical studies were the playthings of bored graduate students, all show Catholics enjoying significantly lower suicide rates than their Protestant counterparts. From this perspective, hardline Catholicism has saved many millions of lives over the centuries.

Outside of the pragmatic, the Catholic reaction to suicide is also a product of the everlasting struggle with moral freedom. Humans have moral freedom, which means they have some free will. God could harden hearts to reason or strike fear in the faithful, but to pull the trigger on a gun, to leap from a building, to take action to end one's life took positive action from the person. Action only the person had control over. Only the most ardent determinists argued otherwise. Free Will; Free Won't? either way, suicide was a choice. Suppress those suicidal *Bereitschaftspotential*, or risk the wrath of God.

Suicide was the ultimate rejection of the Divine. You were not arguing with God, like Lot. You were not lamenting like Job. You were giving God the finger. Life was the gift of linear continuous experiences. Experiences were the foundation of memories. Memories gave personal identity. From identity came purpose. From purpose came joy and wonder. This became creativity. And by taking active part in Creation itself, the individual learned to touch the Divine. To discover love. To realize God.

Through suicide, you said 'Fuck this, fuck you, I'm outta here.'

It was the Ultimate rejection.

It meant the end of faith.

To believe in God one had faith that existence itself, yours in particular, was part of a grand design to increase the good in the world. That despite suffering, pain, evil and vice, God knew there was value in bringing beings such as humans into existence. There was a greater good beyond our comprehension but requiring our participation.

Suicide wasn't to fail the test, it was to rebuke the idea of education.

Rachel's casket lay in St. Lawrence Catholic Church. The Dinkytown church served a mostly student congregation. Father Mike Pavano presided over the service, which was small and informal. Rachel's parents were transporting her body back to Madison, Wisconsin for a formal service at her hometown church. This service was for the students, something her parents felt was important.

About eighty people showed up, including most of The Organization. Every member of all the pro-life organizations also showed. The girls outnumbered the guys two to one; big Frank Wallace was sad about Rachel, but couldn't help thinking about the gender gap in the crowd and his prospects for companionship later.

Even the University President, Malcolm Paulson, showed up. Turnout was low. News hadn't gotten out. Her suicide note had been discovered by a janitor on Sunday. Her body was found Tuesday, hung up on some roots by the river flats just south of Coffman. The coroner found no indications of foul play. The police dropped the investigation prematurely, at the request of the family.

Only the Minnesota Daily covered Rachel's death, with one

article hidden away between the opinion page and the crossword puzzle. At the request of the family.

When a Catholic anti-abortion activist commits suicide, it's hypocrisy. And hypocrisy is the greatest sin among true believers.

Zan wasn't Catholic, felt awkward at Catholic services. So he showed up late and hid in the back of the church. He hoped no one noticed him come in. No one did. Except Ernie Kessler, also not a Catholic. Ernie showed up late too. He sat next to Zan on the back pew.

Father Pavano talked about Rachel. Her years as a volunteer for the Church. Her good works. The importance of her life to her friends. There was no mention of God. There was no mention of how she died. There was nothing to say about those things. She did commit suicide, after all. It was not an act of callousness. Father Pavano had spent twelve hours the previous day praying for Rachel from his knees.

Tomorrow he would do so again.

There was silence as Pavano splashed Holy Water on the casket. Then he led the congregation in a Latin prayer Zan and Ernie didn't know.

Kessler noticed Zan smelled of booze.

"Have you been drinking?" Kessler asked Zan in a whisper.

"I'll splain later," Zan whispered back.

Kessler wasn't happy but let it go.

After forty minutes, the service was called to a close and Rachel was carried out by her family, two brothers, a sister, her parents and her godfather. Everyone was invited to a small reception, held in another room of the church. Kessler led Zan outside and took him for a short walk.

When they were far enough away from the church, in a small parking lot next door, Kessler started in on Zan.

"What the Hell is this Zan? You're fucking drunk. At a funeral."

"Lissin," he replied, slurring his words, "itsa for my head. Isth the only thing sat helps wit ta pain."

"I know all about your head, you should be back in a hospital."

"People die in hosbitals Ernie. I'ma not dying."

"Did you drive here like this?"

"Yeah," he replied, "but itsa not as hard astey say it tis."

Kessler was angry. There was nothing he could do about it. They walked back to the church. A small room on the west side of the church building had been outfitted with folding chairs and round tables. There was soup, bread and coffee at the reception. Kessler and Zan found a seat and Kessler tried to get Zan to drink some coffee. But no going. The caffeine made Zan's head 'schpin.'

The two stayed quiet and watched everyone greet and talk. Rachel's parents, good looking Midwesterners from Wisconsin, were handling things well. Better than Painter, who was openly crying. Painter, Zeale, Witold, Wallace and Horace sat together. They waved over Zan and Kessler. Kessler gave Painter the 'stay there' pushing signal with his hands when Painter got up to visit them. He obeyed, as did the rest of the crew.

Zan had consumed several rolls and looked to be sobering. Some. Kessler hadn't seen Zan since his head injury. It was a more serious problem than he thought. Zan never drank, and now he was self-medicating. Kessler's thoughts were interrupted by Malcolm Paulson.

"Mr. Kessler," he said, "I'm so very sorry. This has been such a tragedy."

"Indeed it has Malcolm," Kessler preferred the familial, "I can't express how I feel about the whole thing."

"What is there to express?" he replied. "There can only be grief."

"Grief and curiosity," Kessler returned.

"Curiosity?" Paulson asked.

"Yes, curiosity...I'm curious if she showed any signs of problems, stuff that should have been caught, but was missed."

"You have to be careful about this sort of thing Mr. Kessler," Paulson stated. "A man can go crazy with the what-ifs in life. Personally, I thought she was handling the new stress of her job rather well. But I didn't know about her boyfriend, or how she was becoming more reclusive. There's nothing we could have done. Really, who worries about a devout Catholic committing suicide, right?"

"Yes, I suppose so."

"And Mr. Chin-Wu, how did you know Rachel?" Paulson asked at Zan, who had remained seated and had ignored Paulson's presence.

"I don't remember," was Zan's only reply. He didn't even turn to look at Paulson.

"A tragedy." With that, Paulson worked his way to the next table and introduced himself.

Kessler sat down and stared Zan down. "You have got to get your act together Zan, this is unacceptable."

"What are you, my mother?" some of Zan's lucidity had returned. "I don't need to take crap from you."

"Maybe it's time you went back to the hospital Zan," Kessler saw the fight coming and tried to calm Zan down.

"I don't need a hospital. I need to destroy that man."

"Who?" Kessler asked, confused.

"Paulson, of course."

"What do you mean?"

"I mean, Paulson took Rachel away from us. And he took Alisha away from me. He needs to be destroyed." Zan's voice had started to rise in volume. "I'm gonna kill him."

"Zan, just relax. You shouldn't be talking like this, now let's go outside--"

"Fuck outside!" Zan got up from the table, then kicked it over. "And fuck you."

Everyone turned and looked at Zan. He looked around at them. He kicked the overturned table and walked out the door.

Kessler walked over and sat with Painter and the rest of the crew.

*   *   *   *   *   *   *

"What is wrong with Zan?" Painter asked Kessler. Painter's eyes were swollen and red. "He hasn't talked to anybody. Hasn't answered the phone. Practically disappears. Then he shows up here like a fucking homeless person and makes a scene. What the hell is that?"

"I don't know," Kessler said, "he was really hurt boxing a little while ago. Nobody really knew how badly 'til he got to the hospital. Then he snuck out before being released."

Zeale asked, "Is he on something?"

"Just booze it looks like, but he might be mixing some other drugs in too." Kessler sighed. "As far as I know, he hasn't left the house until he showed up here today. He even took his phone off the hook."

"You think he's going nuts because of the Alisha thing?" Painter was wondering aloud.

"That's just it," Kessler replied, "he was nuts before. We're all nuts. We have to be. But we have to be cognizant of it. Maybe he's not anymore...or maybe he's just lost the ability to control it."

*   *   *   *   *   *   *

CHAPTER 16

Saturday, November 5

Postering. Parties. Lit-dropping. Phonebanking. Envelope stuffing. Test-taking. Vandalism. Lectures. Papers. Postering. Drinking. Bar Hopping. All nighters. Postering. Fornicating. Arguing. Door knocking. Reading. Letters to the Editor. Chair throwing. Postering. To-do lists. Cramming. Drinking. Laundry. Postering.

THE EDUCATOR

Time flies.

Five weeks can be but a dream.

Rachel was gone, but she had been gone.

Zan went AWOL.

Zeale and Painter pressed on with help from Kessler and Chris Berg. Wednesday nights were still about the Big Ten. The Organization was still a collection of neurotic insomniacs. Politics still drove them to this life of masochism.

But something spiritual was missing.

     *   *   *   *   *   *   *

Campaigning sucks.

It takes all types of people to make a campaign.

And campaigning is fundamentally evil.

The process itself should be taken skeptically. Good can arise from a fundamentally evil process, but the nature of the process still has to be understood.

Politics is social. People become interested in politics only through the social contacts they have. No social contact, no politics.

Bothering people with politics, by forcing them to interact with the politically-motivated, is the best way to win elections.

And in the twentieth century this means phonebanking.

No one enjoys it.

Occasionally some retired woman would take perverse pleasure in calling thousands of people and bugging them to support such-and-such political candidate. Either it was a loneliness thing, or a payback thing. But it was always a woman. Campaigns that were lucky had a few.

In the absence of retired women and young people, local parties pressured the pathetically ambitious for phonebanking.

Or the outright delusional.

It took all types.

Politics is a lesson in abnormal psychology.

     *   *   *   *   *   *   *

"Hello, my name is Gene and I'm calling on behalf of Congressman Rod Gr--Hello?" Gene Zeale checked a name off his call list. Then he dialed another.

"Hello, my name is Gene and I'm calling on behalf of Congressman Rod Grams, I'd like to personally encourage you to vote for Congressman Grams this Tuesday to become Minnesota's next Senator."

The earpiece tinned 'Fuck off' then clicked.

Zeale checked another name off his call list. Dialed another number. No answer. Another number.

"Hello, my name is Gene and I'm calling on behalf of Congressman Rod Grams, I'd like to personally encourage you to vote for Congressman Grams this Tuesday to become Minnesota's next Senator."

On the other end of the line, an aged voice, vaguely womanish, asked "Don't you have anything better to do?"

"Not really...are you going to vote for Congressman Grams?"

"I wouldn't tell you."

"Well you should vote for him."

"And why is that?"

"He'll bring Midwestern values back to the Senate"

"Do you really believe that?"

"No, but that's what this sheet here says I'm supposed to say."

"I'm hanging up now, goodbye."

Zeale checked off another name. Dialed again.

"Hello, who's this?" The voice on the other side was gruff, manly, a little angry.

"Hello, my name is Gene and I'm calling on behalf of Congressman Rod Grams, I'd like to personally encourage you to vote for Congressman Grams this Tuesday to become Minnesota's next Senator."

"Damnit, you people have called me seven times already this month. I'll tell you what I told them all, I'm voting for the man, so stop calling me already."

"That's great, I'm sorry you've been receiving so many calls--"

"Why is that?"

"Oh, that's easy to explain sir. We have research that clearly shows you can increase turnout in midterm elections about five percent among politically-friendly voters who normally only vote in presidential election years. But you have to call them more than five times."

"No shit?"

"No shit."

"Well," said the man's voice, a little less angry, "you got your five phone calls in, so stop bugging me already."

"I'll see what I can do."

Zeale checked off the name, but highlighted it to represent a positive response. Then he dialed the next number.

"Hello?" This voice belonged to a girl, clearly too young to vote.

"Hey there, are your parents home?"

"No."

"Then fuck off kid." Zeale said, hanging up. He checked the name off the list.

Zeale took off his headset and stretched out his arms. Kayla was sitting next to him. She wrapped up a call and took off her headset.

"You know, if anyone from the Grams' campaign catches you talking like that, they'll kick you out," she stated.

"I'm a hundred numbers into a two-thousand number list. They can go ahead and kick me out."

"What's been your worst call so far?"

"Oh, I don't know," Zeale thought for a second, "I think the feminista accusing me of male colonialism has to rank up there."

"Really?" Kayla was disappointed, "I had one guy ask if I had great tits."

"What did you tell him?"

"I said 'yes' of course."

Zeale laughed. "Well, I can't top that."

He put on his headset, checked his list, and dialed. Kayla went back to her list.

The phone rang, a woman answered "Hello?"

"Hi, do you have great tits?" Zeale asked. The woman hung up.

He crossed off the name. And the next two.

It made no difference to him, really.

*　　*　　*　　*　　*　　*　　*

CHAPTER 17

Sunday, November 6
South Minneapolis

Zan took a drink from his flask.

Zan took pride in his work; this was an old-fashioned stakeout. He kept his distance. Stayed hidden.

Zan didn't know why he did all this. It was something to do. It was the only thing he wanted to do. He couldn't go back to his boxing gym. No more martial arts. Zan even stopped jogging. There wasn't much point. Someday, Zan assumed he'd build up the courage to confront Paulson and Alisha. He didn't know what he would do. He'd have to figure it out.

He took another swig from the flask. Alisha didn't work most Sundays. She was at home. Paulson was rarely around on the weekends. His reputation as an outdoorsman was well-earned. Maybe Zan would start following Paulson around on his out-state expeditions.

For now, he was content with Alisha.

Around noon she had done some yard work. Raked some leaves. Watered some plants. Then she left. He followed her to a movie theatre. She was watching the Shawshank Redemption, again. Zan bought a ticket and trailed her in. Easy to do at Har Mar. He liked watching her at the movies. She got involved in the films. Laughed loud. Cried. Got scared at scary points. Zan could maneuver himself really close. Sometimes he'd get the seat directly behind her. She never looked back, Never got up from her seat. Never ate any food. Entering the theatre the world around her was no more.

Zan would sneak out of the movie early to get to his car. Alisha would often do some shopping and head home. Today was no different. She went through Rainbow foods. Zan followed her in, shadowed her. Tried to keep track of what she was buying. Then he let her leave on her own. He caught up with her on 35W. He followed her home.

He had spent the last eight hours on stakeout. Sitting in his car, half a block from her house, he debated spending the night. It was twilight. Another swig from the flask. Before the debate was over, he fell asleep.

*   *   *   *   *   *   *

Tapping. Tapping.

Zan couldn't figure out why the sound of his fists on Alisha's face were making such a sound. Like glass. Glass tapping. A light. The scene evaporated.

Zan opened his eyes. A flashlight was shining in his face. Someone was holding the light, and tapping it against the glass. The fuzziness melted away. Zan realized he was in his car. And that his car was half a block away from Alisha's place.

Zan saw it was a police officer doing the tapping. He swore at himself, and obediently rolled down the window. He hoped his alcohol level had gone down below the legal level.

*   *   *   *   *   *   *

"Sir," The police officer was huge. He towered over Zan at six-foot six-inches tall, and he had to weigh 400 pounds. The officer was also really enjoying this, by the looks of his smug grin. "How much have you had to drink?"

"I dunno, over a lifetime at least several kilolitres," Zan concentrated on every phoneme.

"I meant today."

"Not sure."

"A flask of Jack Daniels maybe?" The officer pointed to the flask on the passenger seat.

"Not sure."

"Did you know Minnesota law prohibits anyone under the influence of alcohol to control in any way a motor vehicle?"

"The law specifically says 'physical control.' I wasn't in physical control, I was napping. Plus, the keys weren't in the ignition. There's no physics to it."

"Smartass, huh?"

"Worse, went to law school." Zan's head was pounding, he needed a drink.

"Do you mind?" The officer held up a small contraption, a breathalyzer.

"I'd rather not."

"You're refusing?"

"I'm just saying I'd prefer not to."

"Minnesota has an implied consent law son."

"Yes, and had I been driving, and had you probable cause, I would not refuse the test."

"You're a smart cookie. But you are still in violation of the open container law."

"No officer," Zan replied, "my container had a lid screwed on. Plus the vehicle wasn't under power. It's legal to transport closed containers of alcohol on Minnesota roads. Or not to, in my case."

The police officer mulled things over. "Can you tell me why you're out here tonight?"

"Not really."

"That's funny, since it was your ex-girlfriend who called you in for stalking. She says you've been following her around a lot."

Zan thought for a moment, he had to be careful. "Napping in an unmoving vehicle is generally not a regulated activity."

"You're dodging the issue...but, yes it is. You're not supposed to be napping in a vehicle."

"Only on the Interstate is a vehicle subject to tag and tow if stopped for non-emergency purposes. Abandoned vehicles are subject to tow if left overnight on public highways. Parking can be regulated locally. But nothing about napping, sir."

"You're definitely a smartass."

"Quite so."

"Now look, I got nothing on ya," Such an admission gave Zan a sigh of relief, "but I can tell you I know what's going on here. I see it enough. One person gets obsessed about another, and it just causes all sorts of problems. Now I told that woman over yonder to go get herself a lawyer and get a restraining order on you. When she does, if I catch you here again I'll throw your ass in jail. Understand?"

"Yes."

"Good. Now do yourself a favor and forget about this chick, aight?"

"Yes sir."

Zan knew if he got in the car and put the keys in, he could get hit with a DWI. So he waited. An hour went by. The officer stayed. Zan's head felt worse and worse. Another twenty minutes and Zan got in his car and drove back home. The police officer followed him all the way up 35W north to Zan's exit. But didn't pull him over. It was midnight by the time Zan got to his place.

He walked up the stairs to his apartment, unlocked the door, went to the fridge, got a bottle of vodka, put a straw in it, and climbed into bed.

*   *   *   *   *   *   *

CHAPTER 18

11pm Monday, November 7
The Steps of Northrup Auditorium

Nolan Painter sat in the dark.

The glow from his cigar the only sign of his presence.

Fall was yielding to the cold of winter. The cold arrived long before the snow did. But the temperature still held autumn's hand. In the dark, leaning against the stone pillars of Northrup Auditorium, Painter was still quite comfortable in a dark fleece pullover and black sweatpants. Forty degrees Fahrenheit was 'Parka and Shorts' weather in Minnesota.

Half an hour went by.

Painter loved the solitude and quiet.

Spags and Kayla showed up, each carrying cardboard boxes and backpacks filled with material. The inseparable pair sat down together, leaning against another of the giant pillars. No words were spoken besides the occasional whisper between the couple. Two-thousand cold phone calls took the talk outta ya.

A few minutes later Bob Restovich appeared; Buzzcut not more than a minute behind him. Tonya Evans and Frank Wallace walked up the steps together. Jason Kang was the last to arrive. The quiet had stopped the moment Tonya arrived. It always did; the woman was an incessant talker. Garrulous. Loquacious. Maddening. But pretty, so all was forgiven.

Conversations sprang up. Some even unrelated to impressing Tonya, so Painter interrupted them all.

"Alright, let's quiet down. There's no reason to let everyone know we're here." Painter waited a second for quiet, then continued, "Here's the deal; we have to tie up as many liberal activists on this campus as possible. They're going to be postering everywhere. So we have to poster over their posters. That way, they have to come back and redo everything. The more of their man-hours spent here, the less they can spend in swing districts."

"Why aren't we going to swing districts?"

"We will. We're pulling an all-nighter. Chris Berg will be picking us up in pairs and driving us to the suburbs for lit-dropping. We're starting on-campus as a big group to try and intimidate the U-DFL. Then we slowly disappear over the night. Chris shows up in an hour. I want Buzzcut and Kayla back here to meet him first, he'll drive up just to the west of Northrup in his big white molester van.

"And it will continue like that. Tonya and Frank go at two. Kang and I go at three. That leaves Spags and Restovich. They're stuck here until morning."

"Hooah," Restovich said.

Spags added, "We'll meet up at the County-D Perkins for breakfast, then we're doing election day phonebanking in St. Paul. Chris Berg and Orson Henning, some of our alumni for you new people, will be driving. Berg has a cellphone--" He was interrupted by some 'oohs' and whistling, "on him so you can call him from a payphone if there's a problem. We're storing our stuff right here, in case you run out of posters or staples or something."

With that the group split off in different directions.

Once everyone had gone, Spags and Restovich took off to the North. There were some kiosks to hit up that way. But mostly, Spags and Restovich were more interested in spending the next few hours in the Dinkytown McDonald's, open until 3am.

*   *   *   *   *   *   *

The posters simply said "Vote Grams" and were printed at the local Kinko's. There was no sense in using any of the campaign's real posters or signage as it would be a waste. The groups circulated about the campus, occasionally running into groups of DFLers who were doing the same. The whole exercise was rather silly. The rules regarding student use of the kiosks stated no posters could be torn down, but they could be covered up.

And both groups of students adhered to the rules. The kiosks were thick with layers of alternating Republican and Democrat posters. The liberals would taunt the conservatives. They had more people, more stuff, nicer signs and more women. Not necessarily more attractive.

Sophomoric behavior among sophomores. A great way to describe all politics.

The conservatives slowly disappeared.

Spags and Restovich walked back to Northrup around three in the morning.

"I think you're wrong," Restovich said, the two had been in the same debate for sometime, "why should a government require you to post signs warning about landmines on your property?"

"First of all, the property needs to be marked in some ways, or else you'll just have a bunch of kids getting blown up finding a shortcut to the playground. Secondly, if you're required to post signs, you no longer need to have any landmines."

"If everyone starts putting up signs with no landmines it will create a situation worse than not putting up signs at all." Restovish retorted. "People will just ignore the signs and it will take a wholesale slaughter to get them to start paying attention again."

Spags thought things out for a second. "Landowners can easily avoid this problem by raising deer and other livestock. That way, occasionally, the livestock will be blown up by landmines. It will be a subtle indication that landmines are present."

"Now you're doing the common liberal thing, protecting a bad regulation with another regulation. Only this one is expensive because it costs the landowners extra landmines and dead livestock."

"There has to be some indication to innocent people that they are approaching private property and should stay away."

At this point the argument circled again. The 'Libertarian Utopia Landmine Conundrum' was a difficult problem that floated around the group, had for a decade. Not only was it an important philosophical question, it also helped separate out the moderate fucks from the group.

The peripatetic discussion took the duo to the steps of Northrup in no time. Unfortunately, when they got there they just found empty boxes. No more posters. No more staples.

"Looks like we can go home and take a nap," Restovich said.

"Fuck that," Zeale replied, "You have a car right?"

"Yeah, it's in Oak."

"There's a Wal-Mart about half an hour from here, open 24 hours. I think we can win this."

"Win?"

"Well, have fun at least. Having fun is basically winning."

*   *   *   *   *   *   *

Gene 'Spags' Zeale was leading Bob Restovich to the toy section. The plan Zeale had in mind was yet to be enunciated. When Zeale grabbed a supersoaker water gun then went over to the kerosene refills in the camping supplies aisle, Restovich figured it out.

"You want to torch the kiosks?"

"Sure," replied Zeale, "how fast can you run?"

"I was blown up by an anti-tank mine."

Bob's statement was answered with silence. He thought for a second. "Okay," Bob said, "we start running around the campus with homemade flamethrowers, we're going to get caught for sure. I've got a better idea. Improvised incendiaries. We do this right, we should be able to time everything so we're nowhere near the kiosks when they catch fire."

      *   *   *   *   *   *   *

They purchased candles, stick matches, duct tape, a half dozen bottles of paraffin lamp oil, several cotton t-shirts, staples and two boxes of sandwich bags. In ten minutes they were back on the road. During the drive, Restovich barked orders at Zeale; an honor not normally given to a first year recruit, but the man was a special case.

"Alright, take the tape and wrap one of the small bundles of matches to the candle...Good, now repeat the process until we have twenty of these candles."

Zeale worked in silence.

Bob's car was a dull green 1979 Caprice Classic 4-door with a modified engine that got eight miles to the gallon. It could hit 140 MPH in a pinch. It just didn't maneuver well. Or stop all that well. But Restovich liked the fact his car could hold its own against a police cruiser.

To what end he didn't speculate.

      *   *   *   *   *   *   *

They hid their materials in one of the cardboard boxes at Northrup. Restovich had explained how everything should work. The sandwich bags would be filled with lamp oil and placed underneath the many layers of posters already on the kiosks. The candles with the bundles of matches were attached to DFL posters near the bottom of the poster kiosks. Strips of cotton t-shirts, soaked in oil, would be attached directly above the matches. They would tape everything in place, light the candle and keep moving.

The candles, mounted sideways on the kiosks, would take thirty minutes to burn down to the matches. Theoretically. The matches ignited the oily shirt strips. Theoretically. Those strips would set fire to the posters. Theoretically. And the bags of lamp oil would fuel the fire until the entire kiosk was consumed. Theoretically. Thus ending the struggle for poster dominance with a scorched earth strategy.

Theoretically.

The conditions were perfect. There was no wind. The candles burned without risk of being blown out. It took some fiddling to keep the candles from setting fire to the posters prematurely. The two men worked quickly setting up their Rube Goldberg incendiaries. They only hit the poster kiosks on the walking platform of the Washington Avenue Bridge and those in the Mall area. Eight total kiosks with twenty little devices. They never did see any of their liberal counterparts.

Starting at 4:45am, the two finished twenty minutes later. Just as their first devices were igniting.

On the West Bank of campus, they decided to walk the long way back to Dinkytown where the Caprice was parked on the street. Zeale lived in a small house just north of Dinkytown with some of the buddies he lad left over from his time in the dorms. The two were excited. There would be time for a nap before breakfast.

At a phone-booth in Dinkytown, Zeale called the Minnesota Daily. They always had someone working the situation desk, 24/7. It was a lonely and boring job. On the tenth ring, the fucker picked up.

"Fires at the Mall in front of Northrup," he told the man. Zeale hung up the phone. And they continued on.

*   *   *   *   *   *   *

CHAPTER 19

5:30pm Tuesday, November 8
Zeale's place on 14th and 7th, Dinkytown

"You want me to get off of you?"

Kayla's question came in such an abrupt and casual manner that it instantly removed Zeale from the post-sex euphoria. Zeale hated it. He always hated it. But she did it every time.

Before Zeale offered an answer, she had already bounced her way off the bed and into the bathroom. The water in the shower was running before Spags decided to move.

The two had spent the last ten hours in St. Paul doing GOTV, Get Out The Vote, phonebanking for Rod Grams. 'Hey, I'm Gene, a volunteer calling on behalf of Congressman Rod Grams, I wanted to encourage you to get out and vote today if you haven't already'

Spags had delivered the phrase almost eleven hundred times during the day. Kayla and most of the other crew had suffered through it as well; except Chris Berg, Nolan Painter and Orson Henning. The three elders used their patriarchal status to take the easiest of election day jobs, standing on street corners, waving campaign signs at passing motorists.

At four o'clock the crew was replaced with yuppie Young Republican volunteers. YRs were brown-nosing boot-licking establishment wannabes trying to whore their way into political work. Generally they were business professionals working office jobs, wearing suits and they couldn't shut up about the weather, traffic or their retirement accounts. Zeale was happy to get out of their presence.

Restovich was stuck dragging everyone to Zeale's place in his car, it took two trips thanks to traffic. Zeale's roommates, fairly knavish gents, were out going to classes. The house was an ancient structure, well over a hundred years old. Falling apart. Rotting. Grime, dirt, garbage and dirty clothes, all strewn about along with dirty dishes and empty beer bottles. Pictures of women in lingerie were scattered about the walls.

In other words, it was a typical collegiate bachelor pad.

The crew had gone out to The Library for some drinks and food. Zeale and Kayla stayed behind long enough to fuck and freshen up. After the shower, they were going to walk over to The Library and wait for the Elders to get back from signwaving.

Getting up from the bed, Zeale walked into the bathroom. Hoping to reclaim his sexual vigor, he interrupted Kayla's shower.

*　　　*　　　*　　　*　　　*　　　*　　　*

"I fucking hate Saint Paul." The booming voice of Chris Berg could be heard across The Library. The Dinkytown bar was quiet, empty. Not unexpected at six in the evening on a Tuesday.

The Library was a great hangout. Good food, good service, clean facilities. The only problem was the clientele. An annoying selection of fratboyish college students and ditzy sorority chicks, and the pathetic yuppie twentysomethings who wished themselves into the college clique.

"Saint Paul is the fat chick that won't take you to prom," Berg continued, "you expect a yes, she's supposed to say yes, but she doesn't."

Kayla and Spags walked over and sat down. Greetings were shouted. Bob Restovich, Nolan Painter, Chris Berg, Orson Henning, Frank Wallace, Buzzcut, Jason Kang and Tonya Hotchick were seated around two rectangular tables.

"What's this crap about Saint Paul?" Zeale asked.

"Bradley at the Grams' campaign sent us to Saint Paul to do the high-visibility signwaving," Henning said, "so Chris tells him we'd rather hit Minneapolis."

"So this guy tells us," Berg interjected, "that we need to do well in Saint Paul and we have a better chance so that's where we have to go.

"So there we are, all damn day on Larpenteur and Snelling. No reactions, no horns honking, nothing. Fucking invisible."

"See," Nolan added, "it's what Zan always told us, working in Minneapolis does something. If only confrontations. So we lose, we're supposed to lose, it's Minneapolis. But at least we'll get noticed. Saint Paul, where Republicans are supposed to do better, sucks. You don't get the confrontation; the press; the crazies; nothing.

"Minneapolis is the hot chick you know will turn you down if you ask her out to prom. But you should do it anyway. Saint Paul is the fat chick you keep in reserve. You ask her when you fail elsewhere. But you shouldn't ask Saint Paul, because she will fool you. She'll turn you down. Then you're fucked. You were turned down by the fat chick. Which is just pathetic. That's why we hate Saint Paul."

"Very poetic," Kayla commented. "So when do we leave for Saint Paul?"

"Kessler wants us there at eight so we can help him setup his suite."

*   *   *   *   *   *   *

Politics is about fucking.

Really, all the activities of mankind are related in some way or another to sex. But politics is simply the pursuit of the tribal leadership power, and the privileges associated with it, leftover from the ancient past of humanity's ancestors. The one male in any group of any species of mammals who has no concerns about reproduction is the alpha male.

People like to believe we are beyond this. On election night, the news is scrubbed of stories pertaining to mistresses, partners, sex or evolution. It's about politicians, policies and electoral results. Speeches are given, gratitude is expressed and platitudes about the 'American Republic at work again' are bandied about. But at the end of the night, the huff and puff of politics is about locking up pussy; and there are few ways for incompetent old fat guys to attract fertile young women except through winning an election.

Power is the ultimate aphrodisiac.

At the Saint Paul Hotel in downtown Saint Paul were gathered dozens of campaigns: candidates, workers, professional hacks, interested politicos and state powerbrokers. Also in attendance were the College and Young Republicans, providing scores of young women, in many cases attractive through youth alone, to participate in the ancient power dance.

In the large banquet hall people mingled. Sharing stories, complaining about Democrats, drinking booze. Tuxedo'd servants walked to and fro, dispensing alcohol and disgusting appetizers. Large campaigns had rented out conference rooms around the banquet halls, with food and liquor available to roaming partygoers. The goal was simple: eat as much food as possible, drink as much booze as possible, and bag some tail.

Modern tribalism at its finest.

Smaller campaigns were stuck buying rooms in the hotel, out of which more food and liquor were dispensed. People walked the halls, looking for open doors and unescorted women.

Ernie Kessler, a wealthy VIP uninterested in being the center of attention, was renting a large suite, the Ordway Suite. The door stayed shut, only those who knew Kessler knew enough to go ahead and knock. The suite had a bar, a large dining area, big screen TVs, Victorian furniture and a buffet of food provided by the hotel.

Kessler lied about needing the crew at eight to set up; hotel employees handled everything. But Rod Grams and his sycophants were making the rounds and stopped by Kessler's room early before the Congressman was needed elsewhere. Polling data showed Grams was up by a few points in the race. A few points in a poll meant nothing for a conservative in Minnesota. The local unions could conjure votes in the twilight of election day thanks to same-day voter registration.

After several minutes of inane chatter, the Grams' crew moved on. The only holdover was a fat man wearing an ill-fitting suit. Painter and Zeale recognized their old tormenter, John 'Shotgun' Underhill.

Shotgun took over a Victorian chair, surrendered by Painter. Then he began consuming a healthy helping of buffet.

"So Shotgun," Painter decided to break the ice with Shotgun, who, when around food, was almost autistic, "how do you like our future Senator?"

"Wynia's right, the guy's a Ted Baxter," the fat man replied, mouth filled with food, "and what's worse is the worthless motherfuckers he surrounds himself with. I kinda hope he loses, I'll probably end up killing myself if he wins and I have to work on his staff."

"What's wrong with them?" Zeale asked.

"It's the same shit," Shotgun replied, "they're either pathetic sycophants or arrogant pricks. And they're lazy. But at least Rod likes to keep a lot of young women around. The guy loves the ladies."

Kessler stepped into the conversation, "Ladies?"

"Yeah, another 'Family Values' candidate who's sleeping with people other than his wife."

"That's not good," Kessler said quietly.

"Who cares?" said Shotgun. "He's never going to win re-election. Chris Berg already ran fifteen hundred or so simulations with his demographic software; even if our immigration patterns change significantly, there's like a five percent chance he wins re-election."

"Let's not get ahead of ourselves," Kessler added, "Grams hasn't won yet."

"He will," Shotgun returned, "Barkley's sitting at four percent right now. He's eating DFL votes twice as fast as Republicans. If he stays right there, we'll be up by a healthy margin. There's no way Wynia gets fifty percent of the vote. It's in the bag."

For a few minutes they sat and watched the news on the TV. The GOP was picking up congressional seats all throughout the south. The night had the early markings of a GOP slaughter.

His plate empty of food, Shotgun began to notice the world around him. "Hey where's Chris? Where'r your undergrads?"

Painter, Kessler, Zeale and Shotgun were alone in the suite, when just a few minutes ago it had been full of people.

*　　　*　　　*　　　*　　　*　　　*　　　*

Republicans despise other Republicans.

The people you hate the most are not those of the opposition party. It's those in your own party.

The hate is natural.

You have expectations of these people. You make assumptions about their behavior. You simply don't have these expectations from members of the other party. You may get along with your opponents, may even be friends, but when you need help in political matters, you don't turn to them. But the people you do turn to can never meet your desires. Any small differences you have with these people becomes exaggerated in the pressure cooker of campaign season. These relationships become stressed, and eventually break.

And the hate builds.

After a while, an activist must find a way to release steam. Some choose to handle disappointment with disappointment. If someone they don't like asks them to work a campaign, they agree; then they don't show up. They promise and don't deliver. Over time, they share and spread the frustration and hate. This sort of attitude is poison for those who wish to climb the political ladder; those who take this road are giving up. But it can be really fun.

Others choose to find some means outside of politics to relieve stress. Food. Alcohol. Strange hobbies involving expensive hand-painted figurines. Shooting stuff. Strip Clubs. Jogging. Hookers. They were all the same. It worked most of the time.

But the best stress relief was cool justice. Defeating an antagonist in a tough endorsement battle. Winning a coveted delegate spot to the national convention.

THE EDUCATOR

Or getting free shit on someone else's dime.

Tonya Hotchick was working the room with this in mind. It wasn't her idea; Chris Berg was the orchestrator. Conservatively dressed in a shiny blue blouse and gray slacks, she still caught the eye of every man who crossed her path. It took almost no effort to convince a man to buy a drink for a girl.

So Berg convinced Tonya to flirt, purr and laugh her way into as many drinks as possible. When she had the drink, she would pass it off to another member of the inner cadre. The crowded banquet room made floating from group to group very easy. Tonya would convince a man to buy a drink for her, he would walk to the bar and return with a drink. She would hold it behind her back, distracting the mark with ample boobage, until Berg or Wallace or Buzzcut came by and passed her an empty cup and took the full one.

Then she'd ask for another drink.

Or move on to another mark.

The targets were preppy suburban white boys from expensive private schools. The worst sort of circlejerk player.

Tonya was collecting phone numbers all the while. Her vagina was locked up until marriage but that didn't mean she wasn't on the market.

Kayla Witold was doing her best to work the scheme as well. As plain looking as nineteen could get, she still held her own in the room. In politics, if you weren't obese, old or had a cleft palate, you were on the doable side of five.

Every fifteen minutes a roar would take over the banquet hall when another GOP victory was announced by the networks. By 11:30 the slaughter was nearly complete. The Republicans had taken back the House of Representatives for the first time in forty years. Not that many in the banquet hall could understand what was happening. Everyone was too drunk.

Life was good.

*   *   *   *   *   *   *

"So what's with Zan?" Shotgun asked.

Shotgun and Kessler were sitting in front of the television, waiting on a couple of congressional races on the left coast.

"Still trying to figure it out," Kessler replied. "I know he got really hurt. As his 'employer' I got stuck with his medical bills, and his doctor calls me everyday to bring him in. I can't get him to answer the phone, and the last time I tried talking to him face-to-face, he pulled a gun on me."

"That's whack."

"It's a chick," Kessler said, "so of course it's whack. He's never had a girl problem. And the funny part is how he was always warning about it too."

"And he's a Baptist, that doesn't help. They don't even believe in dancing, let alone all the fucking and sucking he and that chick were doing. 'A new man in Christ, Baptized in the blood of the Saviour,' he's supposed to be a new person, 'Saved.'"

"And people wonder why Catholics stay Catholics."

"Word."

"He's probably due for an intervention." Kessler said. "But he's been my cat's paw for so long, I figured I'd wait. He deserves it."

"Think you're making a mistake in waiting?" Shotgun asked. "Sounds like you could get him locked in a mental hospital."

"Not a chance. There's not a judge in Minnesota who would grant involuntary commitment because he left a hospital after being declared in stable condition. Plus a man has the right not to answer his phone."

"What about pulling a gun on you?"

"Pulling a gun on a Black man who entered his house without permission?" Kessler pondered, "show me a judge who would see the crime in that."

"You had a key," Shotgun pointed out.

Kessler shrugged. "Details."

The two sat in silence for a while. Another House seat was called for the GOP. It was the 48th pickup of the night.

*   *   *   *   *   *   *

CHAPTER 20

1pm Wednesday, November 9
Zeale's place on 14th and 7th, Dinkytown

Spags' head felt heavy. Heavy, with a dull pulsating ache. His stomach was a fiery stretch of discomfort all through his abdomen. And this was an improvement.

The night had been long. His memories of it were misty.

Someone must have dragged him home. To his room. For that matter, someone must have dragged him from the Saint Paul Hotel, to a car, driven him home and then dragged him to his bedroom. This was a mystery.

A mystery not more important than trying to find a cure for a hangover. Gatorade and cereal were doing alright. Spags had yet to discover coffee.

His roommates were doing the school thing. The house was his alone.

THE EDUCATOR

On the television he watched the Spanish-language channel. He couldn't speak a word of Spanish, but it had the best-looking chicks.

Spags thought about trying to make an appearance at one of his classes later that afternoon. He had skipped his classes and schoolwork for the last week. He was probably very far behind...He didn't care. This semester was going to hurt academically. But he always found a way to pass.

There was a hot Mexican chick with huge breasts and a sexy voice on TV that interrupted his train of thoughts. Mesmerized, Zeale zoned out.

A minute later. Or ten. Knocking.

Spags got up and answered the door, a little surprised to see two police officers on the steps. A little, but not very.

Of the two cops, one was fat, one familiar. Which was bad, since the cop Zeale recognized was the same one he had accused of 'faggotry' earlier in the semester.

"UMPD, we're looking for Gene Zeale," the fat cop stated.

"You're looking at him,"

The fat cop walked up to the top step, and passed Zeale a newspaper. "What does this look like to you?"

Zeale took the paper and examined it. "It appears to be a copy of today's Minnesota Daily."

"Yes, Mr. Zeale. It is," said the familiar cop, "could you take a close look at the picture on the frontpage for me?"

Spags looked at the picture. Good photo. Five pillars of flames from the kiosks billowing up into the dark sky, lighting up Northrup Auditorium in the background.

"Looks like fire."

"Yes Mr. Zeale," Fat Cop said, "Do you recognize the fire?"

"Am I being detained?"

"No," said the familiar cop, "we'd just like to talk about Monday night and Tuesday morning. We heard you and a bunch of other people were out putting up posters."

"Well, I'd be happy to talk to you guys, but I learned my lesson the last time; I don't talk to cops. I'll refer you to my attorney, Mr. Ernie Kessler."

*   *   *   *   *   *   *

CHAPTER 21

Wednesday, November 23

Zan was falling.

Down down down. Grey darkness shrouded the world, roaring with the metallic churn of the waters below. Upon impact, Zan awoke.

It took a moment to understand. The room was bright with sunlight. His head pounded with pain. His bed. His house.

Drenched in cold sweat, Zan could smell the strong sweet foulness of his body.

Just another morning.

Shower. No soap. Just a soak to wash away the night. In his kitchen he prepared breakfast: two beers and handful of Fruit Loops. The clock on his oven said the time was 1:23pm. Not quite morning. Zan wasn't sure if he had adjusted the clock to daylight savings time or not. It didn't matter.

On the kitchen table was a revolver. A nickle-finished Colt Python .357 magnum with a four-inch barrel. A very nice gun.

Zan opened up the cylinders on the gun. One round was chambered. He took it out, looked it over, put it back in the gun, then closed the chamber. Spun the wheel. Four, five times. Without hesitating, he cocked the hammer, put the gun to his temple and pulled the trigger.

Nothing but the click of the hammer falling against metal.

Zan didn't do this everyday. Some days he didn't feel the need. Others? he put his fate into God's hands.

He put the gun back on the table and moved to the couch.

A Bible, a gift from his adoptive parents when he was baptized, was open to Numbers, Chapter 25:

And Israel abode in Shittim, and the people began to commit whoredom with the daughters of Moab.

And they called the people unto the sacrifices of their gods: and the people did eat, and bowed down to their gods.

And Israel joined himself unto Baalpeor: and the anger of the LORD was kindled against Israel.

And the LORD said unto Moses, Take all the heads of the people, and hang them up before the LORD against the sun, that the fierce anger of the LORD may be turned away from Israel.

And Moses said unto the judges of Israel, Slay ye every one his men that were joined unto Baalpeor.

And, behold, one of the children of Israel came and brought unto his brethren a Midianitish woman in the sight of Moses, and in the sight of all the congregation of the children of Israel, who were weeping before the door of the tabernacle of the congregation.

And when Phinehas, the son of Eleazar, the son of Aaron the priest, saw it, he rose up from among the congregation, and took a javelin in his hand;

THE EDUCATOR

And he went after the man of Israel into the tent, and thrust both of them through, the man of Israel, and the woman through her belly. So the plague was stayed from the children of Israel.

It was the passage he read every morning.

Zan had torn, page by page, the Gospels from his Bible. There would be no compassionate God in his life. YHWH was his master. Vengeful. Angry. Jealous. YHWH who could harden the hearts of His enemies. YHWH who used the sinful and imperfect as weapons against the sinful and imperfect. If YHWH wished Zan to stop from his path, the gun would have blown his brains out.

Zan caught an hour of Jerry Springer before leaving the house.

North from Zan's place, on Broadway, was B J's Liquor Lounge. No cover charge in the afternoon, no drink minimum. Five dollars for a table dance. It was dark and dreary, the afternoon dancers melancholic and plain; their skin showed the grainy sandpaper appearance attractive forty-somethings get after a lifetime of tanning. Every flaw was veiled by the club's gloominess. A lone Black stripper had the only smile in the place, and she didn't arrive until late in the afternoon.

It was the dive's dive.

Zan loved it.

Twenty bucks would purchase four hours of distraction and enough drinks to keep a buzz going. The blue collar clientele was quiet. The strippers were desperate shallow people; not flirtatious, just beaten.

In the cramped space, Zan smoked in peace.

When things started to pick up, more people, more strippers, less peace, Zan left. It normally happened around five in the afternoon. Today was no different. He left, drove back towards home, stopping at a liquor store on the way back. There was an hour to kill before he was going to catch up with Alisha after she got done with work.

Time enough for a drink or two.

*　　　*　　　*　　　*　　　*　　　*　　　*

Zan's life was about killing time.

Sleeping, with help from pills and alcohol. Eating, when he could afford it.

The Kessler money wasn't coming in anymore. Zan hadn't seen Kessler in a long time. But Zan had money saved up, and lots of credit cards. You don't need money to kill time, but it helps.

Drinking until he couldn't stand was a necessity. It stopped the demons.

The only other purpose in his life was The Stalk.

Police involvement actually made The Stalk more fun. More exciting. A police car would drive by his house at all hours, checking to see if he was home. Zan learned quickly enough that when he wasn't home, the police sent a patrol car to check Alisha's home in South Minneapolis. Occasionally they sent a car by the Big Ten.

So Zan decided to disappear. He kept the lights off. All the window shades were always drawn. He started parking a couple blocks away from his house. It looked like he was always gone. Police time is precious, so the police had to stop sending patrol cars altogether. Zan had earned freedom of movement.

Zan had Alisha's schedule down.

He could get to campus and up to his hide, a parking ramp owned by the hospital, that gave a great view of the back of the Big Ten.

Alisha normally left to go home around two in the morning.

What made things fun was when she met up with Malcolm Paulson. Sometimes he went to her, sometimes it was the other way around.

Zan soon found Paulson's Uptown apartment.

On Mondays and Wednesdays, the two would go out on a date. Zan figured Alisha didn't want to be around the old crew on Wednesday nights. It was almost impossible to trail them, but they always ended up at either Paulson's apartment or Alisha's house.

Today was the day. Zan didn't know for what. Maybe it was the day he exercised some divine justice on the pair for whoredom. Or he might just beat the crap out of Paulson for shits and giggles. He wasn't sure yet.

A large padlock and a sock were hidden away inside his jacket.

It was Thanksgiving weekend. The campus and the bar would be empty. Zan was certain this was the best day to confront the duo.

Driving into campus, he kept chanting to himself *'tonight's the night, tonight's the night, Divine right.'*

*　　*　　*　　*　　*　　*　　*

Malcolm Paulson loved meteorology.

Hundreds of hours during his grad school days had been absorbed trying to model short-term weather trends. It was a fool's errand. A simple computer program couldn't process all the necessary information. At least not in his day.

But the work had given him an appreciation of weather. It was useful. Rain could erase tire tracks and wash away evidence. Snowfall can cover up a body, hide it for months. Fog can obscure a falling body and muffle a scream.

Tonight was going to be a big night. Three days earlier, the temperature dropped well below zero, forming ice on some small lakes. Then it warmed up into the forties again. The ice disappeared. But the lakes were still cold, near freezing.

There was no snow yet, but it was coming.

A blizzard, expected to dump over a foot of snow all across the Metro, was coming sometime around nine that night. A few hours afterward, the roads would be impassable.

It was all about timing.

If timed right, Malcolm and Alisha could have a romantic walk in the falling snow. Then some fun. Then Malcolm could drive away, the snow covering up the crime. Police would be too busy with cars in the ditch to respond in a timely manner. If really lucky, Alisha's body would remain undiscovered until spring.

Malcolm opened the bottom drawer of his desk and pulled out a small pistol. It was a Bond Arms Company .45 caliber Derringer.

Inside of Hennepin County, only the well-connected could get a concealed weapon permit from the sheriff. And Malcolm was well-connected.

The police were on his mind tonight. They would be out and about, and he couldn't trust anything to chance. Into his Derringer he packed a large .45x70mm slug. A powerful round that should drop a man wearing body armor. In the top chamber he shoved a .410 bore shotgun shell with #9 shot. Not lethal at anything except really close range, but it could mess up someone's face.

His office was completely empty. Just him and his thoughts. At six he called Alisha. They'd meet at her house, have dinner together at the Mai Village, a Vietnamese restaurant in St. Paul. Then he'd take her to eternity.

*   *   *   *   *   *   *

Zeale and Kayla arrived at the Big Ten after the College Republicans meeting. Only a few of the crew were there. Chris Berg, Nolan Painer and Frank Wallace. As they sat down greetings were exchanged and everyone made their orders. No Alisha, which was the new norm. When everything settled down, Painter laid the trap.

"So Gene, we have a little moral quandary for you to solve."

"Shoot."

"Suppose an evil villain has kidnapped your mom and Kayla," Painter said. "And he's trapped you in a building. There are two doors. One leads to your mom, one leads to Kayla. You have to choose one and escape the building, saving the woman of your choice in the process. If you refuse to participate, all three of you die a horrible death. Who do you choose to save? your mom or Kayla?"

Zeale squirmed a bit. "If the evil villain had me trapped, why would he let me go?"

"Because he's an evil villain, that is what they do, and you aren't Spider-Man. You're just some dude he can torture"

Assuming Zeale's objection before he could enunciate it, Chris Berg added: "And remember, you're trapped. There's no other way out. No magic belt. No superpowers. No Hollywood endings. You're stuck."

Zeale dodged, "I would never get into that situation."

"He's an evil genius, you can't avoid it," Painter said. "Besides, it's not you the guy trapped. It's your mom and your girl, now choose."

Valiantly, for ten minutes, Zeale continued to dodge the question while avoiding any eye contact with Kayla. Finally Berg just started screaming at Zeale, interrupting him whenever he tried to say something with "No, fuck you, answer the fucking question."

"Fine," Zeale relented, "I'd pick Kayla."

The table exploded with profanity.

"...Fuck you...you'd pick your girl?...no you wouldn't...you only get one mother...the world is filled with whores...what would your mother say...you're fucking sick...nine months of pain and this is what your mom gets?..."

Zeale, flustered and red-faced, got up and left. "Have a nice fucking Thanksgiving assholes."

Everyone else at the table started laughing.

"I better go then." Kayla got up to leave.

"So Kayla, what about you?" Berg asked.

"Duh, I save my mom. You only get one mom. I can find another boy anywhere."

*   *   *   *   *   *   *

Zan drove by the back parking lot of the Big Ten. Not surprisingly, Alisha's car wasn't there. *On a date. Where?*

Taking a chance, he started for Alisha's house in south Minneapolis. He'd do a drive by first to see if she was home. If not, he could set up shop for a while at the McDonald's on Hiawatha. This would prevent the police from finding him. There was also chance he could run into them at Paulson's apartment.

It took ten minutes to snake his way down to Alisha's home. On the radio, there was talk of a huge snowstorm barreling in to the Twin Cities. *Fuck.* He hated snow.

Zan drove around the neighborhood. Circling gave him a good chance to see any police cars before he violated his restraining order.

Fuck yeah. On his circling tour, he spotted Paulson's big black Suburban driving towards Hiawatha. Slamming on the accelerator, Zan tore through the neighborhood at forty miles an hour to catch up.

Paulson was a good four blocks ahead of Zan. They were going west on 38th street, towards Cedar Avenue.

Zan's knuckles were white on the wheel.

    *   *   *   *   *   *   *

Mai Village was a small Vietnamese Restaurant on University Avenue near the state capitol. It had quietly gained a reputation among capitol regulars for offering great food. It soon become the place to go for power lunches when the legislature was in session.

The small space was filled with ornate Vietnamese imports in bright colors; chairs of carved wood, tables with dragons; on the walls were gold leaf pictures of, what else, dragons. It was gaudy, and even on the day before Thanksgiving, with an approaching blizzard, the restaurant was full. It was that good.

Paulson was still dressed in his work clothes, a dark gray suit with a white shirt and maroon and gold tie. Alisha was experimenting with a single-piece cotton sweater dress, knee high with three quarter sleeves, dark gray. Black stockings provided some contrast. It was commonly understood among Minnesotans that wearing bright colors in November was just weird.

Looking outside the window, Paulson could see the first few snowflakes of the year falling on University Avenue. The sky was getting dark in a hurry. Paulson needed the storm to wait. It took time to finish the huge noodle salads served at the Mai Village.

    *   *   *   *   *   *   *

Zan turned the keys in the ignition, starting his car. Cold was the natural enemy of the Nissan Z-car. Running the engine for a few minutes helped save his battery. It had been over two hours since the happy couple were seated in the restaurant across the street from Zan.

He could see them in the window.

The clock on his dashboard said 8:47. Snow had been falling for about an hour, accumulating on the roads. Listening to the radio, Zan heard reports of eighteen inches of snowfall in Fargo. Expectations for total snowfall in the Twin Cities had gone up. Dave Dahl on KSTP suggested there could be over two feet of snow on the metro by Thursday morning.

Traffic was still heavy on University, annoying Zan greatly. He wanted to get the confrontation done with. *Why would God stay his*

Divine tool?

No matter. The confrontation would come. *Besides*, he thought, *the people at Mai Village didn't deserve bloodshed in front of their business.*

Zan turned off the engine and peaked over at the restaurant; the couple had left their table. He saw them exit the front door and get into their car, parked on the opposite side of the street. Zan expected Paulson to make a U-turn at the intersection to return Minneapolis.

But he didn't. Paulson drove east towards the capitol.

Zan put his car into drive and accelerated down the road, making a hard U-turn to get back on their tail.

*   *   *   *   *   *   *

"So where are we going?" Alisha put her hand on Paulson's knee.

Instead of driving back to Minneapolis, Paulson had taken them East on I94 then north on I35E. Malcolm did this on occasion, working his reputation as a spontaneous romantic.

Alisha normally liked his impulsive nature, but it was late, cold and the snow was getting heavy. However, she was just buzzed enough not to care.

"There's this spot I want you to see," he replied, "you're gonna love it."

"Well it better not take too long, there's a lot more snow coming"

*   *   *   *   *   *   *

They traveled in silence to the Maryland Avenue exit, driving east to Lake Phalen.

The St. Paul lake was a popular recreational area in the summer, with bicycle paths and a large sandy beach. There was a golf course too.

"I don't think Lake Phalen is much of a secret." Alisha had often jogged around the lake when her knees still worked.

"You've never seen it when it's as perfect as it will be," Paulson said, "A little snowfall at night, in the cold, *très beau*."

"Seriously, let's just go home," she said, "I still have to pack for my trip."

"Just trust me," Paulson said as he put his hand on her shoulder. "If it's not the most serene example of romantic transcendence, I'll buy you a new car."

"Would you make it a BMW?"

*   *   *   *   *   *   *

THE EDUCATOR

Zan thought about Job.

"Where wast thou when I laid the foundations of the Earth?" God replied to Job when the ancient Hebrew lamented his woes.

Zan now knew what God wanted.

Paulson had taken the couple to Lake Phalen, taking his Suburban through the gates to the parking lot next to the beach area.

The park would be empty.

The couple would be isolated.

The golf course, with its rolling hills, obscured the view from the west.

The beach, with a large building containing restrooms, changing rooms and showers for the swimming public, blocked the view from the east.

No one would see anything.

Zan drove past the beach entrance and drove around the north end of the lake. There was another parking area on the northwest side of Round Lake, a small pond connected to Phalen.

It'd be a quarter mile trek to the beach parking lot, but his approach would be hidden from their view.

Parking his car, Zan threw on an old blue windbreaker he always kept in his trunk area. A Reagan for President button was prominently displayed on the chest of the jacket.

The jacket barely fit. Zan had put on some weight.

Zan took out the padlock and put it into the sock. The weapon would pack quite a punch.

He started walking down the trail towards the beach-house.

The snow kept falling.

*   *   *   *   *   *   *

"I told you this would be perfect," Paulson coyly intoned.

"Yeah, except for the heavy snow and wind," Alisha replied. She paused and took a breath. "Yes it's pretty, can we go home now?"

"You're such a killjoy."

Alisha was in Paulson's embrace, facing away from him. They were standing against the beach-house to avoid the wind; watching the snow fall on the lake, the lights of the cities reflecting from the clouds. Snowflakes dazzled in the soft light. Alisha saw the peaceful transcendental quality of the scenery, there was just too many things to worry about.

Paulson moved his hands from around her waist up to her breasts. Alisha pushed them back down.

"Will you stop," she said, laughing flirtatiously. "We're not doing anything here. Let's go home."

Paulson grabbed her shoulder length hair, stepped to the side, and pulled Alisha down to the ground. The move took an instant. Alisha shrieked as she went down, panicking. Paulson was on top of her. He grabbed her head in his two hands and started slamming it into the snow-covered concrete. He kept bouncing her head against the concrete until she stopped struggling.

Paulson caught his breath. The adrenaline was pulsing through his system. It was hard to stop smashing her head. But he really wanted her to be alive.

She was still breathing.

Paulson sighed with relief.

He undressed her.

Her clothes were thrown aside, except her panties, which Paulson put in one of his pockets. Once she was completely nude, he started punching her in her stomach as hard as possible. Hit after hit after hit. Then he flipped her over on her belly and grabbed one of her ankles. He twisted it until he heard a pop, using a technique he had read about in a Jujitsu book he found in one of the U's libraries.

He flipped her over again. This time, he sat on her knee and lifted up on her foot until he heard a heart-chilling crack. Both of her legs were now out of action.

Taking Alisha in his arms, he started walking the beach towards the water, still free of ice.

There wasn't time to enjoy this kill. He needed to leave right away, before some serendipitous circumstance got him caught. Still, he was hoping Alisha's death would be long and slow. Torturous. Deserving of praise.

At waters edge he tossed her into the freezing lake. She didn't move at all, so he had to flip her face-up. He posed her body in the snowy sand. Half in the water, half out. Alisha was unconscious but her body started to shiver. Paulson strutted away from the scene. Confident in his work.

*   *   *   *   *   *   *

Zan had found Paulson's car, but no one was in it. The heavy snowfall had covered up any footprints, so Zan decided to wait. When he heard a shriek, he started walking towards the sound, which was towards the big beach-house. Zan figured the two were fornicating. It'd be a great time to confront them.

The parking lot was on a high point, and you had to walk down some steps to get to the beach-house. Zan had to watch his footing on the steps. As he lifted his head from his feet, he saw a dark figure emerge about forty feet in front of him. It had to be Paulson.

Zan put his hands into his coat pocket, and gripped his improvised weapon.

*   *   *   *   *   *   *

Paulson was in the moment.

This little killing was a work of art.

If he got really lucky, the police would turn their gaze towards Alisha's crazy ex-boyfriend. If unlucky, there was still going to be nothing to connect him to the murder. By morning, he would be in New York City to celebrate Thanksgiving by attending a Giants game.

They would find her body in the spring.

By then, Paulson might just retire from the University. Move to Europe. Time would erase any questions about this night's activities.

Working past the beach-house back to his car, he saw someone on the steps.

The elation was gone. The day just got complicated.

It took a few seconds to process who the man was. Then it came to him, the figure was Jonathan 'Zan' Tvrdik. Or Chin-Wu, or whatever he called himself.

What the fuck is he doing here?

Paulson had to act.

He pulled his gun out of his coat pocket.

Zan was too far away for the Derringer, so Paulson briskly walked straight towards him, hoping to catch the little man off-guard.

But Paulson was caught off-guard when Zan started yelling at him. "And I will execute great vengeance upon them with wrathful rebukes;" he said, "and they shall know that I am Jehovah, when I shall lay my vengeance upon them."

Paulson saw Zan take out of his pockets something long and white, and Zan started swinging it over his head. Whatever was going on was beyond Paulson's comprehension, so he fired the top chamber of the Derringer, to end the discussion before it started.

*   *   *   *   *   *   *

The shot stunned Zan; his day just got complicated.

Whatever had been in the gun had hit him in the right arm; but Zan didn't feel any pain. Whatever it was just tugged at his jacket.

Paulson used the gunshot as a distraction to close the gap between them, clutching the small gun in his palm.

Everything happened in slow motion. Somewhere, in the deep recesses of his brain, Zan's body reacted to the situation by charging Paulson with a bull-rush. Head down, body low.

Later, Zan would realize his mind unconsciously conjured

the only solution to the situation. There was no escape in fleeing, as Zan would have been caught on the stairs. There was no way to dodge a bullet. But once, long ago, he had discussed with a police officer at his boxing gym the use of lethal force. In that conversation the police officer mentioned a properly motivated human being could successfully close a gap of ten feet or so on a gunman before the gunman had time to aim and pull the trigger.

Turned out the officer was wrong.

Zan didn't hear the blast from the gun. There was a sharp pain in his butt cheek but it disappeared in an instant. Adrenaline carried him through.

The two bodies met. Zan tried to throw his shoulder into Paulson's gut and knock him down. The bigger man didn't budge. Paulson started pounding the Derringer's barrel into Zan's spine, using his arm like a hammer. Zan felt no pain.

Dropping to one knee, Zan switched to an old-fashioned one-leg takedown.

Paulson dropped to the snow-covered ground, Zan on top of him.

The Professor was a fighter. As soon as Zan lifted his head to start a 'ground and pound' Paulson had an iron grip with two hands on Zan's throat. Zan used his hands to separate Paulson's hands, rolling his head in process, escaping the grip with ease.

Zan started hitting Paulson's face with a series of punches and elbows. Paulson blocked some and avoided others, but the punishment took its toll. Paulson was finally able to roll belly-down and push up to his knees.

Unfortunately for Paulson, this just put him in a great position for a rear-naked-choke. Zan squeezed with all his might while Paulson flailed around. It took almost thirty seconds, but Paulson finally lost consciousness; his body fell limp.

Zan wouldn't let go. He kept the grip on tight. Another twenty seconds went by.

Zan didn't know what to do. The hold would kill Paulson if he left it on too long.

Then again, the bastard did shoot him.

The grip loosened. Zan let go.

*   *   *   *   *   *   *

The static on the radio sparked a little before someone would speak. Deputy Hank Wingard had learned to recognize the sound, though it offered nothing useful in practical terms. It was just something nice to know. The spark sounded.

"Sixteen, dispatch." It was a quick and professional feminine voice.

"Sixteen here," Wingard drawled back, "what's up? over."

"Reported gunfire, at Lake Phalen Park, in the vicinity of the golf course."

Fuck, he thought. "Roger six, ETA three minutes, out."

*   *   *   *   *   *   *

The gunshot wound was on fire.

The adrenaline had worn off and now Zan was feeling the effects of the scuffle.

As far as he could tell, the bullet hadn't pierced anything important; it had just grazed his ass, ripping up flesh but nothing else. There were sharp pains in his lower back, almost crippling pain whenever he tried to take a step.

Paulson was left in the snow, unconscious. Zan had kicked him in the head, after he was choked-out, as punishment for the shooting.

An earlier thought, borne just before the fight, made a reappearance: *Where was Alisha?*

Zan walked to the beach-house. From the air the structure had an L-shape, but there was actually an open space underneath the roof. The two ends on the 'L' contained the changing areas, separated by gender. The stairs brought Zan right to the open space.

The snow had accumulated to four inches.

Panic set in when Zan found Alisha's clothes and shoes.

He could just make out footprints in the beach, and followed them.

Tears welled up in his eyes when he saw the vague lump covered in snow at the water's edge. He sprinted to lump, wiping away snow to reveal Alisha's body. It was freezing cold. Zan couldn't see movement. He thought she was dead.

Checking her pulse, he found one. Weak. But there.

Trying to lift her, he fell face first into the water.

Giving up on lifting, he started dragging Alisha up the beach.

*   *   *   *   *   *   *

Deputy Wingard was annoyed.

Correction: he was pissed.

Working a double shift the day before Thanksgiving made the fact he was being forced to work a long shift on Thanksgiving that much worse. Another double shift would follow. But he was getting Sunday off.

That was not why he was annoyed. Cops worked holidays.

That was that.

Gun play around the holidays? That was annoying.

Gun Play in the middle of the first big blizzard, with dozens of motorists already stranded, roads getting shutdown and during the worst travel time of the year? *Fucking pissed off.*

The gates to the beach-house were supposed to be locked up for the winter. No one was supposed to be back here. The late snow-fall was no excuse, and Wingard hoped to chew somebody's ass out once the weekend was over.

Wingard noticed one car, a black SUV covered in snow. He got out of his cruiser, wiped away the snow from the plates, and radioed it in.

Shootings were common.

If he was lucky, it was just someone taking illegal target practice in the park.

Cooperative, the guy would get misdemeanor for a noise violation. Uncooperative, there were plenty of weapons discharge, transport, carry and license violations to go along with a trespassing charge.

Radio spark, then, "Sixteen, Dispatch, comeback."

"Sixteen, go ahead Six."

"Vehicle registered to Malcolm Paulson, no middle name, no warrants, no priors. Vehicle not reported stolen"

"Roger, thank you."

Wingard recognized the name. Malcolm Paulson was president of the U of M.

What the fuck, he thought.

The wind picked up.

Wingard sensed movement somewhere beyond his vision.

*   *   *   *   *   *   *

Zan was really out of shape. He added at least thirty pounds to a thin and short frame since he was hospitalized. And he hadn't worked out since then either.

With the cold water soaking through his clothes and the indescribable pain in his lower back, he struggled to drag Alisha despite her thin willowy build.

Zan was screaming profanities at himself.

They were almost to the steps. Alisha's only chance was to get to a hospital soon, and Paulson's car was the closest vehicle. The fucker was still unconscious, now covered in snow, so Zan put Alisha down and walked over to him, swearing he'd come back and kill him later.

He checked Paulson's pockets for the keys to his Suburban.

He pocketed them and started dragging Alisha up the steps when an authoritative shout rang out and a light fell upon him.

"Freeze! Sheriff's department! Put your hands on your head!"

Zan froze. There weren't a lot of options, so he went obvious.

"Me so solly! You need hehrp herr, she need hehrp." Zan was hoping his 'me so solly' routine would work; it sounded so stupid, Zan thought it might.

"On your knees, now!"

Zan went to his knees. "So Solly, car amber ramps."

The deputy started talking to his shoulder, "Sixteen, requesting backup and ambulance to Lake Phalen beach-house. Two in need of assistance, one man in custody."

The radio sparked back, "en route."

Zan watched as the deputy moved slowly down the stairs.

"Eyes forward."

Zan was facing the bloody face of Malcolm Paulson, who was starting to stir.

"Lay down on the ground, cross your legs."

"No speak engrish" Zan offered.

The officer was behind him now, and instead of instructions, he just shoved Zan face down to the ground.

Zan knew the next few seconds were about timing. The police officer would move slowly, methodically. But a one-on-one cuff&stuff required a certain level of cooperation from the suspect.

The officer placed one knee on his back. The man was pretty heavy. The next move would be to grab Zan's right hand and place it behind his back as a control. Then the officer would holster the gun and remove the cuffs.

Zan waited.

"I'm placing you in custody, don't move, understand?"

"No speak engrish," Zan said innocently.

The police officer grabbed Zan's right arm and pulled it behind his back, putting a little pressure on it to show control. Zan relaxed his body. When Zan heard the snap of the officer's cuff holder being undone, he knew the gun was holstered and he acted.

Despite the pain, he pushed as hard as he could with his left arm, creating just enough space for him to roll over on his back, loosening the grip the officer had on his right arm.

Wingard panicked, and tried to get up. This created more distance for Zan to work with. He grabbed the Deputy by his shirt and pulled him back down, headbutting him in the process. Wingard tried to grab his gun, but Zan had his legs loose and threw the deputy into a triangle choke with his legs. It took fifteen seconds for Wingard to pass out.

Darkness still surrounded Malcolm Paulson, but his inner world jolted back. *You stupid fucker.* Paulson was more embarrassed than anything else. *The crazy ex-boyfriend. Of all the fucking things.* He could hear some sounds. A scuffle. He tried moving his legs. They weren't working yet. His body ached. Nothing wanted to move. A finger or two were online. Even if he could get back into gear, Paulson knew it was over.

You should have known better. Paulson thought about all that he did wrong. It wasn't just the presence of an ex-boyfriend. Alisha was too close to him. The relationship was several years old. There was simply no foolproof way to kill her and escape suspicion. *Stupid fucker.*

Paulson's eyes wouldn't open. He tried to relax. He could hear someone talking. Yelling. But the outside world stayed distant. The end was coming. Paulson knew he was copped. Even if he could get up. Even if he could fight back. There was no way to escape this situation. His fun was over.

Blame the crazy fucker. The thought kept popping into his head. *Blame Zan. The little fucker was nuts.* From the void his mind had conjured an out his consciousness hadn't realized. As long as there was a cogent story, it would be his word against Zan's. And Zan had gone off the deep end. He could win this. Some energy returned and he started forcing his body to move again. A toe. A finger. His head. His body yielded and he could feel himself coming to life.

His eyes opened. Through the snow he could see a dark figure approach.

*   *   *   *   *   *   *

Zan released his grip on the deputy and got up from under the man. The deputy was five-ten and about 220 pounds, some of it gut. Still a strong and worthy opponent. He slapped the guy hard on the back, and heard the deputy take in a deep gasping breath.

As the officer was taking several deep breaths, he worked himself to his hands and knees. At which point Zan kicked the officer in the head, knocking him out.

Zan removed the officer's gun from the holster, walked over to Malcolm Paulson and fired one shot through his forehead.

In the state of Minnesota, there is no death penalty.

More sirens were approaching. Zan wanted to stay with Alisha, but there was little he could do now.

He started running.

Deputy Hank Wingard was a throwback.

He smoked. He drank. The only exercise he got was walking his dog and throwing a baseball with his kid. He didn't hug. The department's annual 'Psychological Evaluations' represented an opportunity to flirt or bullshit, and nothing more. He went to church on Sundays, but lived by his own moral code the rest of the week; a moral code best understood by watching John Wayne movies.

Being a cop was nothing special. To Wingard, a badge just meant a paycheck and paperwork. If you were lucky, the badge might stop an errant .22 round from a thug's Saturday Night Special. New cops didn't think this way. They thought they were untouchable; above the community, not of the community. Police forces were becoming militarized. Tactics were changing. Wingard didn't like where things were heading. Policemen were not occupiers, they were neighbors. America was a Republic not a police state. To most of his coworkers, Wingard was a dinosaur. At one point, he had been the chief deputy of Ramsey County. Those days were long gone. Now he was along for the ride until his pension kicked in. Happy to be riding alone.

Thus, to Wingard, the scuffle was okay. It was a clean fight and Wingard lost.

Wingard wasn't even going to judge the guy for shooting that Paulson character in the face. Something was going on that he didn't understand; he was just there to do his job. Fine.

But kicking a guy when he was down?

That was wrong.

Wingard pulled a backup weapon from an ankle holster; A little Smith & Wesson .32 caliber short barrel wheel gun. It was one of momma's rules: if you're going to carry a gun, you might as well carry two, in case you forget one.

The second patrol car arrived and Wingard pointed them towards the naked woman, who must have been close to death. He didn't tell them where he was going, this was personal.

He ran off following the footprints in the snow.

*   *   *   *   *   *   *

Zan got to his car.

The metallic blue 1988 Nissan 300zx wasn't going to be happy. At all.

It was not a winter car. It was not a cold-weather car. It did not like snow.

For the last four years Zan forced it to survive in the winter.

But at least he had the common decency not to drive it in a blizzard. Certainly never on un-plowed roads.

As Zan turned the key, the car voiced its displeasure. The engine 'ruhr-ruhred' but refused to ignite.

Zan tried again.

Same result.

Zan gave the car some time. Maybe it would change its mind. The Z-car was capable of it on occasion.

Turning the key again, the engine roared to life. Zan turned on the wipers, hoping it was light snow, and no ice.

Success!

He threw the car into reverse, backed out of the spot, and started forward.

Then his drivers-side window exploded.

He slammed his foot on the accelerator as he heard the unmistakable sound of gunfire.

The unmistakable sound gunfire makes when the gun is pointed in your direction.

A bullet slammed into his steering wheel and ricocheted away.

Zan kept the car moving forward, trying to stay on the road.

He got lucky, you could still tell road from not-road despite the snow.

The gunfire had ceased, and Zan took off towards the southwest.

*　　*　　*　　*　　*　　*　　*

The wind died down.

The world was a beautiful wonder of falling snow illuminated by the artificial lights of the human war with nature.

Zan ventured into the residential area to the west of Lake Phalen Park, hoping to evade any other police cars.

Larpenteur Avenue was just a block north of him. Unfortunately, when he found it there were several patrol cars using it to race towards Lake Phalen. Zan was hoping the blizzard would slow the police down. But Minnesota cops were still Minnesotans and a little weather wasn't about to stop them from showing up to help another officer.

Zan stopped the car to wait them out for a few minutes, hoping they would pass on and he could make a break for Interstate 35E.

It would still be a challenge to get to the Interstate undetected.

Zan started moving again, going west parallel to Larpenteur on East California Avenue. When he passed Payne Avenue, the distinctive blue cherries of a St. Paul Police car flashed on.

Slamming on the accelerator, the Z-car spun its wheels before finding some traction and lurching forward.

The police cruiser was having a better time in the snow, and was gaining.

He took a left turn at Edgerton Street, then another at Idaho Avenue. Just before he got back to Payne, he turned into a smaller alleyway. As he did so, he turned off the lights of his car and made another turn into another intersecting alleyway; a quirk of the neighborhood Zan knew about from the days when he delivered phonebooks in the area.

To the policemen, fighting the adrenaline of the chase and pushing their vehicle too fast for the conditions, it looked like the car had turned a corner and vanished.

It didn't take long for the two in the police car to retrace their steps and find Zan's tracks.

By that time, Zan had snaked his way to Larpenteur.

Less than a minute later he was on the Interstate and gone.

*   *   *   *   *   *   *

CHAPTER 22

1am Thursday, November 24
Lake Phalen, St. Paul

Detective Daniel Longfellow walked around the spot where Professor Malcolm Paulson had died. It was one in the morning and Longfellow had been on the scene for twenty minutes. Paulson was dead but overzealous medics decided to let a real doctor declare the local VIP so his body was transported to Regions Hospital.

Waste of time, Longfellow thought.

The snow was falling harder than ever, two inches an hour, and the wind had picked up. Longfellow enjoyed the weather. His attitude was if you didn't enjoy it, you should get the hell out of Minnesota.

Other than the fact a man had been murdered execution style at this very spot, things were blissful. There was no evidence anything happened. A white blanket of snow covered the whole park. Only shadows of the struggle remained visible. Faint outlines where people walked or where bodies had been. It wasn't too cold. The wind was annoying but the conditions were tolerable.

What Longfellow did not enjoy was getting called out to a crime scene in the middle of a blizzard the day before Thanksgiving. Not that he cared too much--this was his job. And business for homicide investigators had been pretty good lately. It made life interesting.

Longfellow had no idea what he was going to do about this little enigma.

The operation was a disaster in slow-motion.

The lone Sheriff's Deputy stumbled upon an indescribable situation. A fat Asian male dragging a naked chick, picking the pockets of another man who had been badly beaten. Fat Asian Man overpowers police officer, kills the other man with the deputy's gun and runs away.

Then a second unit arrives, is directed towards the naked chick by the original deputy, who did not tell anyone what the fuck he was doing. Deputy fires on another vehicle, but vehicle escapes. Ten minutes later, a St. Paul officer attempts to pull over a vehicle matching the description the deputy gave, and the car disappears into thin air..

A request is sent to the state patrol to start putting up roadblocks. 'Fuck off' comes the reply, the state patrol is too busy with 'the fucking blizzard' to do legwork for the city. Somehow, the Fat Asian Man had made an escape in the middle of a blizzard, surrounded by incoming police cars, in a Datsun. And those things sucked in the snow.

The crime scene was instantly contaminated. The woman and man had been trucked off to the hospital. Medics and police officers had walked all over the place, disrupting footprint evidence. Not that anything could be done to prevent it--the snow covered everything so you didn't know where to step.

Crime scene technicians were stuck in ditches or snowed in. The two St. Paul crime scene photographers were out of town. Minneapolis sent one of their guys, who promptly spun his car into a ditch. Inexperienced traffic cops were trying to collect evidence using ziplock bags, shoveling bloody snow into cool-whip containers. One cop tried taking a plaster cast of footprint, only to destroy the footprint. Another officer was using a brush from her makeup kit to wipe away snow from a footprint underneath, with no luck.

Another officer attempted to cover an area of interest with a large blue tarp, only to see it get blown away.

Not wishing to have this become an even bigger farce, Longfellow immediately ordered everyone except the other St. Paul homicide detective out of the crime scene area. The one forensic technician who showed up, a fingerprint specialist, was working on Professor Paulson's Suburban.

The other homicide detective was Marty Ochoa. He was called in once Paulson had been identified as a victim. Living just eight blocks away, Ochoa knew the area well. Longfellow didn't mind a competitor. It was an extra set of eyes and someone to share the blame when this investigation went from TARFU to FUBAR.

THE EDUCATOR

Ochoa, a short heavyset Hispanic man in his late thirties, hobbled down the steps towards the beach-house where Longfellow found some relief from the wind. Longfellow stood six and half feet, with short brown hair and a dis-interesting pale face of common Nordic features. He was the physical opposite of Ochoa, whose round face resembled that of Cheech Marin, mustache and all.

Ochoa repeated the phrase he'd been using all night. "Ya know, we're fucked."

"I know," was Longfellow's reply. "Any word on the woman?"

"Does'na look doo good, budda you know da rule...na dead 'dil warm an' dead."

Ochoa spoke with a thick Minnesota accent, with long O's and he replaced his T sounds with D sounds and V's with W's. Ochoa grew up on a farm near Willmar, his parents forced him to speak only English growing up, despite the fact they didn't know any. The farmers they worked for had a dozen kids who collectively thought it would be funny to teach the little Mexican boy to speak English like their grandparents. Eventually Ochoa embraced his unique upbringing, handing out a few busted noses in the process.

"Any idea what happened?" Longfellow had his own ideas but wanted a fresh opinion.

"Near as I can figure, da oriendal fella inderrupded a murder. Da Paulson fella brought da woman here, assualded her, sdripped 'er, and dumped 'er body inda water. Da oriendal arriw'ed onda scene and he and da Paulson fella hada scuffle. Da oriendal den dragged the woman from da beach da here," Ochoa pointed at the stairs to the parking lot, "and was looking for keys whenda depudy arriw'ed."

Longfellow didn't laugh at Ochoa's accent, but he couldn't suppress a smile at how ridiculous the man sounded. He was told it normally took a few years to get used to Ochoa before you stopped giggling whenever the man talked.

"The problem with that story is it doesn't make sense," Longfellow said. "Why did the Asian man run when the Deputy arrived? Why did he fight the Deputy? What are the odds some guy is walking around a closed park just as a blizzard is blowing in? Maybe it was the Asian guy who attacked the couple? Beat up the guy and was taking the woman to his car?"

"Ya know, I dinked a'dat," Ochoa replied, "budda why'd 'ee drug her down all da-way to da wader and back? Why sdrip 'er? And how long had he been onda scene? It dyakes dime to ged'da hypodermia, ya know. Why didna' Paulson fire his gun earlier? How'dee oriendal fella ged'da yump on an arm'ed man? Why didna' girl run away? Id donna make sense. Da narradive of an inderrup'ded murder makes more sense."

"None of it makes sense."

"Like I'ah been saying, we're fucked."

Longfellow took out a cigarette and lit it. "There's something we're missing," he exhaled, "what about the girl, any ID on her?"

"Her purse was inda Suburban, no ID."

"That doesn't make sense either, even hookers carry ID." Longfellow's head was aching with thought. He took a long drag from his cigarette and exhaled. "We need some answers before we start asking the wrong questions. Can you take over here? I want to get to Regions and check on the girl, see if there's any evidence on Paulson."

"Okay. I pudda some cardboard boxes over whadda I dink er fo'prins. Udder dan sdyopping da snow, dere's nodda much more da'do."

"Try and find some more forensic techs. Get them from wherever you can. Maybe they'll know something we don't"

"Okay. But I'ma dellin's ya, we're fucked."

*   *   *   *   *   *   *

CHAPTER 23

8am Thursday, November 24
Leaders Airfield, Clear Lake, Minnesota

Zan was falling. Past the snow. Tumbling.

Churning waters below.

A precipice, a bridge, above. Water quickly approaching. Zan turned again towards the bridge. The face of Malcolm Paulson staring down. Then he awoke.

Zan was a giant ache. Except in those places where he couldn't feel anything. He had fallen asleep in his car. Everything was cold. Despite this, he had been sweating in his sleep.

He turned the key in the ignition and the car failed to turn-over.

"Fuck," he whispered to himself.

The cold was overtaking his body. Zan cleared his mind and imagined a ball of flame, the size of a marble, deep in his chest. This ball of flame grew hotter. Into plasma. Into soul. Zan concentrated, made the ball grow. Soon it took over his chest. Heat radiated to his limbs.

Everything still hurt, but Zan could move. Tibetan monks could control their body temperature, spending frigid nights on a mountaintop with nothing more than their thin robes to protect them. The things you can learn at the local dojo.

THE EDUCATOR

For a while, during the two hour drive in the blizzard, as his car nearly got stuck a dozen times in roads on the verge of being closed, he debated stopping at Kessler's Camp Lake cabin. But this might make things too easy for the police. So he stopped at the airport across the street from Kessler's cabin. He was missing the soft bed and warmth the cabin would provide.

The airfield was tiny, with an unpaved grass runway. There was a small population of diehards who flew their planes regularly from Leaders. During the winter, the number dwindled to just a couple of the more daring small craft aviators. The field would get plowed, if requested. But only planes with skis flew in or out when the snow fell.

Zan had parked behind a small building that served as the main office to the airport. There weren't really any official parking spaces, and Zan found a place not visible from the road. With the battery dead, the car was going to remain there a while.

Pushing the door open, Zan fell out of the car into two feet of snow. The sky was the same color white as the ground. If you tried to find the horizon, you could get dizzy. He crawled, and eventually walked, his way to the front of the building. A lone payphone was just outside the main office doors. Zan pulled out his wallet, found a business card and some quarters and dialed the number on the back of the card.

On the tenth ring, there came an answer.

"Hello?" A feminine voice answered.

"I'm looking for Jose" Zan said.

"Who is this?" the voice demanded.

"Tell him it's a friend of Tass."

A few seconds later Jose came on the line. "Damnit, I told you never to call me at this number unless it was an emergency."

"It is. I need a contact number for Fats."

"He won't be happy about it."

"Fuck that, I'll buy him a pie." Zan just needed a place to stay, and Fats was closest. "Oh yeah, and one other thing."

"What's that?"

"Do you remember where we left the keys to the firetruck?"

*   *   *   *   *   *   *

Malcolm Paulson's body lay face down on a slab of metal in the Regions morgue. There was no pathologist available. Instead, Longfellow found himself talking to an intern, in his second year out of med-school.

The farce continued.

Paulson was declared DOA, which made sense since half his

brain was floating vapor near the Lake Phalen beach-house.

No one had told the doctors they were dealing with a murder, though the intern in the morgue mentioned the possibility when Longfellow showed up to view the body. It was all Longfellow could do not to laugh, something that was happening a lot.

Worse, Paulson's clothing had been stripped from him and misplaced. Longfellow shouted at the staff, and eventually some nurses started a search. Longfellow regretted shouting. He'd send a few boxes of pastries to the staff later, as an apology. Until then, he needed to scare the faint outline of competence from those around him.

Longfellow listened while the intern talked about Paulson.

"...Cause of death obvious...gun was less than a foot away...a scuffle...residual black powder...face showed massive contusions... gash above the right eye...if they found the other guy soon enough... plenty of evidence to collect...some marks on neck suggested choking...some sort of sleeper hold..."

The intern was green, but no dummy.

Paulson's clothes were found and brought to the morgue. Upon examination, Longfellow found the surprise of his career. Red panties, wrapped around the driver's license of his Jane Doe. He used a phone on the wall of the morgue to call Ochoa's carphone. Some lackey answered, and Longfellow asked to talk with Ochoa. A few minutes passed.

"Ya?"

"Marty," Longfellow said, "found the name of our Jane Doe, one Alisha Williams, address in south Minneapolis."

"How'dya figure?" Ochoa asked.

"Found her driver's license in Paulson's jacket, along with a pair of panties."

"Da plod'da dickens."

"Send that fingerprint tech down here asap. And have dispatch start the paperwork for a search of Williams' house."

"Will do."

*　　　*　　　*　　　*　　　*　　　*　　　*

Ochoa walked back to the crime scene. Another two inches of snow had fallen. Upside down cardboard boxes, normally used when collecting files and financial statements from white collar crooks, dotted the landscape around the beach-house. Ochoa had used them to cover up some footprints from further snowfall.

The detective played the scene out in his mind. The assault of the girl. The fight between Paulson and the Asian man. The woman being dragged from the water to the steps. The scuffle with the deputy. The escape along the trail. Each scene represented a point on a timeline. Ochoa was searching for the story of the event. The theme that made things come together.

And he came up empty. Paulson had to have been in the process of murdering the woman. The panties and ID card proved it. But there was no explanation as to how or why the murder was interrupted, or why the interrupter fled the scene.

Walking around where Paulson had been shot, Ochoa's foot stepped on something hard. When he reached into the snow, he pulled out something round and metallic.

Ochoa tried to wipe off the snow, then blew it off. It was a ring. Like a class ring. It had a dark blue stone, surrounded by lettering. Ochoa took off his own glove. On his right pinky finger there was a ring with a blue star sapphire.

The two rings matched.

      *   *   *   *   *   *   *

Longfellow watched as nurses worked on Alisha Williams. They were filling used water bottles with hot water from a sink and were placing them around Williams' body. A ventilator forced air into her lungs while IV bags dangled above. A doctor overlooked the operation, writing onto a metal clipboard and occasionally giving orders.

The doctor spotted the detective and walked over.

"Can I help you?" the doctor asked.

Longfellow looked over the doctor. She was short, well-tanned, deathly thin, early thirties, dark brown hair. Attractive in a skeletal sense.

"Detective Dan Longfellow, St. Paul Police," he replied in solemn, official tones, "I wanted to find out the prognosis for your patient."

The woman took a long look at Longfellow's badge. Young women were always suspicious of everything. Finally she smiled, apparently deciding people who pretended to be police officers didn't do it around hospitals. "Okay, I'm Doctor Raleigh."

"Pleasure to meet you," Longfellow said in decidedly unofficial tones.

"Okay," she replied awkwardly, "your Jane Doe came in with a--"

"Alisha Williams," Longfellow interrupted.

"Okay, Alisha came in with a core body temperature of twenty-six degrees, which is severe hypothermia. So far, we've raised her core temperature to thirty-two degrees without incident. We should have her up to a normal body temperature pretty quick. We've been giving her heated fluids intravenously. We'll know more when she warms up."

"Is she going to survive?"

"Like I said," she spoke with frustration, "we don't know yet. I'd say it's still fifty-fifty she makes it. Even if she does survive, she might be in a coma. There could be severe brain damage. She experienced ten minutes of hypoxia, so it's all up in the air. We even found evidence of blunt-force head trauma."

Longfellow pulled out a business card and passed it to her. "Could you contact me as soon as you have more information?"

"Sure," the doctor said, and promptly turned and walked away.

Longfellow left the ICU. It had been twelve hours since he last had some food. He started a search. There had to be a cafeteria around somewhere.

*   *   *   *   *   *   *

Zan was near his breaking point. The firetruck was a big vehicle and took a lot of effort to work. The roads were bad, but this didn't make much difference to the overbuilt behemoth he was driving. Two feet of snow might as well have been two inches. But it had taken a couple of hours to dig it out of the barn, mostly because Zan took long breaks because of the pain in his back. Then it took another couple of hours to drive it to the remote town of Leaf Valley, Minnesota.

There, on a road named for the farmers who lived on it, Zan finally found Mark 'Fats' Nelson. After stealing a hundred thousand dollars from various U of M employees, Mark decided to move in with his aunt and uncle, working on their farm making five dollars an hour. Only Regular Joe knew where Fats was, and it had taken Jose an hour to track down where Regular Joe was.

Pulsing with pain, Zan was desperate to end his misadventure. He found 'Krohnfeldt Drive,' where Nelson was supposedly staying, made the right turn onto the drive, parked in front of the first house, and fell asleep.

*   *   *   *   *   *   *

Epilogue

"There are two ways of getting home; and one of them is to stay there"
-- G.K. Chesterton

9:22pm Wednesday, April 5th, 1995
The Village Wok, Stadium Village

The Village Wok had decent food. It wasn't the best Chinese restaurant in town, but it was the fastest. The menu offered hundreds of dishes, including a section of authentic Cantonese dishes that couldn't be found elsewhere.

Chris Berg and Gene Zeale sat with Ernie Kessler in the smoking section of The Wok. Out the window they could watch pedestrians hurry to and fro along Washington Avenue. On the table before the trio were plates filled with food. Beef Lo Mein. Chicken Fried Rice. Fried Cheese Wontons. Two pots of hot tea.

Kessler was smoking a cigar and sucking down the tea.

"So what's going on with Zan?" Berg inquired.

"Not sure yet. He's got an airtight alibi with the Krohnfeldts, his car treads didn't match those at the scene. There was no damage to his car from gunfire. The sheriff's deputy couldn't pick him out of a lineup, and the deputy mentioned the guy he encountered had a thick accent. Zan passed a lie detector exam and no one can put him in the cities that week, let alone that day."

"So he's in the clear?" Zeale asked.

"Who knows. He's their only suspect. But they have nothing actionable."

"Is he coming back?" Zeale asked.

"Who knows," Kessler replied, "he's actually enjoying dairy farm work, for the love of Christ."

"If anyone deserves a break, it's him," Berg said.

"I'm running under the assumption that he's not coming back," Kessler said, "this means you're my number one guy Chris."

"Yeah I was afraid of that," Chis said, "it's going to be tough going, I'm now a doctoral candidate, I'll be busy."

"Quit bitching," Kessler said, "you'll be making more than enough money at it. Besides, it's easy."

"Easy when you're an unemployed loser who doesn't have to wake up before noon," Berg said.

"Zan's not coming back," Kessler said, "so drop it already."

"Fine," Chris replied, "but as soon as you find someone else, I'm out."

"Not to change the subject," Zeale said, "but we still have some unfinished business. Initiation is coming up, and we don't have a plan for Frank and Kayla. Both are both deserving, and I don't see how we can't initate them."

"Agreed," Berg said.

"South Dakota is out," Kessler said, "we can't chase two people through the weapons depot."

THE EDUCATOR

"Besides, we get caught putting fetuses up around Mount Rushmore again, we'll get arrested for sure," Berg added.

"Boundary Waters Canoe Area," Kessler suggested.

"That's going to be really cold," Zeale said.

"It'll be fine," Kessler replied, "we'll give them the right equipment. Start them off in different areas, scare them with my helicopter--"

"You have a helicopter?" Berg asked.

"I will by the time spring break rolls around."

"I like it," Zeale said, "old fashioned orientation and survival skills."

"No Shotgun though," Berg said.

"We'll make do," Kessler said. "I also had some ideas for our big projects next year."

"Do they involve plastic fetuses?" Zeale asked.

"No, but there's always room for plastic fetuses," Kessler said. "I was thinking we could try Operation Fuck You-Pay me."

"Fuck you pay me?" Zeale asked.

"What we do is we create a whole bunch of student groups really early in the year, and apply for every grant available." Berg explained. "We put a few people on the Fees Committee to assist. The goal is to get as much money as possible and spend it on whatever we feel like. Like the most offensive speakers we can, and piss off students."

"The goal isn't necessarily to bring in convincing speakers," Kessler said, "we only want offensive ones. This makes the papers and students get mad about how their money is spent. Maybe we grow anti-fees sentiment. Maybe all we do is piss off liberals. Either way, we're having fun."

Zeale nodded in agreement. Then checked his watch.

"Alright, Frank and Kayla should be back from postering, I gotta go."

After a round of handshakes and well-wishes, Zeale was gone.

As soon as he left, Kessler passed a large brown envelope to Chris Berg.

"What's this?"

"Slush fund. Ten-thousand dollars, untraceable hundred dollar bills. Use it at your discretion."

Berg took the envelope and stuffed it into his backpack.

"I do have one question Ernie, how did Zan pull this one off?"

"What can I say, the man lives a charmed life. The crime scene was completely contaminated from the beginning. No evidence found there can put Zan on the scene. Bullet holes in a car? Some friend of Fats out in Alexandria has a Z-car the exact same make and model. A

- 274 -

few thousand bucks to grease a trade. Zan put his plates and VIN on the new car."

"What about the cop? Why didn't he pick Zan out of the line-up?"

"After all those revelations came out about Paulson, I doubt a man like Deputy Wingard would ever be able to identify the ghostly figure he encountered that night. Detective Ochoa is pushing the idea it was a Hmong checking some illegal snares for rabbits before the snow covered them up."

"Were there snares?"

"There will be when the snow thaws. Ochoa will guarantee it."

"And Zan's back injury?"

"Consistent with being trampled by a cow."

"Sonofabitch," Berg pondered.

"Indeed."

"How's Alisha doing?"

"Not sure. She moved in with her mom in Florida. She's not talking to anybody from out here. After what she's been through, nobody blames her. The testimony she gave about Paulson...the fucking media hounded her out of the state. Terrible."

After a few minutes of idle conversation, Berg said goodbye and left. Kessler was left alone at the table to enjoy another pot of tea.

*   *   *   *   *   *   *

The crew was already sitting at the Roundtable when Zeale arrived.

Kayla, Frank, Buzzcut, Painter, Restovich, Kang, Tonya Hotchick. Even Orson Henning had stopped by. Zeale took a seat at the head of the table, a round of 'who's this fucker' and 'where the hell ya been' were exchanged with greetings and insults.

"Hey Spags," Henning shouted, "Frankie here had an idea which you need to hear."

The table started laughing in advance.

"What?" Zeale asked.

"I was thinking," Wallace said, "for next year we could do a Malcolm Paulson Day." More laughter. "I mean, we could have speakers and such, maybe some postering, talking about his accomplishments as U prez."

"That's awesome," Zeale said, "He's now been linked to what, three murders?"

"At least. There was that headless corpse in his freezer at his lake cabin, the sick fuck," Frank said.

"And they think he killed that crack whore and the cop in St.

THE EDUCATOR

Cloud," Kayla added.

"The Daily had an entire spread on the guy," Buzzcut shouted over everyone, "It could be as high as twenty."

"No fucking way he killed twenty people," Henning said, "he would've been caught before that."

"What about that librarian last year, the suicide with no note?" Painter suggested, "that must have been him...Oh man," Painter became sullen, "what about Rachel?"

"Oh yeah," Henning said.

"You think Paulson killed Rachel?" Kayla asked.

"No way," Zeale said, "there was a suicide note and everything. The odds she was murdered by a serial killer are almost zero. She jumped off the bridge, that's that."

"Maybe it is unlikely she was murdered by serial killer," Kayla interjected, "except she was working for one."

"What are the stats on Catholics and suicides?" Painter said. "Not to mention gender differences. It's more likely Paulson killed her. I'd bet money on it."

The Roundtable went quiet.

"I know what we can do," Kayla said, "run a cover story about Rachel. The headline could be 'The Story of Rachel Anderson: Malcolm Paulson's Last Victim'. We do it right, we can nominate the story for a Pulitzer. We can get national press out if this."

"And," Painter interrupted, "bring some closure to her family."

The discussion continued for a few more minutes. Zeale wrote down ideas for events celebrating Malcolm Paulson, and that included finding quotes from government officials giving glowing reviews about the job Paulson had done at the U. *It would make a great series of events*, he thought.

Spags' train of thought was interrupted.

"Zeale," the speaker was Bob Restovich, "We got a surprise for you." With him was Kang, the Korean. The two had been sitting together at a booth away from the group. They had stayed out of the conversation thus far.

"What is it?"

Kang opened up his backpack and pulled out an RC transmitter. Zeale wasn't a tech guy, so he knew little about what he was looking at.

"Again I ask, what is it?"

"You know how you're a big fan of pulling fire alarms?" Restovich said.

"I say a lot of things."

"Well, this should make your day." Kang laughed, then pushed his thick black-rimmed glasses up his nose. "This controller is attached to every fire alarm in the Superblock."

"Excuse me?"

"It's a way to take your fire alarm obsession to the next level," Restovich said.

"Explain."

"A fire alarm is just an electric circuit. Anywhere along the circuit we can create our own parallel bypass with its own radio-controlled switch. With help from Bob, we were able to create our own little mayhem maker--"

"The name idea was mine," Restovich said.

"We were able to get copies of all the keys," Kang continued,"that we needed to move around the Superblock. Over the last few weeks I've been putting in our bypasses. I've coded the switches into this transmitter. We can set off the alarms anytime we want."

"How far away can we be?"

"Maybe 500 meters," Kang said.

"Good enough," Zeale said. "How does it work?"

"Well," Kang. "First you would turn on the controller, then if you wanted to hit Centennial, you'd push left on the horizontal lever. Right will get Pioneer. The vertical lever gets Frontier and Territorial."

"How long will the switches be good for?"

"I dunno, we're using simple single-pole single-throw switches. Maybe 100,000 cycles out of each of them."

"That's a lot of fire alarms. Is it working right now?"

"Yeah."

Zeale grabbed the controller, turned it on, and started hitting all the levers.

*   *   *   *   *   *   *

Kessler finished his tea, left a hundred dollar bill on the table and walked out of the Village Wok. It was a short two blocks to his car, parked in Oak Street Ramp. There was a cynical Vietnam vet who normally worked there who would let people out free after ten o'clock at night. Kessler hoped the man was working.

The night air was cool and dry. It was unseasonably warm. The winter started early and died suddenly. Kessler walked around the block and took in the view of Centennial Hall. The beastly building had once been his home.

Walking along Delaware Street, he noticed faint *squawing* above him. Looking up, he saw hundreds, maybe thousands, of crows. They were perched on top of the dorms, along the parking ramps, on the office building to his left, and in the bare trees. The black bodies of the big birds could scarcely be seen--they were little voids in the darkness. Groups of thirty or forty would take off and fly between perches.

It was the spookiest, most transcendental and odd experience of Kessler's life. He stood there, watching the crows for almost twenty minutes.

Then he whispered to himself "The woods are lovely, dark and deep. But I have Promises to Keep. And miles to go before I sleep. And miles to go before I sleep," and continued on to the parking ramp. As he did, lights began coming on in the dorms, strobes started flashing, and students in various states of undress tumbled out of the doors. The high pitched scream of the fire alarms filtered into the night air. The crows took to flight *en masse*.

As the fire engines arrived, something told Kessler it was shenanigans. He began to laugh. He loved shenanigans.

The end.

Author Biography: Marty Andrade

A resident and native of Minnesota, Marty learned politics from the bottom, starting as a volunteer on local campaigns in Minnesota and ending his political career in exactly the same spot. After college, he drifted from dead-end job to dead-end job, including working as a bar bouncer, political hack, antiques dealer, wood stainer, retail clerk, talk radio show host, high school debate coach, day laborer and phone book deliveryman. An irregular blogger, writer, podcaster and author since 2001, he published his first book, The Twin Cities Burger Tour, in 2008. In 2010 he completed an MBA, and promptly lost his job.

This is his first novel.

You can follow him on Twitter @martyandrade.

You can email him at andrade@redpublishing.com

Made in the USA
Middletown, DE
12 January 2019